Looking Glass

EX LIBRIS

_____

Looking Glass

James R. Strickland

FLYING PEN PRESS SCIENCE FICTION

Flying Pen Press

www.FlyingPenPress.com

Looking Glass, a novel from Flying Pen Press Science Fiction, shelve in "Science Fiction"
First Edition, continuous printing on demand, first date of publication June 2007

Author: James R. Strickland, www.JamesRStrickland.com.
Editor: Scott Humphries. Editorial services available at www.ScottHumphries.com.
Cover Artist: Timothy Lantz. Prints available from the artist at www.StygianDarkness.com.
Cover Designer: Kaitlin Porter. www.InfinityCG.com.

ISBN: 978-0-9795889-0-7

Flying Pen Press Science Fiction is an imprint of
Flying Pen Press LLC
18601 Green Valley Ranch Blvd., Suite 112 No. 4, Denver, Colorado 80249 USA
www.FlyingPenPress.com

All Flying Pen Press titles, imprints, and distributed lines are available at special quantity discounts for bulk purchases for sales promotion, premiums, fund raising, educational or institutional use.

Manufactured in the United States of America and in the United Kingdom.
Printing by Lightning Source Inc. and Lightning Source UK Limited.

This novel is a story set in world of large corporations and high technology, based on the author's speculative extrapolation of the technology and corporate environment of the current day. In telling the story, it is necessary to use trade names and trademarks as part of the culture of characters' world. The following trademarks are the properties of their respective owners, and their use in this work of fiction is not a challenge to the ownership of any trademark: AOL® is a registered trademark of AOL LLC. Applebee's® is a registered trademark of Applebee's International, Inc. Ativan™ is a trademark of Wyeth. Bakelite® is a registered trademark of Borden Chemical Investments, Inc. BART® is a registered trademark of San Francisco Bay Area Rapid Transit District. Betamax® is a registered trademark of Sony Corporation. California Zephyr® is a registered trademark of the National Railroad Passenger Corporation. Candy Land® and Monopoly® are registered trademarks of Hasbro, Inc. CBC™ is a trademark of the Canadian Broadcasting Corporation. CNN® is a registered trademark of Cable News Network. eBay® is a registered trademark of eBay Inc. Geodon® is a registered trademark of Pfizer Inc. Goodwill® is a registered trademark of Goodwill Industries International. Gopher™ is a trademark of the University of Minnesota. Iron Chef™ is a trademark of Fuji Television Network, Inc. Motif® is a registered trademark of The Open Group. Mountain Dew is a registered Trademark of PepsiCo. Mr. Coffee® is a registered trademark of Jarden Corporation. Negra Modello® is a registered trademark of Grupo Modelo S.A. de C.V. One Must Fall 2097™ is a trademark of Epic Games. Operation® is a registered trademark of Milton Bradley Co. Perspex® is a registered trademark of the Lucite International Limited group of companies. Schoolhouse Rock® is a registered trademark of American Broadcast Companies, Inc. Star Trek™ is a trademark of CBS Studios, Inc. Trivial Pursuit® is a trademark of Horn Abbot Ltd. ULTRIX32™ , DEC™, and DECTerm™are registered trademarks of Digital Equipment Corporation. VW® is a registered trademark of Volkswagen of America, Inc. Wi-Fi® is a registered trademark of Wi-Fi Alliance. X-Window System™ is a trademark of X.Org Foundation. Flying Pen Press Fiction™ is a trademark of Flying Pen Press LLC. All corporation names are trademarks of their respective owners.

Acknowledgments

For Marcia.

This novel would not have been possible at all without help. I'm naming names. These are some of those.

First, and foremost: Marcia, who read, and commented on every draft of this novel (six major revisions, plus many more minor ones), put up with my writing moods, beat the difference between lose and loose into my head, inspired characters, and in all ways was everything an aspiring novelist could hope for in a spouse.

Then there are my friends, both online and real life, and my family: Badger, Brenda, Bob, Bob, Dick, Jeff, Jeff, Joan, Joy, Lindsey, Mark, MaryKay, Mike, Pat, Ryan, Susan, Steph and Stephie.

Websites: www.wikipedia.org, www.gutenberg.org, and www.nanowrimo.org. Yes. The novel now known as Looking Glass started out as my 2004 Nano novel, then titled /dev/ice.

Hardware/Software: I have this bad tempered urge to write a novel with my manual typewriter and tractor feed paper some year. But don't hold your breath. Looking Glass was written on several Apple Macintosh computers running various versions of OS X, with various (at least three) versions of Nisus Writer Express. www.apple.com and www.nisus.com, respectively. The typewriter? mrtypewriter.com.

Prologue

6:54 p.m. Thursday.

My boss is on the phone. I'm buck naked, and lying in a tank of heavy saline solution. That's not really where I am. That's just where my body is hanging out while my brains are plugged into the network.

"Mr. Conlon, I protected Marketing's server from the net because they failed their security inspection again. It is my professional opinion that the survey software is fundamentally flawed and unsecurable. I won't sign off on that machine being public until it's secure." My brain's plugged into the network through the data jacks in the side of my head, so I'm not actually talking to Conlon. I'm thinking at him. The intervening software and hardware are doing the translation.

"It's not your decision anymore, Ms. Shroud. I've signed off on it," he says. "I got a visit from the director of marketing this afternoon. He says put it online. We put it online. Understood?"

Ms. Shroud? Fucking weasel. "Understood." In the space between Conlon's sentences, I log into the firewall router and open the hole for the Marketing server. "It's online."

Jay's voice comes from behind me, in the operator gestalt. There's a whiff of panic flickering across the gestalt from him. I'm trying hard to care a whole lot. "Ah, shit. Shroud, we've got an intruder alert coming into Softline's server four. Looks like he's trying to get into the order system." Jay works for me. He's my partner, in theory. He's also the new kid on the team. "Weird," he says. "Looks like he's coming from that Marketing server we isolated … wait, what's that hunk of shit doing back on line?"

I have to smile a little. "Gotta run, Conlon. Someone just broke into Marketing's survey server and is attacking Softlines' order system. I'll file a report later. I'll be sure to copy Greer." I hang up before my boss has a chance to argue… *Do small respect, show too bold malice…* Whatever.

"Office politics, Jay. No help for it now. Okay, gang," I tell them, as I take a quick look at the packets. "Let's go earn our pay. Guy's next hop comes from Telefiber in 505 land. That's Albuquerque. Rei, this isn't an East Coast thing, it doesn't look like. You lean on Telefiber and trace this guy home. Jay, you're with me. Everyone, keep an eye on the firewall routers, if this fucker's bluffing us and going after the 'wall, we need to know."

"You pinned it, Boss. He's going after our 88, trying to log into 88a. Freezing the firewall rules and time locking the logins now." Jay says.

"Good work, Jay. Stay on top of him. Also, isolate the Marketing machine again. Full quarantine this time, it's compromised. Company policy. Let Conlon and Greer fight it out with Marketing."

"Understood."

"Stay sharp, kid. Hacker's going to go after the backup router in a sec. I'm going to nail him there."

"Will do, boss," he says. "Go git 'em."

"Tik. You, Kimmy, and Silv watch your perimeter firewalls. This guy's probably got friends coming, and I hate getting blindsided. Rei, where's my trace?"

"Coming, Shroud. Telefiber's guys are on it." Silver and Rei work for me too. They cover our net from Boston, to mind our trans-Atlantic connections to Europe, and our net in the United Christian States of America. Theocratic ghetto, the whole country. You couldn't pay me enough to live there. Tika and Kimmy are the team in San Jose, and they do the same thing for our trans-Pacific net to Japan and Asia, and manage their end of our big pipe through InterStellar Link to the California Technocracy. High Tech land. Nerd Mecca. Yeah, with an average tax burden of about thirty percent. I don't get paid enough to live there, either. Jay and I are at corporate, here in Denver, in the Southern Canadian Province of Colorado.

Anyway. A quick flicker of mental effort and I fly over the net to connect to router 88b. Wait for the intruder. Tell my EII ice to turn my avatar off completely, so the system doesn't announce me. If the intruder knows his stuff, he'll detect me as soon as he gets connected, but at least this way he has to look.

"Boss, he just gave up on 88a. Coming your way, I figure."

"Good work, Jay. You ride herd on that. Yeah, there he is. Coming in on my port 22." Wait for it. Wait for him to make the connection…

"Need help, boss?" Jay again.

"If you want, sure. But mind the firewall. That's your primary concern," I tell him.

The intruder keeps me waiting another thirty seconds, then connects. He sends his public crypto key, so my router can talk to him. I give the key to my attack ice, then hijack his connection. The router's operating environment boils back behind me as I jump down his connection into his deck. "Rei! I need that trace, or I'm gonna lose him here!"

"Hang on … got it!" she says. "2002:44A8:4E1A:: Huh? Where's … oh, it's a 6to4 address, I see. Translates to 68.168.78.26 in IPv4. Half gigabit link. Their install records say it's a back bedroom in a two bedroom condo in Rio Rancho, New Mexico. Main network is registered to a Denise Hall, but there's a subnet registered to a Mr. Crispy. Phonebook says she's got a son, age thirteen, by the name of Jeffrey."

"Excellent work, Rei." It is. Not everyone remembers about 6to4 IPv4 encapsulation. I can feel Rei smile through the gestalt, even as I get to work. Mister Crispy, huh? We'll see about that. His defense ice finally detects me, and dumps my connection. I start a new one directly to his deck. I give my crypto cluster ice the key I stole from him, and between that and the connection negotiation data, the ice identifies his crypto as a reasonably well known piece of downloadable soft, carved onto generic Penguin ice. It's one of my library of thousands of encryption softs I've already broken. And people say I need more hobbies.

The cluster promptly gives me his public and private crypto keys, and I'm into his deck. Three more seconds, and my attack ice has identified it, a Quả-Chuối 2000, and I have everything I need to take control of it. Which I do. I carve one of his ice with a slow acting brain burner and set it to work frying his neurons. This hurts a lot, or so I'm told, and more importantly it paralyses you so you can't get the induction rig off your head. I have a jack. No induction rig. You can't do that kind of thing to me. I also set him up with a time-release virus to corrupt his deck's firmware. *Whiles I see lives, the gashes do better upon them.* The kid's digital screaming flickers back to me. I ignore it.

Company policy says it's bad for our corporate image to fry underage hackers. I say it's evolution in action, and it is legal, but, as usual, it's not my decision. Mr. Crispy is almost certainly the thirteen-year-old son, so I back out of his deck and break into the video feed for the condo. Video player tells me that whoever's watching likes the evening soap-coms, and her credit card name matches the owner of the condo. Crispymom, I'm betting. I put a simple text message across her screen. In big letters. "Ms. Hall, your son is in the back bedroom. You may want to unplug him, while he has some brains left. You may also want to have a long talk with him about breaking into other people's networks. He could wind up dead." No fooling. Company policy says I can come down hard on repeat offenders, whatever their age. I keep an eye on things a few moments. His deck drops offline within fifteen seconds, and I drop out of his network shortly afterward. Bah. He'd have done more brain damage to himself on a good weekend's bender.

Jay says, "Remind me not to piss you off. You chewed him up in what, a minute and a half from when he connected to 88b?"

He's chuckling, but there's a certain edge of fear in it. "Fun?" he asks.

I have to shrug at that. "Just work, Jay. Anyone else come knocking?"

"Nah. Nothing here."

"Tik? Kimmy? Silv? Rei? Anything?"

"Nada." Tik's voice. "No follow-up attack at all. Only wrong call you made."

"Yeah, I didn't figure a thirteen-year-old kid counting coup, you know?"

Tika laughs. It's a warm, happy sound to me. "You sound disappointed."

I turn to face them in the gestalt; look at the eclectic collection of icons of the team. My team. Virtual though they may be. Smile, maybe. Just a little. "Eh. Excitement's overrated. 'Sides, it's quittin' time. Vijay and company probably want their passdown. Nice work, guys." *Cave Canum.* Yeah. Beware of the dog.

Chapter I

6:27 a.m. Friday.

The alarm goes off for the third time.

Three minutes later it goes off again, and this time I'm too awake to hit snooze. I'm already running late. The black sky outside my window is fading to grey; fuzzy with snow, and with the approach of dawn. I watch the window a long moment, watch the snow fall on the city of Denver, my eyes seduced by the motion, jagged pieces of dream slowly melting away as my sleep-fogged brain struggles to come up to speed.

The apartment is plain; the walls are neatly painted off-white cinderblock, and linoleum or whatever the fuck marketroids call it these days, on the floor. Hard over hard, bare walls over bare floor; only the white fabric vertical blinds hung over the window give the room any softness at all. It doesn't matter. I don't close them. I let the lights of the city come in while I sleep. Cool, clean, abstract.

You don't have time for this. Groan inwardly. Such a nag I am. Get out of bed: one hand on the arm of my chair, the other on the grab bar on the wall, lever myself into the chair, settle in. Unlock the brakes. Wheel over to my desk. Punch the button that wakes up my old hand-held OSDeck. In the kitchenette, the Mr. Coffee machine gurgles steadily and I can hear elixir of life dripping into the carafe. Something to look forward to this morning.

Inside the OSDeck, all the ice wakes up: each ice processor comes online, runs the software attached to it, and talks to the deck for its interface with the outside world. Division of labor: the ice does the thinking. The deck does the talking. Kind of like Engineering and Management. The e-mail ice reaches out through the deck's wireless interface to the building network, downstairs into the basement, out through the firewall and onto the big data pipe to InterStellar Link, and from there through the public access gateway out to the public Internet. The ice pulls down my e-mail, and filters out the spam. Simultaneously, the news ice takes a similar path and connects itself to a dozen news feeds, throws away the ads, and collates the results into something resembling order of importance. When both ice are done, they query a third ice: my Environment, Identity, and Icons — or EII — ice, for the rules by which they should display their handiwork. News and mail ice are old friends with the EII ice. They have to be. It's also where the account keys, usernames, and passwords for my e-mail and various news accounts are stored. When they ask, the EII ice rule tells them to open another network connection to my TV, how to lay the windows out, and who gets to use the speech synthesizer first.

By the time the TV flares to life and starts talking, my coffee is ready, so I roll to the kitchenette and pour a cup — black, thanks ever so — before glancing over at the big screen. I'm in a hurry, but coffee and news are important.

So news. CNN.com is the news ice's choice as most important this morning. According to CNN, at 8:00 a.m. Eastern Standard Time, 27 minutes before I woke up, the Holy President of the United Christian States of America in Washington, DC gave a speech, inviting, "…the fracturous pieces of this once great nation to reunite under the glorious UCSA leadership and grand army." Someone should slap his speech-writer. Fracturous is a pretty questionable word.

Looking for more details, the news ice grabs another version of the speech, this one re-streamed out of a TexMex free news site near Austin as of 7:15 a.m. CST. It's the same speech, but the footage has been digitally altered to show the President masturbating as he speaks. In Spanish. They don't think much of him in TexMex by the look of things. Changing streams. Live, on the Canadian Broadcasting Company (CBC) stream, Prime Minister Hilton politely declines the offer when asked by reporters, offering no further comment. Good for him. I voted for him, even though his opponent carried most of Colorado. Not like we need him to comment; his position on defying U.N. Resolution 2651 is well known. No way. Without the Southern Canadian Provinces, Canada goes back to being a minor player in the world, plus we Americans have proven we can't be trusted to handle our own politics.

The California Technocracy has issued no comment at all, but it's only 5:37 a.m. there, and CEO Davis is seldom out of bed before 10:00. Given his two wives and his husband, one can hardly blame him, I guess. Not to be outdone by their Texican counterparts, however, the night shift at one of the CalTech public news sites digitally moved the Holy President to speak from a very large marijuana garden, resequenced his vocal sounds — and lip-synced it, mind you — so he's reciting the lyrics from Jefferson Airplane's White Rabbit. This they streamed out as editorial. Typical. No new revolutions, no new U.N. occupations, economy still sucks, nothing we have to care about in the SCP. There's work to be done, and politics just get in the way. So world news? The usual. Crap.

I don't have unlimited money, so the news ice picks my news feeds carefully. It pulls down 2Quiknews.com, and reads a story about the Houston 281s finally getting busted. Good riddance. I've run into those clowns at work. Apparently the Texas Rangers took them down. Looks like the 281s forgot the old maxim: Do not shit where you eat. They hit some international corp that had a big enough presence in Houston to call down the Rangers. Look for podcasts of the executions while the bodies are still warm, probably by the end of the week. Apparently nobody does an honest-to-goodness hanging like the Texicans. That shit sells, especially in the UCSA. In other news, GenData's entry into high performance virtual-reality decks is delayed again. No surprise there. The big question is whether they'll ship it at all before Nova, Kuroto, and Megadyne take their lunch money.

Anyway. Skimming now: twenty new ice were released, about half of them games and toys, and Super Scriptor 4.0 has been announced, which means I can expect to see new and faster kinds of script kiddy attacks when that ice ships. No skin off my nose. If I can't nail a script kiddy to the wall by now, I might as well retire.

Speaking of which, it's 6:45. Fuck. Fuck. Fuck, I'm going to be late. Finish bolting down my breakfast bar and orange juice, roll into the shower and haul myself into the seat. I can still hear the TV. The EII ice has noticed I'm not in the room anymore and turned up the volume. Wash the hair. Scrub the data jack sites behind my right ear. Do a quick once over the rest of my body with the soap. Haul myself out of the seat and onto my feet. Hold on to the hand rail with one arm like a drowning woman and scrub the behind quickly with my free hand, then sit back into the seat to finish. That gets the old heart going.

6:50. Shit. It's going to be close. Haul myself back into my chair and roll to the sink. I try not to look at myself in the mirror first thing in the morning. *You look forty*. The thought comes unbidden. They say forty is the new thirty. Bull. Shit. Every day there's one more grey hair. Every day the little lines at the corners of my eyes get a little deeper. My eyes get squintier. My boobs sag a little more. You'd think as little sunlight as I get, I wouldn't look my age so much. But I do.

Brush the teeth. Pull a comb through my hair. Think about cutting it short again; it would sure save a lot of time. TV is still talking. Markets are limping along. Consumer confidence is going down a little. Seems as though a recovery, the fourth one they've expected this year in Canada, might need to create actual jobs within the economy that's supposed to recover. Nobody ever seems to consider that. I wonder who writes their economic modeling ice. Here's an interesting tidbit. General DataProcessing has announced an automated net defense system, primarily for military and government nets. GenData's brag sheet says it's whiplash fast and good enough to do first-line defense. *That's what you do for a living.* The thought crosses my mind, certainly, but I've got other things to worry about. Like the fact that I'm almost out of deodorant. *What you do for a living.* Okay, okay, so it gnaws at me a little. I make a mental note to look into non-company housing over my lunch break.

The hair will have to do. Grab my bathrobe. Put it on. Roll out the door to the elevator on my floor and go down twelve stories to the subbasement. Count the seconds as the elevator descends, and the scent of the air changes from dormitory floor to heavy salt water and plastic solvents. The data center. Roll out of the elevator, through the women's locker room and into the tank room. Vijay is already out of the tank and into the shower, and Bobby is on the bitch box. "Mornin', Kate."

Bobby's my safety man, my JAFO — Just Another Fucking Observer. He, alone in the entire English-speaking world, calls me Kate: something of a Shakespearian joke between us, both one-time English majors. *For you are called plain Kate, and bonny Kate, and sometimes Kate the Cursed.* "Hey Bobbo."

"Tank's sanitized and ready to go. Night shift had a busy night, I guess." Bobby's all business today, sounds like he's got a lot of paperwork to deal with.

"Did they? Anyone hurt?"

"Nah. Well, not on our end. Vijay was crying in the locker room, so probably there were some dead hackers when all was said and done. You know how he is."

"Yeah, thanks. I'll check up on that at huddle." I make a mental note to do so.

6:56 a.m. Friday.

I have to be online by 7:00 for morning huddle. I get in the backpack of my chair and slot up my work ice into the tank. Some commercial: word processor, spreadsheet, presentation software, all part of some office software suite or other. Company standard. Some open source: database, e-mail and news, stock ticker. The rest is custom carved: network analysis and debugging tools, crypto, viruses, logic bombs, tank and deck firmware breaking tools. Attack ice. Black ice, as Gibson called it. The fun stuff. My black ice is my own handiwork. All of my network tools are. Wouldn't have it any other way. Finally, I load the last five slots in the tank's main frame with blank Penguin ice. One of the things that separates me from the beginners, the script kiddies, or from any automation is that I can write my own soft, carve my own ice. You can have countermeasures for all the commercial ice in the world and it won't help against me. And with those five blank Penguin ice? They're snappy open architecture processors, and I can write soft and carve them right now, and do things even I couldn't do five minutes ago.

Bobby opens the tank hatch remotely. I glance in. It's a polymer resin cylinder, 1.5 by 2.5 meters, half full of saline solution so heavy that my body will float on top of it rather than in it. Beyond that it's an absolutely quiet, absolutely dark, temperature-controlled sensory deprivation environment; because real world senses slow down the brain's absorption of virtual-reality data. Bobbo's as good as his word. The tank looks and smells clean inside.

Hang up my robe. Haul myself out of my chair and into the tank. Go horizontal for the second time in an hour. The heavy salt water supports my weight. Bobby closes the tank door remotely, and I'm already feeling a little sleepy, a little detached. Fumble around for the optical fibers and plug the tank control line into my old low-speed jack, and the virtual interface line into the ultrafast jack just beneath it. Smile a bit as I settle into the dark warmth of the tank and my brain drops into the alpha/theta-wave state we tankers all work in, and leaves my body to fend for itself until lunch time. Pull up the heads-up display from my low speed jack. I'm on time. *Barely.* Bah, minutes to spare.

Log in.

Darkness on the face of the water. And data says, "Let there be… " And, after a brief shimmer of sensory static, there is. All around me is a world painted in data; metaphors drawn from the real world abstract the streams of data, abstractions of abstractions until the whole world and everything in it can be held in the hand, itself an abstraction. I am changed. I am transformed into a thing of this world, an existence without boundaries, an idealized body of pure black light as defined in my EII ice, submerged in the warren of activity that is our corporate network. Feel it. Feel my network as it comes out of the lull in activity from shift change. Feel the surge as, far away in the real world, thousands of hands set thousands of cups of coffee down on thousands of desks and log in, perhaps with the words, 'I wonder what's going on in the world today?'

Feel. Even without putting a virtual hand in my virtual pocket I can feel each piece of ice, smooth and dangerous like touching the edge of a very sharp knife. I know precisely what each one is and what it's currently doing without the metaphor of hand or pocket. I reach past the metaphors of the physical world to more vague, purely symbolic ones. A new shorthand. New symbols, a new level of abstraction. Home turf for me. What I do best.

A moment of ritualistic whimsy: I raise my arms out from my sides and slide effortlessly upward toward the day-shift operator gestalt, through a twilight sky alive with patterns of light, endless streams of data going from point to point. I could just set coordinates and jump there, of course, but going through the intervening space is more fun. Besides, it means I know where the data path back to my brain is. It makes it harder to do things to it without me knowing. I savor the virtual rush of wind past my virtual face — as good a metaphor of speed as any. A smile creeps over my face as it usually does when I first log in. *Oh I have slipped the surly bonds of earth, and danced the skies on laughter silvered wings.*

Perspective, serenity, at least until I think about the news. Bah. Even if that GenData system is as good as they say — and you'd best believe I'll be watching for CERT advisories to see how fast the hacker scum crack it — it's really for military/industrial nets, working in ultra tight classified environments and all that jazz. I don't work for the military. I work in a net where legitimate users have to be allowed to come in. We're a discount store chain, for Pete's sake. I'm the best at what I do on this site, maybe in the whole province. Me? I work for OmniMart.

Chapter 2

6:58 a.m. Friday.

Log into the day shift operator gestalt. Nothing happens. It's empty, quiet. I'm the first one on, so I get a moment of alone time. I'm the senior operator on site, and the manager of the whole virtual team, so I try to make sure I'm always on when my people get here. I try to make sure that I don't log off until they're all gone, too. Makes for a long day, sometimes.

Tika comes on within a couple seconds. When she jumps in, I'm subliminally, intimately aware of her: her moves, her frame of mind, little tickles of what is being sent to her senses, even what she's thinking when she lets it escape out into the gestalt. It's like being strapped in the front seat of a Volkswagen with someone: a flood of little senses and smells, distracting at first, but in seconds you ignore anything that isn't important. Her voice seems to come from my right and a little behind me, as usual, where my EII ice rule maps her. Where she maps me with her own I couldn't say and don't care. It really is all relative online. "Morning Tik."

"Hey Shroudie."

I learned computer science in the days of keyboards and mice, back when your nick was important. Around that time, my only college boyfriend called me the Bitter Shroud of Death. I've used Shroud as my nick ever since, long after the son-of-a-bitch dumped me — which was the occasion when it came up. Even after nicks stopped being so important with the advent of direct neural interfacing and gestalts, it still suits me. I am old school, and people should know that. "What's new out there, Tik? How's the weather?"

"Oh, you know. Raining when I came in, but it's supposed to be clear by lunch time." She's behind me, so I don't see her virtual representation — her icon — smile. I don't really need to; I'm aware of her mood in the gestalt, and I know what her icon looks like. Short, curvy, dark skinned, vaguely Asian with shiny flowing locks of straight black hair. A sense of humor. The body of her icon is drawn in shades of matte grey with glowing neon blue art resembling circuit diagrams. I don't even think she was born when that movie came out. Hell, I wasn't either, but old science fiction is like viral DNA in this culture. It manifests unexpectedly, frequently as an ironic joke. *Tron, Star Wars*, William Gibson, Elf Sternberg, an entirely unhealthy fascination with Monty Python and *Hitch-Hiker's Guide*. Online culture is a strange thing. It has been around longer than I've been here.

"I have some gorgeous lilacs blooming by my deck, and it's warm enough to wear shorts. It's spring, finally. I thought it'd never get here." As Tika speaks, I can see the flowers, tiny purple beads in clusters like grapes, smell their perfume in warm, wet air, feel the breeze in her hair, sun against her skin beating on her scalp. From her mind's eye, I can see the cool evening over the bay, watch the fog slide down the mountain toward land, feel ice cold water on her feet. That she's breathing some of the most polluted air on the planet does not, by contrast, get passed on. She's still talking, though. "Brian and I are going out to Carmel tomorrow. Probably spend the night at the bed and breakfast we usually stay at there. You know, the one with the fireplaces and the flannel sheets? Did I tell you about that?"

Abruptly the sensations shift to memories of firelight and flannel on bare skin. I try to keep from feeling embarrassed, and more, try to keep from broadcasting the feeling across the gestalt. I try not to cut her off too abruptly. "Yeah. Yeah, you told me about it, Tik."

The sensation memories percolating out of her fade before they go too far into the moist details. She chuckles a little at me. But the subject is about to change. I can feel that too. "How're you?" she asks.

"Awake. Alive. It's snowing here again, or at least that's what the weather forecast said. I haven't been outside today."

Tika's concerned now. It steals over her like a shadow; emotional cues slide over the gestalt as much as the sensations and memories did moments ago. "Have you gotten out at all this week?"

"No. It's still winter here. The weather's been sucky, and I don't have anyplace in particular to go." I send her the view out my window from this morning.

She chuckles. "Mmm. Yeah, I guess I can see that. Got any plans for the weekend?"

Something's coming. I can feel a slightly impish smile coming to her lips. Might as well go along with it. "Not really, no."

"You should catch the Zephyr out here, come down to the ocean with Brian and me. It's really pretty, and I know you'd like it."

The smile, her smile, grows to full radiance; she's amused. I must have let what I felt leak out onto the gestalt: startled, maybe a tiny thrill. I don't even have to look at her graphic to see the smile. I feel it. Try not to let what else I'm feeling go through the gestalt. Try to lock it down, keep it to myself. She didn't mean to make me uncomfortable. This new informality between us is as much my fault as hers. I think back a moment ago to firelight and flannel sheets, and try to keep the twitchy feeling I have now from crossing the gestalt as best I can. Be gentle. "Um. Tik, it's four-and-a-half hours each way, plus passing through customs in and out of CalTech, plus however long it takes to drive to Carmel from Emeryville. Anyway, I'm not fun at parties, I'd just be in the way."

Disappointment. I can feel it from her as she backs off. But she's not surprised. "Aww. You wouldn't be in the way, you'd be welcome. I thought you knew that by now." Now she's teasing. Even smirking a little.

"I can't afford it anyway. Thanks, though, Tik. I do appreciate the offer." I'm her boss. Company policy still has vague issues with that kind of involvement among people in the same chain of command, even if it is on your off time, even if they are in a foreign country, and especially if it's in person. *Of all base passions, fear is the most accursed.* Yeah. That too.

Kimmy arrives in the gestalt. The abrupt third presence in the artificial intimacy of the thing breaks the thread of the conversation, puts us both back into work manners. Thankfully. I barely know Kimmy. I've never actually met either of them, not in person. *Of all base passions...* Quiet, you.

Kimmy is mapped in behind Tik in my private version of the universe. Her icon is a tall, lithe blond with shiny lace up purple leathers and artfully displayed cleavage. No icon dress code for operators who aren't dealing with customers, obviously. Kimmy's a lot more closed than Tik. She keeps her emotional space more private, less intimate. She's more tense than usual this morning, too. Her tension seeps out into the gestalt. "Morning, Tik, Shroud. Sorry I'm late. Night shift guy must have been hitting porn sites after the fight they got into. Had to get maintenance in to flush my tank. Water's still a little cold."

"Ewww." Tika's nose wrinkles. I can feel it, it's almost comical. I want to laugh, but as the boss, laughter is not my prerogative.

"I wondered what had you wound today. Make sure you send e-mail to personnel about that. Trust me on this. They take a dim view of misusing company equipment and bandwidth." A regulation that was made very clear to me not long ago, and presumably to Tika as well. Embarrassing. Enough. "Does someone want to go poke Silv and Rei and tell them to get in here already?"

"Sure, Shroudie, I'll get 'em." Tika jumps instantly across the continent. She isn't as big on flying as I am. Impatient maybe. Certainly her jack hardware is top notch. The only thing that limits her speed is the same thing that limits it for all of us — how fast her brain can absorb virtual data. Tik is as fast as I am. Maybe faster. But *Shroudie?* I need to talk to her about that. Familiarity in a gestalt is normal. Between us it's unavoidable. But there have to be limits, at least while we're on duty. Somehow I have to make that happen. She's still in the gestalt, so we hear through her as she grabs our missing teammates. "Hey guys, stop screwing around, Shroud's waiting."

Silver and Rei come on simultaneously from Boston, UCSA. We got them together. You never see them online separately. They run the same icons, a pair of anime people, color coded so we can tell them apart, one with purple hair — Silv — and one with pink — Rei. What gender they're supposed to be is hard to say, and apparently Silv and Rei like it that way. I'm pretty sure Rei's female. With Silv I honestly don't know. Not like it matters. They're quiet today, probably because they're late. My EII ice tucks them in on my left, one behind the other. Jay arrives about the same time, and his voice comes in from right behind me.

"'Morning, Boss." Jay always comes in last, which is okay with me since he spends the time in passdown with the night shift guys. I'd prefer not to have a partner at all, but company policy requires it. He spends a lot of time monitoring hardware and staying out of my way. Jay and I cover Northern and Southern Canada. Since TexMex is largely illiterate and unconnected, we cover that too, though there are rumors of an Austin site in the planning stages. *Jay has a heart — how shall I say — too soon made glad.* Something like that. He bugs me. It might be that he's more or less a domesticated hacker, the kind of kid who killed my last company and landed me in soulless corp-ville. I don't actually know that; he's never said, but I suspect. In person, Jay is a shy kid with glasses, early 20s, looks 16, with a sad little goatee that looks infinitely less silly on his icon than it does on him. Fresh out of school. I'm old enough to be his mother. He makes me feel old; maybe that's it. I don't know. Anyway, like him or not, he's good. They're all good.

7:00 a.m. Friday.

I start morning huddle. "Okay, gang, it's that time again. Boston. Rei, Silver, you're up. Anything new?"

"Yeah. Night shift here got hit by some splinter of the Righteous Fist of God, out of DC. Usual procedure: we hold them with delay and distract and hand them off to you guys. Vijay did the actual burnout on them. Might be reprisal attacks some time today when the bodies get found. Probably get another protest from the UCSA's embassy since they were clearly doing God's will against the evil Satanic OmniMart. Which, as you know, makes even murder legal here." Rei's bitter this morning, almost seething. Politics. Especially fundie politics in the UCSA. They're enough to piss off even believers.

"Easy, Rei. Stay frosty, okay? We're likely to have a busy day, and you guys will probably be in the front line." I look at the pink-haired icon and make eye contact, such as it is. It's more a gestalt sensation than any meaningful exchange between icons. Doesn't matter, it works the same way. Rei nods. I go on. "Jay, did the night shift guys shuffle the paperwork on that one?"

"Yeah, Vijay sent it off to legal before he logged out for the night."

Poor Vijay. He's a good operator, but the killing bothers him. We always burn the fundies, though. It's the only way to make them stay away. Company policy. "Okay. Anything else, Rei?"

"Nah, other than that, same old same old. Someone billed another pirate line to us. I sent it up to accounting, told them to get their shit together and change the IT department manager's crypto keys. They said the last time they did, someone nearly got fired." Rei's voice has a Southern twang to it. I wonder idly where the accent is from. She turns to her partner. "Silv, you got anything for the boss?"

"Nah, you got all the interesting stuff. Nothing here." Silver is a Boston native, no question. Strong conservation of Rs going on, making it *nothing heah.*

Time to move on. "Okay, Rei, Silv, keep poking those accounting guys, but don't waste too much time on it. It's their problem, not ours. San Jose?"

Kimmy speaks first. "Nothing interesting. They're adding a new branch out here, router just came online this morning. Our network 122. Huh. Must be some secret project, there's nothing on the registration sheet except "Ultra" and Bancrier's signature authorizing it.

Tika cuts in, "Maybe we're finally going to sell porn, eh? We should check it out." Laughter on the net.

"Well, Bancrier's your site IT director, I guess that's kosher. Check it out though, make sure they're obeying policy so they don't try to spring exceptions on us later. Denver. Jay, anything from night shift guys here?"

"Other than Vijay's burnouts? Not much. Hardware stuff mostly. Router 48a is down, BFR's people are en route. Looks like another bad motherboard. 48b is carrying net 48 right now. Oh yeah, G+ Penguin ice shipped finally, I got my first one in the mail. I was up all night playing with it."

He makes me chuckle, sometimes. I remember when technology was fun in and of itself, lo these many years ago. "Okay, keep an eye on 48. That's central accounting, payroll. We'd all like to get paid today. I've got nothing. New version of Super Scriptor's announced, but not out yet. Jay, come lunch break, you can show me your new toy. That's it."

"Will do, Boss." Morning huddle ends. Jay has the last word. He's elated. I can feel it. The cool of mission time has settled over me, the working mindset of frosty professionalism, total focus, efficiency. I may not love my job, but it certainly has enough moments for a long, comfortable — if meaningless — affair.

Chapter 3

7:06 a.m. Friday.

The San Jose team drops out of the gestalt twenty-three seconds after the end of passdown. That happens sometimes when the I-Link pirate crew gets busy chewing on a script kiddy and one of their routers goes down. No biggie.

Tika comes screaming back, voice torn all raw, her icon distorting, writhing, coming apart in glowing fragments. The electrochemical chaos in her head floods into the gestalt like fever dreams: thoughts, memories, emotions flooding out, raving, crying, incoherent. I recoil in shock, drawing back, embarrassed. Tika's brain shits itself, all control gone, a full blown psychotic episode. But I have a job to do.

"We're branched! Scram-Jammers, *Now!* Kimmy, jack out and get your JAFO on the line and tell him to jack Tika out! Do it now!" No time for subtlety, no time now for anything but speed and fury, protect the wounded and attack. There's no reply from California. "Fuck!"

I kick on my own scramble-jammer and crypto ice and try to tune out the bedlam as other voices take up the screaming. Jump to San Jose. Chaos is spewing from Tika's wounded mind, too disjointed even for thought, just noise now. Like blood on the water after a shark bite. I trace the connection to her backwards through the San Jose network. The attacker's coming from InterStellar Link. My connection's exposed; it goes through there.

The intruder is on me. I can feel my connection lag as he starts intercepting my packets, trying to crack them. I jump back out of I-Link before he can get a statistical sample and get serious about cracking my crypto. Local in Denver, Jay's offline, Tika's offline, Silv and Rei are shrieking in unison, and if Kimmy's done what I told her, she's offline and trying to help Tik. I scramble my crypto keys, and send a quick pager message to Bobby.

> 911 911 Bobby, pass the word to all sites.
> Get everyone else out except me, and get
> the I-Link pirates on the horn and tell them
> they're majorly branched. 911 911
>
> -Shroud

Then I dive back in. Fly back this time, full throttle to the largest net site in the world. The virtual environment blueshifts to tell me I'm going fast, plasma heat of virtual air sears my virtual skin. It doesn't matter. None of it matters. There's an intruder in my home; he's hurt my people, and whoever he is, he's going to pay.

The I-Link pirate crew's operator environment is strangely quiet, almost empty, when I reach their home network. They gave me trusted access a long time ago for fixing OmniMart's links to California when they break, on the condition that I not do exactly what I'm doing right now — poke around in their operator environment. But their operator gestalt is gone. Only one presence is here. The intruder. I know he's here; I feel him, but trying to see him is like looking at a hair in your eye. Whoever he is, he's good. I try to relax, let go of the metaphors of the flesh, feel my world, perceive it with my software senses.

There he is, like a ghost, like a poltergeist spreading mayhem. Like a great cat, circling me as I circle him, aware of me. A squirt of packets comes my way, slipping through the

OmniMart network's firewall to slam into my tank's firewall. It's a feint. He's trying to draw more activity, to get a bigger sample of my crypto, so he can break it, so he can jack his signal directly into my brain. Sneaky. I feint as well, take his bait, start a nice virus emitter and transmit the packets to myself, unencrypted. My own antivirus software shrieks a warning at me, but this is a known virus, and my software is already immune. I disconnect from I-Link, lock myself in my home network for a second or two, scramble my crypto keys again and jump back to I-Link to check on his progress. He's gone. Probably retreated to deal with the virus he just caught; exactly what I wanted. I lay my trap for his return. An old-fashioned viral sneak attack isn't going to stop this customer for long, but I've got a trick up my sleeve. He won't know what hit him. He won't know he's been hit at all.

He comes back three seconds later, with new encryption patterns, as expected. He connects right through the I-Link firewall where he did before and right into my trap, a nice little piece of ice I wrote called Ship-in-a-Bottle. The ice gives me a window inside and I can watch him.

The intruder jacks into an environment that looks exactly like the I-Link inside net. It's a duplicate of all the environmental data. He's none the wiser, though I have to move fast before he notices the difference in performance. This type F Penguin ice was top of the line before the G+s came out, but it's nowhere near as fast as the I-Link main environment. While he's lagging I get busy with my own statistical attack on his link. He jumps into what he thinks is OmniMart Denver. Ship-in-a-Bottle picks up his jump coordinates and jumps with him. His connection lags slightly while the ice picks up the new environment and the process repeats. I follow, still nibbling at his connection. In seven seconds I have him. Without ceremony I hit him with a military grade scrambler and a deck toaster I wrote myself, simultaneously sending him a data feed that should give him seizures if he's a jack head like me, and tie up his host software, so I can go jump into it and really do him

dirt. I don't wait to see what happens, I just go. Jump. Good as
he is, he probably won't be disoriented for long.

A brief flash. A gestalt. A cold feeling slides down my
neck, like liquid mercury. Someone else is here with me — the
intruder. The same poltergeist presence huddles in a corner
seizing, pain radiating out into the gestalt. Smile to myself
as I start up my burnout ice, and probe for weaknesses in his
host system. For ways to hurt him. Ways to kill him. *Nemo Me
Impune Lacessit.*

There's a sudden sense of uncoiling in the gestalt, and he
comes for me. Back out, back out, I'm exposed here; burnout
software took too long. My moves are nightmare slow and I
can't get away fast enough. Surrounded, engulfed, I feel incisors beginning to slide through my skull into my brain. Icy.
My mind recoils from them. A burst of static as the environment and I cease to be and I know I'm…

Chapter 4

Out.

Sleep no more! Macbeth does murther sleep. This is what I know. This is what I remember. Blood-bright light through my eyelids into my eyes. Voices. Movement. Something squeezes my left arm crushingly. Something else cold presses against my chest. "Nothing! BP zero over zero, no pulse. Hook her up fast!" Patches taped to my chest. Something forced down my throat. "Clear!" Someone shouts. Hands under my body draw back urgently and I'm alone again for a moment. All is still. Something kicks me in the chest, and everything inside me squeezes tight at the same time for a moment. When it passes, I'm aware of a sudden urgent throbbing in my chest. Gasp for breath. It hisses through the tube in my throat. "We've got a pulse! Blood pressure coming up, one fifty five over a hundred, pulse a hundred and five. Respiration! Pulse/ox is coming up fast. Get the jack EEG adapter."

Open my eyes into the blinding bright. Bobby must have dumped my connection, and sent the EMTs. I'm still breathing hard, like waking from a nightmare. A mass of blue medical uniforms surrounds me, clutch at me, draw me up out of the tank onto a gurney. A white-coated figure bends over me. Bald head. Glasses. He looks relieved that I'm breathing. Look back toward my tank as something's plugged into my head. I should be angry, that's … a little personal, plugging things in there without asking. I reach up to unplug it, but my hand is uncoordinated, fumbling over the spot behind my ear. Some landmark missing. Find the one jack and fumble at the cable. White coat reacts. "She's conscious! Sedate her, quick, before she goes tachycardic again! "

My arms are strapped to the gurney. Bobby's face. I notice him as the needle bites my thigh with a cold burn grown suddenly hot, tendrils of heat radiating from it upward toward my brain. *When the poison reaches the heart...* "Wait!" My brain forms the word, I feel my lips move around the hard plastic tube in my throat, but I can't make a sound. Anger rising within me. I strain at the straps holding my wrists, but I can feel the sedative making my thoughts soft, the urgency draining out, like blood washing down the drain. I look over at Bobby, trying to find my anger under this chemical assault. "Wait…" I try again, but the unbearable weariness washes through me and my eyes slide closed again, and at least superficially, it doesn't matter anymore.

* * *

Light, 2.0. The sun wraps my skin in a weightless, massless embrace, the warmth of it permeating me with a comfortable sense of well-being, and a desire just to lie here. Wind tickles my skin, cooling me a little. I can hear the lapping of water nearby. Smell a saltiness that is probably the ocean. Smell of coconut and pineapple and sweet from somewhere near me, taste it in my mouth. This is such a lovely feeling. I hate to do what I know I have to. I open my eyes … to a cloudless blue sky. Watch a while, uncomprehending. Some suborbital flight or other leaves a con trail through the stratosphere, heading for the vacuum and darkness above. Sound of movement to my left. Motion catches my eye, reflecting off the inside of my sunglasses.

"Shroudie?"

I turn to look toward the voice. But I know it already, even before I see the familiar face, the familiar curvy body, dressed in a low cut one piece swimsuit. Like a dream, before I recognize her, I know already who she is. A glass of something white and slushy and decorated with a gaudy little pink paper umbrella sits on the sand next to me. Beach sand under her beach chair trails out to a gently lapping blue ocean that stretches out to the horizon. Smell of salt water. Of coconut sunscreen. Of body. "Tika?"

Her dark brows disappear behind her sunglasses, furrowing. "Shroudie, are you okay?"

She reaches out to touch my hand with her fingers, and after a moment I take her hand gently. Something. It feels familiar. Like a newly developed habit. I shake my head.

"Tika ... you..." My voice croaks, as though still dry from the endotracheal tube in my throat. I try again. "I ... don't know. I think ... I missed a meeting somewhere, nothing's making any sense, and I don't know where I am."

Tika slides her sunglasses off, baring eyes the color of melted chocolate, pupils drawing tight in the sunlight. "Oh, shit," she says.

Watch those eyes even as they watch me, her brow furrowing, squinting a little, losing the languid quality her tan skin and dark lash line had given them. "Tik ... whatever attacked us ... I thought it messed you up. I was ... afraid..." Squeeze her hand. "I'm so glad you're ok."

She squeezes back gently, but she's sobbing, and something snaps tight in my stomach. "Tika? What?"

"I hoped ... you weren't like me ... I'd hoped you wouldn't get relapses like this. Oh, Shroudie ... I'm so sorry..." Misgivings. It's a foregone conclusion that I'm not going to like what she's talking about, once I figure out what it is. My expression must be sufficiently baffled, though, because she goes on. "What's the last thing you remember?"

Wrack my brain a little. I might have been born the moment the plane crossed my vision and I opened my eyes to see it. But there's more ... it comes to me after a moment. "Jacking out. No, wait. Bobby must have dumped me out. We were being attacked. You went down, everybody was down. I got to the fucker, got into his hardware, and he was on me ... that's when

Bobby dumped the link, I guess. Paramedics were there next thing I remember. They … intubated me and … resuscitated… They… I think I was dead when they got to my tank." A shiver slides down my spine like cold mercury. The memories squirm away from my grasp, and it's hard to pin down exactly those events. "Once I woke up they sedated me. After that…" I look back up at the sky. "Watching that contrail and wondering where the fuck I am."

It comes out more harshly than it should have but I am, I realize, pissed off. Failure. I lost. Whatever the intruder wanted to do, he did. I couldn't stop him. It's a bitter taste, and it poisons the almost comfortable feeling of being where I am. Of being here with Tik. At least she made it. I have paperwork to shuffle, an investigation to start. Revenge to exact. The idea gives me a grim satisfaction I'm all too familiar with.

Tika draws back a little, and again something twists in my stomach. She finally slips her shades back on. I have to look away, and as long as I do, I look around for my chair. "So about now you're wondering where the wheelchair is, huh?"

I look back at Tika and nod. Misgivings again. The change of subject is coming, just like in the gestalt. I can almost feel the change. Body language, maybe. "Yeah." My chair. My life. It seems like a long time ago now.

Tika sighs softly. "They said there might be some relapses even after the end of therapy. You're having a bad one. Shroud, you never were in a wheelchair in the real world. That's implanted memory from the attack."

Her sunglasses reflect mine as I stare at her, and shake my head slowly. "Tik, I've been in a wheelchair since I was a little girl. I was born this way. I've been like this my whole life." I keep my voice calm, neutral, but there's a steely frost filling me despite the sun. Tender subject. Old hate. Or… Or I'm wrong about … everything, and I'm not who I think I am.

Tika nods. "Nasty piece of work, huh? Tries to make you into something you're not. Gives you a whole life that wasn't yours so you conform to some model psychologically. Trashes your sense of identity." She looks over at me. "It does … get better. Pretty soon you can remember both sets of memories together. That … is pretty much where I am. Some pretty messed up stuff in my head, but…" She trails off.

Think about it. My mind recoils from the idea. Force the issue. Another moment of no memory at all, of feeling like I was born the moment I opened my eyes here, wherever here is. I half expect another life, this real life of Tika's, to snap back, to become me, and for me to feel it. But it doesn't happen. The only life I can recall begins in a wheelchair and ends in a tank. I can feel my heart pounding again, and I force myself to take long, slow breaths, the threat of tachycardia and fibrillation still fresh in my mind, whatever the real-time gap between then and now. Vague memories of a hospital. Of a doctor. Bald head. Telling me … asking me… "Do you know where you are, Shroud?" I don't remember. "Do you know?" No. But my name is … my name is … tickle of anger. Reach for my frostiness. Get control. It takes awhile. Thinking. Reminiscing, grasping at my memories. Now not sure if any of them are real. I can't tell. They all feel…

I turn back toward her. "Tik … are you saying … none of my memories are real?"

She looks over at me again. "Some of them are. Most of them, probably. At least, that's how it was for me. The attack ice somehow maps your responses to a series of random images and starts building false memories for you, based on that. Like psych modeling ice, except that it's faster and easier to try and make you fit the model, than to analyze the differences."

My voice is tight, stiff. Like it's coming from a speech synthesizer instead of me. "How do I tell which parts of what I remember are real?" I cling to my frostiness, fighting back the overwhelming feeling of panic. *Did Chuang Tsu dream he was a butterfly, or did the butterfly dream he was Chuang Tsu?* I don't know. I don't know. Worse. Part of me does admire that ice, despite myself. Someone, somewhere, wrote a beauty. And I want to know how it works. No butterfly, I.

Tika closes her eyes, looking away, shaking her head. Her voice is a bare whisper when she replies. "I … the memories I got … were … I guess things I might have done anyway. And they still affect me like they really happened. How do you tell what's real? I don't know. All I've been able to do is ask people I remember doing or saying certain things … and trust them."

That sinks in slowly. A memory, real or not. College. My dorm room. I remember the cinderblock walls there, so very like the place I live now. Think I live now. This is what I know. This is what I remember. My one and only college boyfriend. A fellow nerd, of course, though of the theater persuasion. He's dressing, his back to me, I know he's about to walk out of my life for good. I'm awash in him, in the smell of his shampoo — sweet with awapuhi, the scent of his body, still a little drunk, the enthusiasm for him from earlier in the evening rapidly transmuting to anger. "So you're just leaving then? All of this … meant nothing? Just one last quickie before you say goodbye?"

"You're not a trusting person. You're not a loving person. You're not even very nice. You're like the bitter shroud of death, and I'm too young to die."

Where came you by this goodly speech? It is extemporé, from my motherwit. Yeah. A witty mother, witless else her son. Bah. Theater majors. You've been rehearsing that line, you son-of-a-bitch.

* * *

I met him after I switched majors from English to Software Engineering. Remember the astonishment I felt when he wanted to touch me. Remember that his scent was usually commingled with alcohol, his and mine both. It set the pattern for most of the dating I did later. Remember doing later. This is frustrating. But I remember how much that stung. If it did at all. Frustrating not to know, to feel like I'm looking past something important. But I have to start somewhere. I have to learn to believe again.

"Tik … I remember … um…" Marshaling my memories to something more pleasant, more recent. When the world began and ended at the perimeter of an old-fashioned open bag waterbed; warm, sloshing beneath us, and we shared … and we touched … and we… "Tik, did we ever have sex online together?" I'm blushing. I can feel it. Were I a horny teenager with her first induction rig, sure, this kind of thing happens all the time. But I'm old. I'm supposed to know better. Embarrassing to find out how much of that teenager is still locked away inside.

Tika blushes a little too, but she's smiling. "Oh yeah, that was real. Well, I mean … it was net sex, but it really happened. Well … you know … at least I remember it too, for whatever that's worth." The semantics of virtual-reality experiences are fuzzy, to say the least. She goes on, "I remember talking to you the morning of the attack, trying to get you to come to Carmel with me and Brian. Do you remember that?"

I nod slowly. But in the confines of my skull, I wonder why I'm so relieved that our indiscretions together were as real as net sex ever gets. I could have been fired over that. Force my mind back to the subject at hand. There is a pattern emerging. "Do you remember the intruder?"

Tika shakes her head. "Not really. My memory gets strange right after passdown ended." She shivers, a feeling I know all too well. "Really strange." I look away, decide not to press her on that right now. Tachycardia … fibrillation … I remember that from when I was revived. Something in the implanted memories, or perhaps the interface between implanted memory and real memory … can shut my heart down. Or Tika's, presumably.

A joke. A great cosmic joke. I have to laugh. "It seems like, based on a sample of two events, mind you, that it's only reality that got overwritten, and all the virtual stuff is real. How's that for irony?" Tik smiles a little, a wry chuckle escaping her. But I have to laugh. Where I am right now doesn't seem like a bad place. The life I'm supposed to remember might be nicer too, who knows? Try to believe. "So … you wanna tell me where we are?"

She picks up the subject change as smoothly as she would have in the gestalt, and smiles.

"Cabo San Lucas. I've been here a week, you got here yesterday. They had you in therapy longer. Anyway, the company put you on medical leave for a month, same as me. All expenses paid, and our assignment is to get a tan and get our heads sorted out. Their words."

I snort at that. "Bullshit. Bull. Shit. They're up to something, and you know it. It'd be cheaper to fire us, tie our lawsuits up in court for a few years, and wait for us to starve."

Tika shrugs, but there's a flicker of concern on her face, some of the lightness fading. "Yeah. I kind of wonder about that too, but in CalTech at least, they can't do that. You bring an injury suit against a corporation, the district attorney represents you, and meantime the corp has to keep paying your disability. Anyway, they sold it to me as medical leave, and after a month in the hospital it sounded pretty good. Maybe they're stashing us here to keep an eye on us, see if we go crazy after a while. Maybe they're planning to sell the therapy program for what we got hit with. Or maybe you're more valuable to them than you think, and they wanted to keep you happy so they sent me. So we could compare memories or something.

"A month?" I flop back onto my chair, closing my eyes. A month of real-time? For an operator as sharp as whoever wrote this ice? "And we're supposed to stay here another month? Offline?"

Tika chuckles a little. "Yeah. We're offline. Hard down. Doctor's orders." She looks over at me. Her hand touches mine. The subject has changed again, and I can guess what she's thinking. It might not be such a bad thing, being offline for a month. Here. With her.

I lace my fingers amongst hers, and hope that answers her question, at least, even while I'm picking at her words. That contemplation brings me back to another point that is only just sinking in. "So, you're saying I can really walk." Feel the heart jump at that. But only a little. I'm still cynical. Suspicious even. A lifetime of experience, real or not, is telling me this is bullshit.

She smiles a little, and slides out of her chair. She stands up in a sinuous movement, tugging me by the hand. "Only one way to find out, right?"

She is. And I do. I get up out of my beach chair and stand in front of her. It's a complete non-event, like I've been doing it all my life. But the ground seems so very far away now. I try to remember being used to it, but whatever happened to that memory, it isn't anywhere I can find it. I'm taller than Tik is. Who knew? I feel like a giant. I think about all the things I always wished I could stand long enough to do. And wonder how many of them are things I really did do and cannot now remember.

Tik is watching me. "You okay?"

"Huh?" I've been staring at my toes, I guess. I look at her, feeling sheepish.

"Yeah. Just … taking it all in, you know?" She nods. "I think…" I say, considering the matter carefully. Where do I start? "I think I'd like to go wading." Tika smiles, and I smile with her.

Chapter 5

This is what I know. This is what I remember. It's 1992, I'm 7 years old. I'm sitting in a wheelchair in front of the television watching some religious network. I'm praying, following the words they're saying, pleading for my own little miracle. I know I'll be healed when I'm done. I know that when Reverend Whatzis says to stand up, I can. And Mom will be so proud of me. When he says it, I push myself up on the arms of my wheelchair and let my legs take the weight. Freedom. Healed. Complete. I feel it, the split second I let go of the chair.

The floor rushes up, knocking out both my front teeth with a terrifying crack that reverberates through my skull. I'm dizzy, my nose is bloody, and I've bitten the hell out of my tongue. I'm still there an hour later, bloody and furious, when Mom gets home from work. I tell her the story, words mushy around missing teeth and swollen tongue. She hauls me back into my chair, sends me to the bathroom to clean myself up while she cleans the carpet. Afterward, she imparts words of wisdom about it. Thankfully, I don't remember them right now.

* * *

This is something I always wanted. I walk through the sand with the ocean washing over my ankles. Swing my arms like that little girl I was, holding hands with Tika. Wade in deeper. The water is shockingly cold as my feet pass below the thermocline. Feel myself fly as I float to the top of each wave as it comes by. Flying, at least, is familiar. Landing, feet touching the sand, to be lifted again by the next wave; less so. As the wave runs out, and the water stops supporting me, I'm surprised once again when my legs hold me up. Tika's chuckling softly, and I realize that I'm smiling a small, guarded smile. I still don't quite believe. "This is going to get ordinary some day, I imagine."

"What is?" Tik's fingers are still laced in mine.

"This standing and walking stuff." Tika laughs softly, and I follow suit. But I'm still expecting the ground to come hit me in the face, I realize. Still guarded.

"Ohh. I was afraid you were talking about being with me." That impish smile I've seen online is on her lips again.

My mouth's a little dry suddenly. "Flirt."

Her smile broadens, baring the perfect white teeth. "Damn straight."

"I sure hope not."

Tik laughs and gives my hand a squeeze. "Got me there. What about you? In real life, I mean." My skin flushes at the question, and Tik giggles, but before I can answer, she's going on. Leading me by the hand. "C'mon. Let's go get a drink."

The music in the beach-side bar is all in Spanish, and I don't understand it. "Dos cervezas, por favor. Negra Modelo." That's about a third of my Spanish. I can also ask where the bathroom is, and where the beer and the hookers can be found. And I know enough insults to start a fight, in the unlikely event I should want to. Probably a leftover from my English major days. There were databases of Spanish profanity online then. Probably still are. I slot my bank card in the reader in the edge of the bar. Let it rebound on the elastic string around my neck. Tik giggles at my Spanish, and proves in a sentence or two that she wasn't kidding about speaking the language. "Well, well. Learn something new every day."

She laughs. "Hey, I told you I'm from Austin. My mother was an illegal immigrant in the old U.S. I've been speaking Spanish longer than I've been speaking English. I immigrated to CalTech after the revolution and all that shit. Remember, OmniMart hired me away from Iota Networks?"

"I hadn't exactly memorized your resume, y'know. What about your father?"

"I don't talk about my father." Her smile fades a little at that.

"I never even knew mine. Mom wouldn't tell me who he was. Well ... you know. The usual caveats about my memory apply right now."

"You're lucky," is all Tik says on the matter.

"What?"

"I don't want to talk about it, Shroudie. It was bad, ok?"

"Attack ice found that, did it?"

She nods slowly and reaches up to touch her nose with a fingertip. It doesn't take a rocket scientist to guess the rest.

"Sorry." I take a long pull from my beer. "Man, this stuff must be watered down. I can barely taste it."

Tik pats my hand and smiles a little. "Don't stress over it. No way you could have known. That's the problem with memory, I guess. Real or not, it defines you. Strengths and weaknesses, and you can't ever completely get away from it."

I take another pull of my nearly flavorless beer.

Tik sips her own before continuing. "Gotta live in the present, you know? I mean, think about it. You and I spend most of our time awake online, where nothing's real except that we both remember it as real. And those memories are as much part of us as if we really experienced those events, however impossible some of them are. So what does that leave us, if we stop and try to make sense out of everything?"

"That's how you're dealing with the attack?"

Tik nods. "Yeah. And life. Live in the moment. Feel the real. Enjoy it for what it is, 'cause life's short."

I watch her as she speaks, watch her take another pull from her beer. "Feel the real? Sounds like advertising for a porn virtual."

Tik looks at me sharply a moment, then chuckles. "Well, yeah. You can learn a lot from porn, you know? I keep forgetting you have a sense of humor. It doesn't come across much at work."

It's my turn to chuckle, looking into the dregs of my beer. "Got a reputation to uphold, you know? Gotta keep the newbies impressed." Light, but there's a sick feeling in my stomach as I think about just who that would be. Jay, Kimmy, and to a lesser extent the twins in Boston. "Did ... any of them make it?"

Tik closes her eyes. Shakes her head. "None of them made it. Rei went into cardiac arrest. Silv and Jay had strokes. Kimmy ... nobody's seen her since the attack. She jumped out of the tank and ran off screaming and they can't find her. I don't know where to start to look for her without the net. Brian would, but..."

I look over at her. "But what?"

"Attack ice. It ... used my memories of him to do things. Not ... nice things either. Things I..." Her voice falters, and I pet her hand softly. It's tense, a little cool and damp. Her hand clings to mine, and her voice drops to a whisper. "Things I didn't want to like ... but did. Things I'd never ask him to do in real life. I ... get flashbacks to them every time I see him."

I take her hand gently. "I'm sorry, Tik." I can feel the old fury building up inside me again, just when I thought it was finally ebbing and I might finally be able to just be here. Another long hunt for this joker? This intruder who killed two of us and mutilated Tik's memory, and mine, and Kimmy's, into who knows what. Another long hunt? Bring it on. "I'm going to burn whoever did this. Whoever wrote it, whoever deployed it, and whoever paid for it. Every last one of them."

Tika looks at me and shakes her head. "Don't be like that, Shroudie. We're on medical leave. Let it go. There's already been enough killing. You can't go back online for a month anyway."

"Tika, these people are dead. Kimmy might be too. And you and I don't know which of our memories we can trust anymore, to the point where we don't really know who we are." I lower my voice after that. People in the bar are starting to stare.

"Don't you think I know that?" Tik blinks angrily, wiping at her eyes. "But there's nothing either of us can do about it right now. We're lucky to be alive, and I'm not going to throw that away to revenge this 'foul and unnatural murther.' It won't bring them back, and it won't make us better."

I turn away from her, toward the bartender. "Más cerveza." Slam my bank card through the reader. The card snaps back into my face for my pique, and I'm about to graduate from the low-level annoyance I've been feeling all day to genuinely pissed off again, pausing only a moment to wonder when Tika started quoting Macbeth. She's sobbing again though, and that gives my guts a sharp twist. "Shit. Tik ... I'm sorry. I'm sorry." The anger drains out of me as fast as it built up. I reach out to touch her shoulder, then gently pull her to me, slipping my arms around her. She comes willingly enough and I whisper it again in her ear. "I'm sorry."

"I know, Shroudie. I know. I keep forgetting ... this is all fresh for you. You can't help but drag it all up again."

Chapter 6

This is what I know. This is what I remember. It's the summer, the Turn of the Century, I'm fifteen years old. My mother is at work, and I'm in my bedroom playing One Must Fall 2097 on my PC with my best friend Sarah Wight, and passing a bottle of wine back and forth. It doesn't improve our play any. The game is all about two remotely piloted mecha destroying each other — a nonviolent combat game. I'm busy beating on the character Milano's Thorn with my souped up Jaguar. She's waiting her turn. Sparks and bits of metal are flying from his battered mecha, and Sarah's just chuckling. "Dude, you so need to get a life. You're way too good at this game." She takes a pull from the bottle.

"Sure. Yeah. What would I want to do that for?" And I mean it.

"Because there's stuff you can't do online." She's picked up one of my cowboy boots, soft black leather, etched silver hammered over the toes. Mom kvetched when I spent my Christmas money on them. They're boots made for walking. They still look brand new. Sarah says, "These are nice." *These boots were made for walking…* That was the joke…

"Thanks. Sure. Yeah, I always wanted to get mugged or something. There's a life experience I'd treasure forever." I throw Milano's Thorn into the electric fence and he takes spectacular damage. Not quite dead yet. Sarah scoots closer, until I can smell the wine on her breath. I have Milano on the ground again and am kicking the hell out of his mech. His energy reading is dropping off fast and I'm setting him up for the Jaguar throw move.

"There's good stuff too, you know. The mountains are pretty, and the air up there is fresh and cool, and it's so quiet." She closes her eyes as though remembering something. Smiles. "And there are people. Like … have you ever kissed a guy?" She's starting to throw off my timing by being so close, but I manage to give Milano the coup de grâce move, via a ridiculous combination of joystick moves and button presses.

I sit back a little, resting my eyes. She sets my boot down. I hear it. "No. I haven't."

"How about another girl?" I shrug a little, brushing against her as she leans on the arm of my chair.

"Sarah, I've never kissed anyone, okay?"

All is quiet. My eyes are still closed. Were I sober, I'd probably not be surprised. But I'm not, so I am. She slips her arm around my shoulders, draws me close, and gently presses her lips to mine. If I could feel my toes, I know I'd feel the kiss all the way there. As it is, the sudden electricity trails out in the patchwork of sensation in my thighs, leaving it in somewhat awkward territory. The kiss seems to go on for eternity, making my breathing shallow, palms feel a little sweaty. Then it ends, and she draws back. "Well, now you have." She says quietly, smiling down at me.

* * *

I kiss Tika. All I feel are lips. All I taste are Mexican beer and woman. None of which are bad things. She chuckles a little. "Well, hello stranger." She kisses back softly, tongue brushing my lips. The kiss deepens, her breath on my cheek, fingers twining in my hair.

"Um…" nuzzle her neck between kisses. "We should probably go some place private. People are starting to stare." Tika draws back a little. She's a bit flushed.

"Let them stare," she says. But we do make our way to the hotel.

Tika leads me to a door. I still don't recall ever seeing it before, though there's a vague familiarity. My thumbprint opens the lock readily enough. It swings wide, yawning open with comfortable anonymity decorated with old familiar things. A watch. My watch, I realize. Strange, and yet familiar. It's a bizarre combination of 1960s nixie tube displays instead of LCD, Turn of the Century high voltage electronics, and a modern fuel cell for power. I've seen these on eBay, but they were always too expensive. Never bought one. Don't remember buying one. Wonder where I got the money. It's huge and chunky and it glows in the dark, too. It makes me smile — technological perversity at its best.

I have a purse, it would seem. It's strangely familiar too, though I don't remember ever wearing one. My wheelchair always had a backpack. And of course, my boots are here, shiny and new still, even though twenty-five years have gone by. I'm looking forward to wearing them. Later. I look in the mirror a moment, shocked again by being tall. My hair is tied back, showing my jack. Run my fingertips along it, wonder what it is that's nagging at me about my jack. Still. Has been since I woke up … the first time.

Tika looks at me strangely. "You're quiet again. Are you ok?"

I nod, slip my arms around her, pull her close. "Yeah. Memories, you know? All of this is … is my real life, I guess. It's starting to feel a little familiar. Like … I can almost make out what my life must have been like. Either life I talk about, I've wanted to be here — or somewhere — with you for a long time, Tik."

She smiles and draws close to me. "I know. I've known a long time. It was just a matter of convincing you to come."

Her lips touch mine again, and she kisses me. I relax into it, or try to, if relax could even be the right word. Her tongue brushes mine lightly, and I can almost feel what I should be feeling. Her softness, her warmth is against me. She slips the shoulder straps of my swimsuit down. I let go of her a moment and arch and wriggle out of the suit. Try to stay in the moment. Return the favor. Unzip her. Undress her. Now I'm nuzzling downward along her skin. Kissing her. Tasting her. The salt of the sea and of her skin mingled. Cup her breast in my hand. Feel her other nipple brush my cheek as I kiss her chest. Feel her. Hear her as I take her nipple between my lips. Tease it with my tongue. My senses slowly flood with her flesh, her real. *Feel the real*, she said, and maybe, just maybe, she's right.

Make love to Tika. Making love. How long has this moment been on my mind? How many times have I imagined it, both with her online and without her alone? It's less than that. Imagination is awfully sweet. Awfully attractive. Fulfilling. Sometimes the realization pales beside it. Maybe we should log in… Distracted, but Tika doesn't seem to notice. She's coming, writhing, fingers tangling in my hair, saying my name again and again. "Shroud, Shroud, Shroud." There's a piece missing from this puzzle, and that piece is…

Now I'm on my back, and I'm very … wet … she's licking … arousal now, so close so very … let it … stop analyzing and let me… I open my eyes, turn my head to one side, catch sight of my boots, still pristine after all this time. Missing piece. Close my eyes again. Shudder. Finally … finally getting where I can let go. It's like when I first learned to fly online. Know it's not real, know it will work, but I learned young about falling, and that first leap … I remember how hard it was when I first jacked in … when I first got my jack … just to let go … fly now…

I was twenty-five years old when the first practical direct-neural-interface jacks were invented. They were the old style — slow, an implanted matrix of electrodes put in the brain by a surgeon. Permanent. They would…

I can feel my skin flushing, and I can't catch my breath. Despite my distraction, Tika's caress is … consuming. I feel my back arching, muscles gathering, trembling inside … shiny new boots stuck in my mind… *These boots were made for walking*… Shiny new … let go … fly now…

Jacks were experimental when they came out. More rigidly controlled, limited. That's why I had to … get a new… Soft moan escapes my throat and I can feel the edge of it all. *Made for walking.* Shiny new … already ten years old when … jack … let go … fly now…

Jacks were to help people with spinal injuries and birth defects by letting them control things with thought. Mostly wheelchairs.

People who would never wear out a pair of boots. *Made for walking…* Fly… Fly…

People like me.

I haul up my old jack's HUD. The tank controls come to life. Tank controls. That means … that means… Standing out among the usual heat, water salinity, data throughput, heart-rate, and EEG data displays is a great big red icon marked EMO. It stands for…

The softness is gone from Tika's caresses, and her incisors are slicing through my flesh, rending it, seeking … my mind…

It stands for Emergency Machine Off.

Emergency Machine Off.

In a sensory flash, everything goes dark.

Chapter 7

Stupid girl, don't believe everything you see on TV. Mom's exact words when she found me that evening, still bloody and furious on the floor in front of the television, my faith crushed. My mouth hurts in sympathy to the memory. *These boots were made for walking, but you never will.* More maternal wisdom. It stays dark. Sobbing. Just as well they can't see me. Get control. Get frosty. I can hear myself breathing, panting, heart racing. Tangle of emotions. Rage. Grief. Shame. Arousal. I can smell myself in the tank. Rip the fiber-optic cables out of my skull and lie here in the dark. Feel the water grow chill, the air go stale. Try to flush the images, the sensations, and most of all the emotions from my mind. Hear thumping outside as they try to get my tank open. It's locked from the inside.

Reach up to the tank cover latch and yank it; slide the hatch cover open. The air is cold compared to this artificial womb. Cold, stink of electronics, yellow green of fluorescent lights pouring into my eyes. EMTs again. Blue shirt. Pants like they wore on the Space Shuttle. Big pockets. That's what I notice. This again, except that my heart is hammering quite well enough. "I can get out by myself." They back off. Run my fingertips over my jack site … jack sites, I notice. The old jack. The intruder didn't know about it. The one I always use to control the tank. "I'm fine."

Bobby looks down at me, offers his hand. I slap it away and haul myself to my feet to climb out of the tank. My legs buckle under me. Fight back the sobs again, fight but lose. Bobby can see. He offers his hand again, and this time I take it. *Stupid girl, don't believe everything you see on TV. Made for walking, and you never will.* Mom always hated that about me. I always hated her for it. One of the EMTs drags my chair over to me. I lever myself into it, old, floppy, pissed off, naked, sobbing. No pride left. I don't give a crap who sees.

Bobby's still rubbing at his hand where I slapped it. He looks at me with a stricken look. I have a pretty good idea what he has to say, so I cut him off before he says anything. "What time is it?"

He looks at me, then looks at his watch, as EMTs close around me and I can't see him again. "7:14. Friday. Kate, are you all right? Something happened. Jay's down. He's ... he's dead, I was watching your tank to make sure nothing ... and then you..." Bobby breaks down into sobs. I suffer a moment's wild urge to kiss Bobby, but I don't think he'd understand. Nobody else ever called me Kate. Nobody. Even he never used it online.

I'm his boss. Comfort isn't mine to offer, and I'm fighting back my own weakness. Weakness. Injury. Bobby's a community-college boy with a certification in tank safety team, nothing else, and it'd be a cold day in hell before he has signature authority to do more than call an ambulance. I'm his boss, fifteen years experience, a first generation plughead, and my face is wet with tears, and I'm shivering. Bobby hands me my robe, looks away. His data is all in the packet headers and not the content. His news is bad, but I already knew.

Tika told me.

"I know. I know. Listen. Bobby, listen to me." Shuddering belies the calm authority I'm trying to project. One of the EMTs pumps up a blood pressure cuff around my arm. I stop gesturing with it. "Run down to the main switch-yard and pull the plug on our main and backup feeds to the public net. Shut down the sat-backups, everything, I want us totally isolated.

Then get on the phone with I-Link and tell them they are completely branched if you can get anyone to answer who knows
anything. Use the cell phone. Get going. C'mon, Bobby. Go!
I have to get on the line with Corporate. Someone's pulling
some heavyweight shit in there, and before I'm done I'm going
to paint the wall with his brains." It's easy to lead in a crisis.
People don't know what to do. They want to be told. Bobby
snaps to it. He runs. I turn to get my ice out of the tank's slots.
Habits of life.

The EMTs pull me back from the tank, yank my robe
open, stick ECG pads to my chest. "Ma'am, that's enough.
Will you please hold still? There are a lot of people going to
be working on you, and a lot of stuff happening very quickly. Do you take any medications?" I shake my head. One of
the EMTs tries to stick something into my jack. I grab his
wrist, twist and pull down. It's almost gratifying how easy it
is. Adrenaline. Go figure.

"Do not plug anything in there without asking. Understand?
You can poke me, you can prod me, but do not plug anything
into my head without asking, and do not sedate me."

The EMT looks at me strangely, and I catch him giving a
quick head shake to the one behind me, who was in the act of
peeling a dermal patch; probably a sedative. I let go of his arm.
"Um... Ma'am, this is an EEG connector. Would you please
plug it into your jack?" I take the plug, but my hand is shaking
too much by the time I get it to my ear.

"You ... you'd better do it. Upper jack." The jack I still
trust. The old one. He slides it in, gentle as a lamb, barely hard
enough to latch it. I pull up the jack's HUD and enable direct connections, write only. I see his data screen ripple to life.
Close my eyes. They're moving me again. I let them.

7:21 a.m. Friday.

Hospitals. There's a characteristic stench to them: the mingled odors of antiseptic, sick people, dead people. Vaguely like
urine but not quite, and when I smell that smell I always imagine that all the pathogens known to man are riding that carrier

stench into my unprotected mucous membranes. I've been in my share of hospitals. *Are you Julia Farro's family? Would you come with me, please?* The news isn't good. It never is.

Sterile clean. Hospital stink settles into my hair, my skin. I'm wearing my bathrobe again. The paper gown they gave me is wadded up in the garbage. Hate those things. I changed once I got out of the MRI. I'm sitting on the bed in the emergency bay with a blanket over my legs. They don't feel cold, of course, but they're chilling the rest of me. My patience for being a patient is wearing thin. If I'm just going to sit and wait, I'm going home to do it. Weariness, a brain-deep tiredness, is filling me. I know this feeling. It's a common enough one for me. Too much data flowed through my head for too long. It's the feeling that my inner eye is glazing, over-stimulated. A bit early in the day for that feeling. *How fast were you going?* The emergency room doctor returns. It only seems like it's been forever. I'm watching the skin slide over the bones of his face as his jaw moves. Oops. He's speaking. "…there may be some memory lapses, as your brain tries to integrate two sets of simultaneous experiences."

The doctor looks at me quizzically. He's speaking. "Do you know where you are, Dr. Farro?"

He's a middle-aged man, hair gone black and grey, a bald patch on the top that I can see from the table. He's wearing a white lab coat, pocket full of pens, each with the name of some pharmaceutical corp or other. His other pocket has the end of his stethoscope in it, keeping it warm. His voice is calm, with a professional gentleness. And from the moment I arrived, the moment he first set hands on me, however gently, I've had an uncomfortable sense of déjà vu. "Denver, Colorado. I'm probably in the company hospital, building 27."

"That's good. What time is it?"

Tomorrow and tomorrow and tomorrow… I look to the clock on the wall behind me. "A little after nine o'clock in the morning. Doctor, can we cut to the chase, please? Have you got any results for me? I've got work to do."

His voice is calm, professionally comforting. "Dr. Farro, you've been through a severe neural interface event. Your high-speed jack has a number of neurofibers out of place, and your memory centers are showing symptoms of extreme over-stimulation. More online time is the last thing you need."

"Show me."

He turns on a display screen and turns it so I can see it. "If you look at the MRI images you can see. Your jack is supposed to be connected exclusively to your cerebrum here, and here. As you can see, there are now neurofibers invading the amygdala, which is where emotions are rooted."

I rub behind my ear where my jack is — jacks are — fighting the impression once again that something is wrong there. But something is. The jack's interconnects have shifted inside my head. Artificial neurons, neurofibers, the very development that made high bandwidth jacks feasible, the very nanostructures that intertie my brain with my high-speed jack have plugged themselves into places they don't belong, doing who knows what. Diabolical.

The doctor is speaking again. "— and I think you should stay offline for a while. Take a vacation." I stare at him until he begins to squirm, as I imagine again the neurofibers of the jack squirming inside my brain. It makes my eye twitch, and he squirms in time with it. There's nothing else to say to him. It's time to end this conversation, or make it go somewhere else.

"We have people dead. How do you kill someone like that?" He glances toward the next emergency bay.

So. "Show me."

"I'm sorry, Dr. Farro, I can't do that. Patient privacy…"

I shut him down before he can finish. "I am his supervisor, and he was killed in the line of duty. You know as well as I do that I have access to his medical records as related to this incident."

The doctor sighs, combs his fingers through the fringe of hair at the back of his skull. I can see the tell-tale weariness in him, through the professionalism he's so careful to project. He says, "He's only just been pronounced dead, and we haven't turned off life support yet. The results of the lab work aren't back yet."

"He's in there?"

"Yes."

"Show me." The doctor looks at me, aghast. I look back, giving him my best Shroud steely glare, not knowing if it translates to this world or not. I don't spend much time here. He draws back as though I threatened to bite him.

The doctor walks over to the other bay and draws the curtain back. Jay's pasty white body lies on the bed like a decaying fish washed up on the shore. The smell of rotting fish mingles with the salt sea. I frown a little as that image comes to mind. *You've never even been to the ocean.* He's still wired to monitors and a respirator. Still breathing. But dead.

Lever myself into my chair. Roll to Jay's bed. His face is savagely beaten, and his knuckles are bruised. I wonder what he saw, alone in his tank, what pit of self-hatred the random neural impulses from the jack had unearthed. I reach up to lift one of his eyelids and look at his eye. It's shot with blood, a thousand tiny hemorrhages over the white of the eye. The other is the same. His MRI tells more of the story. His jack is completely rewired, much of it pulled back from his cerebrum and wired into his amygdala. His cerebrum would have been almost sensory deprived while the hacker was deep into his emotional centers and memory. But the movement of the neurofibers isn't what killed him. There's been a massive bleed deep in his brain near the medulla, and the pressure from it crushed the structure against his skull. His lower hindbrain looks like it's been in a blender. You don't do that kind of damage to yourself with your bare hands, and the insides of the tanks are padded. The eyes gave it away. "Stroke?"

Tika said that, too.

The doctor nods quietly. "That's what it looks like to me, yes. We'll know more once the autopsy is done, and you can get those details from the site medical examiner."

I look at the doctor again, staring at the back of his eyes, imagining Jay in his tank, alone, jacked into that ice, jack neurons flailing about randomly in his brain until they plugged into … something … something dark. Something that drove him to try to beat the images out of his head with his own hands … something that pumped his blood pressure so high that the blood vessels in his brain exploded, gushing blood frantically into the confined vault of his skull.

"Dr. Farro?" I blink, find my eyes wet, slump into my chair a little. "Dr. Farro, you need to rest. There's no medical reason to keep you here, and I think you'd be better off if you weren't. I want you to go home. Get some sleep. I'd like to leave the ECG hooked up. We can monitor it from here and send EMTs to your apartment if anything is amiss."

"What about my jack? Those neurofibers that are out of place."

"Only a few of the fibers are out of place. The jack firmware should be able to recognize that and mark them as unusable." He shows me on the MRI. "Don't worry about it."

Something familiar about this doctor. Finally, vague flash, a memory of a memory, his bald head in my almost remembered walking life. White coat. At my resuscitation. Where would the intruder have gotten… "Doctor, do you get online much?"

"I own a deck, yes, but I really only use it to read my e-mail and watch medical journals. Why do you ask?"

I frown a little, thinking. "Does your icon look like you?"

"No, I never figured out how to set that. It's not important for what I do." He looks at me, concerned. "What's on your mind?"

"I'm trying to figure out where the intruder got your image to put in the attack. I know you were there." Fold my arms across my chest protectively. I still remember … kick in the chest, everything squeezing…

"Really? What was I doing there?" There's a voice that doctors sometimes have, more common to psychiatrists. That voice that says, *Yes, what you're saying is important to you, but it's not really real, you poor slob.* The tone people take with children and crazy people. I've always hated that. It made the two times I went to a pro clinic refreshing. The doctor there was cool, businesslike, matter-of-fact. A technician. An engineer. I wish I could afford a service contract with them.

"Resuscitating me. Sedating me. Pretty much the same thing we're doing here, only more directly." Another steely Shroud stare. He fidgets again.

"Do you feel like you're being sedated here?" He folds his arms across his chest as he speaks, mimicking my gesture perhaps, or feeling vulnerable. Like I might jump out of my chair and strangle him, poor mad thing that I am.

"Cut the psychobabble, Doc, I'm just trying to sort out some of the things I saw in there. You were in it, and I want to know where the intruder got your image."

He backs off a little more, then cocks his head. "I am in some training virtuals. I've been in a whole series of them for EMT and tank safety personnel."

"Resuscitation procedures?"

He brightens. "Yes, yes of course. I see where you're going with this. I finished that one a month ago. Do you think it's important?"

I shake my head. "No."

But I file it away, because it is. It's a sharp-edged little puzzle piece that means something, is part of something larger.

9:33 a.m. Friday.

In my absence, the day has dawned, the sun a far-away point of light glowing through the overcast sky. The snow is still falling as I lie in my bed once again. Sit up to look out my apartment window toward the ground, forehead against the glass. The snow is softening the outlines of the city, blurring the edges, making the crisp lines mushy, organic. The bright lights of last evening shine pale in such light as the day allows. Paler, obscured occasionally by a gust of wind sweeping the snow into diagonal motion. I'm supposed to be resting, but I'm not ready to let go yet. My telephone rings — a conference call I've been expecting. Shut down the entire site's outside network feeds, you get some attention. Reach out, put the phone on speaker. Alien. It feels alien, far away. I haven't used the voice line in years. Jack and deck calls, and e-mail, are so much more convenient.

"Dr. Farro. How are you feeling?" Nice of him to ask. The speaker is my boss, Kevin Conlon, Director of Information Technology for the site. He'll inevitably be joined by the usual suspects: Tom Bancrier, Conlon's counterpart from San Jose — assuming of course that they've switched the network back on between here and there — and Reverend Martin from Boston. The CIO is absent, as usual. He's here in Denver, and has been since the corporate headquarters moved after the revolution. He's been away on medical leave for weeks though. It probably annoys them that my phone is so old-fashioned it has no video feed, but that's their problem. If I wanted to see these people I'd fucking take the train and go see them.

"I've been better, obviously, but they tell me I'll live." Toy with the ECG patches on my chest. "They're monitoring me to make sure, though." The pleasantries dispensed with, the meeting starts. I try to pay attention. *This is about your career here.* Yeah, yeah, I know, but losing my job seems like pretty small potatoes suddenly.

The news is bad, but it's pretty much what I already knew. What Bobby told me. What Tika told me. Rei and Silver are dead, heart attack and a stroke, just like Tika said. They have the same jack rewiring Jay did. And I do, though the exact symptoms that killed them vary. Kimmy's wigged, last seen running stark naked down El Camino Real as fast as she could go. Only one detail missing. "What about Tika?"

"Ms. Silverthorn is dead, I'm afraid, Dr. Farro. If our time-lines are correct she was the first to die. It's very likely you saved Ms. Anderson's life. By the time she was attacked she was already in the middle of her logout sequence. You and she are the only survivors." Bancrier speaking. His voice is calm, matter-of-fact. He might be telling me about a stock depression. No, he'd probably be more upset about that.

Close my eyes. Squeeze them tight. But … I can still feel her, here in my mind, that same sense of warmth that the virtual didn't, in retrospect, have. Feel those memories drift, accrete with the softness of her body, with the smell of coconut sunscreen. She can't be ... but she is. And those memories aren't part of this world. Stay frosty, keep the voice level. "You have logs?"

Bancrier says, "Of course, all the way to the start of the shift. Isn't your site equipped with virtual environment logging?"

Conlon jumps in at this point. "Our policy is to log only summaries for evidence to justify homicides. We don't seem to have any logs this time."

"We were a little busy. Sorry." It sounds weak, even to me.

Bancrier says, "CalTech law requires full logging to justify homicides here, and since the operators are frequently too busy to turn the logging on when an incident starts, we log the entire shift."

I jump back in. My patience with bureaucrats seems to be limited this morning. "Look, I don't want to argue policy here, gentlemen, but if you have full logs from the start of this morning's shift, I want copies for my investigation. By courier, please, our network is still compromised."

There is a strained silence. Conlon, my boss, breaks it. "We've already decided that the investigation will be handled in San Jose, Dr. Farro." So. The meeting obviously started before they bothered to dial me in. I keep my voice level and calm, with just a hint of sarcasm.

"You've someone better qualified to pursue the matter there, I take it, Mr. Bancrier? I thought I knew your whole operator staff." I should. I interviewed all of them.

"We're going to hire an outside contractor to look into the matter, Doctor."

"Who, exactly? And why, exactly do we want to involve an outside party in OmniMart internal affairs? Isn't that explicitly against company policy?" Why yes, yes it is. "You are undoubtedly aware that I am highly qualified to pursue this matter. I know our networks and internetworks and, unlike any contractor, I was there."

Bancrier shuts me down effortlessly. "Doctor, the name of the contractor really isn't your concern. As to why, well, to be frank, we feel you may have been mentally compromised in the attack. In any case, your doctor has recommended that you avoid heavy network usage until your jack has returned to normal."

Conlon continues for him, as though they planned this. Which I'm sure they did. However long this meeting was before I was called, I'm sure 'handling Dr. Farro' was one of the topics. I'm sold out, and I know it. How else did that son-of-a-bitch in San Jose get my medical records? Because Conlon got them, and blabbed. He's speaking now, too. "We want what's best for you, Dr. Farro."

Bancrier continues, choreography perfect. "We can't afford to disrupt our operations any further. If word gets out that this attack was successful, every two-bit hacker in the world will come try the same thing. We're going to have the contractor analyze the problem, then we will seal up the holes, and then we will get back to the business of running our network and serving our customers. We're not law enforcement, as you well know, and revenge is not our corporate policy."

I stare at the phone, clenching my fists and tensing like I might jump through it and strangle someone. Revenge isn't corporate policy. Right. "We're going to pretend nothing happened? Is that what you're suggesting?"

"Yes, and corporate legal will take care of that to avoid any unfortunate incidents." An *unfortunate incident* is management speak for a lawsuit. By pretending nothing happened, the lawyers can claim these were normal, work related accidents. The OmniMart legal sharks will do whatever it takes to make that stick. If medical records need to be altered, they will be. And I doubt anyone will notice. Rei and Silver were each others' only family as far as I know. That leaves only Tika's boyfriend. The rest were loners. Like me. I've seen this before. A minimal settlement is paid out to any surviving relatives, and all bodies are quietly disposed of. I swallow my anger and keep my voice level.

"Excuse me, gentlemen. These were highly skilled network professionals, killed using methods that have never been seen before. These people were not disposable. They will not be easy to replace. Our operations are already disrupted, Mr. Bancrier. And if we fail to avenge ourselves even once, then every two-bit hacker with a grudge really will be at our door."

My boss waits only long enough for me to stop talking, as though he was planning what his next words would be. Instead of listening. Just giving me rope. "Dr. Farro, I understand you're upset. I know these people were friends of yours, but the decision has been reached. You've got a lot of vacation time accrued, I'd like you to take it."

"But..."

He cuts me off with, "We want what's best for you," again. Which is management speak for *We want whatever it takes to avoid a lawsuit.* "Does anyone have anything else to add?"

Reverend Martin begins, "Let us pray for the dead." Normally I'd hang up. Normally. Technically it's not even legal in the SCP — to say nothing of CalTech — for the Rev to start in on us like this, but ... it may be the only service they get. I wait to hang up until he's done.

9:45 a.m. Friday.

Shortest meeting I've ever had. That's something, at least. I turn back toward the window, rest my forehead against it, and softly pound my fist against the glass as the world grows soft and indistinct outside.

Chapter 8

This is what I know. This is what I remember. I am in a tank. It's claustrophobically close; a great water-filled sarcophagus around me. Fighting down the panic, forcing myself to breathe slowly. Relax. Let it in. I have to let it into my mind. But I'm afraid. Cold water flows into the tank. Cold water on the warm, streaming into my mouth, damping my scream. Feel for the hatch but can't find it. Fight to hold my breath. Resign myself to die. *You should have died when they did.* Captain goes down with her ship. My responsibility. Resign myself to die. To atone.

In time, always in time, in great long minutes instead of the fragments of seconds I often deal in. In time, the panic passes. As long as I am to die, I should get some work done. Let them find me that way, diligent even in death. It's a comfort. Find the optical cables. Plug in. Calm now, but the fear remains. The fear remains. I am naked in the dark water. Fear, at least, I can do something about. I log in. And there is light.

A sunlit beach. That beach, I realize at once. Except that I'm in my chair; except that my wheels are mired in the sand; except that when I back up they stick hard on some obstruction. Force my way forward. Look down. A body. A corpse. Dead white, black blood pooled around the face, from the ears. Bleeding from the brain. Sand is caking in the blood. The whole mass is only starting to solidify into clotted chunks of gore. Slide out of my chair to sit on the sand next to the body. Roll it over. Gore on my hands, sand between my fingers. Jay. Nothing I can do. Nothing I can do. I slowly begin piling sand on him, as though he were my father, as though he were my brother, as though I am a little girl playing in the sand. Pile it on slowly. Watch the blood soak through it. Pile faster. I have to hurry. I have to have him buried before the tide comes in.

The waves are starting to lap at the mound where Jay lies, and I have to get back into my chair. I have to leave this place. I can't be here when the water comes to claim him. Look back at the chair. Remember that I couldn't back up. Wrench the chair aside. It's light; light enough. The titanium frame was the lightest I could find. But that was a long time ago.

Another body. A wave comes in, splashing over Jay, making me wet again. Drag myself to the other body. I know who it is. I don't have to look. Don't want to look. I start to bury her, face down, no time to turn her over. *Face down, for vampires. Face down for life stealers. Face down for the undead.* I stop. The water is splashing my legs, up my thighs to where I can feel, but I have to do this the right way. Roll her up the beach; drag myself after. Over and over like a crocodile with her prey, blood trailing behind me, soaking me as I drag myself through it. I can feel it, cold, sandy, thick, the smell of iron and death.

I stop. We stop. Roll her on her back. Find a piece of driftwood, and break it for a sharp point. Find a rock. *Do it!* No... I... *Do it!* I pull her grey body-stocking open, baring her chest, noticing the circuitry motif is dead, corroding copper-green in the salt air. *Do it!* I want to touch her so badly. Just to say goodbye. *You don't have time for this, Catherine!* But this will be the last time I can see her. *Do it!* But I don't. I have to say goodbye. The water is further up the beach now, and I can feel the surge of the tide up along my legs again, wetness creeping upward, washing over me. The sun is beating down on me, my skin feels hot. I could almost feel good, as I wash the gore away from her face. Almost enjoy it. *Pervert! Drive the stake! End this!* I've done a good job. She looks like she did when she was alive. Align the stake between her breasts, over her heart. Draw my hand back with the rock to drive the stake home. But her hand is on mine now. She grabs my wrist. Her eyes are open, and that smile is on her lips. *Stupid girl. It's too late. Now reap what you've sown.*

She smiles quietly, demurely as the water washes over us both, until she disappears beneath it, and I'm fighting to stay above it, her hand still locked around my wrist. Squeeze my eyes shut as the tide engulfs me, hold my breath because the air is out of my reach. *Stupid girl. Reap what you've sown.* Breathe. Feel the cold as my lungs fill with water.

I dream ... as the oxygen in my brain is consumed, perhaps, I dream of spreading my arms and sliding into the sky, without even the effort of Daedalus, though my dear one is fallen. Her wings have melted in the sun. Too beautiful her world. Too warm. The sky is bitter-sweet without her. But I revel in it anyway. For myself, and for her since she no longer can, tears in the slipstream as it passes over my face. I soar out over the ocean and weep.

In time, always in time it grows dark, and my thermals begin to fail, and the ground which I despised and the water I despised return to me like a forgiving lover and I skim the cold darkness. There's a pain in my chest, that the flight is ending, that she is fallen, that everything is going dark. Tightness in my chest. Breathe it out. Breathe... *Reap...*

Suck in water, the coldness flowing into my chest, flowing into me from everywhere. Open my eyes, see her Mona Lisa smile, my arm still in her iron grip. Now heavier than water, I sink to her. She embraces me like a long-lost lover, and her lips meet mine in the cold water. Close my eyes.

And she's warm...

And she's warm...

And she's warm...

Open my eyes again. Writhe in the water alone. I'm in the tank, engulfed in the water. The heaviness is in my lungs, the salt taste of the heavy saline below me mixed with the cold, light water over me. I'd resigned myself to death, but I've changed my mind. *It's too late. Reap what you've sown.* No! Rip the optical cable from my jack, try to see, try to focus on the tank hatch; claw at it futilely. No! I still... She's still dead... I'm still ... angry I ... have to ... I ... but I can't fight the urge to breathe anymore, even though I know it's the third breath, the third time down, the last breath. I have to...

Breathe...

* * *

11:40 p.m. Friday

A ragged torrent of air pours into my lungs. I feel my eyes snap open, but all I see is darkness. Only for a moment. Look toward the window. Muted lights stream in: reflected and re-reflected, red and green, yellow and white, flickering like near stars. I breathe, again and again. Swallow, try to catch my breath, and look toward the window. Watch the lights, the incandescent pulse of this city that never sleeps, this warren of busy fireflies, the ebb and flow of the living, of the world. It's still snowing. The white flakes shine briefly in the glare of the building security lights, then disappear once again into the darkness. Everything is soft, everything quiet. The trees are thick with snow, indistinct, poorly focused. Turn inward, toward the room. My alarm clock. 11:41. 11:42. Lie here and watch a while. My heart slowly begins to calm; the pounding in my ears eases to a dull urgency in my chest. Swallow, take deep breaths. My breathing begins to grow more regular and still I lie, still I watch the clock as the last minutes bleed out of Friday night. 11:43. 11:44.

Grab the hand rail and sit up. The phone is next to my clock on my night stand. It too is flashing, mutely displaying the litany of callers that I never called back. I watch it for a while, too. Pick up the receiver, hold it to my ear. Listen to the dial-tone, smell the dust in the microphone. Wonder just when exactly I used the phone last, before the nightmare of today. Was it? Was it only that? *You wish.*

"Building Three Operator." It's a synthetic voice. As always. Machines are never out sick. Machines never have bad days.

They never drink too much the night before. It's never that time of the month. They're unencumbered by families or labor unions. They're infinitely patient. That's what I'm talking to. Just another machine. All of this floods through my head in a second or two. Details most people don't think about: but I am a scientist, an engineer. This is what I do. Run my hand along my leg idly. Feel the numb spots, feel the lack of muscle tone. Same as they've always been. What do I believe? *Stupid girl, don't believe everything you see...*

"Building Three Operator, may I help you, Dr. Farro?"

"Information. Get me the contact number for Tika Silverthorn, San Jose OmniMart. Authorization Farro, Catherine A." Time to do some science. I have to know. I need to be able to trust what I remember. Otherwise ... been there, done that. The machine rattles off the number. I memorize it for the exercise. Hang up.

Dial. The touchtones are the same as they were when I was a little girl. They've been the same as far back as I can remember, and far beyond. But instead of going to some central office switch, they go only as far as the wall box in my room. It decodes them. Translates them to an IP V6 address. Opens a connection over the net. On the other end, another phone box answers. Sends back a sequence number. The two boxes begin exchanging data. 'I'm ringing my phone,' says the box on the other end, as part of the SIP protocol. SIP passes the information to RSTP, which passes it unencrypted to IP, and IP sends it to my phone box across the net. The IP packets reach my phone box, and work their way up the layer cake. IP to RSTP. RSTP to SIP. My phone box dutifully plays a ringing sound in my ear. Ringing. Ringing. Ringing. The phone plugged into me is off-hook. 'I'm answered,' says the other box, which immediately begins converting the analog signals from the microphone of whatever telephone is on that end into digital data. RSTP is told by SIP to encrypt the stream, and so it does. The remote phone box throws the encrypted stream across the net to my phone box; which decrypts the stream, converts it back to sound, plays that sound through the speaker into my right ear. My phone box does the same thing with the sound it hears from my phone's transmitter — sends it in an encrypted stream to the phone box in San Jose. It looks, feels, and for the most part even sounds just like the plain old telephone system I grew up with, in the days of circuit switching, land lines and phone companies selling phone service. But of course, it's not.

"Hello?" A male voice. Light, a little rough. I don't know what he looks like, but the voice tells me what I need to know. It's haggard — little torn pieces of the happiness that once was, caught on the barbed wire sound of grief. It's a raw-throated thing of pain. My own voice catches. I want to hang up. But I don't. I have to know. I have to do the science.

"Um. Hello. Is this Brian?"

"Yeah." What do I say? What can I say? Management training asserts itself. Calm. Keep my voice calm, sympathetic. Stay frosty. Stay professional. *Just like the doctor in the hospital. Remember him?*

"I'm Catherine Farro, Tika's supervisor. From Denver." There's a long silence on the other end.

"What do you want?" The voice is harder now than it was. Tighter. What do I want? I want today not to have been. I want my people to be alive. I want things the way they were twenty-four hours ago. The same thing you want, Brian who-ever-you-are. That neither of us can have. Professionalism demands that I not say that, however. Not in those words. Not in a way that will leave OmniMart more liable than they already are.

"I called to say I'm sorry. Tika was … one of the best." Deep breath. I already know which memory to believe. But it's not scientific. I need confirmation.

"She was a great little worker, before that traffic accident — which we both know she didn't have — killed her on the way to lunch, is what you're saying." The voice is like a knife edge now, through clenched teeth. Traffic accident? Is that what they told him? *Don't make trouble. This is your job.* Bite my tongue and choke back the truth.

"I just ... I'm so sorry, Brian, that's all." My voice isn't staying level very well, and I bite off anything else I was going to add.

"So what? I'm sure you'll find another good little drone just like her. Don't worry. You'll forget all about her." The connection is digital-clear, and I can hear the impact of his receiver against the rest of the phone for a brief flicker before the phone box detects that the phone is on hook, and severs the connection. *What did you expect?* What did I expect? More or less what I got. I have to believe now. Still clutching the receiver. In time, my phone box decides I must want to talk to the operator again.

"Building Three Operator."

The same synthetic voice. I fight back the urge to rip the phone off my night-stand and hurl it through the plate glass window. Irrational. I want so badly to see it fall in a storm of glass shards and explode into pieces on the sidewalk, ten stories down.

"Building three operator, may I help you, Dr. Farro?" Close my eyes. Take a long, slow breath. Squeeze the tears out of my eyes, clench my jaw. The science is done, now it's time to do some engineering.

"Information. Carson Lance. Reno, Nevada. Director of Information Security, InterStellar Link. You dial it and shut the fuck up."

The operator program drops offline dutifully, silently, and without the faintest trace of sullenness, which of course makes the whole exercise completely unsatisfying. Once again my phone box plays a ringing sound in my ear. The voice that picks up is as synthetic as the one that just left, but the modulation, the speech pattern, the pacing all tell me that the synth voice is controlled by a real human brain. I've dialed into someone who's jacked in, and my phone call is being processed by his ice.

"I-Link Reno, Lance speaking."

"Lance? Cath. From OmniMart."

"Hey. Cath, are you all right? After that shit this morning, I mean?" The concern in his voice barely reaches me through the ragged working calm I'm clinging to. Synth voices are programmed to respond as natural voices do; to emotion, to emphasis. It takes a little practice to run one, but there's little alternative in the tank without logging out, plus work can be done in the great long pauses between sentences.

"They tell me I'll live. Listen, Lance. Off the record, we had some problems here. Are you guys okay?"

He's quiet a moment. "No. We're not. We lost the entire day shift, Cath. We're so short handed they've got me in a fucking tank now instead of investigating."

Fuck. *Stop being such a drama queen and get to work.* "Got any leads?"

"Couple. Rumor has it you guys got hit by Righteous Fist assholes last night. That true?"

"Umm. I don't know if I can talk about that, Lance. Non-disclosure and everything."

"You don't trust me?" The voice sounds almost hurt.

"Nothing personal. Just those are the rules, you know?"

"Same old Cath, huh?" Close my eyes again. He's pulling away, I can hear it in his voice.

"Okay. Okay. They came. Night shift burned them. It's public record anyway." *Lance and Diane invited you to their wedding, for Pete's sake. Twenty years you've known him. Not a trusting person ... bitter shroud of death...* Shake my head a little to clear it. Cling to my working calm. Lance is speaking again.

"Mm. Haven't seen it. It'll probably come out tomorrow. Anyway, rumor has it they were working for a guy named Mojo, who used to be out of DC. Old-school cracker, serious crypto guru, ice wizard. Last heard from he was in the Bay Area writing software for NCC or somebody, but I'm betting he's back to his old tricks. If anybody could write software to burn tankers, it'd be him. Or you."

The muscles in the back of my neck snap tight. Swallow, get a grip. A little anger goes a long way to clearing my head. "It wasn't me."

"Didn't think so. Anyway, this Mojo clown has a rep for carving and selling the black."

"How's he tie into Righteous Fist?"

"Nothing direct, but they used to use a lot of his ice. It's circumstantial at best. Mostly rumors."

"Okay, that would explain why he hit us. Why would he hit you?"

"Never know, unless he started when he was in diapers, he's old enough to have kids who are cracking age. You guys might have burnt one. Something like that, at least. Honestly I have no idea. Hitting us doesn't make any sense, so I'm looking for an emotional motive."

It gives me pause. I don't usually think of data criminals having families. Parents. Children. People who will miss them. Maybe. Maybe not. I don't miss mom, certainly. "Hadn't thought about that angle. Got any rug rats tied to him?"

"No, nothing like that. I don't even have his real name yet. Didn't have a lot of time to dig before I had to pull this shift, you know? Aren't you guys short too? I'm surprised they haven't got you back in a tank already."

"I'm on the sick list. I got hit in the attack."

"Jesus, Cath, are you okay?" Lance has that synth voice thing down to a science. I can hear his concern again. It makes my eyes water. Time to cut this conversation short.

"You asked me that already. I told you. I'll live. I'm a little messed up, but … I'll muddle through. Doctor says I should … stay offline for a while…" I know Tika said a month. I can't remember what the doctor actually said.

"Okay." Lance sounds relieved. I lean my head back against the wall, lost in memories, some real, some not. The glass is cold against my skin, and my breath fogs it slightly. Lance goes on, "That's why you're on the voice line, huh? Wondered. I haven't actually heard your voice since we were at Epimetheus."

"I'm in bed, Lance. I've been asleep since I got out of the hospital this morning, pretty much. Modulo a meeting. Leave it to the bureaucrats to waste time in a crisis. Listen, I'm going

to the caf to get some dinner, and then I guess I'll do some digging. I'll let you know if I find anything."

"I thought you were supposed to stay offline."

"It'll be against medical advice then, I suppose."

"Okaaay. I know I can't stop you. I'll keep you posted if
I hear anything, but I'm stuck here for now, and we've got
a pretty full night ahead of us, cleaning up after the cracker.
Listen, Cath?"

I'm about to hang up, but I stop. "Yeah?"

"Thanks for calling. It's good to hear from you."

"Mm. Yeah ... thanks. Good talking to you."

"Be careful, okay? Turns out to be this Mojo guy, he is serious bad news, and he's well equipped with friends."

"Yeah. Yeah, I'll be careful. Thanks, Lance. You too."

"What?"

"Be careful."

"Will do."

And with that, Lance sends a thought to his tank's phone
ice, and the connection between us drops with a soft click in
my ear.

Chapter 9

12:30 a.m. Saturday.

The cafeteria seems strange at night. Whole sections of the lights are turned off, leaving the tables beneath cast in shadow. Empty. Nearly deserted. Only one food line open, heat lamps reflecting off stainless steel, chrome, and aluminum, and the ever-present glass separating disease-carrying humans from sanitary food. The line is serving pretty much anything that will fit in the deep fryer, plus sandwiches and grilled food. The cooking robots stand sculpturally still, waiting for me to speak. The lights that are on are bright enough to make my eyes hurt compared to my dark room, and the smell of hot grease turns my stomach a bit. I settle for chicken strips, fries, a side salad, and a large Mountain Dew. Tell the robots so. They slide into action. No hesitation, no waiting. The fry-bot dispenses my chicken strips and French fries into one of the four baskets and drops it into the fryer without ceremony; the drink-bot dispenses a cup and fills it from one of the taps in its other arm; and the salad/sandwich-bot raises its tubular head to a bowl and vomits a mixture of lettuce, shredded carrots, and cucumbers. It raises a tubular arm, and shaves six slices of cylindrical tomato into the salad.

"Dressing?" The computer is speaking to me again.

"Ranch, please." Salad/Sandwich-Bot spurts ranch dressing over the top from a nozzle mounted over the salad tube. A delivery arm picks up the bowl and puts it on the counter in front of me, then reaches to grab my soda. Fry-Bot raises my chicken and fries. Shakes them the prescribed number of times. Salts them lightly. Deposits them into a paper plate. This too is delivered to the counter. The grill-bot stands immobile, and it's hard not to imagine that it's envious of the others' activity.

"That will be twenty-three dollars and eighty cents, Canadian. Shall I bill your account, Dr. Farro?" Yup, picked up the RFID chip in my corporate ID card. Sometimes they miss it.

"Yes, please."

"Thank you. Have a nice day."

Stupid machines. I gather my tray and roll to a table out of the way, in shadow. Night shift is due to start lunch breaks soon, and I'm not feeling social. Sip the sickly-sweet Mountain Dew a moment, shiver as the highly caffeinated sugar-water goes straight to my bloodstream, and from there to my brain. Now I'm awake.

Gnaw on a chicken strip, mouth full of greasy, salty, vaguely meaty goodness. My stomach settles right down. Guess I was hungry. Plug my OSDeck into the network socket in the wall next to my table. The deck wakes up automatically; it's been a long time since it had a direct connection to the net, instead of a pokey wireless link. Plug a second optical cable into the deck's user interface jack. The little thing must be in deck heaven. I haven't used it for anything other than incidental, non-connected computing in years. It's too slow, really, but for where I'm going, it's the perfect tool. The perfect cover. The perfect sheep's clothing. Except that this wolf's hand is shaking badly as she draws the fiber-optic cable's other end toward her … toward my jack, and it's only through sheer spite that I manage to will myself to plug it into my high-speed jack. I will not be ruled by my fears. I will not. I slot up some basic ice: mail, news network utilities, viral protection, and my EII ice. I trust it. On an outside network, my EII rules won't let any valuable identity information about me get loose.

Munch another chicken strip. Log in. OmniMart's Building
Three net recognizes me; lets me in without hesitation. One
gigabit pipe, probably still 802.3ab. Reasonable speed — a little
slow for virtual links, but the OSDeck's interface doesn't go
any faster anyway.

Take another bite of the chicken strip. Connect to the 2Quik
search engine. Search on Righteous Fist of God and OmniMart,
and limit the search to information posted in the last seventy-
two hours. Anything older than that and Jay would have found
them in his daily search engine troll for crackers on Thursday.
Anything much later than now will be mostly chest thumping
and speculation. There's a spike in the percentage of valuable
information about a given event right before and just after the
event occurs, but the drop-off in that percentage is extremely
steep on both ends. In about a week there will be a harmonic
spike, when people begin to talk about all the facts that have
been gathered, but I can't wait that long.

The search I've done is fairly broad, but it's a place to start.
About a thousand hits. I take another bite of chicken strip and
flip through them. Skim the summaries the search engine pro-
duces for each one. Save all the hits to my network utility ice.
The search engine bills me every time I run a search, as well as
every time I follow a link from the results page to the site, but
each site summary includes the address of the site. By saving
the data locally I can refine my search for free, connect to the
sites I find for free, and most important, not have the fucking
search engine spew ads at me constantly. For Pete's sake, if
I wanted larger breasts, I'd get them done downtown and be
home in time for dinner. Snag a fry from my tray and munch
on it. Refine my search. I get cracker sites. Which, in the end,
was what I was looking for, I suppose. Atrocious spelling and
grammar, excessive substitution of letters with numbers — 3
for E, 4 for A, 5 for S, X for K, and so on. So the first place I find
is Phreax R. Us, only it's spelled Phr34x R. U5. The idea behind this stupidity is to make it harder for law enforcement to
search for data criminals. It's referred to as l33t or lamification,
depending on which side of the law you operate on. It doesn't

work. Even before the days of anamorphic character recognition, it was fairly trivial to create an adaptive substitution table that decodes it. I have a program that does both in my network utility ice. Law enforcement has had them for years.

On the Phreax R. Us forum I find this:

> **Dood:** Rightous Fist hit the big Os in Denver. Nobody got out alive.
>
> **Spamminer:** Could have told them that, those OmniMart guys don't fuck around.

Good. We work hard for that reputation. Worked. Still do, most likely.

> **Dood**: I could take 'em.
>
> **Spamminer**: Don't, man. Don't even go there. Supposedly Mojo was going on that run, but he got delayed or something.
>
> **Dood**: Mojo? I heard he was in CalTech. I heard he went legit. Carving ice for somebody.

Sounds like I found one of the same sites Lance found.

> **Spamminer**: Yeah, any idea what he was working on?
>
> **Dood**: He's Mojo. Probably carving black ice for them. Man's an artist. I bought some black of his for a project I was working on.
>
> **Spamminer**: Get out, you poseur. You did not.
>
> **Dood**: I did. I bought it from a guy at Haxxor Hell. He knows the man himself.
>
> **Spamminer**: What guy?
>
> **Dood**: I'll PM you, shoot me your addy?
>
> **Spamminer**: 5p4mm!n3r@3x4m!n3r.w4r3z. misc.

Hideous. Spamminer@examiner.warez.misc is how it's read.

* * *

This is what I know. This is what I remember.

I'm sitting in a classroom. In sweats. CS530. First thing in the morning. All I really want is my coffee, but instead … lecture. Complexity. Intensity. This is serious.

"The weakest link in any security plan is the human link. Crackers know this." The speaker is Dr. Thurn, a small man with blond hair and a mustache that makes him look vaguely like a sea otter. I'm twenty-two years old. This is graduate school. "From the cracker's point of view, it's much easier to get a user to give out passwords, use unsecured software, transmit confidential data unencrypted over wireless, and so forth. This is a cultural problem. You have to know your culture to know where the weaknesses are. Try to know your quarry, think like him, so you know what his weaknesses are, as well."

* * *

Know your quarry. I do a little digging on Spamminer, both in clear text and lamified. He's a fairly active poster, mostly on video-game and hacking forums. A few minutes of reading his work, and I have a reasonable picture of who he is. Younger, probably early twenties from his slang use. Posting times tell me he's mostly on at night; given his age, this equates to a college student, most likely. There's a certain stiltedness to his writing that reinforces that feeling. He sounds, in short, like someone who writes a lot of college papers, probably in a technical field. He leaves feedback with suggestions for the writers of pornographic fanfic. I have his number now. I know his kind. I've been around people like him my whole life. A body'd think I might have gotten laid more. Except that I was never quite that desperate.

I change my icon. Use an old one, the Woman in Black; a fairly unimaginative icon I built up from my own picture and a starlet of the day named Christie Keeley, when I was in graduate school. Tall. Willowy. White hair. Black pin-striped suit. Boots. *These boots were made…* Yup, those boots. Spurs.

Black leather gloves, for that slight hint of class, and of malice. It seemed like a good idea at the time. I unbutton a few buttons of the blouse in the name of sharpening my tools.

Showtime. A quick connection to an onion routing server for anonymity. I get a warning that my bandwidth is limited to a gig and a half, which is still faster than my OSDeck can go. Not a problem. Make a quick private message to spamminer@examiner.warez.misc. Sensible people ignore unsolicited calls like this, but there are advantages to having your gender flag set to female. Spamminer answers after a few seconds, and we get a somewhat slow virtual chat connection going. Spamminer's icon is a great metallic spider, and the environment is, naturally, webbing.

"Come into my parlor, Ms. Shroud." I'm supposed to laugh at that. I give it a try.

"Cute. Thanks for answering. I saw your post on Phr34x, and I'm looking to buy serious ice. Can you tell me where you found your contact?"

Spamminer laughs at me. "I know you? No. I care what you're looking for? No. You could be a cop for all I know, let's just check."

He can't map back through the onion routing to me any more than I can map to him. It's encrypted and randomized. But my network utilities ice informs me he's probing my deck through the chat server. I pretend not to notice. "Little girl, take that antique deck and go back to school."

"Hey c'mon now, don't be like that. Everyone's got to start somewhere. That's what I want the ice for, so I can make some cash for a decent deck. Got my eye on a Zhang D50 or a Megadyne 205."

"They are so not worth it. They're crap. You want the good stuff, get a Domaru. Even a couple years old, a Jap deck will stomp anything made in China or CalTech. Night and day from a damn OSDeck." I listen, trying to appear enrapt and vaguely ignorant. The latter, at least, isn't difficult. A fast deck is a cracker's toy, my OSDeck is the only one I've ever owned. I'm

a tanker. Deck jockeys like him only wish they could get the
kind of speed I'm used to.

But it's time to jiggle the bait a little more. Smile, fold my
arms across my chest, lean forward a little. He looks. And
smiles, in a vaguely spidery way. "I might be able to help you.
Let's talk."

Smile back. Turn down the bandwidth to a crawl, practically analog modem speed. Draw gloved fingertips to my lips.
"I hoped you'd see things my way." Even with his spider icon, I
can see that he's starting to get frustrated as my presence comes,
goes, and pauses randomly while his deck waits for more signals from mine Eat lag, hacker scum.

"Fucking onion routers. Look, why don't we cut all this
anonymizer crap out and get to know each other. My real address is peter6972@lunchrat.com. Call me there." Hook, line,
and sinker. Gotcha.

I drop the connection, leave the onion routing network,
and go to Petanet. In fifteen seconds I've rented a gigabit connection to the public net. I make a note of the charges, I have
an expense report to think about. Technically I'm not supposed
to be investigating this matter. Realistically, when I nail this
Mojo character, assuming he turns out to be my guy, forgive-
ness should be much easier to get than permission. The new
link comes up. I pause a moment to grab and read some stats on
Domaru deck firmware. Connect to Petey-Spamminer's home
address. Reach out in the outside world, unslot my news ice and
slot up some black ice. Tools for the attack. Lock and load.

He smiles, icon assuming a more humanoid shape. "Now
then, where were we?"

"Right about here." I hit him with a pain stimulus attack.
Simple, direct, and to the point. He's got no security running
against me, functionally naked. Pitifully easy. Let him writhe
for a while, undoubtedly twitching on the floor in real life as
much as his icon does, while I feed my deck-breaker ice what
it needs, then take control of his deck so he can't log out, can't
break the connection, I've got some time to talk to him before
he can get his hands up to the induction headband and get it

off his head, freeing himself from the deck. Smile. "You were going to tell me where to find the guy who sold you that Mojo ice."

"Fuck off, bitch!" That's about enough time. I let him writhe some more. Can't have him unplugging himself unexpectedly. I give him a whole minute before backing it down again so he can hear me.

I smile sweetly at him, still showing considerable cleavage through the partially unbuttoned blouse just to help out that attraction-avoidance complex. Why not? Curious detachment. They're not, after all, my boobs. They're not even Christy Keeley's boobs anymore. Last I heard she'd gotten a gender re-assignment and goes by Keith. With the advent of clone tissue transplanting, it's the latest thing in Hollywood. "We're going to go all night like this, Peter. Nice and slow. And this isn't the nastiest ice I've got, either."

"Fuck … you…"

The sweet smile again. Pretend I'm the kind of sadist I sound like. Watch him squirm as the attraction-avoidance complex gets worse — he looks at the cleavage I'm showing. "I don't know, Petey, I don't think you'll be up to it when I'm done with you." I adjust his deck's output level up slightly, raising the current of the signals it's inducing in his brain. "Feel that? That's your induction current. It's way up. I've read you can feel the brain damage happening. What's it like?"

But he doesn't say anything. "Mmm. Don't feel like talking? Well that's dull. You won't tell me what I want to know, and you're not keeping me entertained. I guess I'll just turn the pain software back up and go eat dinner. Okay. Have a nice night."

"Wait … wait … please…" His icon is starting to flutter a bit, the spasms of motion becoming more seizure-like.

"Yes?" I turn up his level of pain a little anyway, and look back toward him, giving him my best manifestly bored look. Your pain means nothing to me little man. At least, that's what you're to believe.

"H4xx0r H311. He's always there. Please! Turn it off!"

Look down at my glove, run my thumb along the seam of my finger "I know that, Petey; you posted that. I need a name. Sorry." Turn my back on him and begin to walk away.

"Shogoth ... please ... something's happening to me ... please, turn it off!" Smile over my shoulder, keep walking.

"Goodnight, Peter."

"No!"

I tell his deck to shut down the induction interface. Copy his EII ice. Load some deck burning ice and run it. It systematically erases all his ice, then writes its viral payload over his deck's firmware. His deck drops offline, and the chat session terminates. Best-case for him, he'll be hours cleaning up the mess I've left him. Worst-case, the hardware is permanently damaged. But he'll probably live. Though he may never live down having his deck toasted by some girl with an OSDeck. There was a time when a win like this would have made me smile. Register myself an e-mail address at lunchrat.com. Yay. So professional.

Open my eyes to the real world, I look through the plane of the virtual world of my deck at my half-eaten dinner, and think about Jay lying on the medical examiner's slab in Building 27. Watch the grease congeal on my chicken strips. Log out. Finish my Mountain Dew and play with a french-fry a few minutes, trying to remember the hunger I came in with. Throw the rest of my dinner in the trash on my way out of the cafeteria.

Chapter 10

1:05 a.m. Saturday.

I know this place. I've lived here long enough. I know that in addition to the tanks in the data center downstairs, there is a second tank room on the fourth floor. I interviewed Jay here on my day off two years ago; ran him through his paces as an operator; tested his knowledge. It's generic office space: windowless, white walls, grey-speckled white tile floor, orange-red stripe around the perimeter of the room near the ceiling just in case the people who work here have forgotten the corporate colors, and of course the ever-present smell of salt water from the tanks. There are three of them today. Two are older GenData 15 slotters, taken from the data center and moved here for interviews and training. The third is a new Nova 7170, here for testing and evaluation. I'd be tempted to use it but there's no water in it, and it takes hours to fill one and get the salinity right. We're really just sitting on it. The only reason we're testing Nova tanks at all is to lean on GenData to cut us a deal on the fifty slot tanks we're supposedly going to order. Politics. It all degenerates to politics. I choose one of the two GenData 15s, roll around to the side, check the water quality, water temperature and network connectivity. Press the standby/active button. The tank's skid pack hums to life, warming the water for me.

Load up my ice. Open the hatch. Watch the water circulate in the tank. Smell it as it grows warm, as it rises to blood temperature. Squeeze my eyes tight shut to fight the feeling of panic. I will not be ruled by my fears. I will not. And yet I can remember the feeling. Remember the flood of water into the tank. Remember feeling the cold water rush into my chest when I breathed it in. I know that it didn't happen. But I remember it just the same. Despite growing up in Denver, I've never even met a horse. But I'm starting to understand what that means to climb back on one after being bucked off. It's not just a confrontation of your own fears, it's a confrontation of your own fears and — sometimes — the horse's deliberate malice.

It is about deliberate malice somewhere. One doesn't tear apart a large corporation's whole security shift in a few minutes by accident. Tika and Kimmy, Silver and Rei and, hell ... Jay and I. None of us were creampuffs. I hired everyone except Silv and Rei. I know they were capable. My people. And this butcher took them down. Took us down. All of us. The cold anger steals through me, pushing the fear to a small corner of my mind where it sits and winks at me. Fine. So be it. Lock the brakes on my chair. Open the hatch. Lever myself out of the chair and into the tank. It's a little chilly, not quite up to temperature yet, but close enough. Look up at the ceiling a long moment, watching the light, then close the hatch of the tank, and plunge into darkness. But not for long. Habit guides my hands to the optical cable. This is a GenData 15. It's only got the one. All the tank control stuff is manual. *You'd be dead now if you'd been in this tank this morning.* Yeah. Whatever. *You're not a forgiving person.* Forgive who, exactly, this Mojo clown? I think not. *Stupid girl...* Oh, do hush up. I try to relax a moment, try to let go and float, to prepare my brain to sieve through data quickly. Like the flood of water ... like the tide ... I log in, and my brain fights the data feed a moment, the images coming in spasms. Guh. Haven't had a login this rough in years.

It clears in a moment. I'm standing in the test environment. It's deserted, as expected. Feel the relief that gives me, back in my body. It means I'm not fully under, not out of body. Not enough. I set jump coordinates and jump to the boundary router between the test environment and the rest of OmniMart's net, open the door, and slip into the sky.

Vijay buttonholes me almost immediately. He's on the ball — that's good. "Shroud? What're you doing here? Conlon said you'd be offline for days."

Nemo me impune lacessit. Yeah. Nobody hurts me and gets away with it. "Conlon's an asshole. Did he fill you guys in?" I know I'm being relayed to the rest of the gestalt while Vij talks to me. Strange to be on the outside.

"Yeah. I'm really sorry to hear what happened to you folks. It's got us all a little shaky tonight. What brings you?"

I look at Vij a moment, watching his eyes. "You have to ask?"

"I thought the investigation was supposed to be run from San Jose." He's being careful now, walking on eggshells with me. It doesn't take a gestalt for me to see that. I know the man. My being angry with anyone, friend or foe, always made him uncomfortable. *You're not even very nice.*

"It is being run from San Jose. I'll make sure to forward any information I gather on the matter to Mr. Bancrier in the morning. It's his investigation, I'm doing this on my own time." The environment glitches a moment as I lose my theta wave state and am back in my body. The bandwidth through my head drops to a trickle. "Oh for fuck's sake!" Reach up to the controls and turn up the heat in the tank a little, the green digits on the display glow brightly a moment, telling me the temperature I've selected, then fade to darkness. Feel things speed up again slowly. "Sorry, Vij, I didn't get what you said. This tank's heater sucks."

"Shroud, I don't think this is a good idea. I think you have an awfully good chance of getting hurt. You're not at a hundred percent, obviously." The concern in his voice is evident. It annoys me, here and now. This is Vijay. He's a fine operator. He used to be my partner on day shift, before he got promoted to team lead at night. I trained him from a pup, but the one thing he never quite learned from me was the importance of staying frosty. In the end I wasn't sorry to see him take the other shift. *A heart too soon made...* I didn't wish Jay dead, damn it. Vijay's icon is practically an animated 3-D model of him. Tall, dark skin, black hair. The icon frowns, watching me.

"I'm fine. And that bastard's still out there somewhere. I have to find him." Vij steps back a little, as though afraid I might bite.

"Why you? And why now?" If he really wants to, Vij can refuse me access to the outside world on the big pipe. He is, after all, the lead operator on duty, whatever goes in or out of this network is his responsibility. I stare at him, just for a moment, until he squirms.

"Because four people are dead, and two more injured, and it will be a cold day in hell before I leave this investigation to bureaucrats and politicians. Understood?" Frosty. The cold sense of purpose slides through me at last, and the distractions fade into the background a bit.

Vijay folds his arms across his chest. "Understood. But understand this. We can't back you up. If you do this, you're on your own." Vijay's own voice is a little heated too, and he stares right back at me. This is new. I nod.

"Got it. Thanks Vij. Be safe." I go before he has a chance to reply. A quick jump vector to the gateway router, the line between that-which-is OmniMart and the unwashed outside. I load my copy of Spamminer's EII and become him for all casual observers.

Chapter II

I need a shower. Haxxor Hell is typical of its species: a chat room with a pseudo-bar from which psychedelic software experiences can be bought, and from the moment I cross into its virtual environment I feel contaminated somehow. There are a number of private sub-rooms. Espresso and hard liquor flow for free at the bar, though the sensory experiences they offer are pale imitations. The room is decorated with liquid metal walls, floor, furniture and the odd liquid metal person as well. A brazier lights the room in reflected flames, and the music is thunderous house/neo-rave music. For someone on a deck, the sensory experience would be nearly overwhelming. I scuttle Spamminer's spider icon up to the bar.

"Quad espresso mocha." I give the bar-bot my best tough-boy-wanna-be impression through Spamminer's voice. He seemed like an espresso kind of guy.

"Spamminer. Long time." Turn toward the voice. The speaker is a furry — an anthropomorphic animal. Seven feet tall, obvious cybernetics, generally lupine features, horns, wings, and … yup, the enormous bulge in his jeans that suggest he's true to the basic stereotype. More advanced versions would have breasts and both sorts of genitalia. I find myself thankful for the spider icon's lack of facial subtlety.

"Dude." It's a greeting and a guess as to his identity. Fortunately spelling in a virtual environment chat room is no longer relevant. "You seen Shogoth? I heard he's got connections to The Man, you know?"

The big furry saunters over. "No shit, man, I'm the one who told you that, remember? Funny thing, he got burned last night. Story is he was screwing around with Domaru's site, probably trying to get himself a free deck. You didn't mention his name to anyone, did you?"

Look around. How many of the people these icons represent will miss Shogoth? When I hang my head — such as my icon allows — it's real enough. And I never even fucking knew him. The world glitches on me again, but apparently the theta wave state just flutters and doesn't really go away. *You're not at a hundred percent, obviously.* Vij was right. I shouldn't be here. It's too soon. I try to pick up the conversation. "Shit. Um. Shit. I got a run, I need quality ice. The best." Stupid kid, this Shogoth. Got himself killed before he could tell me how to find my real quarry. And now I have to dissemble more than is safe; it's only a matter of time before they figure out I'm not who I'm pretending to be. "C'mon, man, I need help here, or I'm gonna get burnt."

"Try D4rk H0m3. But Spamminer, y'don't summon The Man. He summons you." The big furry … whatever eyes me curiously. "Man, you're tight about all this. You don't wanna do a run all tight, you'll get nailed for sure. C'mon, let's go loosen up." He gestures toward the back room. And moves close to me. Very close.

"I'll be fine." This conversation so needs to be over, before I laugh at Dood or nausea sets in. "Thanks, man. I'll go see if I can find him at D4rk H0m3." He's still watching me strangely as I leave and step into the sky. Safer this way, flying. This way I know where my connection is routed through. I just have to remember to keep my speed down or folks will notice I'm not using a deck. Brain bandwidth equals speed.

I reload my own EII, and the Lady in Black returns. It still feels dishonest, but at least now I'm only lying about my age. Not that anyone would care in this place. It feels infinitely cleaner, too. At least I know where this icon has been.

* * *

What I remember is this — I'm seven years old. Seven. It's 1992, and I'm in second grade. Westwood Elementary has a brand new Internet Initiative — a prototype for all the networked schools that would come later. They put a DecTerm on each of our desks. The smell of new plastic is sweet and laden with chemicals, none of which are likely good for me. I watch as the thing starts up. Tells me it's connecting to the network; that it's booting. I wiggle the mouse and watch the pointer on the screen move. And suddenly my screen springs to life. I know the names by the end of that year. Motif, Ultrix32, xTerm. By the end of the month I can make Gopher, ancestor to the web browser, do what I want it to. By the end of the week I know telnet and ftp. By the end of the day I know how to start and use a word processor. And along the way I realize something magical. That there are other people in this magic window, and we all live together in a world of ideas, of our own making. Of our own choice. And all I have to do is sit and type.

I'm good at sitting. Typing comes reasonably quickly.

It's 1992, the same year AOL first offers limited internet access. Ever since, the net's been about preserving islands of good things in a rising tide of sewage. *O brave new world, that has such people in't.*

* * *

Dark Home. Another wade through the cultural sewer. This time the theme is Gothic, replete with bondage and fetishwear, several people dancing in cages, whips, chains, leather skirts. Really. Walk in. Watch the white faces and blood red eyes, a sea of blood red eyes. Two dozen of them asserting individuality in exactly the same way. Goths haven't changed much in twenty years. They probably never will. Walk to the bar. Listen to the hollow thud of my footsteps on the floor, the *ching* of my spurs. They seemed like a good idea at the time.

"I'm looking for a man." The bartender smiles. He's pale, of course. Dressed in an Edwardian ruffled shirt under a leather vest. Pretty, in an androgynous sort of way. Evidently he's being run by a real person. 'Bots don't usually get such care on their icons. Except for sex-bots.

"Mm. I don't doubt it. A particular sort of man, or will any … victim do?" The resolution is pretty good. Everyone's eye has a sparkle. But it's the tiny details of dirt at the seams of his shirt that impress me. I smile at him. I try to keep it to that. People indulging in digital sexual fantasies don't like being snickered at.

"I'm looking for a specific man of peculiar talents. I understand that he goes by Mojo." The bartender's eyes narrow a bit, and he draws back from me.

"Mr. Mojo has been known to be here. But he is not to be approached lightly. When I see him, who shall I tell him called for him?"

"Tell him … that in light of his recent work, a professional organization wishes to retain him. Tell him that the reward is rich, but that time is short. I can be reached at Shroud@lunchrat.com." I allow myself to show off a little and produce a business card with a flick of the wrist, where there had been no card before. Stupid ice tricks. I coded that up in less than a minute.

"I doubt we shall see him tonight, Ms. Shroud. Perhaps if you check back in a few days, I'll have news for you." And with that the bartender saunters over to another patron, who reaches out, pets the bartender's cheek, then hauls his head down to the bar and bites his neck. I walk out, trying not to let my disappointment show.

The strip online is almost infinite — an endless dark alley in the bad part of a theme park populated by people who want a taste of the gritty side of life without taking the actual risks of going there. There are as many chat rooms as there are bad clichés: strip clubs, bars, fight clubs, Roman orgies, superhero hangouts, opium dens, and a dozen or two copies of each one, spawned when two groups of users of a given place stop getting along. An infinite number of monkeys and no sign of Shakespeare yet. I've looked. Talked to bartenders. Been hit on in subtle and unsubtle ways. It's become apparent that Mojo doesn't spend a lot of time hanging out in virtual bars. His use of them is sporadic at best. He's the hidden master, the one who exists by reputation but that few people, if any, actually know. You have to work for a reputation like that. Plant the seeds. Make the runs and survive. Sell the ice. I could have a reputation like that, except that I'm a corpie. Except that I've got a few scruples. *Are you Julia Farro's family?*

And except that I'm an idiot. It dawns on me slowly. Lance said Mojo was old-school. He's known in places like these because these are his customers. He's an ice pro. Like I am. And do I spend a lot of time in places like this? Before tonight? No. Embarrassing. How much link time have I wasted? How much money on the outside link through Petanet am I now going to have to pay for rather than put it on the expense sheet under, "Because I'm a moron?" I carve ice. Write a piece of software that will generate random plausible EII values and send virtual people — 'bots — into a hundred places at once. It takes me ten minutes or so — pretty straightforward stuff.

Run it. And the chaos begins.

Each 'bot displays its point of view as an icon in my field of vision, limited to me only. Each one walks into a place mentioned on any of a hundred cracker forums and finds somewhere to sit. If spoken to, each one will ask if Mojo is around. That's all this ice does. But sooner or later, each one is addressed by someone. Hit on by someone else. When that happens, I have to look out through the 'bot. Play back what was said. Respond. The context switching is making my head hurt. But there's a pattern emerging: after thirty more minutes and three changes of bars, for a total sample of three hundred bars, I have a sample large enough to do some loose statistics. As expected, he's not around. But if I were creating a reputation like that, I'd be sorely tempted to put a 'bot in the average bar, then start to accumulate statistical hits on my name. I'm betting he'll think the same way. If he's my perp, then I know he likes to control, subtly. To manipulate. Then destroy. He'll know I'm looking for him. If he's as good as they say, he'll know where to find me.

I log out of Petanet and emerge back on the outside of OmniMart's firewall.

And he pounces on me. There may be such a thing as being too right.

I don't have time to admire what he's done; traced me back through Petanet, or somehow picked me out of the thousands of connections into Petanet. It doesn't matter. My defensive ice has detected a lag in my connection. He's spoofing me two-ended, so I'm effectively routed through his hardware, where he can work on my crypto. I pull back from the route, back out of his equipment, and hit him with a scrambler-toaster attack. He dumps me out of his hardware completely, and we're back in neutral territory. His icon is black on black, hard to see, as though a man had been sculpted of obsidian. Even his teeth are black. The icon of a veteran. Hard to see; yet another hardship for the metaphor-dependent, certainly, but different. Slippery, this one. A moment of uncertainty. I haven't faced a cracker of this caliber outside the OmniMart network in longer than I care to think about. What else have I missed? I keep my tricks more subtle, and embed a time-to-live counter in each packet when I speak to him. As the counter expires it generates an error where the packet expires and tells me where it happened. If the counters have progressively higher values before they expire, I get a trace all the way to where he is. A variation on a classic network tool. All I have to do is say something. My throat shouldn't be dry. Can't be dry, it's not ... *Of all base passions...* "Dr. Livingstone, I presume. Or shall I just call you Mojo?"

"You presume a great deal, Lady OmniMart." His voice is low, vaguely hollow, like muffled thunder; designed to push the usual cultural buttons of authority, even awe. Glacially calm. Speaking softly. "You have gone to a lot of trouble to seek Mojo. You have found him." My virus detection ice goes off. His communications transmissions are loaded too. Nice touch. "What I want to know, Lady OmniMart, is why."

"You know full well." The words come with a snap. The freezing fear within me is thawing in the heat of an entirely different feeling. I have to be careful. I have to be sure he's my guy. "You've been here before." A brief adjustment to my ice and my icon begins to corrode, just exactly as though the virus had hit me. Let him gloat.

"Of course I've been here before, Lady OmniMart. I had reason to be. An interest I was paid to have. It was not a personal interest, I assure you." My trace completes, but I don't act on it, not yet. Let him believe I'm not in a position to act on it anymore.

"Paid by who?"

He laughs, obsidian teeth glistening wet. The man's got style and puts a lot of care into his icons, certainly. "If you don't already know, I can hardly tell you, now can I? I do have a professional reputation to consider." A suspicion. Most groups of fundie hackers like the Rightous Fist of God operate on a shoestring. Operated, in their case. They don't hire the likes of this guy. Someone else hires them, and him.

I know his own trace is coming. I stutter the output of my EII ice a little more, making myself look vulnerable. Show weakness. Route my own traffic through Ship-in-a-Bottle. Let him trace me inside it. My defensive ice tells me he's tracing me, and I block the trace from exiting the Ship-in-a-Bottle. All he has to do now is believe. Fall for my best trick a second time. "They paid the Rightous Fist assholes too, didn't they?"

He smiles again at that. Calm, waging life and death electronic warfare with me and still taking the time to be calm, relaxed. What does he know that I don't? Or is this all bluff? "No. Actually I paid the Righteous Fist in ice. Though it apparently did them no good. Is that what this is about? The pathetic efforts of a group of deluded children?" So much for Lance's theory. Mojo is moving again, though. He's fast. Tanker fast.

He believes. He jumps to what he thinks is my tank environment and sets to work cracking my crypto, and things begin to accelerate. I unspoof myself and set to work cracking his, even as he begins to probe the bottle environment. It takes him less than a minute to realize the nature of the bottle and drop out of it. But by then I've cracked an underlying weakness in his crypto algorithm and broken his crypto completely. I fly to the results of my trace against him, plasma hot and blueshifted — no sense hiding my speed now — and take control of his connection at the source, following his routing all the way through. "No. This is about you, and me, and mine." I start my probe ice to suss out his hardware.

His voice is serene. "You underestimate me, Lady OmniMart." And a moment later I know that I have. In the time it's taken to break his crypto algorithm, he's brute forced my crypto key, and he pours data into my connection, and from there into my brain.

Flashes of images. They begin slowly, grow faster. Random images taken from the net, faster than I can perceive. Sun. Beach. Naked bodies on the beach. Pictures inside a tank. Pictures of the sky. The beach. Burying the bodies. No wait … that came from me. The water filling the tank. Sounds. A baby crying. Revulsion. Too much. Too much too fast. I try to close my mind's eye to it, but it flows in unabated. The limitations of the flesh, of the mind. He's flooding me, pouring junk into my head. Has this happened to me before? I think it has, there's a … feel to it that feels … familiar … *Nasty piece of work, huh? Tries to make you into something you're not.*

The shiver slides through me, mercury cold down my back, the fear making my responses to his sensory-overload flood more frantic, more blurred together. Could he write memory this way? Could he rewire my jack? What is he doing to me? Is this what happened to the others? That rock of pain provides me a refuge in the sensory deluge to gather my thoughts behind. My thoughts. And they're all of blood and rage. The sensory flashes come faster, more urgently. Frosty. Got to stay frosty. Let the data flow through me. Resist by not resisting. He knows. He knows I'm trying to control this interface.

And in another moment I have it. Reach out from the refuge in the flood and change my crypto key, and all the packets of sensory garbage begin to bounce. The junk he's pouring into my brain stops abruptly, leaving nary an echo in my head. My crypto-analysis ice tells me he's changed his key as well, and, by virtue of having broken his entire algorithm, my ice promptly breaks his new key as well. I hit him with the pain-inducer software, at maximum intensity. It gives me time to think. To focus. He's in a tank, as expected, some newer model from Nanoframe. Erase his crypto ice. Re-carve it to always bring him right back here. To me. "This is about you, and me, and mine, you son-of-a-bitch. You attacked my crew. And before you die, you'll pay for it." He's rising through the pain flood, mastering it just as I did moments ago, resisting by letting it flow through him. I send him scrambler packets along with it, and I can feel him start to seize, the studied calm, the artful organization of his mind begs to be scrambled, like stained glass church windows with their pious cartoons beg to be hit with a sledgehammer. I indulge.

I use the time to carve a custom piece of ice. Its teeth are the same scramble and pain combination he's enjoying right now, along with an addictive pleasure mode. Its senses look for any sense of focus, any response to the questions it will ask that is less than immediate. Its voice is mine. I segue it in in place of the attack ice I've been running for the last ten minutes. "Listen to me, Mojo. I want to know who paid you."

Apparently he stopped to think. The new ice lays into him with pain and scramble mode. I use the time to have my search ice pull down everything it can get on this Nanoframe tank. A new product, a way to get tank performance on a medium-to-high end deck budget. Cheap. Reasonably fast, but they cut corners to keep the price down. Most notably, the tank control system is just a piece of ice connected to the tank's main frame. A fatal bug; the last thing a tanker should ever let intruders get ahold of is their tank controls. In pricier tanks they are completely separate computing systems.

It takes me a few minutes to break the control ice and control the tank directly. Tank heat controls here, fill and drain controls here, air handler here. Induction controls here, for those not jack-equipped. Mojo is plugged into the jack interface. I'll have to decide at some point whether to kill him by asphyxiation, heat stroke. Or open the fill valve on his tank and drown him, I suppose. Another shiver slides down my back.

The conditioning ice strobes into pleasure mode and the gasping sigh from Mojo is audible. He's stopped resisting, apparently.

"I asked you who paid you."

The conditioning ice flickers into pain mode again as he stops to think, but it goes back into pleasure mode almost immediately. He's talking. The conditioning is taking hold. "Private … private account. Aliased. Swiss bank account. Instructions … some corporate covert account. Don't know."

"What account? And what were your instructions?" The conditioning ice flickers back and forth between pain and pleasure, hundreds of trials a minute, shaping his behavior. Breaking him. He speaks again.

"BlueViolin … the account name. Instructions … retain … third party. Provide them with … tools and technical assistance. Hit OmniMart first thing in the morning on Friday."

The words are wrung from him, like twisting a washcloth to get every drop of water out. It's bad for the fabric, but it works. "They hit us Thursday night. Explain that."

"Jumped the gun. They. Jumped the gun. Sent me e-mail about … not wanting to work on Good Friday. Imbeciles. They were supposed to wait for me."

"So you came in on Friday to finish the job."

The conditioning ice flickers once. "No! I never … attacked you."

"Then who did?"

"I don't know. I don't know. I don't…"

From a software standpoint, he has to be telling the truth. He's conditioned to it. With what I've done to him, he could no more lie to me than he could wet himself intentionally.

Conditioning is a powerful thing. But he's not my guy. He's not my perp. Of course, he was associated with the Righteous Fist of God raid Thursday night, and he did attack me minutes ago. Legally that's grounds to burn him. *Hasn't there been enough killing?* I've ruined his mind. I've broken him. That will have to be enough.

Abruptly it's no longer my decision. Somewhere a link drops, and I find myself back inside OmniMart's network. The system tells me we're cut off from the world. Again. I jump back to the operator environment. "Vij, what's going on?" There's no reply. I can't log into the operator gestalt without a password, either. A quick virtual phone call to Tom, the night shift JAFO. It rings and rings, but there is no answer. Something bad is happening. Has happened. I log out and jack out. Open the tank. My head is beginning to ache. Again.

Chapter 12

3:45 a.m. Saturday.

Haul myself out of the tank and into my chair and bathrobe. Roll out of the fourth-floor tank room and take the elevator to the data center. EMTs. Close my eyes. Not again. It has to be another virtual. Another game Mojo is playing with me. Has to be. The gurney that rolls past me first on the way to the elevator contains a body bag. Look at the EMT. He recognizes me from yesterday. "Who?" I nod toward the bag.

"Vijay. He's gone. Kamio too." And with that, he disappears into the elevator.

3:50 a.m. Saturday.

I'm still there, by the elevator door, watching; my mind's eye glazed again as Kamio's body is rolled past. Still watching, watching nothing, thinking nothing. Not resisting. I have to control this interface. A security guard comes through the elevator. "Dr. Farro?"

Turn toward him. Try to recall where I've seen his face before. If I've seen it before. "Do you have virtual access?" He looks at me blankly. "Please. It's important."

"No. I use a keyboard and a mouse when I need stuff online, Doc. Conlon wants you. He's pissed. He said to bring you up there by force if need be." The guard is big, and the stun baton at his belt has the thousand little burn marks in the paint that suggest that it's been used. I don't doubt he'd use force. Not for a moment. I look down at my feet. Try to move them. Nothing happens. Both jacks reassure me they're offline when I check them. Which means ... which means...

"Okay. Let's go." I roll into the elevator followed by the guard.

3:54 a.m. Saturday.

Conlon's office. The guard's hands are heavy on my chair. He's standing behind me. I can feel his body heat. Smell him. Conlon is sitting behind his desk. He looks freshly showered and hastily dressed, but neat. Clean. Corporate. By contrast, I reek of tank. My hair is drying in tangles, and the saline is starting to dry on my skin, leaving a faint crust of salt. I really do need a shower. Conlon is speaking. "Dr. Farro, I have just one question for you. What were you doing online?"

"What's going on?"

Conlon glares at me, and I shrink back into my chair a little, ashamed of my own weakness. Too much. Too fast. "I'm asking the questions here, Doctor. You're answering them. Your job is on the line here."

I almost wish I felt more threatened. But I'm numb. "I was investigating yesterday's attack. I had a lead I wanted to follow." My voice is strangely flat, even to me.

"Did we not agree that the investigation would be handled in San Jose?" Something stirs in the numbness within me. It gives my voice a snap that is just as strange as the flatness moments ago.

"You and Bancrier and Martin agreed. I don't recall having a choice." Conlon flinches a little at it. Press home the advantage. "Bancrier's not going to investigate. You know it and I know it. He's going to sweep this under the rug or blame someone else."

Conlon doesn't back down. "Doctor, do you realize the position you've put me in? Bancrier's gunning to be the next CIO of the whole company when Greer retires. I will be working for him." This I did not know. "Whether it's right or not is irrelevant. You are out of line. I'm putting you on thirty days unpaid leave. You are not to access OmniMart's network. You are not to be on OmniMart property. At the end of thirty days' time, I'll review the matter and you may, I repeat, may be re-instated if and only if you stay the hell away from this matter. Do you understand?"

"Did anyone on the night shift survive?" Conlon looks at me as though I'd offered to eat the bodies.

"No. Nobody survived. All three sites are down. And I'll remind you that that fact and any other internal business of OmniMart is covered by the nondisclosure agreement you signed as a condition of your employment here." He turns away to the monitor on his desk. I have the feeling we've had an audience. I just watch him, angry and numb, while we wait for the personnel drone to come with paperwork for me to sign. *Stupid girl… Are you Julia Farro's family? One short step away from unemployed.* Mom would be so proud.

Chapter 13

6:05 a.m. Saturday.

I've been back in my apartment for a bit over an hour, packing. Which I hate. Every damn thing I touch is a memory, most of them mindless, pointless vignettes that mean nothing, and are only distracting. It's a stock-taking of my life I really do not need just now. But I can't leave it here. Stuff disappears around here when the owner's not around to keep track of it. Shake my head. Ten killed, another possibly driven insane, and the investigation is going to be a whitewash to avoid lawsuits. Turn around, and petty bullshit like this virtually guarantees employee lawsuits against OmniMart. Most of their problems could be avoided with the barest hint of planning, and maybe a touch of consideration for customers and employees. I feel the cold anger settling on me again, feel myself go frosty. Good. I need it right now. I pull up my bank ice. Check my balance. Not including my retirement fund, I have about 700 euros in savings. That comes to nearly 1400 Canadian dollars, and the relationship fluctuates daily, usually to the detriment of Canada and the SCP. Yeah. That's why my bank is in Zurich.

8:34 a.m. Saturday.

All my important belongings are in the backpack on my chair, and I'm on a train called the Zephyr bound for Reno, Nevada. I lucked out and got a seat in the dome car, and I'm watching the landscape fly by in a silent blur, just on the other side of the perspex, just beyond my reach. We pass through some town, possibly Cheyenne, Wyoming. Beyond the perspex, beyond the chain-link fence that keeps townies off the high speed rails, are cars. Are people. Are lives. They're gone in a few seconds, passing behind us at 800 kilometers an hour. The train bumps almost imperceptibly as a couple of passenger cars and a long string of refrigerator freight merge with us, and together we blast out across the empty plains, with nobody to notice except the coyotes as they hunt in the snow.

I have time to think. Too much time. Every time I close my eyes, I can see Vij or Kamio wheeled by in a bag. Or Jay, bright blood against pale skin. Or Tika. I get out my OSDeck. Squeeze my eyes closed and plug it into my skull. Pull up the train's local wireless network. No password needed. If you're on the train, you paid for net access from it.

Now what? I've proven I can stay connected on the train. Today that's no big deal. It's expected. The train communicates with its control center in Omaha over the same network, and over that same network the whole merge-fork process of train operations is coordinated. It has to work. The net has to work. It has to work on more than just a physical or data link layer. It has to go all the way up the layer cake to applications. It has to be secure. It has to be reliable. If the train's communications with a given station or with the central control room fail, the train doesn't work. Cars can't leave or join the train. Track management becomes nonexistent. And if the communications are intentionally changed, the timing screwed up, a station deleted from the plan, then the train doesn't split to let cars fork out at that station. The track switches and the train derails at that point, at eight hundred klicks an hour. Thousands of tons of metal and composites are thrown around like toys. People die. The net's not the scientific curiosity it was when I first encountered it. It's like the air. Everything depends on it, and nobody thinks about it anymore save for we few, we happy few, who operate it, defend it, make it go. We band of brothers.

I don't think I can leave this alone. I am going to have to play out the hunch that put me on this train heading west. The hunch that the attacker came in from InterStellar Link. I-Link is contracted up the ass with OmniMart. They know me. Lance knows me. I play by the book most of the time. This time ... if I just tell him I actually am doing an official investigation, I doubt anyone will check up on me. It could, of course, cost me my job if they do. It might be illegal, though in Reno I doubt it. Nevada is contested territory between Canada, the Texicans, and CalTech, and Reno falls into the demilitarized zone. The only law that applies there is Shoshone and Paiute tribal law, which is remarkably short on information technology law or anything else lawyer-serving. If you don't mess with the casinos, and you don't mess with the native peoples, you can pretty much do what you want. I don't want to lie to Lance, but I'm not sure I have any options. I'll burn that bridge when I come to it, I suppose.

Consider my facts. Who did this? Who was served by burning two full shifts of OmniMart's operators? Don't know. It's not like we make a lot of friends in our business, but this is above and beyond the usual life-and-death hostility. Why was it done? Don't know that either, it will probably be more obvious when I find the Who.

How? Okay, I have some data there. I consider the attack I was in. It's rather like my own Ship-in-a-Bottle. If I were writing Ship-in-a-Bottle ice to model real life, what would I need? Ship-in-a-Bottle copies its virtual environment data from the virtual environment it's run in. A virtual environment is a minimalist representation of the world. Simple. Small. To model the outside world you'd need ... very close information on the life of your target: who she knows, what kinds of things she says, where she lives. You can get all of that from our inside network once you are in, if you penetrate beyond the public access system and into the corporate data areas. My life would be an open book to you. You would have to simplify the environment as much as possible. Edit out the parts you don't have data for. Keep me, the victim, off balance while you deploy whatever the weapon is. How would that model even work? The real world is … real. Complicated. Dynamic. And the people within it contextual. I'd be likely to notice serious mistakes. *These boots were made for walking ...* or maybe not. I managed to miss some pretty big ones. Or more exactly, to be distracted from them. Or was letting me walk itself a distraction to keep me from noticing the other mistakes?

Know your quarry. Think like him.

Look out the window a while. We're running out from under the snow storm that's blanketing the Front Range, blasting westward toward Utah along the old I-80 corridor. The train lurches again, the cars spreading out, making room, making time so that individual cars can be switched out — forked — without derailing the following car that is staying with the train. The train lurches again as all the remaining cars close ranks and the magnetic couplers lock up, and yet again as the new cars merge with the end of the train. I wonder about the people who have joined our westward pilgrimage. Moving between cars is allowed, but it's discouraged. You don't want to be in the wrong car during a merge or fork.

I'm looking through the world of my deck, then at the high plains of western Wyoming. Laramie is behind us, but it's still snowing. This storm must be immense. It only takes a moment to pull a real-time weather map up. All that data. Just … out there.

Okay, let's start with that. If I were building the model to attack someone at OmniMart after penetrating the home office network, how much could I get? Lots. I manage that network, there are hundreds and hundreds of nodes, massive databases with all kinds of stuff in them. I could find out who you are, get a picture, definitely know the kinds of things you buy, where you live, who gets let in through security to visit you, medical records, dental records, psychiatric records … all this would give me a pretty good model of you, but it doesn't help me build your world. Or does it?

If your purchases are all in one area, even one store, I can constrain what parts of your world I need to have good details on. If I know your bank account, I can take a guess how far you travel ... and make sure I move you someplace else, like Cabo San Lucas. Keep you disoriented. Give you one of your heart's fondest wishes. Two of them. To walk into a motel room and take Tika to bed, in my case. But where would I get that particular data? If the point of the ruse is to get some kind of a handle on your specific mind, I'd need that data, and the company didn't have it. Except for ... shift logging on the California end, from the time Tik and I fooled around. Personnel records too. And it's probably in my psych profile.

I feel naked again. Embarrassed. I may have endangered my life by acting like a horny teenager with her first jack, and her first net lover. But I didn't know California logged everything. Should have suspected it, and Tik, rest her soul, probably should have told me. Fight back tears. Again, damn it.

Of course, there are a few glaring holes in my theory. The biggest is this: I can model a piece of the net in Penguin ice because I can throw the same codes at your client that the actual environment does. Your client does all the work. From my OSDeck to my big GenData tank, that's what they do. That's why we have them. Just accumulating the data that's on the net about the real world would take a staggering amount of computing power and network bandwidth. No single-processor, half-terabit ice chip is going to do this. I'd need a ton of computing power, and exabyte-scale storage. It might be possible, but doing it would cost far more than hiring crack squads of corporate commandos and just having you shot.

Of course, there's another place all this information exists and is preprocessed and stored — inside my head. But once again, the Ship-in-a-Bottle explanation is feasible only if you have access to my head, and its purpose is, itself, to get access to my head, so you can ... do what? The recursion goes the wrong way. It doesn't make any sense.

Rub my temple slightly. This line of reasoning is getting me nowhere. Salt Lake City goes by in a blink. It's practically a ghost town. It's fallen a long way from when it was a terrorist stronghold. Most of the Mormons who survived wound up in prison camps after the U.N. armored invasion. They were gradually deprogrammed and relocated. The city itself is still recovering. On the other hand, the stories I've read say they're legalizing prostitution after heavy lobbying by the union. They're also legalizing polygamy. Embrace the twenty-first century, Utah.

Okay. Let's look at the teeth of the process. The only direct results I've seen of this attacker's handiwork were the mess he made in Jay's brain. I have a pretty good idea about what happened. Jay's jack was rewired into his emotional centers, and then over-stimulated, bringing his body along for the ride. He went to maximum fight or flight response and stayed there until something broke. The beating ... the beating was probably the result of something he saw in the dreams that resulted as his cerebrum tried to make sense of the emotions pouring through it. The way the jack was wired at that point, there wouldn't have been much going directly to the cerebrum, and sensory deprivation can lead to insanity fairly quickly. I rub my high-speed jack port, trying to remember what the jack manual said about security and safety.

Frustrating. I should be able to remember this. I read this paperwork carefully enough before I got the damn thing installed. Finally I give up and hit NeuroGen's website and look it up. Give them the serial number of my high-speed jack. They're forthcoming with the manual.

The NeuroGen N1000 Ultra data jack is, like all modern jacks, a fairly conventional optical interface capable of terabit transfer speeds. What separates them from their predecessors, like my other jack, is that on the other end of that hardware they have 30 centimeter-long neurofibers that can do two things. First, they move, albeit slowly — a brain full of thrashing nanowire of any kind is fatally bad for you. Second, they can interface with synapses, where they capture some of the neurotransmitters that go by and then use those neurotransmitters to transmit and receive messages to those receptor sites. All of this fueled by the same thing that fuels your brain. Glucose. Let's see.

Blah blah blah, marketing spooge ... okay. The jack is installed by drilling the jack mounting hole in your skull, making a small incision in the dura mater, and then running the installing software on a dedicated controller plugged into the jack, and waiting while the mass of neurofiber spaghetti threads its way into your brain. Simple, neat, outpatient surgery. Yeah, unlike my old jack where they took the top of my skull clean off to put it in. I still have the scars, but they're under my hair.

Blah blah blah, more marketing spooge ... geez, where do they get these guys? Use this jack, get laid. I guess every advertising campaign comes down to that on some level. Ah, here we go. When they're done with the install, there's a command that burns out a fusible link in the jack hardware that prevents the neurofibers from being externally controlled. That should prevent the kind of thing that happened to Jay. That's exactly what it's designed to prevent. Okay, that, and it prevents these very expensive jacks from being reused when you die. Yeah, they make sure that part works. Blah blah ... normal time for full integration and control by a first time implantee is about a month. I had the basics down in a week, and was ready to work in two, but that's not abnormal for repeat customers.

From there, the manual gets more technical. Optical protocols, local hardware, specifications on the neurofibers, contraindications, pre-implant testing, side affects, and so forth. In CalTech, just like in the old U.S., they'd make me sign a nondisclosure agreement to even get some of this data. But I'm from the SCP. I'm legally Canadian. In Canada they figure if hardware is in your skull, you probably have a legitimate need to know about it. So the manual has everything — including the command sequences used by the install controller. I go back to the schematic and check the fusible link. It really does sever the hardware connection between the jack and the neurofiber motion controls. Once that's done the fibers only move in response to the same chemical messages that make your brain rewire itself. When you learn something.

12:01 p.m. Saturday.

I'm jarred from my OSDeck's reverie for the third time.
This time it's not an empty fuel cell on my deck or a full bladder, but the train itself, the "please return to your seat" alert.
Right on time. I jack out, put the OSDeck away, buckle my
seatbelt. "Please be sure your seat backs and tray tables are in
their fully upright and locked positions." Hard to believe they
used to pay someone to say that. I look through the perspex at
the train, watch it spread apart, the microwave links providing
power and communications between cars little inconvenienced
by the doubling of their transmission range. I can see the T1
itself, the big fission reactor on wheels, as it goes into a turn
to arc around the switchyard. A light jolt and a flicker of the
lights in the car tell me the fork is complete. I watch the train
streak away, only a few cars diverging from it to join up with
the car I'm in as we turn away from the main line and hit the
brakes, decelerating toward the station, the g-forces pulling
me against my seat belt a bit at first, easing down as we slow.
Not so different from a jet landing in the old days, and much
more gentle than a sub orbital reentry, or so I'm told. Safer
than both. There are almost always survivors in a train wreck.

Chapter 14

12:30 p.m. Saturday.

It's the heat of the day in Reno. There's an extra 300 meters of sky pressing down on me, wringing the sweat from my skin, making me feel greasy. I roll my chair out of customs. The customs guys give me the usual warnings about fruit, and chuckle a little at my OSDeck. "It's paid for." I tell them. If this were the UCSA I could have been in trouble for having black ice — the attack stuff — but here they — do — not — care. They don't even scan it. Something to be said for the frontiers of civilization. All they care about is that I not leave any ice behind. Tech waste is a problem, they tell me.

I wasn't born when Steve Wozniac asked his famous question of what on Earth we'd do with all these CPUs, put them in doorknobs? Yes, Steve, they're in doorknobs. And in everything else. Ice isn't just a microprocessor, it's a multi-core device with, usually, some very fast RISC processing, some DSP, hardware crypto to protect your intellectual property — important, since the laws on that change from country to country — and the thing will run autonomously in any given deck you slot it into, using the interfacing resources the deck provides. Whether the deck is my four slot OSDeck, which really is the size of a deck of cards, hence the name, or the new fifty slot GenData, a porno-house coffin, or my tank at work, they sort out how to display what the ice sends them, and the ice chugs away doing whatever job it was built to do. When that's not useful anymore, you wipe it, sell it, donate it to Goodwill, give it away, use it as a coffee stir stick, or fucking throw it out for Pete's sake. And therein lies the problem. Ice is almost as common as dirt, but infinitely more toxic. In some places there's talk of mining landfills for technology. Recycling the lead, the tungsten, the gold, possibly even sieving the molecules of the devices apart and reusing them. I've read that they're already doing it in the UCSA. They don't have a choice. They're poor.

Anyway. Customs passed, I roll out onto the sidewalk, looking for a place to stay. InterStellar Link's security perimeter closes at night, because even now, even in Reno, people still have the idea that crime is easier when it's dark. Besides, the next train heading east is 9:00 a.m. tomorrow morning.

There's very little left of old Reno. Reno the gambling town, the Las Vegas Lite. Only the bones of that remain, even now. It's something like fifteen years after the war, and nearly that long since Reno was nuked. For no reason anyone has ever been able to fathom. Which means it was probably done by one of the religious factions. Reno today looks like an Old West frontier town, built on a concrete landscape surrounded by a junkyard. New Main Street is a battered chunk of freeway with a hodgepodge of shacks, prefab buildings, and the odd, slightly radioactive stone building left from before the war. But there are people, buying and selling, doing what we humans have done probably as long as we've been human. Trade. Commerce is like a cockroach infestation. It thrives in garbage.

There is one thing and one thing only that makes this dump worth stopping at, and its name is InterStellar Link. They are the landline gateway for everything to the east of the Sierras to talk to everything to the west of the Sierras, unless you go around the long way across the Atlantic, Europe, Russia, China, the China Sea, Japan, Hawaii, and the Pacific Ocean. The lag alone going that route is fierce, and the cost severe. It's just as bad going by satellite. Putting birds in orbit and keeping them there is expensive, and the quarter-second surface-orbit-surface lag times start to add up when you're using multiple birds.

Finding a cab in Reno is an impossibility. They don't exist. There just isn't the market. So I roll out to the street. It doesn't take long before a battered VW van rolls by. I wave him down. "Gas, Grass, or Ass, no one rides for free." That's what the sticker reads. I already have a handful of two-euro coins ready. Paper currency doesn't carry the weight in either the currency sense or the brass-knuckle sense around here, and alcohol for fueling these antiques is expensive. The driver leans out the driver's side window, his blond dreads hanging down. "Hey baby. Want a ride?"

You know, when I was little they always said I should stay away from people who said that. Instead I hold out the coins. "I'm headed to I-Link's compound. Could I get a hand with my chair, please?" He helps me in, swaying a little as though to some inner beat that I can't hear. Smokes too much pot, probably. I remember people like him in college. As for the car? Some people collect internal-combustion-engine cars, and reminisce about the glory days of the big V8. Me, I've done my time in noisy, stinking, pollution-spewing old cars and vans like this hunk of junk. Not only can I remember being able to buy gasoline, I can remember when people still bothered to call it unleaded. I remember cars like this. I do not miss them. Technology marches on.

1:30 p.m. Saturday.

The InterStellar Link compound looks exactly like the compounds the Montana Militia would like to build if they had the money. Where the Militiamen use barbed wire and fence posts, I-Link has a meter-thick, reinforced-concrete wall topped with razor-wire. Where the Militiamen's guard towers tend to be crude tree houses with guys with rifles, the I-Link towers are on sturdy steel superstructures: probably recycled transmission towers. The boxes on top have a low-slung, armored look to them, and what are almost certainly gun barrels sticking out. The various shacks are pretty much the same as a militia compound, as are the Quonset hut barracks for the people who work here and so forth. Most of the people dress the part, too — camo fatigues seem to be the dress code, and you can't tell the security people from the working drones.

I'm being cleared through security. Getting dressed again. My rear feels a little greasy from the body-cavity part of today's fun. The guards are going over my chair with an explosives scanner, and my OSDeck and my ice are being thoroughly scanned. They're being careful. After yesterday, I don't blame them. It's a sick feeling in your stomach when you know you're vulnerable, and letting someone into your Network Operations Center, or NOC, without being sure — really sure who they are can be suicidal. The finger wave? Hell, some people pay big bucks for that kind of action.

By the time I'm fully dressed, they've finished going through my stuff. My personal security guard is young, intense looking, probably Native American: black hair, high and tight in front, long in back. Eyes hard enough to cut glass. W&S 25 slung over his shoulder. He's watching me as I get dressed. I should be offended, I suppose. Or flattered. I don't bother with either. I can see the very professional disinterest. I wonder how many times he's had to watch this today. He stiffens a little, getting data back on some jack of his own, probably. It must be under his hair. He's probably got a wireless transceiver in it. "Okay, the NOC has cleared you. Here's your visitor badge. Do *not* lose it. If you're caught in here without it, you're likely to get shot. Anyone asks to see it, you show them. If you do lose your badge, as soon as you notice, get on the ground, face down, arms and legs spread, and wait for security to come get you. Understand?"

"Yeah. I've been here before." Yeah, I'll worry about my legs then. Right.

"Well then, listen up, this is new as of yesterday. We are in lock-down status. No unauthorized transmissions into or out of the NOC. No unauthorized access of any of our systems. And you do *not* go into the tank rooms for any reason. Got it?"

"Got it." You don't try and reason with an 18-year-old with a submachine-gun in your face. You say, "Yes, Sir." You say, "No, Sir." You reason with the people he's protecting.

2:00 p.m. Saturday.

The I-Link NOC. I'm underground. I'm not even sure how far, but if I had to guess, I'd guess you could drop a nuke on this place and not inconvenience anybody down here. I'm talking to Director Carson Lance. *If you did what you're told more, you'd be a director too.* Lance is fresh out of the tank, his hair still wet from the shower. He's wearing the tanker's usual clothes. A bathrobe. Underwear for meetings. I feel overdressed. "Hey, Lance."

"Cath. How long has it been?"

"Well, since Epimetheus folded up … what … eight years ago now? Been since then, I guess. Been out here a couple times, but…" But it was awkward. But I didn't want to bring back a lot of memories from Epimetheus. But I've forgotten how to have real world friends, maybe. Lance looks at me a little strangely, raising an eyebrow.

"Are you okay, Cath?" He gets out of his chair as I sink back into mine.

"Just … woolgathering. I've been doing that a lot since the attack. It … stirred things up." Well that, and I am planning to lie to an old friend. "How is Diane?" Change the subject. Distract.

He flinches. "I wouldn't know. She moved to Austin a year ago."

"Shit. I'm sorry, Lance. I really am. She got the crotch monkeys, I assume?"

Lance looks at me, snorts softly and shakes his head, chuckles a bit. "Do you know how long it took to get Christie to stop calling herself that? She thought that was the funniest thing. Her teachers were not amused."

I shrug a little. "Nice to know I managed to corrupt a four-year-old, I guess." His smile must be infectious, I'm starting to do it myself.

Lance chuckles ruefully. "Christie's with me. She's quite the hellion, too. She's sixteen this month. Kelly graduated from high school in December. She's starting college in Montreal. She went with her mother."

"Did you get Christie her shots?"

Lance scowls at me a moment, but nods. "Of course I did." Despite the topic, he's relaxed a little, talking about his family. Something I knew he would do. People with families want to talk about them. It makes it hard to find things in common with them when you're single, childless, and not interested in breeding. He goes on. "I think it encouraged her, though."

"Lance, you know as well as I do that when you're sixteen you don't need encouragement. Shots just limit the consequences." I still get mine. An unplanned pregnancy or a sexually trans-mitted disease can get you fired from OmniMart. It's a sign of poor judgment, they say. It's also cheaper than treating you after the fact. More importantly, shots suppress your period if you're a woman. Technology marches on. Glory hallelujah, does it ever.

Lance steps back a few steps to lean against his desk. "Yeah, yeah, I know." He grows serious. "So I assume you're here about yesterday's break-in?"

"Yeah, exactly. We had some deaths, like I said." Time for business. Time for professionalism. Time to lie to Lance.

"Your company's still officially denying that, by the way," he says. No surprise there. Policy. Been afoul of that once al-ready. Might as well go for broke. *Funny you should put it that way.* Oh, do hush up.

"Lance, do you have logs of the event?" Lance watches me a moment. If he's like me, he's settling into engineer mode. And probably trying to sort out what I'm up to. I have to be cautious.

He nods. "Partial logs, yes. They don't start the instant we were attacked, but we have a pretty good record of the attack on OmniMart's network."

"So you don't know where the attacker came from."

"I'm sorry, no. All I have before the start of the attack is the operator voice log. I've been digging on this Mojo character more, and he looks like our boy. Or looked. Someone snuffed him last night."

It's my turn to stare at Lance. "What?" But...

Lance chuckles a little. "I keep my ear to the ground, Cath. C'mon, Cath, level with me. You went on another of your little tiger hunts and got the bastard." His smile fades as he sees my expression.

"Um. No." I didn't. This guilty twisting of my stomach notwithstanding.

"You mean to tell me you're not here to collect the reward?"

"I'm sorry, Lance. I didn't do it. The timeline's important, though. I need to know when he died. And where was he?"

"Check your news." Lance looks at me, more than ever trying to figure out what I'm up to. I know the expression. I know the man.

"Authorization to use your local wireless?" I pull my OSDeck out of the pocket on my chair.

Lance rolls his eyes, then reaches down to his desk and picks up a fiber-optic cable and jacks it into his head a moment. "Yeah, go ahead, you're authorized. I can't believe you're still using that thing." He pulls the plug out of his head.

"It's paid for."

The OSDeck reaches out to the I-Link office wireless.

So. News — local feed. The death toll in the last twenty-four hours was seventeen, a record low since the end of the war for Reno. Five suicides, one down-on-his-luck cowboy with a shotgun in the mouth, one jail cell hanging — a minor-league criminal rumored to have attracted the affections of his cellmate. Two slashed wrists, or four, depending on how you count them — a teenage lover suicide pact — and one John Doe, Caucasian, twenty-something, white collar guy found stark naked and beaten to death, apparently by his own hand, in an enclosed tub. Time of death looks like 1:00 a.m. Saturday. Other deaths were police raids, sled races gone bad, accidental impalements, murders, even two or three of natural causes, including one of old age. Pretty much the normal for Reno.

Four dead at InterStellar Link from unknown causes, probably remote homicide. Incident occurred around 7:00 a.m. Friday. I'm not surprised. The pirate crew at InterStellar Link would have gone after the intruder in a big way when it first touched their network. They're why I'm here. I'd mourn them too, but I'm a little numb right now. I scroll through the news on the OSDeck's screen and read the summaries. "Yeah, and…?"

"The John Doe. His real name is Arthur Rusbridge, from D.C. A friend of mine at Interpol says they're ninety-percent sure that's Mojo's real name. Come on. Level with me, Cath. Are you sure you didn't nail him?"

I shake my head. "I didn't, Lance. The man was alive when I left him. I caught him, and I broke him, but I didn't kill him."

Lance raises an eyebrow. "Why not?"

"Because he wasn't our guy. I broke him. I conditioned him to tell me the truth. He was the mastermind behind the Fist of God attack, but he was adamant that he had nothing to do with the follow-up attack. And he was already broken when…" *Nondisclosure Agreement…* Fuck it. Lance and his people are still at risk. They need to know.

"When what?" Lance's face is tight, apprehensive.

"When whoever it was hit our night shift. We lost the whole shift this time. While I was fucking around with Mojo." Stare into Lance's eyes. Watch him fidget. I don't really blame him for the bad lead. I don't really blame him for my not being there when the night crew got killed. Without his lead I'd as likely have been hitting the search engine all night. Vij wouldn't have let me sit in with his team. *You're not at a hundred percent, obviously.* I didn't know. And Lance didn't either. Right? Look away.

Lance's expression isn't quite shock. It isn't quite puzzlement. It's an amalgam of both, and the look of a bright man who is rethinking the scenario after having his facts pulled out from under him. "Shit. I was so sure … the timelines matched up. He didn't go after us at all last night. We didn't log anything except the usual noise-level attacks." I thought it was over. Lance doesn't say it aloud, but I can see it.

And I know the feeling. Look away.

So we start at the beginning again. I ask, "How did the attack start for you guys, Friday morning?"

Lance nods. "Super Scriptor attack. Script kiddy shit. It got one of my guys to go over the firewall like that. Ten seconds later the guy flatlines in his tank, and a second after that, the intruder barrels through our firewall like it wasn't there. He could have done that all along, but he wanted to make sure we came after him. He wiped out my whole night shift team."

Lance blinks a few times, then holds his eyes wide open for a few seconds. I know what he's doing. Blinking back tears. I look down, let him have his moment. I understand completely. But there's something fishy here. Something easy for both of us to miss, more even for him than for me, he's older, he runs a bigger network, so he's got more experience than I do. Lance looks at me. "What?"

"I have … a bad feeling, is all. May I see your logs? I'd like to at least upgrade to a theory before I shoot off my mouth."

He looks at me, a little puzzled now. "Yeah. Sure. Don't you have your own logs? I know your CalTech branch logs everything to keep their asses out of court."

"We do, but they were on their way to Denver by courier when I left to come here."

More wary. "So why didn't you just wait the extra day? I know this isn't an easy trip for you." Engineering again. He's watching me, observing, testing theories. Time for the big lie. I'm sorry, Lance.

"I wanted to move this investigation, nail the perp before he can get away. Parallelize. I'm not the only one who can analyze our logs, but I'm the only one you guys know well enough not to shoot on sight. Plus we all know your security guards are hot for me. They always get out the rubber gloves when I come to visit." It's a little like online combat. Feint, dodge, use any detail that wandered by and apply it right now. Flash some body to distract, divert. It's so much like online that I have to pull up my old jack's HUD and check it for connections. But I'm offline. For sure.

"You want to set up a conference call and see what OmniMart's analysis team has come up with? We can compare notes." He's not buying it.

"They won't. They're trying to keep this hush-hush." Lance is drawing back from me, whatever comfortable familiarity we had is going fast.

"You're right. That is the OmniMart corporate way. I worked for them in CalTech for a few months. Site IT director there is a hand full of engine grease. Bancrier, right? He never struck me as the kind of guy who'd do the right thing when the easy thing was easier. He's why I quit." Oops.

"You never told me."

"I left a message on your machine."

Correct that. It's nothing like online combat. I'm better at online combat, this face to face stuff is for the birds. Come on, you've caught me with my pants down, get it over with.

"Cath, why don't you tell me why you're really here?"

We used to be friends. Now I've come to use him, and he? He has become corporate. Maybe hooking wouldn't be such a bad way to earn a living. By the time this friendly shark's done with me, it might be the only license I can hold. I stop, look down. I've lost again. I'd better stop that, I'm liable to get used to it. And then I'm broken. Useless. I go with the only thing I have left. The truth. "Payback."

Lance nods. "Thought so. Another tiger hunt, huh? Any idea what your gang got hit with? Sounds like scramblers. Looks like it from the traffic patterns, too."

I shake my head. "Nothing commercial, that's for sure. I got hit, and I didn't even know it at first."

Lance looks startled. "Your defense ice didn't notify you?"

"It never detected the attack, even after it was over. And I write my own. I used to think I was pretty good."

"I used to think so, too. So what happened?"

I look at Lance sharply and he leans back a little, expression concerned. I wonder if he meant that to sting. Corporate. So probably yes. Close my eyes. "Ever written a Ship-in-the-Bottle ice?"

He whistles. "They're tricky. You have to be in the environment they were written for.

"Not mine. It copies the environment from where you run it, then tracks your jump vectors and jumps with you. All you see is some lag."

"I'd love to see how that works, some time." Playing good cop to your own bad cop now, Lance? Sneaky.

"No promises. Anyway, the point I'm making is that I hit the intruder with that. Then I cracked him and jumped down his connection into his home hardware."

Lance goes quiet. When I open my eyes, he's staring at me. "You tracked him home?"

"No, I was in a hurry, I just hijacked his connection. Two ended-spoof." That draws a raised eyebrow, and I start to feel like I have some control over this … this interface. This conversation. Whatever.

"You cracked him? He's got some intense crypto."

"So do I. That's why he didn't burn me right away. Anyway, I got to his home machine, and … it was like I was in a gestalt with him. No entry points, no login, nothing, just bang, into the gestalt. But if that's what it was, it was some really sick custom-carved gestalt ice. And next thing I know, I'm in *his* bottle. But get this. His bottle does the real world. Hi-res, interactive. Not perfect. I think he was getting his data online because he missed important details like my wheelchair, but he covered for it well enough."

Lance whistles again. "How did you get out before he could burn you?"

"Cussedness, I guess. I finally muddled through some of the confusion he was giving me and EMO'd my tank." I turn my head to tap on my ear, where my two jack ports are. "NSF jack. First gen, remember? I keep it plugged into the tank controller so I can check on my body while I'm away.

"I remember. Saved your bacon big-time. Did you talk to our boy while you were in his virtual?"

I don't blush, as a general rule. I'm a tanker, I spend most of my life buck ass naked soaking in an artificial womb, and I get born again at 7:00 p.m. every night. Even when I am dressed, most of the time it's just that damn bathrobe. But this time? Whoosh. Feels like my skin is cooking. "Not much, no. He modeled a friend of mine convincingly enough to take me to bed."

"You fucked him?"

"Um. Her."

"Oh. Sorry. Didn't mean to be sexist."

Oh, quit looking so astonished. "Yeah."

"Did it feel real?"

I have to think about that one. "Not ... exactly. The resolution was plenty high, good level of detail, no noticeable repetition or cloning but there was ... something missing. I wouldn't have fallen for it except that he caught me off balance and kept me that way." Look down. "The hacker made me believe I could walk."

"And then modeled your friend to the point where you could be seduced by her. Was she one of the victims?"

"Yeah. The first one, so far as I've been able to tell. They won't fucking let me see the San Jose logs."

Lance nods slowly. "So that's why you're really here."

"That's why I'm really here, Lance. I'm on suspension for being online with Mojo while the night shift was getting killed."

"Why didn't you just tell me, Cath?"

I look over at him. "Because I play..."

He cuts me off. I think it may be only the second time I've seen Lance angry. And the first time I've been on the receiving end. "By the book, I know. You always used to, at least. But you're not exactly now, are you? If you're on suspension you're probably supposed to stay away from this investigation."

"Yeah, that's about the size of it."

Lance nods. Once. It's stiff, too. "Well, if we're going to make any progress with this, I need you to decrypt the log of OmniMart's tunnel."

"I can't do that. Giving away the tunnel access codes goes beyond firing me, which is probably a given right now." *Probably? Certainly.* "That goes into hit-man territory."

Lance folds his arms across his chest. "I'm not asking you for the access codes, I'm asking you to decrypt the data." I hesitate. This was supposed to be a pseudo-official visit, some quick log perusal, and then I go off on my tiger hunt and leave these people alone. He goes on. "Cath, I thought we were friends, but you've put me in a bad spot. Please realize that you've committed two acts of corporate espionage against I-Link already. You've jumped into my local operations environment, and you've come here under false pretenses to get my logs, which could leave me open to a lawsuit. For all I know, your company could be setting us up for one. I could lose my job here. I should just call OmniMart and tell them to come pick you up."

"I'm sorry." And humiliated. And disgusted, mostly with myself. But he's not done.

"Look, Cath, I'll make you a deal. I'll take you through my logs from where they start until where the attacker jumped into your network. You decrypt the tunnel data and take me through everything that happened after that. We each monitor the other for illicit logging, and we take away only what we can remember the old-fashioned way, and if anyone asks, this is informal cooperation between individuals for the betterment of both companies. That way it's in neither of our best interests to blab."

They say the truth hurts. They're not kidding. My metaphorical ass is starting to get metaphorically sore. I suppose I should have expected the captain of this pirate crew to be good at playing the game. That's why he's moved up to be a suit, and I'm still a tanker. "You gonna tell me I have a choice, Lance?"

He looks away, eyes closing. "Would you believe me if I did?"

"Okay, let's do this. You have a deck around here somewhere? My OSDeck is a one-holer."

"You should really get a better class of equipment, you know?"

I roll my eyes. "Come on, let's get this cooperation thing going while we're still friends."

Chapter 15

2:24 p.m. Saturday.

Corporate decks suck. The resolution is only adequate but the environment they come with … everything has this fresh-scrubbed, shiny gleam. Perfect weather indoors or out, with a tasteful perfume in the air and the echo of smart heels on clean tile floors every time someone walks. That shit impresses newbs and suits, but I feel like I'm on the set of Iron Chef reruns. This stuff is easy, quick and dirty, you can buy it by the ream. You want to impress me? Give me weathered rock, carved with stairs, in a thunderstorm. And the hard part? Make it slippery.

"Okay, I'm in. How do you suits put up with this place all day?"

"C'mon, Cath, you know I wasn't always a suit. I was a tanker just like you until two years ago. What did you think, I meet people in my bathrobe out of eccentricity? Look, we buy these decks to make the corp types we sell to feel comfortable, and that's my job now. Besides, I'm starting to get slow. I don't belong in the tank anymore."

"Still having coverage problems?"

"We lost our whole night shift. And finding good people in Reno is damn near impossible."

I've thought about working for I-Link once or twice. It pays a little better than OmniMart, but at the time I had friends in the company I didn't want to leave. Now I don't, but I don't have any friends here anymore either. Stupid. What was I thinking coming here? I was thinking four of my people got killed in that attack, and six more the next night, and damn the consequences, I will have the guy who did it, bones, blood, brains, and balls. I'll worry about tomorrow if I'm still alive then. "Yeah, good operators don't grow on trees in Canada either."

Lance doesn't move, but the playback starts. He's good. No metaphor-dependency for him either.

The log starts in chaos. But it's thirty-one hours old now. I can be objective. Scriptor attack on the firewall, the transcript log flooding, network asking for help. One-and-a-half seconds after the attack starts, Beak, which a glance at the identity block just at the top of my field of vision shows, aka Henry Beakman. Born, 2001, New York City, learned the trade in night school there after a stint in the Grand Army of the UCSA. Night shift junior operator. New jack. This was his first real job. He goes over the wall. I have to smile, he's even yelling "Arrr!" We call these guys the pirate crew for a reason. Called. They have flair. Had.

The deck's software provides a standard intruder icon. I stop the playback with a thought. Lance looks at me. "Something?"

"Yeah. Tell your deck to stop filling in null icons. I want to see it how Beak did." The icon vanishes, I relax. Let my cyber senses, the ones with no human analog take over. I get the amalgam of data the log recorded about him, the rough, less detailed analog of what my counter-intrusion ice grabs for me automatically. I'm used to these things running my way. Being in this deck is like wearing someone else's underwear. But he's there. The intruder. Harder to see without my sharpened tools, but it's him. "That's our boy. Look at him go." I smile grimly. But I'm doing the talking still. "He's screwing up again. Look at the malformed packet generator he's using. It's a classic scriptor script, but look at the counts."

Lance does some quick statistics. "You're right, that's more bandwidth than Super Scriptor can generate."

Smile a moment. "Not exactly. They just announced a faster one yesterday. It was in the news."

"Think it's one of Super Software's people? Running prototype ice, maybe?"

Shake my head. "No. I think it's a ruse. He found the stats online and didn't check to see if the product had shipped yet. He's emulating vaporware."

"But that means he would have had to carve the ice yesterday morning before the attack."

"Yeah, that's exactly what it means. Did you get a trace on him?"

Lance says, "Nothing legit. Hijacked connection. Forged headers and crypto. Our trace said the connection was coming from you guys." The log steps forward again, everything in slow motion. A tenth of a second has elapsed. Beak finishes his jump. The intruder cracks his crypto. I pause the log. "…the hell?"

Lance nods. "That was my question when I first saw this log. There's no way even the fastest computer on Earth could brute force that crypto that fast. He's cracked the algorithm."

I can think of a dozen ways to do it without resorting to brute force, but I wrote my thesis on cryptography. Not everyone has that kind of background. "Do you have Beak's ice still?"

"Oh yeah. It's all locked up in security. They have Beak's body there, too. I went through Beak's crypto. It's a little basic, but solid, he should have been okay with it." I guess I'll have to check that to be sure. Another tenth of a second. The encrypted transmission between Beak's brain and the environment he's in doubles in bandwidth. I freeze the playback again, and back us up two tenths of a second, and tell the deck to generate a data subset of the data that was being sent to Beak in such a flood. It gets represented by the deck as a reel of mag tape unspooling from Beak's head to the reel on the floor, growing larger quickly. Mag tape? Okay, that's going back a ways.

I tap the connection with a fingertip. The deck helpfully displays the bandwidth of the connection of Beak's that's just been broken into. It's jumped to half a terabit, approaching the limit for Beak's jack. A .75TB Mercury Bio jack. I looked at those. Cheaper, to be sure, than the one I got, but I tend to think that cheap is not the most important thing for hardware going into your skull. "That's a healthy traffic spike. I wonder if it's on anyone else's traffic stats?"

He eyes me. "Maybe you should ask around for their logs, too." Ouch.

We watch the tape pile up on the floor, magically spooling onto a tape reel that never seems to fill up, all courtesy of the corporate deck, until Beak's mental signal goes unstable and he drops offline. Save it out as a separate log. Play that back. A quick burst of random images spews forth. It goes on for a while. At full speed it would have been too fast to react to. At least, consciously.

"What's he doing?" I know Lance is talking about the intruder through the somewhat cordial, arm's length gestalt we're sharing. I tap the deck mentally, forgoing even fingers this time, streaming the burst of images slow enough that we can look at them. I've seen this before. I know I've seen this before.

Riding a deck isn't like tanking. You still have some awareness of your body unless the deck actively suppresses it, or you do it yourself by long practice. So I can feel, really feel the hair on the back of my neck prickle. "He's flooding Beak with sense stuff. Looks pretty basic. Beach. Pretty naked girls sunbathing. Naked man with an erection. Smell of food … there's something here."

Lance goes quiet. He's watching me. I'm probably staring at the scene. I've been at this beach. Drunk in that bar. Gotten laid in that hotel. This version's a little different, more canned, less carefully made. It's exactly like a porn virt, where the beach needs to be convincing enough for you to get it on with one of the pretty people on the beach, but not so convincing you get sand in sensitive places. There's no resonance. The sun is warm on the skin, but the body temperature never changes, there's no sense of well-being. It's a picture, a simulacrum of my beach. Of our beach. "I've been here."

"Where is it?"

"Online. But I've been in a *much* more detailed version of this model. Use your outbound link?"

Lance nods. That's permission. Search on beach. Cabo. Porn. Bar. It takes 2Quik Search seven seconds to find it. Costs me about half a euro. A hole appears in the universe, and in it a miniature version of the scene we're looking at. It looks like a porn virt because that's exactly what it is. *Sex on the Beach 16*, starring Autumn Brieze. She's been edited out, but most of the rest of the cast is here, among other random faces and genitalia.

Somewhere here, staring me in the face, is something important, though it hasn't quite percolated into my forebrain yet. Back the log up and play it forward slowly. This time instead of watching the beach virt, I watch Beak's transmissions. I can decrypt them in real-time. The intruder blasted Beak's crypto keys in the clear to hijack his connection.

It reminds me a lot of when Tik would send us her little 'happy world' postcards, actually, except that Beak's reactions are less happy, more tainted with self-loathing. Beak was from New York. New Yorkers tend to think their city is the best in the world, but Beakster left as soon as he got out of the Army. It could be a coincidence, but I'm a cynic about those. I know the UCSA passed some pretty nasty anti-homosexuality laws as soon as the U.N. pulled their garrison out of Washington DC. And I can feel Beak's emotions change as the beach scene feels him out. Finds the chink in his armor. All the naked bodies, and the only one that catches Beak's attention on any visceral level is the man. It radiates out from him like chum in the water, faster than he can lock it down, so fast he may not have even consciously perceived it. And then the weird stuff starts. "Tell the deck to stop rendering unrecognized sequences already."

"You're onto something."

"Beak was in the closet."

"No kidding."

"Yeah, but he was ChrisAmerican and in the closet. Ever wonder how the guy wound up in Nevada?"

"Is it important?"

"He came here so he wouldn't be persecuted, but most of the persecution he was feeling was coming from inside. It got him killed." I would have thought I had the self-loathing to do the job too. Puzzling. I play the sequence back, and this time the deck renders only what it understands. The data going in is still pictures, random images, sounds, scents, tastes, interspersed with pictures of the cross, of Jesus Christ, naked men, stern-looking minister, hell. The emotional gradient is coming off Beak like a lighthouse, but there's something else Beak is radiating as his sensory system overloads trying to sort out the flood of random images. These sequences the deck doesn't recognize, doesn't know how to render. But I've seen similar sequences before. I read about sequences like this on the train. "These are jack control sequences, the ones that control the neurofibers. That's the attack. Right there. It's bypassing the fusible link in Beak's jack by making his brain generate the signals from the inside. And it's got all kinds of brain chemistry to home in on to hook the jack to Beak's emotional centers. Once he's got Beak's amygdala wired up ... yeah, there he goes. See the signal change? Feel it? He's streaming emotions into Beak ... and there. Beak just cracked."

Beak's brain is thrashing, spewing everything he knew out onto the link through the parts of the jack still wired to his cerebrum. I don't need to see his tank log's timestamp to know that whatever systemic failure killed Beak is already starting to occur. Beak's mind shrieks out the flood of memories for seven or eight seconds before the flood of his mind degrades to the random noise of dying nerve cells, then silence. Lance is quiet, watching. A feeling of horror radiates from him. I can feel it as the playback flood of Beak's death fades away to silence.

Lance breathes slowly. It's a gesture that comes to one, even in virtual space. "Holy shit. Ho ... ly ... shit. This guy's some kind of genius. He's ... found a way to really go after tankers. We'll have to be a lot more careful from now on."

"I'll give him that he's fast, and this ice is devious as hell. But I've known geniuses. He screws up too much. Counts on speed to cover for him too much. That deck of his, whatever it is, must be serious shit, though. Or he's another tanker."

Lance looks at me a moment, then shrugs. "Get decks like that in Japan. Kuroto's high-end stuff. I've seen induction guys keep up with plughead tankers like us with decks like that."

"See many of them on this side of the Pacific?"

"A few. Corporate Ninja types have them sometimes. You can get them on the grey market if you know where to look. I've actually seen a couple around here. Expensive though. Ten thousand euros for a naked one, you start putting ice in it, and you've got a serious fortune spent. They come with both flavors of connection: induction and jack. The corpies use jacks. Either way those decks induce the theta wave state in you. They say it's almost as good as being in a tank, and I've tried it. I believe them. If we didn't have Kuroto's factory reps saying, 'Wait until you see our new line of tanks' we'd be setting up a deck shop for the Vancouver site."

"Vancouver?" Lance doesn't answer, just gives me a wan smile. That slipped out. I change the subject back to what we're doing. "Corporate ninja. That'd explain a lot."

"Don't you get that shit going on at OmniMart?"

"Not much of it, no. Last scuffle we got into was sorted out in board rooms. Considering how our stock took a dip, I'd say the company that was attacking us probably got bought out. I imagine a few upper management types at Great Central got wireheads behind the ears, but I'm not at a level of abstraction where they'd tell me that."

"We see that kind of shit all the time. There's only so much land going up over the pass into CalTech, and I-Link pretty much owns everything that doesn't have rails on it. And we've got a contract with the Railroad that keeps them out of our business in exchange for free bandwidth. But yeah, everyone wants a piece of us. We're privately owned, so the only way they can get us is to crash our business. Buy us out at liquidation. Lot of folks have tried."

"Can't blame them. Owning your big fat pipe over the mountains would be worth it."

"Anyway. C'mon, I've showed you mine, time for you to show me yours."

"Yeah, yeah, I hadn't forgotten." But it does sound friendlier that way. *For someone giving me the 800-pound gorilla treatment, he's being generous with the pillows and the lube.*

I roll the log forward, letting Beak's attack wind out. It takes eight seconds for Beak's jack to rewire and his brain to come unglued, in a burst of noise all too familiar. The stimulation the attacker is sending Beak's emotional centers is bizarre, rapid images like fever dreams, and speaking of anal penetration, there's gobs of that. I finally have to lock out sensory feedback on my link. Then there's the dive through the mighty I-Link firewall, like it's not there.

The other I-Linkers are good. They're using some very fine techniques, and they get the attacker with a viral attack, at least one infinite dive attack, and a good scrambler-burner combo attack that ties him up for nearly a minute, dead still. More than time enough for them to trace him. He comes back for more. Cracks each one of their crypto links in turn, though not with the ease he broke Beak's. Experience teaches you to practice safe crypto. Beak didn't learn that in night school. Once the hacker is into their connections, he burns them together, each attack preceded by floods of images, each more realistic than the last, fleshed out with details that hadn't been there before. One is windsurfing in Carmel, and you can feel the cold water move inside the wetsuit. Joy, it would seem, is as effective a beacon as turmoil. *Pause the log. Consider.* "Are we looking at a team, do you think? One guy running the combat, one doing research and upgrading the models?"

Lance nods. "Could be. Maybe more. Or some awfully sophisticated ice doing it in the background."

"If this attack had just been on you guys, I'd say it's a prelude to a corporate war. Have you had any security incidents out in the world?"

"That's why our security is beefed up. We're expecting an attack. But so far, nothing."

It's harder to stay frosty when we crack open the encrypted pipe to OmniMart, starting seven seconds after the I-Link pirate crew stops screaming. I see myself come in. Smiling. Doing my Daedalus thing. Tika jumps on, and that presence comes through even in the log. Lance freezes the log, just at the point where Tika's inviting me to visit. I glance over at him. "What?"

"I'm trying to think like the intruder. Looking for weaknesses. Even without cracking your crypto I can see you're reacting emotionally to this one. It's like watching a feedback loop rise and fall." Oops. Somewhere along the line I guess I thought Lance's getting out of the tank automatically made him a stupid bureaucrat. But now I'm impressed. You think of an encrypted link as secure, that no sensible data can be extracted from it. Lance had just proven to me that it isn't necessarily. And slipped a piece of the puzzle into place.

"You just solved my chicken and egg problem. I'll show you when we get to that part of the log."

From I-Link's vantage point I can see where Tika and Kimmy were attacked, and why we couldn't see it. The intruder reset I-Link's mainline router, dropping the link from OmniMart to Nevada at the Nevada end. "Doesn't want to get gang-banged again, it doesn't look like." I try to sound casual as I say that, but there's a lump in my throat. I have to watch this. They're the last sane moments Tik had. The ones I never saw. Before the screaming started.

Tika notices the dropout. "Oh fuck, Shroud's going to be pissed, can't those I-Link jokers keep their net running?"

I look over at Lance, who's watching the playback intently. If the insult bothers him, he doesn't let it cross his jack.

Kimmy pings the links to Denver and Boston. "Yeah, dead in the water at I-Link. I hope they come back, the satellite links are too damn slow."

The operator environment security alarm goes off. Tika turns, all business now. "Kimmy, we're branched. Trace that incoming connection!" And that's the last sane word we get.

The intruder dives into the OmniMart Denver net and re-boots the router to Boston, just as the Reno side of the link comes back online. I see my log-self looking vaguely annoyed at the continuing dropout, then flinching as San Jose comes back online, and the screaming starts. I have to watch, I have to unwind what this guy is sending Tika. The screams. *Things I didn't want to like, but did.* I slow the log down. Watch the parts I'd hidden from at the time. See my own emotions radiate through the gestalt to the intruder's ice. I know now that he's picking them up. Analyzing them. Tika's brain begins seizing. It vomits forth emotions, thoughts, memories. And I have to watch. I have to watch, even has her brain begins to die from whatever damage the overstimulation has done to her body, and her flood onto the net is reduced to noise and fades away.

Lance freezes the link again. "Shroud? Are you all right? You're shaking."

And I am. "I know where he's getting his data."

"Where?"

"From that. When … when the minds go, he's got … some kind of ice sucking up the data. We all work in gestalts, we all know a lot about each other." I look down. "That's how he knew how to blow through your firewall, too. Because Beak knew. Probably even knew the keys. That's why he's killing everyone. It's a stepping-stone attack."

"That's impossible. Logging the data is one thing, but that explosion was over a terabyte of data, her jack was running flat out. It'd take hours to process that."

"Would it? Even on the Kuroto decks you were talking about?"

"They're still only as fast as the ice that's plugged into them. They're very specialized machines. They do all their environment and interfacing in custom electronics. They're not programmable."

"I know the deck/ice architecture, Lance. The deck's internal communications speed does matter a lot if you cluster the ice. "

"Cluster it?"

"Yeah. Old-school technique, before decks, back in the Linux days. Spread a computing task across multiple cheap CPUs. Probably before your time."

"It was not before my time, I remember where the Penguin people came from, I just wasn't studying computers back then."

"I was. The technique goes back to the 1970s. Digital Equipment invented it."

"Well, you started freakishly young. Can you do this with clustered ice, though?"

"Depends. I do my crypto-breaking with a six node cluster of F+ Penguin ice."

"So you think what, he's running some kind of parallel analysis on the … brain surge to develop material for the next attack?"

"That's what it looks like."

"That's impossible. Even if he does have the model built that fast, how is he going to generate the virtual on the fly?"

I think about that for a few moments. No answers come. I shrug and roll the log forward again.

The intruder attacks my log-self. Kimmy starts her jack out process. Nowhere to run — the intruder is in their home environment. I watch her a moment, look at the data going from the system to her. But she's run the trace from her tank. I can't see the results. They never crossed I-Link.

"I have to get this to the outside."

She says it so loud I can hear it over the gestalt. The intruder hears it too and launches a second attack against her, after booting Silver and Rei offline in OmniMart Denver's NOC. But I heard … I stop the feed, step it forward, just before I jump to I-Link to attack the intruder. "Look what he's gotten on me already. Look what he's sending me. This is the chicken and egg stuff I was telling you about. He gets ahold of my head here and the rest was the actual attack."

Screams. The intruder'd gotten the sudden intensity of emotion when Tika screamed, and had synthesized screams for Silver and Rei. In the log it makes me jump again. In real-time

I react only slightly. Lance looks at me. I look at him. "I barely knew them. I try to stay frosty."

Lance nods slowly. But I imagine his opinion of me has dipped a little more. He probably thinks I'm a callous corporate bitch, who doesn't care about her people much, except the one she wants to sleep with. And in the hindsight of the log I have to say he may be right. I tell myself it's professionalism, but I'm still numb, almost indifferent about Rei and Silver; not to mention the entire night shift. And Jay, for Pete's sake. Jay, who I abandoned when I felt the intruder chewing into my crypto. Jay, who the intruder turned on with…

With me.

I'd never been able to figure why Jay bugged me a little. The intruder makes it obvious. What did Jay respond to? Me. Images stolen from Tika's head probably, memories of the evening we both stayed after work to misuse company property by using it to play at having sex.

Those images get Jay killed. With his crush on me, his emotional system lights up like a spotlight, while the intruder cracks his crypto and rewires his jack. I don't have to imagine what Jay saw while he was being killed. I can see the images. The self-hatred? Rejection. Simple and direct. It makes me hang my head, even in the virtual world, and Lance stops the playback again. "Are you all right?"

"Ohh, Jay. Stupid kid. I'm old enough to be his mother."

"That doesn't make a lot of difference sometimes. Did you and he ever…"

Look at Lance. "No. I didn't know, he never told me."

"Would you, if you'd have known?"

On the one hand there was nothing to particularly recommend Jay for dating, or even for a one-night stand, probably well-marinated in alcohol, like most of my dating since college. And certainly another run-in with personnel could have gotten me fired. On the other hand … he might have been alive today if we had.

Lance nods. "Crushes are like that."

I look at Lance, then back at all that's left of poor Jay and roll the log forward. The intruder kills off Silver and Rei as easily as it did Jay. I never realized they were a couple, but his attack ice picked right up on it, and he takes them down together in one swift motion while I'm attacking it.

The virus attack. The Ship-in-a-Bottle.

Lance nods. "Impressive. That's some slick ice you've got there. Did you notice this, though? It's only a few seconds before he uses the same technique against you. You don't get the flood. He already knows you well enough."

I let the log run to the end of the event, until I EMO my tank. My objectivity is gone, and I just don't want to see what he sent me a second time. When we reach my EMO, I stop the log. Turn off my decryption. Jack out without another word.

It's gotten personal. Most crackers, hackers, script kiddies and assorted scum — even when you kill them — don't know you. You don't know them. But this guy ... has a model of me. A copy built up from the snippets of information from other people's minds, and from watching me when he had me in his own bottle.

Lance is out moments later. We're both quiet a long time. We've both been reliving the deaths of people we worked with. Some of them friends. Oops. Lance is talking now. "... and then he just ... disappears. Gone. One second he's there, the next, pift."

"So. Is I-Link going to investigate?"

"We are investigating. I'm leading the investigation in any spare time when my ass isn't in a damn tank keeping script kiddies from raping us while we're short handed. CEO approved a bounty on this asshole this morning. A hundred million yen. He's shopping it around CalTech. I thought you'd come here to claim it."

I do some mental calculations. About three-quarters of a million euros. I look at Lance, and he watches me knowingly. He knows what OmniMart pays, probably. That kind of money isn't life changing wealth, but it's enough for a house up the mountain or wherever it is Lance keeps his dreams. Put a couple kids through college and retire maybe.

"That's blood money, Lance. That's lower on the food chain than I care to go. That's lower than management, even."

He winces. "I have a daughter to finish raising. I can't be taking this kind of risk anymore."

It's my turn to wince. "I guess it's good that I'm still expendable. Someone's got to keep the place safe." *We few ... we happy few...*

Lance turns away from me. "That's not what I meant. Cath, don't you ever get tired of fighting? You've been doing this ever since GodWire hit Epimetheus."

"They killed Epimetheus, Lance. You remember what that logic bomb did? To our customers? Not to mention our bottom line? People don't pay to get seizures. You know what? I got them. I nailed every last one. Carthago. Delenda. Est."

"So you burned the city, sold the women and children into slavery and sowed the fields with salt. Did it make you happy, in the end?" Lance reads, it would seem. Who'd have thought?

"You going to tell me I had a choice? The net has to work, Lance. You work for fucking I-Link. You saw what they did to us at Epimetheus. You were fucking there and I have to tell you this?"

"Cath, there is always another company. I worked for NCC fresh out of college; then Epimetheus; then TurnTek ... bet you never heard of them; then OmniMart, and now here. It's a job. It can be replaced. You can't. Maybe it's time to let some domesticated hackers do the job. You were an engineer, Cath, and a damn good one. You created stuff. Now look at you. This job isn't making you happy, it's killing you. I don't doubt you'll get these guys. I want them taken out too, but..."

"But you don't want anyone you know taking the risk. You really are management these days." Wait ... I didn't mean that ... I've been too long in soulless corp-ville ... too long in Denver, a city I never liked, even when I was growing up there. Maybe Lance is right. But it's too late now. All too late.

It's about payback now. That's why I'm tracking this bastard and I'm going to burn him no matter what it takes because this bastard — or bastards — killed four of my crew, six of the night crew, and payback is a bitch.

Lance blinks at the cheap shot.

I'm sorry, Lance. I'm sorry…

"I think you should go, Cath."

Close my eyes. Nod. "I guess I should."

He's turning away, but he stops. Turns back toward me. His office is quiet. I can hear it. "I hope you'll come back and collect the reward if you get them."

"I'll get back to you about that."

Lance nods. "I'd still appreciate any leads you can give me."

Open my eyes again. Look at him. Think. Wonder what his dreams must be like. Probably all about a bigger house, better school for his daughters, and finding some pretty young bimbo to hook up with. *Alas, poor Yorick.* I knew him back in the day. "Here's one. There's some connection between him and Mojo. I'm sure of it. Mojo wasn't the perp, but there's a software similarity."

I surprise myself with that comment. But when I think about it, it's obvious. Just like the attacker built up a model of me, I'm building one of him. In the game industry you can tell when you're inside a virtual by a specific team. Every image, every sense, every detail of the place that was filled into make a complete picture instead of just being part of the spec tells you about the people who built the game. When I was in the industry, I could recognize styles well enough to tell who was on a given team, and the old skills still serve, apparently. In this case I can backfill the rationale pretty easily. Lance eyes me.

"The image flood. The one the attacker didn't hit me with, so I didn't know about it until today, was practically identical to Mojo's attack ice from last night. The attacker's ice evolved from Mojo's somehow. I'd bet money on it."

I look at the corporate deck we were both inside a few moments ago, and unslot my logging ice. Think about the pieces of world it contains. Turn it over between my fingers. Shove it in my chair backpack. Lance watches me as I roll back from the table. I nod. Look at him a moment. He's not young either. His burliness and gym-built physique are starting to sag a little, and there's grey hair at his temples. And those blue eyes are looking a little faded, like the light that's gone through them, the images they've seen have bleached some of the color away, and the sunny blue color they were has been worn to cooler colors. I used to think having a family made you prematurely old from the stress of a house full of screaming crotch monkeys, but there are times I wish I'd chosen that life. Because you grow old anyway.

I look away, tangled. Try to ignore the sense of seeing more of someone than I wanted to. Like the first time I figured out that not only had my mother had sex at some point before my birth, she was probably still doing it. More than I wanted to see. More than I wanted to know. He's growing into a corporate shark, sure, but even they are better than hackers. "Hey, Lance?"

"Hmm?"

"Be careful in there."

"Yeah, you too." A wry smile from him as I roll past. "Give my love to security on your way out."

I smile a little. The best I can do right now. Hold one finger up, and give it a suggestive twist. "Sure, but I think they get plenty already." I get a snort. Just a snort. Comedy never was my thing. Nor, for that matter, was flirting.

Chapter 16

4:30 p.m. Saturday.

Reno, Nevada. Fifteen hours before my train. I've been up for nearly thirty hours. I am way too old for this shit.

It's been a long enough day that I roll through the honest-to-goodness swinging doors of the first bar I find. It's made up, by some enterprising recycler, out of half a dozen shipping containers all welded together. It is called Black Jack's. It's small. It's dirty. The ceiling is only centimeters above some of the tallest patrons' heads. The bar itself is chicken wire with an uneven coating of concrete covering most of it, with a slab of glass epoxied to the top. The floor, the furniture, and the tables are recycled plywood, covered in graffiti. Most importantly the air conditioning is aggressive, and it sucks away the cigarette smoke and the outside heat with equal thoroughness. The place is loud. I can barely hear myself think. This is a good thing.

Life fails to imitate art and Tika doesn't come through the door looking to get lucky. She told me she used to slum a bit in places like this, both here in Reno and what is now TexMex, where she was born. I remember being surprised by that, I'd never thought of her as a Texican. That's why the Spanish surprised me in the virtual. In the very throes of the attack.

Squeeze my eyes shut. Maybe I need to find a louder bar. If I do, I'll probably wind up with hearing damage, though.

When the waiter shows up, I unclench my jaw to order my first bourbon of the evening, and a beer to chase it with, and a bowl of the house chili. I've had better days, but I'm trying not to reflect on that anymore. I am focusing on the bits of unidentifiable meat stewed all day in hot, spicy, flavorful sauce, soybeans, and beer, served with chives, sour cream, and cheese. It's good chili. After draining my drinks and a number of their brethren, I'm in a position to reflect on that.

It's Friday night at a dive bar. Full of people who've worked hard all week. Unwinding, getting smashed, having some fun. Eventually it grows dark and cool outside. I'm fairly sure that's about where I leave. Fortunately I don't have to stand up to get around. My balance is not mission critical.

Somehow I find myself sitting at the curb on New Main street beside a burned out pickup truck, watching prostitutes take their dates to the mattress in the bed. One, after another, after another, but there never seems to be any contention for the pickup. Nobody's ever waiting long. Each man stands with a prostitute. When one couple exits the truck, the next takes their place and the first couple parts ways. The man disappears back into a bar. The prostitute cycles back to the street to pick up another. Time-sharing by intelligent agents. There's probably some great revelation for operating system theory in that someplace, but of course nobody bothers writing multitasking OS's much anymore. Why share a CPU when they're so fucking cheap? Eventually a wind shift brings me the smells of the process and I go on my way. Watch the stars for a while, clear and bright over the dim lights of Reno. "Good night, Tik. Wherever you are. Miss you." And then, somehow, I find my way to my motel.

* * *

This is what I know. This is what I remember. Or what I think I know. Or think I remember. Or remember thinking. Or something. He's there. In my mind with me, in the gestalt we shared, demon lover, deprived of zombie flesh to take me with, hiding in the shadows, watching, but I know he's there. I can feel him with my senses that aren't senses, eyes upon me. I reach to him, pull away the mask and look into the emptiness, the hole in the world where it was, and see the … room full of vacuum tubes, smell the smell of hot dust and Bakelite, feel the heat as it radiates from the false world to my skin like the warmth of the sun in Cabo. If I close my eyes, I can almost taste … pineapple, coconut… Opening them again, I look into the ten thousand filaments, red eyes of Legion, and I know I'm in trouble because my pockets are empty, no sharp smoothness greets the fingers of my mind. The hands reach out to draw another mask up, pull it over the head like a hood, mask of skin and hair, dripping with blood, soft lips white and limp. It kneads the face a few moments, and when the hands come away, the face flushes once more with healthy color, and the eyes open, and Tika's white teeth smile at me. But I can see through the eyes, the lie does not deceive me a second time, the filaments glow through.

"What do you want?" I ask.

"Everything," he replies. "Everything."

Chapter 17

6:27 a.m. Sunday.

The alarm goes off, but I'm already awake. Thrashing against the covers. Heart pounding in my chest. Trying to choke back a scream. Disoriented a moment. Look around: bad art, mismatched wallpaper and carpeting, smell of old cigarettes and beer. The mattress whiffs of sex as I roll over; old, dried up, dusty and horrible. I sit up, fumble for the light switch. The power is off again, so I wait. In a little while the light flickers on and I can start my day.

My OSDeck beeps. Now that the power's on, the news ice has run its morning sweep using the motel's wireless connection, but it's unsure where to display it. I pick the little deck up, press a few buttons, and the room TV, a prewar CRT type, flickers to life, color badly distorted, jittery.

I press a few more buttons and read the news on the OSDeck's little screen. Skip the local feeds. I'm already tired of Reno. On the wider front, it's Sunday, so not a lot of new product release information. A dozen new worms to exploit the clowns who are still trying to use PCs. There've been better options for a quarter of a century. If people are too dumb to use them, that's evolution in action. Even OmniMart doesn't use that shit anymore, I personally scrapped the last PC server in the Denver systems room. With a sledge hammer. It was one of the better parties I've been to. MSIE is one certification I'll never use again. I'd rather hook for a living. I must be getting morals as I get older or something.

I roll into the bathroom and wrestle my way into the bathtub. I chose this hotel, not because of its stunning view — the scrap yard — or the pleasant rooms or comfortable beds. I chose it because it's the only hotel in town with bathrooms that are remotely accessible to someone in a wheelchair. Convenient? No. Workable? Yes. Once I'm in the tub I take a fairly leisurely bath, in no small part because of the leisurely water delivery. At least it's hot. That's good, because by the time the shakes and crying are over with, it's tepid at best.

8:00 a.m. Sunday.

Breakfast time in the city of Reno. I'm in a train car, the only one joining the Westbound today, waiting for the train to get within 30 kilometers so this car can link up with it. The Zephyr again. *Zephyris with his sweet breath hath bathed every vine in such liquor, of which virtue engendered is the flower.* I try to relax, I've got a half-hour train ride to San Francisco. And no, there will be no flowers in my hair, I'm going to meet someone. Hopefully. If I can find him. I have Tika's home address. If Brian still lives there, if Tik and Kimmy were close, if he knows Kimmy well enough; then maybe, just maybe, he can tell me where I might find her now.

It's all very iffy. Hell, it's a long shot — odds I'd be insane to bet real money on. I'm not sure what I'll do if I lose, either. My ticket home isn't good for a week, and the Bay Area's an expensive place. But I don't dare access OmniMart's corporate net to look up private phone numbers. If I raise periscope on their net they'll know I'm not taking a much needed vacation, and I'll probably be fired and locked out of their network for good. And that's a card I'd like to hold a little longer. I'll need some net access, of course, so I jack into the train's wireless net again with my OSDeck and buy five days unlimited subscription to CalTech's NFWN — the National Fast Wireless Network, one of the largest wireless networks in the world. It's not fast — CalTech law allows half the bandwidth to be taken up with ads. It's not secure, either. Security is strictly bring-your-own. Going online there without industrial-grade crypto and a firewall protecting you is only slightly less stupid — but much faster acting — than cruising for sex in Five Points back home. Before shots were invented, at least. Everything's different now. Anyway, if you want fast and secure you pony up to Telefiber or one of the other big providers and start selling them your internal organs. Speed is money, how fast do you want to go? NFWN is free for CalTech citizens, but for foreign nationals like me it costs. Everything costs. My bank account takes another small dip. If I'm careful about how much I eat, and I can find at least three nights' lodging for free without hooking for them, I should be just about broke by the time my ticket deposits me back in Denver. Not including my retirement.

I'm pressed back into my seat as the train car goes into boost mode, accelerating at one full G on Reno city power. A lot of people on the train have their eyes shut, and it's not a bad idea; if we run early, we derail the train, then hit it. If the power sags again, we get dumped out onto the main line late, and we coast to a stop and wait until the yard engine comes and gets us. If we're really unlucky, another train comes through and clobbers us. Bigger stations have a bailout switch line where the car can be diverted away from the main line if the timing is messed up, but Reno is old-fashioned. Only one pair of rails each direction, linked to a switch. I watch. If I'm going to die, I want to see the show.

No show. Just the usual lurch as we merge with the end of the train and head west. It's a short hop, but hunger eventually overcomes the wretched shape my stomach and head are in and drives me to the food machines at the back of the car. I slot my bank card into the machine, which, after a moment, spits it back out with the message "Declined" on the little screen. Bah. Vending machines' network interface must be down or something. Fortunately I have some cash left over from Reno, and the machine does still seem to recognize euros despite being cut off from home. I'm rewarded with a sausage-egg McLugnut. I give it a sniff to make sure it hasn't gone rancid, and throw it in the microwave built into the food machine. Some more coins in the soda machine give me a bottle of water and a Mountain Dew, the choice of computer people since before I was born. *By Caffeine alone my mind is set in motion. By the juice of the bean, the thoughts acquire speed, the hands acquire shakes, the shakes become a warning. By Caffeine alone my mind is set in motion.* Frank Herbert must spin in his grave every time someone says that.

I roll back to my seat, set my lunch on the arm, and haul myself out of my wheelchair and into the seat, fold the chair up and shove it into my luggage space. Going to the bathroom requires similar planning, so it pays to think ahead. Maybe that's why the world and I don't get along very well. It's not designed for me. At least that doesn't become a problem on this leg of the trip.

8:45 a.m. Sunday.

I roll out the door of the car. The Zephyr ends here, so the whole train actually stopped, a process that took thirty kilometers. The locomotive crew gets out here, and the locomotive is inspected, switched to another line, coupled to a new train, and becomes the Super Express. Then it accelerates down the track towards the bay, headed for the suspended tunnel to Hawaii and Japan. It's gone by the time I'm through customs.

People. Emeryville is easily the busiest station I've ever been in. It handles the transcontinental traffic on the Zephyr, the transpacific traffic on the Super Express, and the Coastal Starlight going up and down the West Coast. Busy place. I get bumped a few times, nothing serious. CalTech law makes those of us in wheelchairs a privileged class, so people are pretty careful around me. Civilization has its perks.

I change my euros for yen at the train station, which adds two orders of magnitude to the number on the bills. It actually lowers my spending power as the money exchange takes its fee. I'll need to hit a cash machine soon. Another perk of civilization. My bank's cash machines. Lower fees.

Of course the air is vaguely yellow, and it makes my throat raw to breathe it, even though combustion engines have been illegal here for years. I roll to the other wing of the station to catch the BART. The Bay Area Rapid Transit system is a valiant attempt to provide mass transit for one of the worse examples of urban sprawl in the world. It's a hard problem, impossible to do efficiently particularly in terms of time, but this is CalTech, where people never let impracticality stop them from doing something they want to do. BART works for me. It goes all the way to Redwood City, where Tik lived. I feed the ticket machine a few hundred yen and pass through the wheelchair gate to the car in the train specially made for people like me. Being coddled like this is nice, but it makes me nervous. I expect the other shoe to drop any moment.

It does, of course. When I hail the cab in Redwood City to take the last hop to Tik's home, I get one easily. It glides to a stop smoothly, electric motor going into regenerative mode and turning its inertia back into electric power. Waste not, want not. I slot my card into the car's side, so the driver will open the door, and the message comes back. Declined. Nothing more. Now I'm annoyed, my bank doesn't make this kind of mistake. Normally. My cab leaves without me.

I stare at the card, like a Neanderthal contemplating fire.

9:00 a.m. Sunday.

I'm on the phone with my bank, digging alarmingly into my diminishing store of yen to pay the pay phone. Moving up in the world, now I'm merely Nineteenth Century instead of all the way back to Neanderthalism. Annoying.

"Consolidated Swiss Bank, may I help you?" The girl on the phone has a charming German accent, despite thorough fluency. It's just enough to make me imagine sipping cocoa and schnapps in an Alpine resort somewhere, and to absolutely assure me that I'm talking to a human being and not a machine. I wonder if it's intentional.

"Yes, my name is Dr. Catherine Farro, I'm a customer of your bank."

"Very good, please slot your card now to verify your identity." I slot it in the phone. "I'm sorry, your card has been deactivated. It's been reported stolen." Hey, it's another shoe coming down. How many feet does fate have?

"This phone has a thumbprint scanner, can we verify my identity that way?"

"Of course."

I press my thumb to the faceplate of the phone.

"Please stay on the line, we're having some difficulty with the phone's verification system."

Occam's razor suggests that CalTech is probably not having a massive data corruption on its lines to the world. It's conceivable, but not likely. I'm starting to have a very bad feeling about this. "Is there a problem?"

"We're still trying to verify your thumb print, please stay on the line, we're reversing the charges on the telephone call." Without my card, I have no power in the world. None. I wait.

9:17 a.m. Sunday.

I'm still on the line, waiting, like a fool, when the police car shows up, and the two CalTech police officers get out. I ignore them as background noise until one of them reaches out to hang up the phone. I look up at him, annoyed. "Excuse me? I was on the phone with my bank."

"Yes ma'am, we know. They called us. You're under arrest. Please don't try to escape, or we may be forced to stun you." I stare at him. The idea that I'm being arrested is ridiculous. The idea that I might somehow roll my wheelchair down the sidewalk fast enough to escape two healthy young men on foot? That's just funny. Who are they kidding? But the smile on my lips fades away before it gets started as the blue coats take both my hands and zip tie them together. "I'm sorry, it's department policy to also zip tie your ankles. We've had people in wheelchairs get up and run away."

I nod slowly. My voice is a feeble croak when I finally speak again. "What … am I being arrested for?"

"They'll want to discuss that with you downtown. In the meantime, you have the right to remain silent. Anything you say can and will be used against you in a court of law, and all contact with the two of us, as well as any other officer you meet will be recorded by the officer's onboard hardware. Do you understand this right?"

I nod slowly. The other officer asks, "Do you have anything in this backpack that will hurt me? Knives, needles, anything like that?"

"No, I … All I have are clothes and ice and my old deck." As the first officer speaks again, I'm fighting back tears. Dammit, No tears. I'm not … I have to stay frosty, keep my cool … stay rational. I hate the real world. Hate it. Online I never cry. I'm strong. In the real world, I'm pathetic. Weak. Embarrassing. I try to get ahold of my emotions, but my lip is starting to tremble.

"You have the right to an attorney, if you do not have, or cannot afford an attorney, an expert system will be provided for you to defend yourself. Do you understand this right?"

I nod again, realizing that no, I can't afford a lawyer. I don't have access to my own bank account. But expert systems? I've used them. I've written them. They're a damn poor substitute for knowing what you're doing. I'm trying to keep my diaphragm from going into the spasms that are sobs. I know me. I know what happens. I take long, slow breaths, feeling my breathing shudder.

"If you decide to answer questions now without an attorney present you will still have the right to stop answering at any time until you talk to an attorney. Do you understand?" I nod again, but my vision is going blurry. I blink, trying to clear it.

The officer searching my backpack returns with my Canadian ID card and my corporate ID. He studies the pictures in both, then my face. Please let him realize that's me. Please. But if he does, he doesn't say anything. He just zips them into an evidence pouch along with my bank card, and both officers push my chair along the sidewalk.

In kindergarten, my teacher would ask who wanted to push me to lunch. I had a huge hospital chair, and I wasn't very big, even for my age, and wheeling myself around was a lot of work. And the kids would raise their hands, enthusiastically, like pushing me around was the most fun thing to do in the whole world. I was special. I was a kindergarten celebrity. And then one day they started asking if they could go for rides in my chair. Without me. I sat there on a regular chair, watching them all go have more fun without me, wondering if I'd ever see my wheelchair again, and knowing beyond a shadow of a doubt just who the celebrity was, and here's a hint, it wasn't me. I hate being pushed. I hate being … I hate … I hate being carried. I hate crying like a … fucking baby like I'm doing now, even while it goes through my mind that if I'm really online with the intruder … I'll be dead in about five seconds.

Chapter 18

4:12 p.m. Sunday.

Nope. Still here. Here, as it happens, is the San Mateo County courthouse. My fingerprints and DNA trace and picture have been taken. And I'm waiting. Doing a lot of waiting. I'm staring at a telephone from a hospital wheelchair that smells like disinfectant. I've had all day to think of who to call. I get one shot.

The obvious choice would be work. OmniMart has a large presence in San Jose. If I call them, they could have some flunky down here to pay my bail, and a first class attack lawyer to get this whole mess straightened out and leave my bank and the Redwood City police quivering in fear that I'll sue them all penniless. OmniMart Corporate is relentless in screwing over anyone who gets in their way. Of course, that cuts both ways. If OmniMart is aware that I was in Reno, that I'm here, it doesn't take a super-genius to figure out what I'm doing here. They might just as easily fire me on the spot and add data crime charges to my woes. For that matter … for that matter, I would not put it beyond them to list my identity as stolen in the first place if they found out where I am. But how would they know? Occam's razor suggests Lance, dear, sweet corporate shark, bent me over the table at the first chance he got. Lance went ahead and told them about my little visit. The razor suggests that I am where I am because OmniMart and I-Link cut a boardroom deal. And that I am a first class sucker for ... looking for a kindred spirit in a soulless corpie.

The only other living person I know in CalTech is Kimmy. If she's sane at all, she could come here. She might not be able — or willing — to post my bail, but I could probably have her subpoenaed to verify my identity, then hire my own lawyer to go after the police and the bank, and maybe OmniMart if I'm feeling suicidal. Of course, so far as I know, she's been incommunicado since the attack, and nobody knows how to reach her. She kept her phone number and residence secret from the company, which CalTech law lets you do, to prevent discrimination against the homeless.

That really only leaves one choice and I take it. It's an unlisted number, but I know it by memory. I dial. The phone rings. And is picked up.

"Hello?"

"Hello ... is this Brian?"

"Who is this?"

"This is Catherine Farro ... I um ... I called you night before last?"

There's a long silence. Please don't hang up. Please don't hang up.

"I told you people to contact me in writing through my lawyer, and I have nothing further to say on this case. Don't call here again, Dr. Farro." I know that script. OmniMart's dicked him over and he's suing them. To him I'm just a minion of the nameless, faceless bureaucracy I serve. I squeeze my eyes shut, vowing not to start crying again. I need my head clear. It's not obliging.

"Brian, wait! Please!" I don't know why he waits. Maybe ... maybe he hears something in my voice. Something like panic. Or maybe humanity.

"What?"

"I'm screwed, Brian. I was coming out here to talk to you ... I'm trying to find out what really happened, but all they want to do is sweep the whole thing under the rug. These were my people, Brian. My responsibility and..." It comes out in a rush before I manage to shut it down. People are starting to stare. There's a long pause.

"What are you doing at the San Mateo courthouse?" His voice is incredulous. Mine is quivering, the words flowing in a rush again. Unprofessional, but I don't have any professionalism left. If Brian hangs up, any chance at finding out what's going on evaporates. I go to prison for twenty years, and Tika goes to her grave unavenged. "Someone's reported my identity as stolen, I think the company found out what I'm up to. Please help me, Brian, you're the only person I know in CalTech who I don't think is in on it. Please help me ... please ... I can't ... I can't go to prison." *You knew you'd say those words eventually. Just like Mom did.*

There's another, even longer pause. I know what he's thinking. If he's got any sense, he's thinking that this is a sucker play. He's thinking that OmniMart is playing mind games with him now, that I'm to be good cop to their bad cop. I don't blame him for thinking that one bit. If I'd been as proactive I wouldn't be where I am now. Never trust a corpie. Didn't I say that somewhere? I trusted Lance, and look where it got me. Corpies. Well, I am one. And he has no reason in the world to trust me.

"If I help you, will you help me find out what really happened to Tika? And will you testify in court about it?"

It's my turn to hesitate. Someone else is looking for a piece of my metaphorical ass, and it's still pretty tender from yesterday's screwing. If I testify against OmniMart in a lawsuit, I'll never work in the industry again. If I get caught investigating something they want covered up and make them liable, they might even have me killed. But I'm no better off in prison, and the only way I can prove they tampered with my identity — also a form of identity theft, nicely giving me grounds for a lawsuit of my own — is to get out of here, to get online. It's personal. It always was, but now OmniMart's on my payback list too. And payback is a bitch. "Yes." *So much for non-disclosure, hmm?* So much for it. So be it.

"All right, I'll come get you."

"Will you know me to see me?"

"Are you anything like your virtual self?"

"More or less. A little older. Less ultra-violet. More in a wheelchair."

"Okay. Tik showed me a log. I think I'll recognize you. I'll be down there in about ten minutes. Don't wander off." Does he think that's funny?

5:30 p.m. Sunday.

Brian is here. I'm wheeled out to meet him in my own chair. They hand me a provisional ID with just a case number and my picture on it. Legally I'm nobody now. Not a citizen. No qualifications for anything. A human organism. Beyond that nothing can be trusted about me. In some circles this is called being free. I don't live in any of those circles.

Brian's younger than I pictured — as young as Jay was, maybe younger. He barely looks legal. His hair is no more than a centimeter long anywhere on his head, dyed black with red tips and waxed into little spikes, giving him a punk porcupine look, which his black leather jacket festooned with spikes, leather pants, and honest-to-God paratrooper boots do nothing to change.

He's wearing Utanium wrap-around HUD shades, I notice. Shatterproof. 360 degree vision, radar sense. Physiological stress analysis. They're street fighter shades, designed to make you nearly impossible to sneak up on, give you that little edge when someone pulls a knife or a gun on you, to give you a hint, telegraph their motion a little. We see a lot of that in Canada, despite the ban on handguns. I'm surprised the shades are even legal here. CalTech likes to ban anything that could be used as a lethal weapon, except for military and police use. Been that way since the days of the old U.S. Even the corpies can only carry stun guns. Theoretically. Yeah, right. And people call the SCP conservative.

"Doc?"

"Brian?"

"Yeah."

I breathe a sigh of relief. "Thanks for coming. And for bailing me out." My words sound heartfelt, even to me. And they are. Brian's being here doesn't solve any of my problems, but it buys me some time. He doesn't react at all.

"Let's go." Expressionless. Frosty. Like a real world version of my online self, I realize. *They come like sacrifices in their trim, And to the fire-eyed maid of smoky war All hot and bleeding will we offer them...* Eyah. Henry IV Part 1. I saw that play once. On Betamax video tape. It was recorded in 1981, four years before I was fucking born.

Brian doesn't offer to push. I go down the hard way — use the stairs and my forty years of experience. Balance on the rear wheels and just go, because I want it that way.

We sit in traffic a while, even on the surface streets, but it gives me time to recover my own cool. To get frosty. To clear my head. Neither of us has anything to say. I watch the city go by through the window. Strip malls are like islands in a sea of traffic. The sun is already hot on the roof of the car, even this early in the year. There is, I notice, no middle ground in the buildings. They are either brand new and sparkling clean, or they are faded, mildew-flecked, and slowly being engulfed by vines and overgrown landscaping. As though the climate is so fast moving and corrosive — or the buildings so poorly made — that the passage of only a few years requires their replacement. It's a city built of toilet paper. No past. No real future. Disposable. *My name is Ozymandias...* It makes Denver look positively antique.

Eventually he parks by a curb on a small street in a suburb. A row of small, practically identical older honest-to-God houses, surrounded by huge, mature trees. I stare a moment. This kind of standalone structure is slowly going extinct in modern cities. They take too much room. They're too inefficient. They reap no economies of scale. Above all, they're too damn expensive for the workers — like me — who live in a city to own one. "We're here. 508." That's all he says. A little blue one story house. Brick facade, blue siding on the fascia. Low, flat roof. Somewhat overgrown, patchy lawn. It's obvious that the trees are fighting the grass for water. And winning.

It's a struggle getting out of the car. There are tree branches in the way. It's a struggle getting up the stairs to his porch, too. I have to go backwards, using the back wheels of my chair again. He holds the door for me. I stare at him, meeting his gaze through those dark shades. A slight smile quirks his lip at that and he hands me the door and goes in first. He seems to understand. Respect me when I earn it — not because of my chair or my pussy, or anything else I had no say in.

Chapter 19

7:30 p.m. Sunday.

We're sitting in the living room. The sunlight filters in through dirty windows, past a curtain made from a U.N. flag. That quality of light makes the room seem more yellow, the house more full of stuff, the air closer. Collectors live here, and the things in the house tend to run in families. Dolls, lovingly dressed in club wear, their glass eyes everywhere looking out into the living room, unseeing. Sculpture welded up from junked technology. Animation cels, some from series I even remember. Art is plastered to all the walls. There are toys. Board games. Video games. Half a dozen game consoles from the antique models of my own childhood through the present. A whole shelf of game ice from Epimetheus Games. My old company. They're displayed prominently, and some of them I even remember having a hand in. Too much of that, time to look at other things.

I look around at the board games — Operation. Trivial Pursuit. Candy Land. Candy Land? Hell, I've played that. It's one of the earliest things I can remember. I'm lying on my belly on the scratchy carpeting of mom's apartment and playing Candy Land with her. I'm too young not to think she is the best person in the world. Monopoly. I'm older. Same living room. The carpeting is more threadbare. The game is more cutthroat. "Money doesn't grow on trees, Catherine. It's serious business." Mom says that, as I land on Park Place for the third time and her hotel bankrupts me. "That's how this world is. Get used to it. No pity. No mercy."

* * *

These are not my things, I remind myself. They are some-one else's memories. Someone gone.

There are home decks wired together, a Devuzhka and a Zhang. Newer than my OSDeck, faster. They're connected to a wireless switch, connecting them to the NFWN. Brian is sit-ting on a lumpy looking couch, toying with a battered looking pillow and afghan there, lost in his own memories, perhaps.

"So you're Dr. Catherine Anne Farro." He says, enunciating with excruciating precision. Even my first name gets the three syllables to which it's technically entitled.

I look over at him and nod. "Yeah. Not what you were ex-pecting, huh?"

"Not too far off, actually." He shrugs a little. "I know the type."

"I'm of a type now?" He nods. Small talk is awkward. We're both having that hippopotamus in the corner problem. The one thing, the only thing we have in common is… "Listen, I'm really sorry about what happened to Tika…"

"Really?" The face is neutral under those shades, the body language carefully guarded.

"Yeah. Why do you think I'm here?"

"I think you're chasing a ghost. To be honest." He's watch-ing me behind those shades. Taking my measure. Sizing me up.

I wonder what kind of impression I must be making. But I'm tired. I've had what you'd call a bad day. So now I don't actually give a shit about making a good impression. This is me, Brian, warts and all. "It's about paying my respects. By finding who killed her."

He's still impassive. Maddeningly so. Barely moving at all, even to speak. "Then what?"

"Then they'll die." No reaction. None. He could be playing video games in those glasses for all I know.

"Then what?"

I look at him. Until this afternoon, I'd assumed I was going back to Denver. To OmniMart. Probably quietly inject the results of my investigation where they'd do some good. Or back to get fired, go find another job. Either way, I'd expected to go back to something. To my life, such as it is. "Don't know. My plans have gotten changed out from under me."

"Yeah. So why *are* you here?"

He's starting to annoy me, but I can feel my old skills clamping it down. A lifetime on the line, swallowing my emotions, keeping myself in check. Staying frosty. "I just told you."

He stares at me a long time. Long enough that I'm sure he's looking at his HUD instead of me again. So be it. Finally he leans forward, raises a hand in a lazy gesture, pointing toward me. "So of all the people she knew, why are you the only one who's here now, digging at this?"

"Because I cared about her. That doesn't happen much to me."

He shakes his head. "You never knew her."

"I knew the parts she liked well enough for people to see. The parts she thought were worth sharing."

"Yeah?" He stares at me again.

"Yeah."

I meet the plastic covered gaze, staring back at him. He finally looks away, and a humorless chuckle escapes him. "I can see why she liked you, Doc. You're a hardass, and … Tik liked that. But there's something human about you. I didn't think so at first. I don't know what to think anymore. I was thinking this was all some kind of a corporate con, about the lawsuit I filed yesterday. But if they were going to throw an assassin my way…"

"It wouldn't be one in a wheelchair."

"Probably not."

"They can't just make you disappear. It makes your local authorities ask a lot of difficult questions. The corp is nailed down; they can't pick up and move the assets they've got here. Plus you have a lawsuit on file. Vanishing plaintiffs are the

kind of things that make Interpol curious. The last thing any
big corp wants is to have Interpol sifting through their records
to find every little misdeed they've ever done. It's the kind of
thing that gets executives killed."

Brian looks down. "I'm not a lawyer. I'm just a hired-mus-
cle kind of guy, you know? I get a phone call, I show up, they
jack me in, I do what I'm told for a while."

I look at him curiously. "You're a tech-ninja for hire then?"
He laughs a little, the first almost living expression I've seen on
his face.

"No no, I'm not like that. Guys in my biz call those guys
jack whores. And it actually takes a lot of conditioning to be
able to lie back and let someone else jack in and do the driving.
I know guys like that. They tend to be really really psycho.
Nah. What I do is more plug the receiver in, let them give me
the walk through. I'm still driving, and I'm still responsible."

I nod slowly. He looks at me a while, and it's my turn to
look away, but there's no safe place to look in this room. He's
quiet, then reaches into his pocket with a quick movement. A
very quick movement. Very, very quick. I've seen this kind of
thing before. It's from neuro-wiring. Take a jack's neurofibers.
Connect them from the motor synapses of the brain to the neu-
romuscular junction synapses. Congratulations, now you can
send stimuli to muscle nodes directly, and neurofibers conduct
their signals at electronic speed instead of the rather pokey
seventy meters per second of the average neuron's propagation
speed. You get very, very fast reflexes. For a price, naturally.

I looked into it once, with the idea that it might bypass the
sciatic nerve buds in my spine. That maybe it could fix me. It
was the first time I'd ever been to a Pro Clinic. I've never been
rich, so I had to save for over a year to get even the evaluation
done. The doctor who gave me the results was young, sharp,
professional, a little cold, but you want that in a Pro Shop doc.
She was disappointed, she said, to tell me that while my nervous and histamine systems were more than tolerant of the
implants, there was very little point in doing them. The leg
muscles I can't already control, she explained, are so atrophied

that being able to send them control signals wouldn't buy me much without years of physical therapy. Which both of us knew wasn't going to earn me the kind of money it would take to pay a mortgage on my implants. I went back to that clinic two years later to get my high-speed jack done after I got laid off from my first job.

I'm woolgathering while Brian is showing off his wired nerves. I don't worry about it, if he intends to shoot me there is bugger-all I can do about it now. He hands his PocketPDA 2020 to me after a moment, a picture displayed on its little, hi-res screen. "This is Tika. It's from last winter."

I'm looking at the picture, like the long-lost friend that it is, drinking it in. Tik was shorter than online, fleshier. Spending twelve hours a day nearly sleeping in a tank of water doesn't give you a tone, trim body unless you eat practically nothing and Tik was no more immune than I am. She had a tummy, and the beginnings of an abdominal roll. Her hair was different too, which I'd expected. Online she'd had long, flowing locks of shiny, straight black hair. Her real hair was the same color, but much shorter, and in this picture tied up in braids, one on each side. But she's not so different. Older than online, probably early thirties. The face is the same, except that in the real world she wore glasses. I remember her mentioning that once. The eyes are the same. And the smile. And the white teeth, contrasting with her skin.

"Eternally tan."

"Hmm?"

"Tika told me that once online. That her skin is … was…" I have to stop, I can feel my lip starting to quiver a little. I clamp it tight against my upper lip and force myself to breathe slowly and evenly. "May … I copy this?"

Brian watches me through his shades the whole while, as though studying. As though this was a test. "Sure. Copy the whole directory, they're all of her. Some of them are nudes. She ran around naked a lot. But I figure…" And then just a flicker from him, a swallow. He looks down a moment. No test then. This is someone he loved. A tiny flicker of humanity from him. As though his frostiness until now has been something of a lie, but one designed to protect him. "I figure she'd have wanted you to have them. She ... wanted to get you out here this weekend. I guess..."

I look down at the pictures, flipping through them as dispassionately as I can. When he says that, I don't even look up. "She wanted to get us all in bed. Yeah. I know." I wipe my eyes roughly. Because I've cried enough today. Because I have a job to do here. Because I have to stay frosty. Because I don't want his emotions on top of my own, there has to be distance between us. I have to give him back his own frost. Brian's head snaps up as though hit with a stun gun. He stares at me through the shades and takes a slow breath as well, letting it out. "Okay, Doc. Your call. What's our next move?"

Better. Professional. Problem solving; something I'm good at. "Find Kim Anderson."

"What for?"

"You know any other survivors of the attacks?"

"Attacks?"

I look up at Brian a moment. "Yeah. The night shift got hit the night I called you. No survivors at all." I look back toward the Visor.

"Jesus."

"Unlikely." My attention is still occupied with his Visor, shutting it down, unslotting its ice. It's little more than a frame and a display without it, fundamentally the same as a Quả-Chuối GamePet, only its ice comes with office tools instead of tools for school and games. And ice is ice. As usual it's copy-protected with some lame hardware encryption. My icebreaker – another Gibsonism – makes short work of it, and I copy the whole thing. It's easier that way. The software won't run on Penguin ice, of course, but the data formats are standard.

Brian's quiet a while, looking down as though thinking. "Will you tell me what really happened?" I look at him a moment. I thought we'd agreed to keep this professional. But okay. We're both after the same thing. The truth. If he wants this part of it, I'll give it to him. He lost someone he loves. It's his truth as much as it's mine.

"Okay. Here's what I have so far. At 7:23 a.m. Denver time, Friday, someone, possibly a group of someones, penetrated I-Link's operations network in Reno, killing all their on duty operators with a sophisticated anti-neural-interface attack. They then broke into our secure tunnel through I-Link, and rebooted the Eastbound I-Link router, dropping the rest of us out of the link, and went after the San Jose team first. By the time the link to Denver came back up, Tika ... was already being killed. We responded immediately. I told Kimmy to jack out and get Tik clear and I went after the intruders. We in Denver got hit next, and while I was slugging it out with one of them, apparently, the rest went after my partner in Denver, and the Boston team."

"What did this attack do to her?"

I look at Brian again, but his face is stony behind the plastic visor. Street fighter. He's seen worse. "Without seeing her MRIs I don't know exactly. If the damage is consistent with what was done to Jay and to a small extent to me, they hit her with very sophisticated ice. It caused her data jack to be rewired, effectively reprogramming it relative to her brain."

"I thought that was impossible."

"It's supposed to be. But what makes these jacks so useful is that they adapt, they move just like real neurons, and they link up with your synapses. The jack can learn, after a fashion. That's how it's installed in the first place, but there's a fusible link in the hardware that they burn out before they release you from the clinic, so other people can't tell your jack's neurons where to go."

"Then how..."

"As I said, the jack's neurofibers can still move and form new synapses, and they do it in response to your neurochemistry. If you manipulate the target's neurochemistry, you can control the jack's neurofibers and where they go. It's a psychological attack with a data content. It sent her some kind of scenario that got a strong emotional reaction. A very specific one, which causes the brain to produce the signals to rewire the jack.

"So what was her jack reprogrammed to do?"

"Migrate most of its connections to her amygdala. Which is the primary center of emotions." It's getting easier to talk about this. It's a technical issue; a cold, precise, engineering problem. Almost comforting. Staying frosty becomes easier.

"She died of this?"

"Once the attacker had direct control over her emotional system, he used it to extract memory and then probably to over-stimulate her sympathetic nervous system. Triggered the fight or flight response. In my partner's case, this led to a massive stroke. I assume it was similar for Tik." I'm trying to stay clinical. To keep this detached.

Brian looks down. His face is impossible to read behind those shades, but not impossible to guess at. "She got fucking FastBalled."

"What?"

"In my biz, one way to kill someone that's hard to detect is to hit 'em with … it's called FastBall. It does just what you said, goes for the nerves, pumps you way way up until something pops. Looks like normal neurotransmitters unless your lab guys are really good. Target dies of a heart attack, or a stroke, or shakes blood clots loose, or whatever else breaks. Big time hallucinations, really bad trip too. A really healthy guy will sometimes actually beat himself to death. Looks like natural causes. If you're smart you stick a Chill patch on you someplace before you go on a run.

"Chill?

"Yeah, it's a mixture of Geodon and Ativan. Autodoser patch. It monitors your heartbeat and blood pressure. They go sky high? Autodoser patch slaps you up with the drugs. After that you're so fuckin' mellow you can hardly stand up, but you're alive, unless someone does something else to you. I've been hit with FastBall. Had my Chill patch go off. Sucks. Hangover like you wouldn't believe."

"How long has this stuff been around?"

"What, FastBall? I dunno. Couple years, maybe. Chill patches came out last year, when we started seeing a lot of FastBall going around."

I'm thinking about Jay. His stroke must have been a mercy to him. And wondering about the news from Reno. Mojo ... found beaten to death, no weapon found ... I doubt it's a coincidence. And of course, there's... "Oh shit. We have to find Kimmy right now, if she's still breathing." The mental image of Kimmy beating herself to death moments before we can find her are all too real for me.

Brian looks at me. "If she's been FastBalled or something like that? It's way too late, Doc."

"I don't know. I don't know how far she'd gotten in her logout before it hit her. Come on, we have to find her." I'm going for my jacket, but Brian hasn't moved.

"So what does Kimmy know that you don't?"

Paranoia. I want to keep the few cards that I have private. It's probably why I don't have many allies at this point. Or friends. Or maybe it's just that I'm afraid to get my hopes up, or I'm too embarrassed to admit what little I have to go on that got me all the way out here. "I'm not sure, but she was there, and she was in San Jose during the time they were cut off from the rest of us."

"They don't make logs of this kind of shit?"

"They do in San Jose. But you and I both know they're not investigating, they're covering this up. They wouldn't let me see them and suspended me when I started to investigate on my own. And when they found out I'm not on a beach someplace trying to forget all this, they're probably the ones who listed my identity as stolen, knowing that takes forever to sort out."

Brian whistles. "For a plug head, you've had a pretty busy weekend. Anyway, traffic's going to be jammed up pretty much all night with all the people coming into the Bay Area to go to work tomorrow. It'll ease up about 10:00 tomorrow morning, and we'll go find Kimmy then."

"You know where she lives?"

"I got an idea. She had me and Tik over for Christmas last year. Little apartment in Santa Clara, nothing special. We can give her a call, though."

I think about it, and shake my head. "No. Especially if she's cracked up and paranoid, telling her I'm here and giving her 24 hours to run could guarantee that we never find her. If she's even at her place."

"I could call her."

I shake my head again, and look at Brian a long moment. "If she's as screwed up about Tik as we are, that could actually be worse."

Brian looks down. "Kimmy and Tik weren't best buds, and they weren't fucking, if that's what you're thinking." He looks at me a long time, then looks down again. "I loved Tika. We were talking about getting married, for fuck's sake. I loved her, but I knew her. She was an ordinary girl, not some magical force of nature that everyone loved like she came across on-line. She tried to be that in college. She got burnt, and it was a long time before she trusted anyone like that again, and even then. It was a very small circle she was inviting you into."

I sit back a little, watching him. I can feel my eyes narrowing a little, taking on the familiar dimensions of the infamous Shroud stare. "You get a lot of data out of that thing, don't you? Thermal scanning, maybe? Or voice stress?" He's scanning me. He has to be. Because we're not jacked in, he can't be reading my mind, feeling my emotions as if we were ... but we are in the same room together. Reality. Bites me.

He watches me a moment, then looks down and slides the shades off, baring hard, light eyes, strong eyebrows. Slight lines of a face that gets too much sun, lives too hard. Young, but battered. "Better?"

Nod slowly. "Yeah. I was starting to wonder if you had eyes."

"No. You're changing the subject."

"Why would I do that?"

"I don't know. You cared about her. You said so yourself, and I think I believe you. But you can't seem to handle that she cared about you. Specifically."

I look Brian in the eyes, and he does the same to me. His eyes are green, I notice. Unusual. I focus on that for a while, I look down at my jacket and shrug it back off, since we seem to be staying home. "If you say so."

He looks down at his shades, as though considering putting them back on, then sets them on the coffee table and gets up. "Listen, I'm going to make some dinner. Want some?"

A slow breath, and I let myself relax just a little. My stomach growls. "Yeah, I guess so. Please. Tik um … Tik always bragged how good a cook you are. She and Rei were big-time foodies."

I'm not expecting a laugh from Brian, but he surprises me. "Foodie, Tika? Nah. She … just liked to eat. Liked to taste. The pleasure of the senses. But she got that from Applebee's malts as much as anything fancy we ate. Last time she was on a diet she swore those malts off for three months. When she gave up on the diet and we went there that night. It was like she was going to get off from it, you know? Same look."

That's easy to picture, too. It makes me smile. "I used to say she lived in a beautiful world."

Chapter 20

The smells coming from the kitchen of the little house make my stomach growl again. There's something sizzling in a pan with the aroma of onions and bacon and … cilantro, maybe. Cooking. Real cooking. My kitchen never gets dirty except around the fridge. I roll toward the kitchen to watch Brian cook. Who knows, maybe I'll learn something. Brian's talking about Tika still.

"…nah. She um … she just made a point of seeing beauty in the world she did live in… Fuck!" A pan clatters to the stove top.

"What's wrong?"

"Oh, nothing. Burned myself." He shakes his hand out, as though that will make the pain go away.

"Let me see."

He glances over his shoulder at me. "Nah, I'm all right, really."

"Let me see. Now."

He eyes me as I roll into the little kitchen, but dutifully holds his hand out. "See? I'll live."

"You should put some ice on that." Brian is quiet for a moment, stirring with his other hand.

"Yeah. Yeah. You're right." But he's sobbing when he gets to the fridge. And I know it's not the burn. "Oh fuck. Oh fuck."

I roll over to Brian. Reach up to touch his side. He flinches, then turns and lifts me out of my chair and into his arms, in

a rush of motion that it's hard to even see. I hold onto Brian
firmly, pulling my legs under me as though I could stand. He
holds me tight, I return the favor. Push down with my legs
as much as I can to try and ease the feeling that my breath is
being crushed from my lungs. His arms aren't that tight, and
I can breathe well enough, but the feeling … persists. My legs
buckle, and I cling to him. He draws his head back a little to
look at me, holding me up, his eyes wet. He sniffles a little, trying to exert control. "I'm … sorry, Doc."

I shake my head. "Cath. Catherine."

He backs me up against the cabinets. Lifts me up a little.
Props my bottom up on the counter top. I'm a little taller than
he is like this. He doesn't let go. Neither do I, and he buries his
face in my shoulder, sobbing, tears soaking through the thin
old T-shirt to my skin. I'm fighting back another flood of tears
— my own. Swear vengeance against whoever did this. Clench
my jaw hard enough that I can hear my fillings creak. My eyes
are closed tight when his lips first brush mine. My eyes aren't
closed for long afterwards, certainly. He draws back a little.
Shakes his head, but I stop him. "It's okay."

There's nothing more said. Another soft press of his lips to
mine, mine to his. A hug that presses my body tight to him,
almost crushingly. Cling to him as much as he clings to me. His
tongue brushes my lips and I try to remember how to kiss like
something other than a gagging goldfish. I finally have to draw
back. Try again to catch my breath. My eyes are tearing a little
in spite of me. "Um … no good can come of this."

He snorts softly, tensely. "Nope. None at all." And then all
talking ends, because his mouth is against mine. Jaws relax.
Tears flow, and it does not matter. I'm almost consumed in this
dance of tongues and hands.

Tika wanted this. She wanted all three of us together.
Wanted there to be sharing. Would want there to be in her
memory. Is it love? No. It's not even really passion. All we have
to share are memories of her, and comfort for a few hours, maybe. Even so, this kind of thing doesn't usually happen to me, so
I make a quick, paranoid check of my old jack's HUD, just to be

sure, but it gives the usual "No Connections" message. This, apparently, is as real as it gets. "Hey Bri? Turn off the stove first, okay? Last thing we want now is a kitchen fire."

It gets me another snort. "Right." He leaves me propped on the counter and goes to turn off the stove. I have a few moments for second thoughts. What will this solve? Seriously, what good can possibly come of this when we're both more lucid later? No answers, as usual. He comes back and picks me up. I'm being carried for the second time today, or the third, depending on how you count them. I let it slide this time. I've had my shots. How bad can it be?

Chapter 21

The bedroom is dark, and there's the scent of cologne, of laundry, mingled with the food smells that came from the kitchen, and the smell of man, and of woman. Tika is suddenly a very intimate presence for the moment. Her scent rises from the blankets. I'm not sure Brian notices the difference. The weight of him presses against me. Lips to my lips. Caress of tongues. Urgency and need carry us through the awkward parts of two almost-strangers getting undressed together. He expects the moves and cues she gave him. But I haven't done this often enough with anyone for it to be anything else but awkward. He needs — he takes me. I need — I accept him willingly. We need together, and need desperately. He offers his ablutions to the dead inside me. I'm offering my own. Cling to him. Hold him tight to me, like a drowning woman clutching at straws.

He lies on me afterwards, his weight on one of his hands. I reach out to touch his face. His eyes are wet from crying and coming. So are mine, I guess. We're catching our breaths. Kissing as though being together like this is the most natural thing in the world. The tightness in my chest isn't gone. Not quite. It lingers in the background far away. Slip my arms around him again. "And to think I wasn't planning to come here this weekend."

It was a feeble attempt at humor, though the pun was not intentional. It gets a feeble chuckle. He's quiet a long time, even after he slides off of me and lies beside me. It's not long before we're in each others' arms again, bodies tight together. He tries his attempt at small talk, mine having so obviously failed. "You're pretty buff for a plug head."

I look down at my arms. Uncurl one from around his chest. Really look at it. Admittedly my arms are pretty solid. Muscular. I raise that hand. Watch the muscles and tendons in my forearm as they move in concert. All I ever notice about my arms in the mirror is that I'm growing old lady wings. My body's always been a source of betrayal for me, from the first time I can remember realizing that I'd never be able to walk. As I grew up I got into books and computers, retreating into my mind. My world is in my head. My body just gives me a way to haul that around. Has always given. So I look at my arm, the muscles of forty years powering a wheelchair carved in it, and I'm surprised. *Know thyself much?* I let my hand fall back to him. Play my fingers through his spiky hair. Feel it brush the calluses on my palm.

He looks at me. "Something on your mind?"

I look over at him and smile a little. "Lots of things. I'm kind of ... marooned in the real world, you know?"

"Is that such a bad thing?"

His nose is about a centimeter from mine, it's easy to tilt my chin up and kiss his mouth lightly. "It has its moments, certainly." I close my eyes, rest my forehead against his. I have a million things to think about, but the only one my endorphin-soaked brain seems to want to deal with is the vaguely indecent little proposal Tik had for me Friday morning. And how the memory doesn't hurt quite so much as it did before. "Just ... thinking about what might have been."

In a moment, his head moves, His lips brush along my collarbone; a sensation that gives me goose bumps. His fingers slide along my thighs. He's exploring the patchwork of sensation I have there, and the contrast between the three states, numb, tingly, and alive makes me shiver. It's probably a contextual thing. Run my fingertips downward along his side. Watch him shiver as well. Yup. Contextual.

Brian, it would seem, needs more comforting. I'm not the woman he's wishing I was, and I know it. But I'm willing enough to comfort … and be comforted. When all is said, I'm sitting in his lap. Facing him. Engulfing him. Cuddled close. We rock together slowly. There are worse ways to say goodbye to someone, though it's a strange feeling to have the sobs followed on closely by an orgasm. And when all is done, I have to say that this spooning stuff I've read so much about? Is lovely.

Chapter 22

Brian's quiet. All I can hear is his breathing. I've started to think he's fallen asleep when he finally speaks again.
"Still hungry?"

I unlace my fingers from his and turn towards him onto
my back. Look over at him. My stomach growls on cue, more
insistent this time. "Starving. Still up to cooking?" It gets me
a smile; I quirk one of my own. He gives me a soft kiss on the
mouth which I return. Hey, all this practice and I'm getting
better at it. He slowly disentangles himself from me and the
rumpled sheets, and heads to the kitchen. Now, I happen to
think it's distinctly not safe to cook when you're naked. One
bit of hot grease splatter and you're going to an emergency
clinic, and you just know they're going to chuckle about you
when you're gone. But whatever. I have my own concerns. My
bladder, like my stomach, has demanded my attention. "Hey
Brian, could you shove my chair in here?"

No response. I sigh inwardly, and pull on my jeans to protect me from rug burn and climb out of bed to the floor. Glance
out the bedroom door toward the kitchen. He's not there. He's
in the living room, jacked into one of the decks. I continue my
crawl to the bathroom. The OSDeck in my pocket presses un-
comfortably against my hip. I'm not angry with Brian. There
are probably a million and one things that are automatic to
you when you can just get up and walk that don't occur to you

until you're in a wheelchair or know someone who is. Being freshly fucked certainly seems to improve my outlook. I decide to make use of the tub, as long as I'm stranded in the bathroom. Since my OSDeck is waterproof it seems like a perfect time to check my e-mail.

9:27 p.m. Sunday.

My OSDeck wakes up and the security ice informs me that my network connection is not secure. A little poking reveals why. The wireless connection I'm on is coming from the living room. That network, in turn, is bridging the entire NFWN into Brian and Tik's living room network rather than routing it. No encryption. No firewall. No nothing. The network is naked. I decide to check it out; to make sure nobody else is taking advantage of that weakness. Fire up my sniffer ice. It puts my OSDeck's wireless interface into promiscuous mode, which gives me a flicker of amusement. Brian's encrypted connection is the only active one on the link. I let the sniffer run to keep an eye out for intruders. Make a mental note to delete the log the sniffer ice generates later. Make another to fix Brian's wireless setup so every scum-sucking war driver can't come by and steal bandwidth. Go go mail and news ... whoops.

I stop the news ice just in time. News costs, and my bank account is frozen. This rosy world-view business is softening my brain. If I'd let that ice run it would have set off alarms all over the place and pretty much guaranteed me a trip back to jail.

E-mail — my spam filters have reduced my personal e-mail level from a hundred-twenty-six thousand e-mails to three. One of those is promising me a larger penis. I think I'd be sore. I add that one to the spam filter and go on. E-mail from my bank indicating that my account is frozen due to my recent identity theft and the criminal has been arrested in Redwood City. How thoughtful. I have my doubts they'd accept an e-mail from my account informing them what really happened, and my life is complicated enough right now without having my personal e-mail account frozen too. Lance has e-mailed me. How nice. My mailer ice is set up to never ever run executables that it's been mailed or hand them off to other ice, or in fact do anything other than display the mail without asking. I have it dump Lance's e-mail character codes in hex. A few minutes' review tells me that not only is there nothing fishy with this mail that would, for example, tell Lance that I've received and opened his mail, but that Lance is old-school enough to keep his e-mail seven bits clean. Even I don't bother doing that. Any bytes expecting to be executed by my ice should be at least eight bit words, so this mail looks cleaner than clean. So I read it.

> Shroud:
>
> I've had a chat with the owner and he agrees that if you're interested in leaving OmniMart, we could definitely use someone with your abilities here. Day shift, pay negotiable. Please reply at your earliest convenience.
>
> -Lance

Sneaky. Go after me where I'm weak, in the real world and not online where I'd own him. Very sneaky. Just in case I somehow get off from the screwing the company is giving me, Lance has a fail-safe. If OmniMart can't fire me for anything else, like insubordination, they can fire me for negotiating for a job someplace else. My investigation, any political pull I might have to use the results, and I, would all be on the wrong side of the security wall. Save the message. Make a mental note that if I am still employed when all this is done, to give it to personnel and let them complicate Lance's life. Stealing employees from your customers is seldom a good idea. Lance is on my list now, along with whoever he set me up with at OmniMart. And payback is a bitch. I feel much more like myself now.

Brian has logged out. The smell of good things cooking has begun to waft from the kitchen, so I unplug the little deck from my head and finish my bath. Pull my clothes on. Crawl back toward the doorway from the hallway to the kitchen and living room. "Hey Brian. Could I get my chair, please?"

Without facing me, Brian reaches across the kitchen to roll my chair in my general direction. I'm not the only one who's grouchy tonight, it looks like. I lock the brakes and crawl into the thing, thankful to have it for a change, then unlock them and roll toward the kitchen. "Bad news?"

"Business. Don't worry about it."

"You have to go out tonight?"

"I said don't worry about it."

But his shades are back on, and I do worry. I try to remind myself that he's not my lover, that what happened between us was about Tika, about trying to come to grips with her being dead. I was right. No good will come of this. I nearly got myself arrested with the news software, and now … I'm confronting reality about the whole situation once again. And I'm functionally alone again. Which is how I like it. Or will like it. I can feel my frostiness returning. Let myself get distracted and this happens.

Dinner is quiet, a little strained. Which is too bad, because Brian can cook to make the angels sing. Spices — ginger, garlic, and I don't know what all else fill my mouth with a near-perfect balance of hot and sour, salty and sweet. Even I've absorbed enough kitchen-ese to know those are the four axes of Asian cooking in general. Dinner seems to be some kind of stir fry and lots of rice. The meat seems to be chicken, and what the sauce is I couldn't say, except that there's fish sauce and soy sauce in it, and the meat is vaguely yellow from the spices it was cooked in.

"This is really good." Brian doesn't say anything. Whatever rapport we'd established is gone as if it hadn't been there. Back to work. "Any feedback from your friends on where Kimmy is?"

He shakes his head.

"Not yet. Morning. I gotta go out tonight though."

I nod. "I figured. Be careful, okay?"

Brian looks at me as though I've stabbed him with my fork. Stares at me a few moments. Then nods and looks back into his plate. "Blanket's on the couch."

I nod a little. I guess I expected that.

10:15 p.m. Sunday.

I'm in bed, chair parked next to the couch. Brian's still gone. I check the fuel cell on my OSDeck, set the ice up to pull only my e-mail tomorrow morning when the alarm goes off. I notice the sniffer's log is still there, and I drag it to the trashcan. Then glance toward the door. A panicky feeling. If something happens to Brian, I'm pretty well stuck here until the Redwood City police come and get me. And once they do, they're probably going to have some awkward questions if he's turned up dead, especially with the trace evidence of our little tryst. I look at the OSDeck again, slip out the ice with Tika's pictures in it, and slip two nodes of my crypto-breaking ice cluster in, and drop the log into the crypto-breaker instead. It leaves a bitter taste in my mouth. But my betrayal is postponed. Brian's crypto is first-class, and my ice is going to take hours to days to crack it. I turn my attention back to what I need to do, hopefully tomorrow. And think about how I can get what I need from Kimmy.

Chapter 23

9:22 a.m. Monday.

I awaken to the door slamming. Brian. He looks tired. Look at my OSDeck. The alarm is still beeping as it must have been for nearly three hours. Fuck. Sleeping in on Monday morning. What next?

"Turn that fucking thing off, would you? Get dressed, we need to roll. I thought you'd be awake already."

I kill the alarm and haul myself off the couch and into my chair. This getting dressed business is a nuisance. But I bathed last night, so I can hurry. Brush the hair. Wash the face. Brush the teeth. Clean underwear. Last night's jeans. T-shirt. "Bring your jacket," Brian says. Okay, black leather jacket. Unlike most women I can be up and running in 15 minutes if I don't have to shower.

"What's up?"

Brian's in the kitchen again, and there are more good food smells coming from there. I roll into the kitchen, and he turns on me, wire-fast. "Are you in all the way on this, Doc? Are you willing to do what it takes to find Kimmy?"

"Like what?" *Sounds like an invitation for your mouth to write checks your ass can't cash, doesn't it?* Well ... yes.

"Like not asking. Are you committed to this, or not? All or nothing, I can't do this without data support." Brian scrambles eggs vigorously. They're in with onions, cheese, mushrooms, some kind of hot pepper, chicken, and curry. The scent alone is making my mouth water. I roll toward the back door and crack it open. Smell the lilacs. Flash back to Friday morning. Two days ago. Tik was sending me these very flowers' perfume. The smog makes me cough a little, so I close the door again. *This is not your beautiful world.* No. It's not. It might have been. But it isn't. That's reason enough. "Yeah, okay. I'm in. What do you need?"

Brian rolls up two burritos and wraps them in paper towels. "Fill you in on the road. We gotta get someplace you can link safely."

Close my eyes. "I'm not going to like what you want me to do, am I?"

Unexpectedly, Brian chuckles. "You might, actually. Tik always said she had the fun job."

I must be staring. Tika Silverthorn was … it does explain how they paid for all this. House. Car. Stuff. "Wait. What are we talking about here? Exactly?"

"Are you in this, or not?"

I nod after a moment, fighting the instincts of my whole life. Justice. Law. Order. *The instinct to not be like mom.* Yes. Exactly. But … I don't see that I have a choice. *Did mom?* Shut the hell up, okay? I answer Brian. "Just … trying to plan my day."

It gets me a grim smile. Brian says, "Tik always said you'd come around." I stare at him again. Oh Tik, what have you gotten me into now? "It wasn't just about getting you in bed. We were starting to get jobs she couldn't handle technically, and she said you were a lot better." He pauses in the living room, all mirth fading into seriousness. "Okay. Here's what I've got. It took some digging, but I tracked Kimmy to The Asylum."

"A mental hospital?"

Brian shakes his head. "It's a place in San Francisco. Down in the Tenderloin. If you're crazy sooner or later you wind up there. If you don't get killed first. Lot of empty buildings, hasn't been rebuilt since the war. It's not a big area, couple square blocks."

"And you need … what?"

"An army to search it. Or some kind of electronic recon. Real-time or very recent." Brian gets into the closet and fishes out a gym bag. When he sets it down, it makes a plastic sort of thunk, and a scent wafts from it. The sound and the smells of new electronics. I look over at the decks near the TV. Slip into my jacket.

"Better pack up Tik's deck, then." He looks at me. I know. Under those shades, I know his eyes are narrow. Touched a nerve.

"Why?"

"Are you in this, or not?" I meet his gaze levelly. He looks away almost instantly, down at the deck. He gives me another long look, and goes to work unslotting all of Tik's ice and unplugging it from the network they once shared. I look away. It's like burying her. Disturbing her things, moving the things that she last touched. Answer him, somewhat belatedly. "Because mine's an antique, and yours has to be plugged in." It's hard for him, I know. But what he's asking of me is hard for me, too. And there isn't much alternative for either of us.

9:30 a.m. Monday.

We're stopped for juice for the car. Brian's standing outside the car, leaning against it while the juice pump's ammeter blurs as it counts up. The price meter counts faster. It's counting in yen. "How long?"

Brian glances over at me. "About five minutes for ninety percent charge."

"Use your credit account?"

Brian snorts. "No. Get in the bag, it's got some cred cards."

I get Tik's deck out to use the time. Fill the fuel cell with alcohol. Plug in my EII and net tools ice, and log in. The deck slides its virtual-reality up behind my eyes every bit as smoothly as my OSDeck. There's the sense of barely contained speed, barely touched capabilities that the OSDeck never quite has. There's also an ineffably chunky feel to the power it's offering. It lacks the subtlety the OSDeck is known for. The

OnoSendai guys were ahead of their time. Pity all they make are game machines anymore.

Enter the access codes for one of Brian's unnamed accounts. The total pops up — about ten thousand yen. I head to my old friend 2Quik Search. Switch to the map and satellite information service. Log into it. I know that I'm paying by the byte for the data they're sending me, so I start my logging ice. Tell the service to give me satellite views of the area bounded by Larkin and Ninth, Taylor, Sixth, and Mission Street. It gives me the god's eye view. Streets are laid out in geometric precision, and each space in the road grid is stuffed with roofs. I tell the map and satellite service to give me the lot at maximum resolution. It's not quite close enough to see faces, but it gives me bones to hang the rest of the model of the area on. Store it, and move on. I'm down about a thousand yen now. They go fast. Brian's done with the car. He gets in, presses the power switch. We're driving again as I pull down a couple scientific papers I need to re-read for this.

Lean back against the headrest. Close my eyes. Dump the papers into my brain at speed. It only takes half a minute or so. I have the concepts and background knowledge to hang the information, on courtesy of my days at Epimetheus, so I can load fast and still retain it. Real world model-building is nothing new to me, but it's been a long time since I did any.

When I open my eyes, I look through the virtual view of the deck to the windshield, and through that to the road beyond. I've done nothing illegal. Not yet. The information I've downloaded so far is publicly available for a small fee. I tell 2Quik to erase all records of transactions with me. CalTech privacy laws ensure that they really do, right now. Unlock Penguin ice 1 and start carving. Brian's quiet. He lets me work.

10:00 a.m. Monday.

We're at a place called the Thai Orchid. I happen to think that it's a little obvious to roll into a Thai restaurant with a deck in your lap, a wheelchair backpack stuffed full of ice, and a twitchy younger man with sunglasses at ten o'clock Monday morning. Obvious that we're looking for bandwidth for nothing good. For nothing legal. But then, how many people go looking for bandwidth at a restaurant, anyway? Brian leads me to the kitchen, in the walk-in freezer. My chair barely fits through the door.

"This," I say, "would be why I needed a coat, wouldn't it?"

Brian nods. "Yup. Freezer makes enough radio noise that electronic signatures can't be traced through the walls. It's also bulletproof and easily secured."

"This is standard cracker procedure, then?" The words are bitter in my mouth and hang in the air equally bitterly, laced with the cold scent of chicken and spices.

Brian smiles at me "Nah. Corporate ninja standard procedure. Now c'mon, let's get going, I've only got enough money for an hour here. If we run late they'll call the cops themselves. Plausible deniability."

I plug Tik's deck into the high speed fiber-optic jack cunningly hidden behind a hanging carcass and log into a full terabit fiber line. Good response. Nice, low latency. "Plausibly deniable that this high speed optical fiber happens to terminate in their freezer? Who are they kidding?"

Brian chuckles, a flash of white teeth. "Plausible deniability. These good, honest citizens who run this link for legitimate covert corporate customers, local police, CalTech feds, and the odd undercover Interpol agent wouldn't let just anyone off the street use their facility. Which side of the law you're on can be pretty fuzzy sometimes."

I turn my head and let Brian glue a wireless transceiver to my head just in front of my left ear. Patch the signal through the deck and over the line to the transceiver he's glued behind his own ear. He patches his HUD shades into his transceiver and I have video, too. Looking at myself. I minimize that context for now.

"Okay, Bri. Can you hear me?"

"Five by, Doc."

Shake my head. "Shroud. Online it's always Shroud."

He raises an eyebrow. "Whatever."

Close my eyes. Take the last breath I'll ever take as an honest woman. Dive in. Go directly to the City of San Francisco's network. Decent firewall, good encryption, probably a team of pros behind that wall just waiting for … for someone like me to try their wall. *We few…* This isn't about direct confrontation with their security people. I'm not about to try and hack through the city's firewall. I could do it, but it would set off alarms from here to Oakland. If the city's data-security people don't get me themselves, they'll call down the thunder of the local cops. Presumably the city is one of the local police's customers. No good can come of that.

So I wait a minute. Two. There. Some supervisor's mail ice logs in through the firewall from the NFWN. Pretty common occurrence. I catch his connection as he logs back out. Break the crypto. Send a bogus message along his connection to the San Francisco city net. I tell the city net that the supervisor has arrived somewhere with high-speed access. That the roaming system should hand his connection off to his new provider. To me, in this case. Lesson for the day: no matter how important a person is, no matter how secure they promise to be and how tight they say their crypto is, nobody should have roaming access to the inside of the firewall. Fought that battle at OmniMart once-upon-a-time.

I have about five minutes before the supervisor's ice comes back to check his mail again. It's the minimum standard delay between mail updates. Net admins get pissy if you update more often than that. When the supervisor's mail ice logs back in, the system will notice that there are two connections under his name, log the event, and kick me out. If their security people are any good that will get noticed when it's logged. If that happens, within seconds — again, assuming they're any good — the City of San Francisco network security team will jump down my fucking throat. And I'm on someone else's deck, in a walk-in freezer in the Thai Orchid in the Mission District. *His horse is slain, and all on foot he fights…* Yeah. My kingdom for a tank.

I head to the city planner's office. Pull the files for the
Tenderloin and the Asylum. Water, sewer, data network,
street lights, traffic lights … bingo. Traffic surveillance cameras. The plans give me the exact location of every camera, and
of the dedicated fiber-optic network that goes under the street
to serve them. Dedicated fiber-optic network? For street cameras? You gotta be shitting me. It gets better. The dedicated
network is not directly connected to the public net or the city
backbone. I literally can't get there from here. Swell.

I drop out of the city's network and open my eyes. Look
up at the ceiling. It's featureless stainless steel with a rather
grimy looking light fixture in it. Look over at Brian. "Whatcha
watching?"

Brian is leaning against the freezer wall, plugged into another net through his Visor handheld. "Perimeter surveillance.
Nothing exciting. Did you get what you need?"

"Um … no. The only surveillance I found in the area were
traffic cameras. They're on a dedicated fiber network."

"You saying we're dead in the water?"

Close my eyes again. Look at the traffic surveillance network plans a moment. I don't do this kind of thing. I'm one
of the good guys, one of the people who keeps the net going.
We few. We happy few… I'm not a cracker. I'm not a criminal.
*You broke into the city network. That's a twenty-year sentence
already when they catch you.* Don't remind me. Open my eyes
to look at Brian again. *Are you in this, or not?* I guess I am. "Got
any bridges? Say, a nice Penguini with OC3 passthrough and
wifi?"

Brian's lips curl into a smile. "You're gettin' serious about
this." He holds up the little piece of electronics from the bag.
Basically an open architecture penguin processor with bridging
and routing software and various network interfaces. Common
cracker tools. Also handy for network testing, which is how I
know about them. The two overlap a lot. Both dig deep into
how the network works.

I look at him steadily, then down and away. "Brian, I've
already crossed the line. Turned to the dark side. Something

I didn't ever want to do. I have to live with that now." Look
back at him with the Shroud stare. His smile fades. "And if you
think for one second that I'm going to back down now, and live
with doing all this and failing, you don't know me very well."

Brian nods slowly. "Yeah, well, we just met, remember?"

"That didn't slow you down last night."

Brian snorts again. An amused sort of snort. "So what's
the plan?"

I pull the schematics and a map up onto his HUD. "Okay.
There are 2,600 cameras in the system." They light up on the
map as I mention them. Standard presentation stuff. "Each one
is connected locally to its intersection switch." The intersection switches in the picture he's seeing highlight themselves
obediently. "Each intersection switch, in turn, feeds one and
only one of thirty-six regional hubs, over an OC12 fiber line."
Light up the regional hubs. Zoom the map to the Asylum.
"These hubs feed the central traffic monitoring facility, which
is in the city government complex."

Brian raises an eyebrow. "You want to break into city hall?"

I shake my head. "No. We can't take over the whole traffic
surveillance and control system without people noticing. We
don't need to control the whole system anyway, we only need
one regional hub." I pull up another map. "The hub we want is
here. Number 27, serving the Tenderloin, Mission district, and
Civic Center areas. TurnTek M300 real-time switch. We're in
its coverage area right now. The hub is in a utility closet in the
Civic Center."

"So all I have to do is go where the hub is and patch you in?
Should be pretty straightforward."

"Not so fast. I have to reconfigure the hub, and that's going
to mean rebooting it. Which means the last thing these cameras see will be you breaking into the Civic Center. They cover
themselves. One imagines the Civic Center also has surveillance cameras of its own."

Brian frowns. "That's bad. Is that the best you can come
up with?"

Shake my head. "No. The system is designed so that a single fiber cut won't take out monitoring and control for an intersection. Each hub is also connected to an adjacent hub by an OC3 fiber line, so if the main line from the hub to the control center is cut, the backup line can be used to maintain control while the main line is fixed. Hub 27's adjacent hub is 28, at the corner of Oak and Grand. It's in the systems room of a parking garage." Pull up the plans of the parking garage. "Underground. In the elevator equipment room. Break in, unplug the OC3 line, plug in the Penguini, plug the OC3 into it. Should be pretty straightforward. Right?"

Brian looks over the building plans. Nods a little. "Should be, yeah. It's the simple ones that get you, though. I'll be back within thirty minutes. If something happens to me, just disconnect and go. Take the deck with you. Catch a cab and go home." He drops his house key in my lap. "Oh yeah. Don't forget to keep an eye on your security perimeter."

"Be careful, Brian."

He leans toward me, then stiffens. Straightens up. Nods a little. Then opens the freezer door. "Yeah. Yeah. You too." With that, he's gone.

Except that he's not. Pull up his context. I can see through his shades, hear through the transceiver. It's like a live action video game. He heads out to the car, climbs in. Hits the switch. Accelerates alarmingly out into traffic. I let his context drop into the background a moment, where I can see it and hear it, but it doesn't occupy my full attention. There's a detail I've been glossing over. I've never even seen a TurnTek switch. I have no idea how to set one up. Everything is BFR Systems on OmniMart sites. We like our networks to work.

Chapter 24

Dive back into the net. Look for documentation. When all else fails, RTFM. Read The Fucking Manual. Should be simple. Go to TurnTek's website. Except of course that there isn't one. News site hits. Archives. TurnTek went under five years ago. I'm dealing with genuine, unsupported legacy hardware. *It's the simple ones that get you.* I take the risk and run an open web search on TurnTek M300.

Two hundred hits. Pop the first one. And what do you know? The setup and configuration manual. The switch looks like a pretty simple animal. Configuration is 2-D graphical, basically no security at all. Which isn't all that surprising, since they're designed for dedicated fiber networks. Pretty easy. Basically I log in. Tell the thing what I want it to do. Add the new port in and set the bridging rules up. Reboot. Simple.

> The Phreax R. Us forum is the second hit.
> From: Sh0g0th@3x1t.net

Well there's a familiar name.

> To: EVERYONE
> Subject: TurnTek Manuals Online
>
> URGENT! TurnTek manuals online are honeypots. B34rN423 got *burned* on a

> run last night using one of them. He got
> into the surveillance net in C. City, and the
> city cops came down on him. They shot
> him, he's gone!

Well that's just lovely. There are a thousand explanations. From what I've seen a lot of hackers just aren't very good. Shogoth himself, obviously, wasn't cautious enough some- where along the line. The victim in this case could have set off any number of alarms along the way getting into the switch in the first place. *It's the simple ones...* Yes, yes. It could also be exactly what poor dead Shogoth says. Some operator got cracked one too many times and has left something nasty in that switch for the perps. There but for the grace of God...

Brian's voice. Loud and clear. "Shroudie." Shroudie? Again? "Need the side view of the parking garage, elevator shaft." He's there already. Shit. I send him the plan model of the building. Pop it up on his HUD in wireframe. Skin it down to the center core. "Thanks."

I watch Brian's feed a moment. He's parked on the top floor of the parking garage, the sun beating down on pave- ment bleached almost white. Row upon row of cars, reflecting it back at him. The HUD sunglasses darken automatically. He pauses a moment, probably looking at the diagram, then clears it. Opens the trunk of his car and withdraws the gym bag. Digs into it. Then walks with purpose over to the elevator and presses the button. When the door opens, something happens. He does something but he doesn't look at his hands, so I can't tell what. The elevator doors don't close after him, though. He waits a moment, then walks back out.

I'm curious, so I ask. "What did you do?"

"Spray on condom over the optical sensor. Busy now, hon." He leaves the confused elevator stuck on the top floor, and jogs down the stairs to the floor below. Close my eyes. Hon is a habit of speech for some people. It doesn't mean anything. And even if it did, so what? *The simple ones that get you...* Yes, yes, I know.

I move Brian back to the corner of my perception and get busy on the switch problem. TurnTek … Catherine, stop thinking like a hacker and think like a professional. Network. Who do you know who might know these switches?

One name leaps to mind. The question is, do I trust him? I watch Brian a moment. He's wedged the elevator doors open on the floor second from the top of the parking garage and is looking down the empty elevator shaft, then up at the bottom of the elevator car still parked on the floor above. Vertigo makes my head spin a moment. He reaches under his coat to his belt and withdraws a small device that looks like a set of brass knuckles. Reels a … his HUD sensors come up automatically … it's a carbon-nanotube monofilament line. He clips it to his belt, and casually reaches into the elevator shaft and squeezes the grip of the device in his hand. There's a muffled report, like a gun shot, and more monofilament streaks up through the darkness and hits the bottom of the elevator car. And sticks. Carbon nano-hair tipped, apparently, like gecko feet. He gives the line a tug, then nonchalantly steps into the elevator shaft and drops, a stomach-churning visual drop. I can hear the line reeling out of the handgrip, arresting his fall, see the flood of darkness as the elevator doors above him slam shut. See in the dark through his shades.

I put Brian in the background again and pull up the phone. What, exactly, is left to lose? Dial Lance's number. "I-Link, Carson Lance speaking." He's in his tank again.

"Lance, Shroud. You son-of-a-bitch, why did you turn me into OmniMart?" Well, that … could have gone better.

"What are you talking about?" Lance sounds genuinely confused. I used to know the man. In the old days this would have been all I needed to prove his innocence. But I don't know him anymore. Do I?

"Who all did you tell that I'd been there?"

"Just the owner, and he knows when to keep his mouth shut. I told him it was important to keep this confidential, in case you didn't want to work for us. Shroud, what's going on?"

"I got picked up for identity theft as soon as I got to CalTech and tried to use my card."

"Shit. Shit. Um ... are you calling from the courthouse? I can't seem to get a trace back on your location. I can come testify as to who you are, no problem." *Not a trusting person...*

"Thanks. That means a lot to me, Lance. I may need you to do that at my court date, but that's not until tomorrow. Right now, can you tell me what the security systems on a TurnTek M300 are like?"

There's a long pause, and I'm starting to get very afraid. "Do I even want to know what you're up to?" he finally asks.

"No. You don't. I don't either, but nobody ever said tiger hunting was easy, you know?"

Another long pause. Long enough to call the SFPD in another context. He's in a tank, after all. He finally answers. "Understood. Okay, an M300. Been a long time, but all the municipal RSTP/IP switches TurnTek made were pretty much the same security-wise."

I glance at Brian. He's crawling through a wiring tunnel. He emerges inside the wiring closet. Nice.

Lance again. "They have a stealth security system. They look wide open, and it looks like you have full control the moment you jump in, but you're in a bogus environment and they're tracing you. Real communications from hub to hub or from control to hub are encrypted. You know the RCP44 algorithm?

Brian's looking at the rack of equipment he's just emerged from. I talk to him quickly. "Next rack over, Bri. That's the elevator controller. High voltage."

Brian worms his way over to the other rack. "Now you tell me."

"Sorry."

Turn my attention back to Lance. "RCP44. Yeah, I know that one."

Lance says, "Good. Oh yeah, one other thing. The alarms go off if the fiber times out. That would probably be bad. And don't forget these aren't BFRs, you have to reboot them when you change stuff."

Switch contexts to Brian again. "Brian, freeze." Brian freezes, his fingers on the optical fiber connection. "There's a wrinkle. You have about five seconds between when you break the fiber connection and when it has to be back up before the fiber timeout starts logging error messages and people start noticing. Turn on the Penguini. I need to set it up. We're going to have to plug it in hot."

He lets it go gingerly and gets into a pouch on his belt, getting the Penguini bridge out. "Shroudie, when we get out of here remind me to talk to you about your timing. Okay, bridge is on, standing by."

Lance is talking. "Hey Shroud? You still there?"

I switch back to the phone call with Lance while I log into the Penguini bridge, set it to go straight through and repeat what it hears to the blind drop site I picked out ahead of time.

"Thanks, Lance. Listen, I need to go. Thanks for your help."

"No problem. Tell me about it some day?"

"No promises."

"Okay. Be careful."

"Yeah, thanks. You too." Close Lance's context.

"Brian. Okay, the Penguini is ready to go. Five seconds, remember?"

"I remember, I remember." Brian's hands are fast. He unscrews the plug on the fiber line. Five seconds. Four. He screws the fiber line into the Penguini. Three. Two. Screws the cable from the Penguini into the switch. One… "Done."

"Okay, get out of there, if that thing's turned in an alarm, the cavalry will be arriving presently."

Brian dives into the bottom of the high voltage rack again, pausing to pull the cover on behind him, and begins worming his way through the tunnel. I can feel myself hyperventilating. Brian makes it to the elevator shaft. In time to see the elevator car coming down at him. "Brian! Look out!"

Brian snaps into motion and hauls himself down and back into the tunnel. His shades can keep up with the sensory flow of his motion, and so can I, with the deck. Barely. It would be easier in a tank where I've got serious bandwidth and my own body's feedback isn't making me tense. I let out my breath. He holds up the handgrip and squeezes it again. It immediately winds up all the slack in the monofilament.

The Penguini has begun relaying data. I set my cracking ice on it. If Lance is right, I should be able to see whether the alarms have been set off or not. If he's wrong, if he's selling me out... *Blow, wind! Come, wrack! At least we'll die with harness on our back!* Well, on the bright side, at least my retirement will be taken care of.

"Here we go. Going up..." And so he is. Brian's elevator has begun heading upward. He levers himself out of the tunnel as the clearance increases, and the elevator effortlessly hauls him up underneath it. He pays out some line and swings to the second floor door, clings to it and gets out another tool. Then glances upward to see the elevator starting down again. "Uh oh..." is his only comment. He sets to work furiously on the doors with his pry-bar.

I'm faster. The Penguini has let me know about a few other wireless networks it can touch. I relay through it. Break one of the other networks. Jump into the elevator controller and send a command. It tells me it can't stop the elevator between floors. I send another. Watch Brian's context. Hold my breath. The doors open. He rolls through, and squeezes the handgrip a third time, severing the monofilament line.

Passengers' knees are showing through the open doors as the elevator slides down behind them. Brian stands up, dusts himself off, as the elevator stops at his floor. Brian nonchalantly steps into the car. "Going down?"

Breathe again.

My ice cracks the RCP44 encryption without too much difficulty. It's an older algorithm, solid enough for slightly sensitive data on a private network, but not really up to front-line service. I can see Hub 28 talking to 27, mostly exchanging messages that amount to, "I'm here. You there?" "Yeah, I'm here. You there?" The social lives of computers are not to be envied.

Brian emerges from the elevator and gets into his car, drives to the entrance, pays his parking fee, and drives out.

I log into Hub 27 gingerly, via the encrypted communications from 28. Set up the new switching rules. Pull up Brian's context. He's stuck in traffic. "Hey Brian, got any ideas on how I can get some kind of real-world thing going on at the Civic Center that will make people not notice when I reboot this stupid hub?"

"Sure, no prob," Brian reaches into his pocket. Pulls out a brand new disposable phone. Turns it on. I can't hear the other end of the conversation, but I don't really have to. "Yes, I think you can help me, actually," he says. "I represent an organization called the People's Will. We have planted a radiological contamination device somewhere in the civic center's HVAC system. It will go into dispersal mode in sixty seconds. You may wish to evacuate the building." Then turns off the phone, opens the door of his car, and tosses it under the wheels of the car next to him. "Give 'em an extra minute, to be on the safe side."

I just stare for a moment, eyes open, looking through the virtual world at the deck in my lap. He basically called in a bomb threat. With no more concern than calling out for pizza. *Man, proud man, Dressed in a little brief authority... Plays such fantastic tricks before high heaven As makes the angels weep.* Close my eyes. Tik what have you gotten me into? Feel the Real. What have I gotten myself into? I wait two minutes and reboot the hub. It works as advertised.

Chapter 25

10:57 a.m. Monday.

Still at the Thai Orchid. Brian and I have a somewhat early lunch. I don't know Thai cuisine, or in fact any cuisine other than American fast food, so Brian orders. Tom ka gai, it seems, is a soup made of coconut milk, chicken, ginger, lime leaves of some species I've never heard of, mushrooms, miscellaneous other flavors, and chili oil. It has a light, fine burn that lingers in the sinuses, and a rich chicken flavor that balances it out. There is also a noodle dish called Pad Thai. Rice noodles, tamarind, peanuts, garlic, shrimp, along with a vague, wonderful fishiness I can't identify, scrambled-looking eggs, and chilies. Some kind of sprouts over top. Sweet and salty with a mouth filling flavor and searingly hot a few moments later. Oh yes, I think Thai food is my new favorite thing. The noodles are finished before there's much talking. They're that good.

Brian nods a little as he eats his soup. "You did good back there."

I poke at a mushroom with my spoon. "All this … isn't somewhere I wanted to go, Brian. I've got this thing about law and order."

Brian nods a little, taking another spoon full of soup. "She told me. About your mom, I mean. I guess I understand, but … I grew up different."

Watch Brian a while. In a moment he looks back at me through those shades. "I imagine she thought I was over-compensating. Mom turns out to be an embezzler, daughter naturally goes to the other extreme."

Brian nods again. "Some of that, yeah. Some of it … not. Anyway. We do what we do here. What we have to do, you know? Corps hire people like me … like Tik and me … to do shit to each other. We take the risks. They pay large for it."

"And then she'd turn around and go back to her work-a-day job defending against people like you. And her. I feel like … I didn't know her at all anymore. Because I don't under-stand how she could do that. It's like betraying everything we fought for."

"Doc, Tik fought for a paycheck. That's all. Sorry if that blows your image of her. She really liked you. But it was like … she liked *you*. Not your job."

"Me, or my skills?" I keep that tone strictly neutral. I try not to feel proud of my technical accomplishments today. Try not to admit to myself that on some level the run we just made was illegal. The fact that I can now control, at will, all of the traffic cameras in the Asylum. The fact that while we eat I have the deck sifting through data I'm picking up from the blind drop, looking for Kimmy. I try not to admit to myself that on some level I really am proud of these things that I've done. Try not to admit that I've had fun. *Like mother, like daughter.* My stomach twists on me a little, curling up around the heavy dose of chili oil already in it. But I'm still hungry, and the soup is too good to waste.

Brian leans back a little stiffly. "Would you believe me if I told you? Since I have a vested interest now?"

Play with a mushroom in my soup. Watch it bob. The deck beeps softly in my mind at that juncture. I close my eyes, look within the machine world at the model my cameras and my ice have built. Fly down over the virtual streets. Play back the feed. Watch a hooded figure disappear into a partially collapsed building. "Got her. Wrecked apartment building, at Broderick and Fell."

Brian leans forward, all business again. "Can you get internal surveillance of the building?"

Shake my head. "Doubt there is any. Shouldn't need it though. I'm not out of tricks yet."

Brian nods. "Okay then. Let's roll."

"You gonna tell me I have a choice?" Brian looks a little startled. After a moment, though, he chuckles. I must be getting better at the comedy thing, too. Roll out to the car. Lever myself into it. Fold the chair up and shove it into the back seat of the car. The chair's made for this. We drive off.

He gives me a sidelong glance. At the next traffic light he reaches into the glove compartment and hands me something. Something small and lethal looking, bright yellow on black plastic. I pick it up, and the grip vibrates momentarily in my hand. "A gun? Jesus, Brian, I could go to jail just having this in my hand. So could you, just having it in the car."

"You shoot?"

I look at it, turn it over in my hand. It's trouble, pure and simple. "Yeah. I learned when I was in junior high. I hung out with the guys. They took me shooting a couple times. Taught me the basics. It's been a while though. Once the SCP became part of Canada, I figured one more skill down the drain, you know?"

"Good. You'll like this thing. JenArms Yellow Jacket. Disposable. 150-round magazine, 4.4 mm wireheads. Muzzle velocity of about Mach 2. Fuel tank will keep you shooting all day. It's keyed to your hand now. You want to give it to someone, hold the safety down until you feel the grip vibrate again. Otherwise … boom."

"Boom?"

"Thing is mostly PBX, except for the barrel liner. It's got biometric sensors. Someone picks it up who's not authorized, the frame and the fuel tank blow up. Blows mono-mol wire everywhere, too. Bad for bystanders."

"Nasty."

"These are for people who do *not* want to get caught. The whole gun goes away, no evidence that it was there at all except for the crater and the shrapnel. No prints, no hair and fiber, no DNA. You can also use it as a grenade. Hold the safety on and pull the trigger. When it starts vibrating continuously you have three seconds. Throw hard."

I nod a little. "Are we expecting to have to shoot someone?"

"Maybe. Bad neighborhood. Just a precaution."

I look at the deadly little thing, wondering just how much trouble I'm already in. Safety there, safety turns off there. Wireheads. Nasty business. A 4.4 mm wirehead going supersonic will punch through most types of body armor including steel plate. When it hits flesh, however, the sudden increase in heat wakes the memory metal up, and the bullet expands into a coil of about a hundred meters of mono-molecular wire. This takes place inside the wound. It also fails to have distinguishing rifling to be traced back to a specific gun. They're assassin bullets, plain and simple. Perfect for this gun. I slip the nasty thing into my pocket, after making darn sure that safety is set. The gun hangs in my pocket like an albatross around my neck. The problems with the bank weren't my fault. The stuff with the city network this morning? Possibly recoverable. I'm a first offender, after all. This? Possession of a firearm, let alone a handgun in CalTech? That's a major felony. *A gun now, hmm? Even Mom never packed.* Didn't she? A gun. It gives me pause.

But only for a moment. I'm already risking my life, my safety, and my freedom. So is Brian. I didn't kill Mojo, but I left him for the wolves. I fully intend to kill again when I find out who hit us. And I've made a career out of burning script kiddies who attacked OmniMart. So it's a little late to start having second thoughts now. If I was going to back out, the time to do it was before I got on the train to Reno. That's what I tell myself.

I darken the windows a little and withdraw the gun from my pocket. Take the time to learn it. Not much to it. The gun is completely sealed, including a foil seal over the muzzle. Its small frame and light weight don't give me much enthusiasm for firing it, despite the muzzle brake which supposedly suppresses the recoil. I make sure the safety is set, shove it back in my pocket. Swallow my apprehension. Reach for my frostiness. This isn't so different from being online. The risks are different, the means are different, but the song remains the same. I tell myself this. In time I start to believe it.

Chapter 26

11:12 a.m. Monday.

I have a theory. In order to survive in the long term, every city needs a neighborhood where vice thrives. The alternative is that vice distributes itself through the respectable parts of the city. It's like a form of sprawl. Manage it, or it manages you. In Denver, you'll find it in Five Points. Regulated and unregulated brothels, unregulated drugs, unregistered clinics, slavery, guns, it's all there. Nobody hires the law to go in there, unless things get really out of hand.

In San Francisco, there is the Tenderloin, and we are heading deep into it. Past the legitimate businesses selling fetish wear. Past funky restaurants hawking fast Indian food. Past the Alcazar Theatre, more curry places, a theater offering a showing of *The Green Door* ... which I think is porn ... gay bar ... gay bar ... transvestite bar, I think. We pass them all. Past the dive bars, the neighborhood suddenly goes from bad to ruined. To dead. It begins abruptly, in the middle of a block. Houses are boarded up, knocked down, burned. There are crowds of people, even the drug dealers and streetwalkers are gone. "Welcome to the Asylum," Brian says.

"What happened down here?"

"Dirty bomb. Retributive strike. Christian Front, I think. They hit the Civic Center, and this is where the cleanup ran out of money. The Asylum is still a little radioactive, especially when it's dry outside, and the dust kicks up. Nobody lives here who has any damn sense. It's okay for short trips, but ah ... don't eat the natives. I'll try and keep them from eating you."

I stare at him a moment. I'm pretty sure he's serious. "I should have stayed in bed this morning." I recognize streets. Time for the cameras to look somewhere else. I send them commands, and they all happen to be in the wrong places in their arcs to see us as we drive by. As Brian gets out of the car. As I get my chair out from the back seat and unfold it, then climb in. So far everything is quiet. I take this moment to pull on my wheelchair gloves, the kind with no fingers but thick leather palms. I don't wear them a lot, but I can already see I don't want to touch anything here.

"Yeah, yeah, you did stay in bed this morning. What room is she in?"

I pull the model of the Asylum up onto his HUD, and tell my camera control ice to play the hand it's got. Eight cameras at two intersections swivel to face the apartment building from different angles as we zoom in on it. Meanwhile a second ice plays back loops of the pictures they took a few minutes ago. Not much changes in the Asylum. Turn on the laser infrared illuminators and step all the cameras in precise steps over the building, on a high angle over the roof and from the side. Not all cameras are mounted on the same plane.

Grab the data from each camera. Combine them all, like a panoramic picture except in three dimensions. Classic synthetic aperture techniques. Now go back to the original data. Rectify each image to a common coordinate system, so they're square to each other. Map only the pixels that are turned on. Add the images together. Digitally generate and remove a flood-lit version of the image. Use that to make a matte. All the points that reflected light are opaque, all the points that didn't are transparent. Feed that back to the cameras, shoot another image set in the same pattern. Let the matte exclude the façade and roof of the building, and only illuminate what's inside through the magic of infrared. Combine this confocal image with the synthetic aperture image. The result? X-ray vision, in real-time, at fifteen frames a second. Move the synthetic focal plane of the image through the building, slicing it like a cake. Pick up the huddled figure hiding in the ground floor apartment. Watch her move. "You never told me if it was me, or my skills that Tik liked."

Brian stares at what's going on in his Heads Up Display and whistles. "If she'd known you were this good, she might have had a harder time deciding. Okay. Wow. Okay. I'll go first. You wait here. Anyone gets too close, drop 'em. No questions asked. Okay?"

Catherine Anne Farro, what are you doing here? Mom's words the one and only time I ever took a cab and visited her at work. My moment of pride slips away. I look at Brian, fighting back a mix of worry, possessiveness and the strong feeling that I must not be sane to be sitting where I'm sitting. Paranoia. There is literally nobody around. And in a big city, for a big city kid like me, that's cause enough for paranoia. "Brian. Be careful."

He gives me a smirk and trots off. I slip my hand into the pocket with my gun. Brian looks like he's having fun. And why not? He loves this stuff. He's wired for this stuff. It's what he does, and he's good at it. Adrenaline junkie. Maybe even idiot. He wouldn't have taken Tika out for a morning like this. But then, I remind myself yet again, we're on a run together. Coworkers. Not lovers. Try to keep that in mind. Try to stay frosty.

Chapter 27

Brian's gone only a couple of minutes, when his voice whispers in my digital ear through his transceiver. "Okay. Got her. Come on in." I slip my hand out of my pocket. Wrestle my chair and myself out of the car. Lock the car doors. Take a quick look around, including behind me. Roll towards him as fast as I can go. The street's in rough shape under me. I can almost feel the Asylum getting into my gloves. Think about throwing them away when this is over. Gloves are cheap. Roll across the street. It takes time. "She's in here." But I knew where she was. I watched him glue the fire door that leads to the stairway shut with an epoxy sheet. Watched through his shades as the sheet heated up as the chemical reaction happened. Watched him find her. I spy, with my digital eye.

I follow Brian, wrestling the chair through the rubble of collapsed ceiling tiles. Leave wheel marks in the mold. Stir up the stench of a hundred refrigerators gone bad, to mingle with the chemical smell of the epoxy sheet. Feel the floor creak beneath me, and hope that it holds. And all around is a faint ozone tinge to the air. I imagine I can feel the radiation digging all the way into my bone marrow, corrupting the DNA data by which my body is maintained. *Live by the hack, die by the hack.* It's probably a good thing I'm not having children.

I have to do some fancy maneuvering, side slipping and such, to get through it at all. But I follow Brian. I can hear his familiar voice nearby. The room he leads me to is dark, illuminated only by a couple chem-light sticks. Above, the ceiling, and presumably the next floor up, are sagging badly. The smells of wet wood, sodden plaster, and decay fill the air. Keep the cameras focused on the building. I can see the three of us. Brian, though he's barely an outline; some property of his clothes is infrared-opaque. Must have some kind of cold storage built in, or he'd fry. Only his face shows beneath his shades. I show up like a beacon in my jeans, T-shirt, and leather jacket. The deck glows in my lap as it exhausts the heat from fuel cell and electronics. And Kimmy. She huddles up against something, making rhythmic, spastic movements. Her head snaps back. Her arm moves. Fist lashes upward.

Into her own face. Hard. Again, and again, the impacts making a solid, plastic sound. Like smacking a watermelon with a carbon fiber baton. Brian shines his flashlight into the closet. I've never seen Kimmy in person before. She definitely does not look like her icon online. That's normal. She's fairly new, and she grew up on *The Matrix*, so online she had that shiny leather look, the lace-up shirt, the artfully arrayed cleavage, the long black hair. In reality she's short, vaguely mousy looking, hair brown with a lavender stripe. She's wearing a soaked woolen blanket and huddled in a corner, her face and body a mass of bruises. Blood trickles from her nose, and her lips are bludgeoned thick. She looks at me and screams. Brian looks at me quizzically. "Not what you were expecting either, is she?"

I shrug a little. It's hard to hear over the screaming, but at this point I'm starting to get used to it. That doesn't seem like a positive thing. "Kimmy. Kimmy, it's me, Shroud."

The screaming goes on, unabated, grating on and on, digging into my head like a knife that's being slowly driven into the sutures of my skull. I shout to make myself heard. And because it's getting on my nerves. "Kimmy! Shut the fuck up!" The screaming stops abruptly and Kimmy goes back to cowering and whimpering. Not necessarily an improvement, but quieter at least. "Do you know who I am?"

She shakes her head no, then nods. "Boss." A smile. She doesn't have many teeth left.

"Kimmy. When you jacked out, what was happening."

"I … you told me, 'Kimmy, Jack out!' And I … and it … no! No!" The screaming starts again, and her fists begin to lash up into her face again, each impact making a sodden smack on her battered skin. I try to stay frosty. She's had her jack rewired. That much is certain. I know what was done, and I know how it was done. I'd allowed myself to think I had some little mastery over it. This is a little more visceral. Messier. It makes my stomach twitch every time she hits herself.

Brian looks at me. "Not much left." His hand is in his pocket, and he's starting to slide it back out, a hard set to his jaw, his lips tight. It doesn't take a rocket scientist to figure out what he's about to do. He's about to put Kimmy down. It also does not take a rocket scientist to figure out what he's thinking right now. This went on in Tik's head, too. Had he been there, far from saving her, the only thing he could have done for her was…

"Wait. Not yet."

Brian looks over at me and slides his hand, and presumably his gun, back into his pocket. I never even saw it. "This isn't a kindness to her, Cath. What're we waiting for?"

"She's all I've got for leads, Brian. She's in bad shape, but she's all I've got."

"What are you going to do?" he asks. Kimmy is incoherent now. On some level she's picked up what Brian wants to do to her.

"Take her into a gestalt. Talk to her."

"Yeah, well, what do you want me to do if it turns out to be contagious?"

"Put both of us out of our misery." I look at those lenses of his, and for just a moment his cool slips and he stares at me. His mouth hangs open. Then clamps shut. The muscles along his jaw bulge out. Then his mission cool reasserts itself and his face goes neutral again. He nods once. And I know he'll do what I asked if it comes to that.

Kimmy's face is a mass of blood now, her fists making soft, wet sounds as they continue hitting. I rummage in my backpack for the right kinds of ice, trying to ignore her for a moment. She spatters me with blood. I look up at Brian. "Hold her, will you? And if you've got any tranquilizers, they might help."

Kimmy's screaming rises to frantic shrieks as soon as he touches her, and she lashes out at Brian immediately. But she's a tanker like me. He's a universe faster, and a lot stronger. He wrestles her to the ground as I casually load more ice into Tika's deck. It has ten slots. Six are filled already. I add the jack manual. Add a virt called *Camping in the Woods*. It was a gift, something Jay bought me for my fortieth birthday.

"You need a vacation, Boss," he'd said at the time. "So I got you one." The memory makes me smile, in spite of Kimmy's slowly declining shrieks, in spite of everything. The rest of my ice are blank Penguin ice.

"Tranqued her?"

"Yeah." Brian's voice is a little strained. Kimmy's eyes are rolling around like those pictures of spider monkeys on crack you used to see on TV, back in the day. I'm not really looking forward to strapping myself into a gestalt with her like that, but at least she's stopped thrashing around for the moment.

I nod. "Good. Got any extra Chill patches?"

Brian looks at me. "What are you planning to do?"

"I don't know yet. But I don't want her popping on me while I'm in there. And I don't want to go that way myself, either. I'm old. Stress she's in would probably have already killed me."

Brian snorts, but he rolls Kimmy over. Slides his hand up under her blanket. Slaps the patch to her back where she can't reach it. Good thinking. He tosses me one next. I pull up my T-shirt and slap it on my belly. Nothing happens, but at least in theory the patch is now monitoring my vitals, keeping track that they stay within reasonable ranges.

I pull an extra optical cable from my backpack and plug it into the second port in Tika's deck. Roll over to Kimmy. Reach down, and gently press it into her jack. *Do not plug anything into my head without asking.* The memory makes me shiver a moment.

Tell the deck to establish a gestalt. The deck comes up in a slow onset, like drifting into a light nap. The deck is starting to work hard now. Two users, and a gestalt, and my image-processing ice. I turn off the cameras for the moment to free up some bandwidth. Let the deck run the video loops back to the control center. Brian glances my way and I nod to him. He takes up a position at the doorway. This time he slides his gun fully from his pocket. It reflects green chem-light in the darkness.

I miss my OSDeck. But it couldn't do this. The OS guys didn't keep up with the times in the deck world. Shortly after the release of the OSDeck they changed focus, to making game machines. Screwed everyone who invested in them, too, because that focus shift was announced after the stock went public. Tik's Zhang is ten years newer, far more powerful. Last year's model, I vaguely remember her mentioning. I wondered at the time what she needed this much deck for. Now I guess I know. My OSDeck fits in my pocket. And it's paid for.

Kimmy's gone quiet, sitting in the gestalt, her mind beginning to settle down to a more normal state. We're sitting in a tent, in an evening full of stars in the Rocky Mountains near Denver. It's a good virtual. The thin crispness of the air, scent of campfire, sound and feel of the wind against the tent are all convincing. I start from scratch. "Kimmy? It's me, Shroud."

Kimmy's icon is generic. Without her EII ice, the deck has no idea how to render her, so she is a vaguely human-shaped metallic blob. A digital ghost in the tent with me. "Hi Boss. We're branched. Bad."

"I know. Are you all right?"

She shakes her head, and runs all the fingertips of her right hand over the space where her icon's lips would be, as though wondering why they're not so battered as they were before she jacked in. "No."

Kimmy fades out of the gestalt, chaos bubbling up from her brain. Like snow. Like a blizzard of static. I've seen this before. I know what is happening. I saw it in real-time once, and then again in the log at I-Link. Tika's brain made noises like this, and worse. The hair on the back of my neck prickles again. I can feel it. In a few minutes, eons in deck time, Kimmy fades back in.

"What are you doing here, Boss? Where are we?"

"It's a vacation virt. Jay bought it for me. Remember? I gave him a hard time about sucking up to me?"

Kimmy chuckles a little, stops abruptly. "Boss, something's not right. In my head. It's like…" And she's gone again. It gives me time to think, I unlock the write-protect on Penguin ice number 4 and start carving a quick program. A simple machine-language assembler/monitor, really. Something I can send control sequences to, and have it yield control sequences back, monitor the results. I lock it up, and unlock a second, Penguin ice number 5. I build a small analytical program that takes the raw data from the jack's neurofibers and tells me what the stimulation patterns are.

Kimmy comes back, fading back in in a burst of static. I know how that feels. Disjointed. Incomplete. The feeling that someone has used a sleight of hand and done something you should have seen, would have understood, had you only been able to see it. Like a hair in front of…

"How are you, Kimmy?"

"I can't … think." Kimmy begins to fade out again, but I can't let her. I know that outside, in the real world, we're sitting in an apartment building contaminated with heaven knows what, in an environment full of people as crazy as Kimmy. Maybe worse. And I can't ask permission, either. If the tables were turned, would I want her to fix me? Practicality sets in. The alternative is to give her a wirehead behind the ear to put her out of her suffering. If this works, if I can fix her, maybe she can live. I try to justify it to myself that way. But that isn't honest either. The truth is the same one that dragged me into this wasteland in the first place, that dragged me to California in the first place, landed me in jail, landed me in Brian's bed, involved me in some pretty significant criminality, and led inexorably to where I'm sitting right now. Kimmy ran a trace before she logged out. She was the only one inside San Jose's network who was still sane enough to do it. She was the only one who might have been able to see where the perp really came from. I have to know what she knows. I simply have to. So I key Penguin ice number 5 and hope it doesn't kill her. Or if it does, that it's at least quick and painless.

I assemble a short program for Kimmy's brain. Build up the images it needs with some web searches. Run the program. Hope I'm guessing right. The intruder's program was designed to stimulate the emotional centers. Mine goes after the forebrain, the cerebral memories, the high consciousness. And stimulates them. Uses the same mechanism the intruder did to make Kimmy's forebrain generate jack control signals. To the amygdala, my ice sends calm, placid water feelings.

Kimmy jumps back into the gestalt in sharp focus. A low keening comes from her. Parts of her brain are wired together that were never meant to talk directly, probably, but the stimulator is working. Her frontal lobe signals are loud and clear, while her emotions are growing calm and serene. I key up Penguin ice number 4, the assembler/monitor. Theoretically I'm moving the neurofibers of her jack, but I'm flying blind. The fusible link in her jack prevents me from any access to her jack's neuron controls. My assembler/monitor ice generates the signals the hacker sent to the brains of his targets to reprogram them from inside, and I'm watching the progress on my analyzer. It's fairly simple. The sequence I need to send is the same one used to install the jack in the first place. A jack shouldn't ever talk directly to your amygdala. The poor old lizard part of your brain isn't up to the stimulation; the world's long since gotten too complex for it. That's why we have a forebrain now. It's designed for this stuff, and it's the only part of the brain a jack should talk to.

The ice processes, the two programs comparing notes, refining the simulation, resending some commands. It would be much easier if the fusible link was intact and I could just tell her jack's neurofibers, "Do this." But then the hacker would have found it awfully easy to do what he did, too, had that been the case. The assembler/monitor tells me the sequence has been run. I shut it down. Let her brain's stimulation levels go where they want.

"Kimmy?"

"Yeah?"

"How do you feel?"

"Different. Fu … fucked up. Why … are we in this?"

"We needed to be somewhere. This was handy."

"Jay … bought this for you. I remember … he was … asking what kinds of things you like. I think … he has a crush on you." I start to wonder if everyone knew about this except me.

"I know that now. I wish he'd told me."

"He wanted to. Tik told him to keep it to himself. Didn't want … anyone to get hurt."

"Kimmy, do you remember the last time you were online at OmniMart?"

"Yeah. We got branched. Bad." I can feel the wave of panic sweep through her through the gestalt. I brace myself for the explosion, and probably for her to go comatose when the Chill goes off. But she has some control. She hauls it in gingerly, as though testing the ropes. "Tik got hit, Boss. I didn't know what to do!"

"I know. I told you to jack out. Do you remember that? I told you to do it. 'Jack out, get your JAFO on the line and tell him to jack Tik out.' Remember?" Kimmy nods.

"I remember … but … I had a trace running. Tik told me to trace the guy."

Tik's last sane words. I remember from the InterStellar Link log. "Did you get a result?"

"Yeah, I did."

"Do you remember where it went?"

She pauses a few moments, brow furrowing, then nods. "Uh-huh."

I try to stay calm, not to tilt the fragile balance that is giving her this clarity by letting my own emotions leak into the gestalt. "Key it out the way you remember it, okay?"

"Okay." The numbers start to appear in a block.

Kimmy types them in air with her virtual fingers. "2001:A1AA:FE14:007A:0240:63FF:FEC0:8D14" Her voice is sing-song as she recites the digits.

I try not to let my disappointment show. "You're sure that's right?"

"Uh-huh. They taught us to memorize them in hex. Said it's too hard to memorize 32 bit numbers in decimal."

I take a slow virtual breath. "Okay. Are you ready to jack out now?"

"Do we have to?" Kimmy's expression is pleading. As though she knows the shape her body is in now.

"Yeah. We're not anywhere safe."

"I remember seeing Brian. Is he really out there?"

"He'd better be. Go ahead and jack out."

Kimmy does. She drops out of the gestalt and offline in a smooth jump. I hope Brian is ready for her. I stay a moment. Look up at the stars. "I'm sorry, Tik. I'm so sorry. I thought for sure Kimmy'd have the answer for us."

But Kimmy doesn't. TCP-IP addresses, whether they're version four or version six, always go from the biggest network to the smallest. 2001 makes it a unicast address, which it should be. But I know the next two network numbers, A1AA:FE14, like I know my old U.S. Social Security number, like I know my Canadian Social Insurance number, like I know my phone number. A1AA:FE14 is OmniMart's own network. I was hoping Kimmy's trace would lead me right to the bastard, but either the hacker came in through a spoof attack, like he did coming into I-Link, or Kimmy botched her trace. I'm at a dead end. Without the San Jose logs, there's nothing more I can do.

I jack out a few seconds later.

Chapter 28

Kimmy's quiet, leaning against the wall, breathing tiredly. I wipe my eyes once as a preventative measure and look around. Brian is pressed up against the barred window, he turns his head to look back out.

"What's up?" I whisper it.

"'Bout fucking time. We gotta get out of here now. All the screaming has the neighbors' attention."

"Can we get to the car?

"Kimmy's fading in and out. She can't walk."

I'm disappointed with Kimmy, frankly. A trace is basic stuff, she should have been able to get the thing done and get a good result. But not that disappointed. She's not my virgin daughter, but I'll not do as Lot did. I'm not throwing her to the crowd just because she didn't have the data to save my bacon today. "You carry her. I'll cover you."

They're gathering around the car like zombies, trying the door, shaking it a little. Nobody's organized enough to hit it with anything hard yet. Brian and I get to the lobby of the building. Kimmy is slung over his shoulder in a fireman's carry.

Kimmy drifts back into consciousness. Looks around. Her expression is more puzzled than anything else. "What's going on, Boss?"

"Shh, Kimmy. Let Brian carry you." I unplug from the deck. Unslot all the ice that's not busy controlling the surveillance cameras. Stick them in my coat pocket. Cleaning up — it's automatic for me. I follow Brian back out to the front door of the apartment building.

"Okay." I look up at Brian and reach out to pat his arm. "Good luck."

Brian snorts slightly. "Luck is for beginners."

"Go. Now." Bah. I'll take any luck I can get. I pull the Yellow Jacket out of my pocket and aim it towards the ankles of the person nearest the car. Pull the trigger. The report is enormous and the cheap little gun lurches in my hand. The wirehead bullet explodes in a cloud of monomolecular wire as it strikes the pavement. I've drawn attention to myself. *That was the plan, right?* What plan? I'm making this up as I go.

So far it works. The loud noise and the promise it carries is much more interesting than one man carrying off some girl, probably for a snack. I can hear the murmur in the crowd. "She's got a gun. She's got a gun. She's got a gun."

It transforms the crowd. Some cower and flee. But a disturbing number turn my way. Walk toward me. When you're beaten down, when you're the throwaway people nobody wants, and you've gone away to die in a radioactive hole like this, any power you can grasp feels like salvation. Any power at all. And a gun is power you can grasp. The power to fight, to resist, to assert control over your own life. Which is, of course, why they're illegal.

I have a line drawn on the street in my mind's eye. The line across which nobody gets to walk except Brian. It's twenty yards away, which is a good pistol range, one I used to be able to hit things at. As the first zombie crosses it, I find out for sure. I raise the pistol, pull the trigger. Its pancake flat trajectory isn't even visible behind the gout of flame leaping from the muzzle brake, but the wirehead bullet slaps into the zombie's chest, and he drops, twitches once, blood pouring from his mouth and nose, and stops moving. His innards are shredded by the cloud of monomolecular wire that just unwrapped it-

210 James R. Strickland

self inside him at high speed. I try not to think about that. No time. In three shots I take down his two nearest companions, the explosion of wire inside the one I double-tap tearing him in half, a mass of squirting tissue and a considerable distance of pavement between his shoulders and hips. *Don't debate. Just act.* Messy. "Come on, Brian. Come on!"

Nobody else seems interested in crossing my line. They mill back from it a little, as though they too can see it; a few dragging the bodies away. My heart's pounding in my ears, forming *basso profundo* for the ringing from the gunfire. And then, by degrees, I hear something else. As the ringing fades back I can hear it. Another sound. Outside my head. The steel fire door, the one Brian epoxied shut to secure the floor, is being kicked down.

"Oh. Fuck."

I throw the selector switch on the Yellow Jacket to full auto and turn toward the stair door so I can try to cover both directions at once. Which just means I see what's happening in both places at once. Sudden movement to my left, at the front door. A zombie goes flying, another screams as the car rolls over him. At the same time, the stair door slams open. *Don't debate.* Act. I pull the trigger again. Send a hail of wireheads at the three zombies ... the three people who push their way through the stair door. The cheap gun jumps, climbs badly. I don't know if I hit anyone or not. *Yes, you do. You did.* The gun is hot in my hands, then against my side as I shove it in my pocket and roll out the door to the car. Brian opens it immediately, and I throw Tik's deck and the backpack in unceremoniously and bail in after it. Look back to my chair, but Brian's already closing the door. "Leave it!" he says. And I do. He stomps on the accelerator and we get the hell out of Dodge.

I can't hear anything but my own breathing, my heart pounding in my ears, the road whispering by. *Your chair ...* my chair... I look out the back window as we drive away. They're fighting over it. Over my chair. Close my eyes. How long have I had that one? I don't even remember. Years. Decades. Look again. They've torn the wheels off by the time we turn the corner and I can't see anymore.

Brian is grinning, high on his own adrenaline. Freak. I feel like throwing up, but I'm not inclined to roll down the window.

"Hey. Cath."

Look over at him. He sees something in my face, I suppose, because his smile fades a bit and he says only, "You wanna set the safety on that thing? Before it goes off, kills us all?" He turns back to watch the road. But I can see the smile creep over his lips again. I carefully reach into my pocket and switch on the safety. Turn the gun off. Conserve its fuel. I have the feeling I may need it.

Chapter 29

3:00 p.m. Monday.

Monday. I'm at the house, in a wheeled desk chair. Brian has gone with Kimmy to try and get her some medical help. And I'm worrying again, damn it. He was still smiling occasionally with the adrenaline high from our run, such as it was, when he dropped me off. But I'll take my life and death thrills online, if it's all the same to everyone. I jack into Tika's deck for another few moments, pick up camera control in the Asylum one more time. Close the connection to the blind drop site, set the camera hub to pick up its normal settings the next time it's rebooted, and program the Penguini bridge to throw away the data the hub sends it. Then lock myself — and everyone else — out of the Penguini. Log out. *You can't undo what you've done.* No. I can't. But I can leave their network more or less as secure as I found it. Brian will have to deal with the lost Penguini. They're not expensive. Unslot my ice from Tik's deck.

Brian. What am I going to do about him? We're in a relationship of mutually assured destruction, but all of a sudden I care what happens to him. And he hasn't got any damn sense. He's a street fighter, he gets off on this stuff, and my stomach's still full of butterflies and my hands are shaking. They're calmer by the time I get this stupid desk chair to the bathroom. Wash my hands carefully. *Will all great Neptune's ocean wash this blood clean from my hand? No. This my hand will rather the multitudinous seas incarnadine, Making the green one red.* Look in the mirror. I don't feel like a killer. *Killer.* Yeah. I guess so. I have been for a long time. *More personal when you can see the bodies, isn't it?* Even Mom never killed anyone. That's not quite true, is it? Besides, I'm sure someone committed suicide when they found out what she did to their retirements. Prison would have been too kind. *Fuck you.* No, fuck you.

My OSDeck is beeping again. It's on. It's still in on from last night. One node of my crypto-breaker ice is still chugging away, without the help of its usual cluster-mates, trying to crack the industrial strength crypto of the phone call log. I slot up my EII in my OSDeck again, and jack in.

And immediately I know I'm screwed.

My deck has been on all night, and on an unsecured link, at that. Damn it. I forgot. I have enough time to kick myself once or twice. The OSDeck isn't very fast, and neither is the link I'm using — 802.11n only goes half a gig per second at best — but the hacker is here. And I'm jacked in alone, like an idiot.

"Hello, Shroudie." She smiles. Perfect white teeth against her dark skin, and I look at her. She is as she was online, smooth bellied, flowing hair. I eye her critically, staying cool this time.

"Who are you really?" I try to raise my hand and unplug myself from the deck. It fails to move. How?

Tika chuckles. "Don't you recognize me?"

I force myself to chuckle slightly, wishing sincerely that I had serious crypto tools at hand. If I did, I could break this son-of-a-bitch again, and this time... But I choke my anger down, along with any residual pain at Tika's likeness being used again.

"I've missed you, Shroud. You left in the middle of things last time."

"Yeah, well, sucks to be you, doesn't it?"

Her smile fades. "So have you fucked him yet? You know ... my boyfriend? Was he good for you?"

"What makes you think I'd fuck a professional thug adrenaline junkie half my age, hmm?"

Tik smiles. "You did, didn't you. You probably said it was for me, in my memory or something, right? Justified it that way to yourself. But I don't believe you. He doesn't believe you either."

"Who are you?"

"Don't change the subject, Shroud. You're fucking my boy, and I'm angry with you about it."

"Aren't you forgetting something important? Like the whole 'death do us part' thing?"

Tika laughs, a chilling sound like ice cracking. "Oh that. Well … it's inconvenient, you know? I kind of miss having a body. So what *did* you do to poor Kimmy? She looks like she's been run over by a car."

Stare at her. What does she know? How could she know? I feel the hair on the back of my neck prickle. Crush the sudden creeping panic as fast as I can. Stay frosty.

Tika touches a fingertip to her brow, a gesture of respect. "Almost, hmm?"

"I'm onto your ice."

"Oh, you think so? You've certainly had enough time to sort it out. You're supposed to be so good, but how good can you be, leaving your deck lying around running, stuck in some pathetic attempt to crack crypto on a file?"

"The real world fucks me up sometimes." I have to do something. I can't just sit here and chat with this … apparition. But the only non-busy ice in this deck is the copy of Tik's pictures. I summon my self control, stay as calm and frosty as I can, unlock the ice, and erase it.

Tika changes immediately, her body taking on the profiles of her real-life self. "Look at me, I'm fat!" She laughs, like a cheese grater against my skull, as she plays with her tummy a little, setting up standing waves in the tanker flab around her waist. My mental eye can't close, never could. She's found a back door into my memory. The reality of Tik that I never knew. As much a construct as she is with me now. "Am I prettier like this, Shroud? More real? More flawed and human? You can picture me like this, can't you. In bed with Brian, fucking him while you watch, knowing that your turn is coming…"

I can feel the tampering start, feel that she has me, that she's already broken my crypto. The OSDeck is so slow I can feel it. But I know how long this takes, I can do this. The hacker isn't omniscient, and she thinks she has me. Got to keep her talking, but I can feel…

A sodden rush in my guts. Sense of warmth between my thighs.

You know, I'd almost expected her to go with pain or fear or something else I could fight.

"That is the key to you, isn't it? The chink in your armor. I see now. All your life stuck in a wheelchair, and human instinct isn't really about reproducing with the defective, is it?"

Feel myself grow reassuringly cold at that comment.

And then there are two of me. Then four. My simple ice program has come online. We, my alternate selves and I, speak as one. "Maybe. Maybe the real world isn't mine. But you are on *my* turf, bitch. You play by my rules here."

"Oh, surely you don't expect this little ruse to…" She does what I hoped she would. She shows off. Pops one of my illusionary selves. The projected Tika evaporates as the ice locks onto her as soon as she touches it. The ice is faster than the deck. The deck can only forward packets so fast, and my ice is vacuuming up the packets she's sending me as fast as the wireless interface can forward them. All I could think of. I tell the deck to jack me out, but it's sluggish; its internal communications are overwhelmed.

The deck picks up a little as it freezes my perceptions, locking me in place as the jack out process slowly occurs. I get an indicator. Penguin ice one has crashed. My quick and dirty gambit against her has ended, and her packets are coming at me again. I expect to jack out momentarily, but things stay slow. The news ice counter blurs, begins downloading megabytes of bogus news stories. Sneaky. She's flooding my news ice, keeping the thing busy, which is keeping the limited bandwidth of my deck busy from its most important job, jacking me out.

Paralysis. I can't even defend myself. I can feel the signals, feel my emotions running over again. See the bogus news topics titled: Bitch, Bitch, Bitch." even as she pours a torrent of memory into my head, trying to rewire my jack from the inside. And a moment later, I can feel my heart beginning to pound, far away in the real world.

And then, everything goes black.

Chapter 30

5:33 p.m. Monday.

5:33 p.m. 5:34 p.m. I open my eyes slowly, looking at the room uncomprehendingly for a moment, watching the edges swim in and out. A face looks down at me. My stomach roils, and if I could muster … could muster the strength … I…

A hand reaches down and the world rolls sideway and I'm facing into an abyss. Smell of vomit. Taste of it. My stomach feels like it's been kicked.

"Areyouallright?

"Wha?"

"Yourchillpatchwentoff. Toldyouitwasabadtrip." My mind has very few edges right now, but slowly, slowly it starts to dawn on me.

"Chill?"

"From thismorning.

Chill. Geodon. Anti-Psychotic. Ativan. Tranquilizer. Euphoric. Two great tastes … taste … great together. "How … long?"

"Couple hours. You're going to be out of it for a while longer. What happened?"

"Hacker."

"Here?"

"My deck. Left it on."

"Fuck." Brian seems concerned. I probably should be. Something is bothering me. Some tidbit, something the hacker said. Hard to think. Hard to focus. I'm drifting off to sleep. Oh yeah. Have to … have to … ask about that later.

Chapter 31

8:40 p.m. Monday.

I have to pee.

Sometimes it's the little things that get you. For me it should be some secret super ice I hide in my jack itself that wakes me up … hmm … interesting idea.

Ugh. As I was saying, some day I'll have to figure out a technological method to snap me out of drug-induced sleep. It'd be nice to have such a thing. But I don't. My insistent bladder does it the old-school way. Wake up, I'm full. I percolate back into consciousness. The smells of cooking give my stomach an uncomfortable wrench. Open my eyes. Try to ignore the great nail of pain that drives into my eyeballs. Look around for my chair. Bucket … okay … glance downward along my body. I'm on the couch again. The desk chair is down toward the far end of the couch, so I reach for the back of the couch to sit up. The effort is titanic. I must have groaned. Brian comes back.

"Feeling better?"

"Adjectives from the family of 'good' … do not apply." I try to sit up. The world spins alarmingly and I squeeze my eyes shut. "Fuck."

"Vertigo?"

"Big time."

"Easy. Just lie there a while."

"I gotta get up."

"What's the rush?"

"Bathroom." I have done some embarrassing things in my life, been exposed, been weak, been vulnerable. But since I was a little girl I've never had to be carried to the bathroom and helped onto the toilet. If my head were spinning any less so that I thought I could hit it reliably, I'd probably put the Yellow Jacket in my ear and pull the trigger.

Brian doesn't say anything.

* * *

Dinner is quiet. After that initial twist at the smell of food, my stomach announced itself as the next major need on the agenda. Perhaps I'll live after all. Dinner is sausage sautéed with onions, peppers, and wine. Mushy peas, which are far better than they look or sound, and fresh bread out of the bread machine. I wait until after dinner to speak. Find my energy. Find my bearings. Find my voice — at least a whisper. "Thank you."

Brian looks at me. "For?"

I nod toward the bathroom.

Brian shrugs a little. "You needed it. I mean really, what else was I going to do?"

"Still. You're kind. When you're not…"

"Working," he says. "When I'm not working. I am what I am. Sometimes that isn't very nice."

I nod slowly. "Sometimes it is. How do you keep the two separate? Work and life?"

That gets a chuckle from him. "Sometimes not very well."

"You saved my life today. Thanks for that, too."

Brian shrugs again. "That was just work. You go on a run, you don't let your partners die, you know? That was some pretty decent shooting by the way. And some righteous hacking."

I shrug this time, then chuckle at it.

"What?"

I watch him a moment before speaking. "I was just noticing. Sometimes we seem like we're a lot alike."

Brian nods. "Yeah. Well, you know. Tik liked us both."

It's obviously meant to be a light comment, but it hurts him halfway through, like finding tinfoil with your teeth in the middle of a pork roll. I reach out to touch his hand, inwardly thinking that this is pretty much how things started last night. Comforting. Wondering if I'm up to it again. Not really, I'm forced to admit. He cuts me off before I can speak, gently resting his hand on mine. "Can we talk about something else, please?"

I nod a little. "Um … okay. How's Kimmy?"

Brian nods. Work is a safe topic, for both of us. "Dunno yet. She was getting a little twitchy at the hospital."

I frown slightly. "What hospital? I thought you were taking her to your clinic."

Brian eyes me. "Cath, that clinic is expensive. I have a maintenance contract with them for me, but it doesn't cover anyone else."

"So … where did you take her?"

"OmniMart's company hospital. Obviously."

I stare at him, snatching my hand back from his. "You took her to OmniMart?"

"Yeah, what was I supposed to do with her? She needed help."

"Brian, they're suppressing this investigation. Lance went to them and they're probably the ones who filed the ID theft report. You handed Kimmy over to the people who are trying to sweep Tika under the rug, dammit!"

Brian slaps his hand on the table in front of me, his hand only a blur. I flinch backward reflexively, and he pounces on the weakness verbally. "They're also offering her the only care she's likely to get. I don't know where you think you are, or what year you think it is, but the days when you can walk into the emergency room of any old hospital and get care for free are long gone. Your fucking company was offering a bounty for her."

His hand blurs again into a pocket to slap the table a second time. "*This*, by the way, is your share of her bounty, minus expenses. I was feeling fucking generous this afternoon. I was

222 James R. Strickland

thinking, hey. You're good. Maybe you could stay, and we could work together again. We make a pretty good team. But I was wrong. You're fucking nuts. You're obsessed and paranoid. I saw your face when you jacked out. You got nothing from Kimmy. And even if you could find this hacker, even if you nail him, even if you survive, you know what? That's not going to bring Tik back. Nothing is. But you can't let it go, it's always got to be about the fuck that got away, doesn't it?"

I stare daggers at Brian, and he stares them right back.

"Fine," I say. "I'll be going then."

"Like hell you will. I bailed you out of jail, remember? Until your court date, I'm fucking responsible for knowing where you are. Plus that's my desk chair you're sitting in, and I want it back."

I've already pushed back from the table when he says that. I noticed the chair again right about then. It's my turn to bang a fist on the table in frustration, hard enough to make the china jump. How could I be so careless with my chair? How could I let myself be so dependent? "Great. That's just lovely."

"Yeah, next time I'll bail out an Oakland whore, she'll at least be better in the sack." He kicks his chair back from the table and stalks out onto the porch, slamming the screen door behind him. I can feel my face burning. Emotions and drug hangover. My stomach ties itself in a knot, ruining the pleasantly satiated feeling I'd been enjoying a few minutes ago.

Chapter 32

There is no containing the flutter in my diaphragm, the trembling of my lips. I don't even try. I have no strength left to fight with. I have nothing left to fight for, either. I've given away my integrity for what? To fight the good fight? To keep one last little thing in the world good? Out of some sense of devotion? Revenge? My vision blurs as the moisture wells up, and my breath comes only in sobs that wrack my body in deep spasms, like an orgasm of pain, of tears. None of it. None of it means anything.

There's a word that resonates through me, knocking memory loose in razor sharp fragments, like the pictures of Pennsylvania Avenue after *Walpurgisnacht,* where the glass of every building is on the street. Mental images. Flashbacks. Every one is sharp. Every one cuts.

You're fucking my boy and I'm angry with you about it. Hug my arms around my chest. How could I have? What was I thinking? I can still feel his arms around me, face buried against my shoulder, feel him inside me. Comfort in sex with a total stranger? *You're not even very nice.* What comfort did I offer? What kindness have I been able to give him? Comfort like driving splinters in his eyes.

Failure.

She's got a gun. She's got a gun. Squeeze my eyes shut and try to blot out the memory of shooting six people to death. But

I can feel the gun jump in my hand with each pull of the trigger. Remember the wet smack and the almost ultrasonic hiss as the wireheads come apart inside them. Not zombies. Not video game targets. Real flesh and copious blood. People. Mojo too, his mind broken, lying in his tank waiting for some opportunist to take pity on him and end his life. I remember his screams as my software conditioned him, without remorse, without pity, without humanity. What have I done? What have I become?

Failure.

Kimmy! Shut the fuck up! Another brain hack. I can remember her expression of horror as the software steadily bounced signals and images out of her mind. I threw them around with such … impunity. Such carelessness. But I was playing with her mind. Everything that made her who she was, and who she probably isn't anymore. And I still have the gall to be disappointed as she reads back the trace, and it goes the one place it can't possibly go. And my entire plan for tracking the hacker goes to hell.

Failure.

I think you should go, Cath. How could I have been so wrong about Lance? I lied to him. I gave him the third degree about deaths in his own team. I remember him choking back tears, and I remember him reaching out to me. I repaid his kindness and his suffering by lying to him and by hitting him with a cheap shot. And then I used him without a second thought when he had information I needed. Why? Why do I keep people at arm's length and abuse them? Lance was my friend. Twenty years he was my friend. Not anymore. *Not a trusting person.*

Failure.

Tika. Oh, Tika. This is all my fault. All of it. I am to blame. I was the leader. I was responsible. If it weren't for me, you and Brian would be together in Carmel, enjoying the flannel sheets and the fireplace I can still feel from the bed and breakfast I've never been to. I'd be home reading a book or something and watching it snow.

Instead, I'm here.

And you're dead.

Failure.

You're not a trusting person. You're not a loving person. You're not even very nice. You're like the bitter shroud of death, and I'm too young to die.

Yeah. Well. Here I am. I don't have a choice. I go to court tomorrow. And from there to prison. If I'm lucky it will just be for the crime I didn't commit.

I can't go to prison.

I don't have a choice.

Alone.

Stupid girl. Reap what you've sown.

Alone.

The stink of burning clove wafts in with the smog through the screen door. Try to choke back the tears, to catch my breath. It doesn't come. I have nothing right now, no control, no effect, I don't even have wheels I can call my own. Immobile.

Alone.

The only people I know in this city are dead, in the hospital, with the company, or that nutcase on the porch sucking on a clove cigarette.

Or the hacker.

What? Wipe my eyes. It … it's a stupid conclusion. Brian's right, I'm obsessed with this place, and maybe it really is about Tika and that I was too much a coward to come out here and screw her the times she invited me, not to mention join her and Brian's little corporate mercenary ring. Should I have? Would I have?

Shiver. Wipe my nose with my napkin. I can imagine doing it, actually. Close my eyes and imagine … saying yes on Friday. Coming here. Damn it, I can still feel her arms around me from the first attack. How long … how long would it have taken to say yes? To throw away my ticket back to Denver? How would they have broached the subject of what they did for a living?

It would have been in bed. Obviously. I don't think I'd have taken it well. There would have been shouting. And they would have asked … Tik would have asked … just like

Lance asked. *Don't you get tired of fighting?* And I don't know what I'd have answered. And she'd have kissed me and said, *Feel the real.*

It's easy to imagine being … seduced, if you want to call it that, by the quick rewards, the easy money, by Tik and Brian, by all of this. *Not a trusting person...* Would I have trusted Tika? You already know the answer to that. Yeah. If I had, I'd have said yes when she asked me to come out in the first place. And it wouldn't have made a particle of difference.

You trust her now that she's dead. Wait. That's not fair. *You sanctify her memory now that she can't disappoint you anymore. But if she were alive, you still wouldn't trust her. You don't trust anyone.* Tik was different. *How, exactly?* Tik was my friend. *And this means what?* It means that I owe her. *You owe her what? This crusade? You didn't trust her as much as you've already trusted psychoboy outside.* She's dead, it doesn't matter anymore. *You're still alone.*

A whirlpool of crystalline memories. Each one cuts. I bleed tears until I have none left, until my napkin is soaked, until my eyes are raw with them, until my chest and stomach tell me that the sharp glass of memories is all inside me now. Until I physically can't cry anymore. An emergency room truism. All bleeding eventually stops.

How do you tell what's real? I don't know. All I've been able to do is ask people I remember doing or saying certain things … and trust them. Tik. Oh Tik, I've really made a mess of things, and I'm all broken inside. I wish I'd known you.

There's no reply, obviously. She's dead. All I have is my own model of her, based on … based on … the hacker's model. There's a reassuring shiver of pure fury sliding up my back at that. Grab it. Hold onto its pure cold sharpness. It will cut me too, eventually, but the cold is worth it. The clarity. Is worth it. Frosty. *All I've been able to do is ask people I remember doing or saying certain things … and trust them.* Okay. Okay. Let's look again. All I have to do is log in. Yeah.

Take a deep breath. Look at my OSDeck. A few thumb presses on its buttons and I've turned off its wireless interface.

No surprises for me this time. I verify that all my ice hasn't been mucked with. Erase Penguin ice one, making sure it shows completely empty and no cycles executing, and throw it in my backpack for safekeeping. I also do a hard restore on my news ice. It's commercial, so all its code is in ROM, can't be written to. *Just like your jack, right?* I look at it and throw it in my backpack too. E-mail ice gets erased, it's just a Penguin ice, and an old one at that. I can re-carve it later with open source soft from the net. That leaves the deck, me, and my EII. Environment, Icons and Identity. The most basic of all ice. I've never heard of EII ice being cracked. It's barely ice at all, just a series of programs that store your preferences, who you are, and how you represent yourself and your stuff. I've had this same ice since my first jump onto the net that didn't involve a keyboard and a mouse. And now I don't trust it. *Not a trusting...* I slide its permissions slider to read and write but not execute, slot it into the deck, plug the deck into my low speed jack, jack in.

Nothing happens. I look at myself. I'm the default icon. Humanoid, gender undefined, covered in a mirrored finish. A newb. It's not too much different from how I feel. The net has changed under me. It's not the place I left it.

I flush my EII. Reset it to its factory defaults. Time to start over. I configure the bare minimum of things. Color, rendering — turn rendering of unknown streams off, set resolution to maximum modulated by speed. Set force metaphors off. Jack out. Pop the ice out. Move its slider to execute. Pop it back in. Jack in. Close my eyes and look inward.

Very little changes. I'm local in the deck. Just me and what I bring in with me. That's fine. The rest can wait. All that software gets to be a crutch after a while.

Open my eyes. Slot up the dangerous stuff: the ice I attacked the hacker with, the monitor and logger from fixing Kimmy. The only data I've got beyond what I remember. Set them all not-executable. Close my eyes. Feel them burn behind my eyelids, and pause to wipe my nose again. Then look into the electronic world. Again, nothing happens. Again, that's good. I go to my hastily carved attack ice. Play back its log file. All the packets it received came from 2001:A1AA:FE14:007A:0240:63FF:FEC0:8D14. Great. Just great. A1AA:FE14 makes it an OmniMart address. Why would the hacker go to the trouble of spoofing an OmniMart address to attack me on the NFWN? *All I've been able to do is ask people I remember doing or saying certain things ... and trust them.* Ask who? But no one answers. So I stare at the address a while. Read it aloud to myself.

An IP V6 address is a long, ugly hunk of data. Even so, after some practice you can pick them up like phone numbers, so that the sound, the rhythm, the phrasing of an otherwise innocuous series of numbers associates with a memory of the person whose phone it rings. It's like that with IP addresses after a while. The sound sticks in your mind. Or at least in my mind, anyway. There's a familiarity to the phrasing, like when you listen to someone recite the preamble to the Constitution of the old U.S. and can tell they learned it from that Schoolhouse Rock song on TV. And when I read the address aloud, it dawns on me that I've heard it before. Heard it. Not seen it written down, heard it. *Ask people ... and trust them.*

It takes me only a moment to find it, on the log of the ice from fixing Kimmy. The log spools out, slowly. She rattles off the address. "2001:A1AA:FE14:007A:0240:63FF:FEC0:8D14." Stop the playback. The same address. The last eight blocks, 0240:63FF:FEC0:8D14, are the interface ID for Pete's sake, the hardware ID of the network interface. It's almost the serial number ... of the device the hacker came from. *Not a trusting person ... ask people ... and trust them.*

It can't be that simple. Can it? Can I prove that this address isn't just a spoof? I've done that just today. Masqueraded as someone else from some other address. But to spoof the address you have to know it. Spoofs normally come from router addresses, web servers, or tanks. Machines that touch the outside world frequently. As a result, I usually recognize the spoofed addresses. This one before ... Friday ... I never knew it existed. *All I've been able to do is ask people I remember doing or saying certain things ... and trust them.* In God we trust, all others we polygraph. This is science. What other data do I have?

The attacker's used that same address both times. That's definitely not good spoofing behavior; it gives the people defending against you a standing target. So. If that address is legit, what does it tell me? 2001:0000. That makes it a unicast address. One machine on a network. Most IP V6 addresses you encounter have that. A1AA:FE14. That's OmniMart. Every address on every machine on OmniMart's net has those two blocks of address space. That amounts to a knife in the back, if it's real. 007A ... Oh, for fuck's sake. If my legs worked I'd have to kick myself. Hard.

Human beings have ten fingers to count on, so our numbers are base ten, decimal: zero through nine, add a digit for ten. In the old days with IP V4, we represented blocks of the network address in decimal as well, so you might have 129.82.169.3 or something like that. IP V6 addresses, because they're so much longer, are represented in hexadecimal. Count zero to nine, then continue on A, B, C, D, E, and F, then add a digit for 10, which is equal to decimal 16. Decimal 169 becomes A9 in hex. The network section of the address the hacker came from is hex 007A. In decimal, that's 122. And what was it Kimmy'd said at morning huddle, a lifetime ago now? Ultra. OmniMart's secret San Jose network 122. When did they come up? Early Friday morning. It could be a coincidence. But I doubt it.

Ask people ... and trust them. If I trust ... if I trust Kimmy's trace, where does it get me? Test the hypothesis. Try to fit the puzzle pieces into place. Why didn't the I-Link pirate crew get a good trace? They did, but like me, they didn't believe it. It doesn't make me feel any better. But why was my trace wrong? What if it wasn't? What if the hacker came from San Jose and jumped out at I-Link, just as I did later to attack him, then jumped back in from I-Link into our network? From where I sat, he would have come from I-Link. And the final piece of evidence? Where would he have had to come from to attack the San Jose team while the I-Link routers were down? West of Reno. Like San Jose.

Dumbass. How could I miss all this? *A tale told by an idiot...* Thanks. It gets worse. How could the attacker know about Tik's sensual nature and how to attack her? Betcha he's been into the logs at San Jose, where they log everything, including the evening we spent making love online. It gives me pause. I contributed to the information he used to tear Tik apart. That doesn't last long. Rationality slams an iron fist down on the idea. The hacker went through the I-Link pirate crew cold, and in less time than it took him to kill us. Tik and Kimmy were good, but the I-Link crew was just as good. All those logs did was maybe make Tik's last moments a little nicer.

Okay, fine, I'm an idiot. What do I know about the hacker? How can I be sure OmniMart San Jose isn't just a waypoint for him and he's coming from Japan? Well, I know he learned some of his tricks from Mojo, who was rumored to be in CalTech contracting for someone. I know the attacker's not coming over the satellite links. His attacks came on too fast, and if he's rich enough to afford to use that kind of bandwidth on the birds, he'd hire hit men instead of hacking us. I know he knows CalTech's National Fast Wireless Network. In fact, I know he's either sniffing them or he's into their accounting, because the last transaction I made on my bank account was to buy access on the NFWN. I suspect he's into their accounting. NFWN's a mesh topology network instead of a leaf and trunk network. The only place it forms a single data flow is where it jumps onto I-Link's feeder network. And watching all the packets from the entire California Technocracy as they go over the mountain to connect to the rest of the continent? That'd be like straining a major metro sewer with your teeth.

Stupid girl, don't believe everything you see on TV. Yeah. My facts are all circumstantial. But I can add more. Theoretically net 122 has no connections to the outside world except through the corporate firewall. The very same firewall all six of us guarded. Yet he hit us and we didn't detect him until he was through it and into our gestalt. Even if he had come from out-side on an unauthorized link, the kind of bandwidth he's been using would have shown up as a monster traffic spike on some router somewhere. It would have set off the alarms. We'd have seen it.

Okay. Okay. Let's stack these hypotheses up higher. If the hacker is inside OmniMart San Jose, when did he show up? Don't know. I know that once network 122 came up, he hacked I-Link, then us, then NFWN, and he's been keeping an eye on me since then, because he was waiting for me in my deck when I logged in. He's been a busy boy.

A few things aren't adding up yet. The big one that leaps to mind is, why me? *The fuck who got away...* Kimmy got away too. Except of course that Brian and I just gave her back to the company. Oh shit. That would mean...

Brian. A man lodging a suit against OmniMart just walks into the corporate hospital with a semiconscious OmniMart employee slung over his shoulder and they pay him his boun-ty and send him on his way like any other pro? *Ask people ... and trust them ... not a trusting person...* Pull up the log of his phone call. The data is still encrypted, so I just look at the packet headers. Who sent the packets, and who received them. Decking is not like tanking. I'm still aware of my body. I can feel the shiver run down my back again. The call is a deck to tank call, all digital.

One address is Brian's. I saw it when he was on the phone. The other is 2001:A1AA:FE14:007A:0240:63FF:FEC0:8D14. The same address. The hacker.

I have to crack the crypto on Brian's phone call now. Have to. But I have to have Tik's deck for that, at least, which would involve explaining. *Not a trusting person...* How can I trust him? He's been in contact with the enemy. For all I know he's work-ing for ... whoever within the company ... to tie up the loose ends. Kimmy. Me. Would he work for them if he knew they were probably the ones who killed Tik? Whether he knows or not, he's a suspect. I jack out. Ask people ... and trust them.

I lean back in the desk chair I'm sitting in, and set my OSDeck down on the table next to my empty plate. Close my eyes. Take a deep breath. The dining room still smells like food, mingling with the stink of pollution, lilacs, and burning cloves coming in through the screen door from the backyard. The moisture in the air has a vaguely grey water sewer smell, too, and I'm only just noticing it now. Beautiful world. *With such people in't.* Would Brian turn me in? Has this all been a set up? *Tik fought for a paycheck. That's all. Sorry if that blows your image of her.* But he has as much to lose as I do. Maybe more. He does this for a living. *Don't you think he has the legal angles worked out? Corporate legal will be on his side.* He also saved my life twice today. *Twice?* Yeah. Once with the car. Once with the chill patch. If this was a setup, why not leave Kimmy and me to the zombies? Damn it. *Not a trusting...* You, shut the fuck up. This is what I've got. It's all I've got, but it's something. There are answers to these questions. I have to have them. And they are all inside OmniMart net 122. I have to know where that address goes, because whoever was at that address on Friday morning is going to die tonight. After that ... whether I die in the attempt or whether they convict me and send me up for twenty years for identity theft tomorrow ... well ... I'll take my lumps. I'm good at that.

I'm not going to get in there on an OSDeck, though. Even Tik's Zhang is too slow. Too clunky. I need a tank, ideally, or maybe, just maybe, one of Lance's ultra-high-speed Kuroto decks, along with all my ice and then some. That means money. Pick up the bank card Brian left on the table. Wonder how much it's worth.

Engineering. Planning. This is what I do. And I'm good at it, too. *You're planning a run.* Yeah, I'm planning a run. *Not much planning.* Not much time. *You're not at a hundred percent, obviously.* Obviously. But I have to do this tonight if I'm going to do it at all. I may not be able to after tomorrow. I'll have twenty years to think about what I do tonight. I need to do this right.

I'm going to need a high-speed link, but it seems likely that any place with a tank will also have high-speed access. Axiomatic, in my book. *And you're never wrong...* I thought I told you to shut up. The other thing I need is a safety man. I need someone I trust who can pull the plug on me if my vital signs start going berserk without having a chill patch that will leave me drooling for the police or corporate security slugs to pick up. I need someone who can watch my perimeter security. If I'm going to do this, I'm going to do it. I don't want the hacker to get away from me and get off scot-free because he sends some flunky to go open my tank and put wireheads in my skull. I really need someone like Bobbo.

Like Brian. Whose side are you on? Look, I can't trust Brian. I know he's involved somewhere and there's more going on than he's telling me about. I also have no reason to expect him to go along with this plan. *Have you got any connections in this city?* Well, no. *Got any better candidates then?* No. I don't. I don't have anyone else. Not in this city. Possibly not at all. Alone. Push myself toward the glass door in this stupid desk chair, and lean against the glass. Look out onto the porch. Above Brian where he's pacing. At the stars. Wait for them to stop blurring. I know what I have to do. *Ask people ... and trust them.* "Hey, Brian? Can I talk to you?" Nothing. "Please?"

His shadow turns, and the cherry on his cigarette glows bright a moment, then falls like a meteorite to the ground and flares as he stomps it out. I honestly don't know why he comes back in, not really. But I'm grateful. I feel it wash through me, like warm bathwater on a carrier of chill hangover. Crow, it would seem, is a fine dessert.

Chapter 33

Brian sits at the table, looking at his hands. He smells like cloves and tobacco. It's not altogether unpleasant, though certainly not healthy. "What?" he says.

"I'm sorry, Brian." I expect it to be thrown in my face. A sign of weakness. *Not a trusting...* No, I'm not, really.

Brian sighs softly, looks down at his hands again. "Yeah. Me too. Especially about the Oakland whore crack."

"What?" We are not on the same page, I don't think. "Oh. Forget it. We're both screwed up about the whole thing."

"No, it's important."

Why, oh why, does he want to talk this out now? I'm in a hurry and my grip on frostiness is tenuous at best. But we're not going anywhere if he's not willing to come with me, so I push, shove, and pull myself and the stupid desk chair back to the table. "Okay."

Brian is looking at his hands again as he speaks. "We keep winding up fighting, and I want it to stop."

"Like I said, we're both pretty messed up about everything that's happened."

"It's more than that, Cath. Tik and I fought. Pretty much all the time." I look at Brian, watching him. He goes on. "I don't want to go there with you. I don't want that to happen again."

"Why? You loved Tik. I should be flattered." I regret the words as soon as they're out of my mouth. Brian reacts as though I slapped him. I fumble on, quickly. "Wait. That didn't … I'm serious, Brian. Tik said you made her happy. And she was big on sharing her thoughts directly about it, so I know she wasn't just saying it. If the two of you fought, maybe that's just how the two of you were together. And here I am in her space before either of us has really grasped down deep, that she's gone. I'm flattered. I mean okay, it's flattery like butt sex – nice, but you know you'll be sore later. Still."

Well, it was a joke. A desperate attempt to lighten the mood a little.

Brian doesn't laugh. His eyebrow quirks a little is all, then he shakes his head and looks at his hands again. "You're wrong about me, Cath. I know she's gone. I've lost people before. In my biz you learn to let go of the dead fast; grieve later, preferably with a bottle. It's important to me because I've got these feelings for you … I think I'm…" It's awkward for him, as though his feelings are alien to him, to his vocabulary.

It's a sensation I'm familiar with. Take his hand gently, and cut him off. "Don't. Please don't say it. Brian … please … not tonight. If I go up against this hacker with a brain full of warm fuzzies and complications, he'll nail me to the wall. If I win, there'll be time, and if I don't you'll just have to let go of me too."

Brian blinks at me. We're still not quite on the same page, I guess. He closes his eyes. "We've been through this. Catherine please. Please. Let him go. You don't have anything left to go on anyway."

I shake my head. Fuck. Part of me desperately wants to do just that. Let go, I mean. Stay here. Live my life. Be happy for once. But I know me. I've known me for forty years. This would gnaw at me for the rest of my life, poison everything I might get by letting go. Especially now. *Stupid girl, don't believe everything you see on TV.* "I think I know where he is, Brian."

It's as though someone else is sitting in Brian's chair, suddenly. Someone sharp. Someone dangerous. As though he'd put aside his anger, but not let it go. Any more than I have.

Now he's picked it up again, and it's still loaded. He stares at me. "Where?"

"He's inside OmniMart San Jose. You were right to be paranoid about the corporation. We both were. This is some rogue inside the company, in some secret project called Ultra."

"Ultra?" Brian's guarded, suddenly. He looks away as though Ultra is a name to conjure with. One he already knows. I can see the wheels of his mind turning, putting his own puzzle together, I imagine. *Or trying to figure out how to cover his tracks.* Ask people ... then trust them, isn't that what Tik said? *Do you remember when she said it?* Yeah. When the hacker was modeling her. In the attack. *Stupid girl...* You got any better ideas?

"Brian? Okay. Truth between us. I have a pretty good idea something's up between you and OmniMart. The company hospitals are secure facilities, but they let you walk in, and now you know about Ultra. I need to trust you, Brian. Level with me, please?"

Brian looks down at his hand, still held in mine. "Nothing gets by you, does it? I'm on contract to OmniMart Ultra. Just basic thug work, go here, guard this, kill anyone who crosses your security perimeter without an ID. Last night, after we made love, I got a phone call from my boss on the Ultra project. He said he'd gotten word that I'd bailed you out of jail, and asked where you were. I figured, you know. Company cares about one of its best security people. So I told him yeah, I knew where you were. He said he'd get in touch today."

"Your boss. Are you sure?"

"Same guy I've been talking to the last week, Cath, though it's the first time he's ever called me on my deck. It was a rich contract, I was planning ... to use the cash to have a wedding."

"I mean you verified his ID, right?"

"Of course. Word-choice analysis, source address, the works. You're not the only one with ice around here, you know.

I nod at that. But I had forgotten Brian is technical. Oops. "Has he been in touch today?"

"No. I was expecting a message in my inbox, but nada."

"I think maybe he left a message with me instead."

"What?"

"Old-fashioned message. Here's what happens to little girls — and boys — who screw around in my business. Your boss was the one who mugged me this afternoon. I don't think he expected to nail me in my slow little deck. It would have taken days to transmit all the data on NFWN, not to mention being totally insecure. Your net isn't even locked."

Brian looks at me. "It was. Why'd you unlock it?"

"I didn't."

"When was this?

"While I was on the pot. There wasn't much else to do, and I wanted to check my e-mail. Your router was the closest link point."

"It let you in?"

"Yeah, security was totally turned off."

I hesitate here, looking down at Brian's hand. I'm thinking of Lance, actually. And realizing that I can't just lie to Brian, or not tell him. This trust stuff cuts both ways, but never doubt that it cuts.

"What?"

"I was packet sniffing your network the whole time you were on the phone. I was looking for anyone else coming in, I didn't want to lock up your net without at least telling, but I didn't want to let some scumball in either. I forgot to delete the log, and later … you were acting so weird, I've been letting my deck run cracking software on your call. That's why it was on when we came home, and that's why the hacker was waiting inside it."

Brian looks at me, then down again. "Jesus, Cath."

"That wouldn't have been my first guess, no."

He looks at me again. "You bugged my phone? You didn't trust me?"

"I sniffed the line. It didn't become bugging until I decided to crack your call instead of throwing the fucking thing away like I should have. I'm sorry, Brian. Not too sorry because now I find out you're working for the guy I'm after, but I'm sorry."

"What are you talking about?" The warmth in his voice has shut down again. He stares at me.

"Do I have to spell it out, Brian? The IP address your phone call originated from is the same as the hacker who killed Tik and attacked me Friday morning. It's the same address Kimmy traced to, and the same one that attacked me again this afternoon."

"So they're on the same network."

"No. The same address, all the way across. Same interface ID. Everything. That doesn't tell us who was using it at the time, but it's likely that even if your boss isn't the perp, he's sharing a tank with the guy, at the very least. I'm sorry."

"Yeah, I'm sorry too." He withdraws his hand from mine. A freezing chill slides down my spine to sit soggily in my guts. Dammit. I trusted. I did. It's not my fault this time. *Stupid girl...*

Brian's voice is as flat as the day we met at the courthouse. "I'm in, how do we burn this guy?"

I was afraid he'd say that. *Wasn't that what you were trying to talk him into?* Yes, but that was before Brian said ... almost said... "I'd like you to stay clear, Bri. All I need is taxi stuff."

"No. I'm going with you."

"Brian, I have to do this. I can't let it go. He's hurt me, he's hurt Kimmy and may be messing with her in the hospital. He's killed pretty much everyone else I know or care about. More importantly, he's a danger to every other operator on the entire net. For better or worse, that's something I have to fight for. So I have to do this. But you don't."

"He killed Tika. He hurt you. Isn't that enough?" The voice is almost a growl.

"Brian, if you get involved now it'll cost you your contract. OmniMart tends to think breach of contract is a good reason to hire hit men. And I don't know what rich is to you, but it's probably enough for you to start a new life, move someplace else, start over, no matter how this turns out."

He looks at me and slides his shades on, and I know that we're no longer negotiating. "I live in California."

Chapter 34

10:00 p.m. Monday.

Brian and I are in San Francisco again, this time in Japantown. A maze of color and light, Japantown is slowly being made over in Tokyo's image: huge neon displays, enormous televisions hawking everything imaginable, all in Japanese, frequently with pretty naked Japanese girls involved. Distracting. I have a bounty of a million yen to spend, and a bad feeling about what part of OmniMart it was that paid a bounty that high for Kimmy. My eyes grow a little overwhelmed. I can feel the lights spilling into other areas of my brain, like the hacker's attack tried to, even in the slow confines of my OSDeck, like Mojo's attack before it. Probably the tail end of my chill hangover still screwing with my nerves, too. *Not at a hundred percent, obviously.* No. But it will have to do.

We check the porno houses first. No, scratch that. First, we buy a plain, matte-black polymer wheelchair at a clinic. You know, I remember chairs costing a lot more, but I guess technology marches on. This thing is half the weight of my old one, too, despite having an active suspension. I remember being more attached to my old chair, too. But it's just a thing. Things can be replaced. Now we're checking the porno houses.

A modern porno house is all about the virt — the virtual experience. Anything you want short of a real prostitute, they try to make as real as possible in a virtual environment. The high-class places even hire their own engineers to custom-make environments for customers. One of my coworkers at Epimetheus got caught moonlighting in a porn house. She got fired. The company, we were told, had the right of first refusal on any virt we created while we were employed by them. So porno houses are virtual heavy. They pack a lot of hardware into a small space, and they're all about the custom ice. And for the customers? They call them coffins, and they're custom made for porn houses: induction rig, Tempurfoam lined, soundproof. Usually rigged up with an automatic cleaning and sanitizing system. Most houses don't bother with coffins, though. It's usually cheaper to just buy used or surplus general-purpose tanks, and hire someone to scrub the interior between customers. Or not bother until the tank gets too scrofulous. *Not a trusting person...* Hey, this is porn. *You can learn a lot from porn.* Model or not, that sounds like something Tik would have said.

The tanks in this place are a mishmash of different types. We look them over, one at a time, all thirty, though we frequently have to wait for customers to finish a virt. We're not the only couple inspecting tanks. Nobody gives us a second glance. Or a first. Porn houses are like that. Most porn consumers are married or involved. They don't want what they're doing to be noticed by anyone. Particularly themselves.

"Hey. What about this one, Doc? It's a ... Nova 11/735. Looks like eleven slots." He's calling me Doc again. I'm not entirely sure why. Brian goes on, "I know it's induction only, but it solves the jack problem, right?"

"Yes and no. I can crack an induction rig and brain-burn someone a lot faster than our boy can reprogram my jack. Plus I've got a skull full of silicon interconnects with my old jack. I'm really not induction compatible."

I pass by a GenData 850. Jack interface, sure, and maybe just enough slots with eight, but it's a first generation tank. It belongs in a museum. It's way too slow for what I want. Tika's deck is almost as fast.

"What we're looking for is a high-end Megadyne or a modern GenData 15 slotter. Or a Nova 4000 series.

"Probably gonna need a better class of porn shop then. Maybe one of the interactive places would let you rent their master tank."

His reasoning stands up. An interactive porn house's master tank is where their interactive artists — and she's always called an artist — lies, spending her evening spinning out sexual encounters for as many as a dozen customers at once. They're really interacting with her ice, rather than her, but she keeps the experience tailored to them. They say the interactive houses are where old tankers go when they burn out in corporate-land. They're right. I shiver.

Brian notices. "What?"

"I was signed up to work a place like this when OmniMart offered me a contract."

"You?"

Brian's incredulousness brings back his comment about how I was in the sack. "I was studying for it. Learning the moves. Learning how the game works. It was all I could get."

Brian just chuckles and pats me on the shoulder. "You'd have been good at it."

Finding a place with the right level of seediness is difficult. They either have the right equipment, but aren't inclined to rent it out for what is obviously a run, or they are seedy enough not to ask too many questions, but their master tank and their networks are antediluvian, and not up to what I need. Several of them seem interested in hiring me as their tank mistress, and Brian gets his ass grabbed more than once in the gay interactive house. The real problem is, of course, that without their master tank, the place has to shut down for the evening. The kind of place with the equipment I need makes more in one night than I make in a year, so I suppose I can understand their reluctance. Frustrating.

"Brian?"

"Yeah?"

"If you wanted to buy a state of the art deck, fresh off the boat from Japan, where would you go?"

Chapter 35

11:50 p.m. Monday.

Still in Japantown. I'm sitting in the back room of an Asian market, the stench of not-so-fresh fish mingling with spices. And with gun oil. The room I'm in is a small warehouse. Plastic pallets of Yellow Jackets from Indonesia. Hundreds, maybe thousands of the cheap, nasty little pistols. There are a few wooden crates, the open ones appearing to contain honest-to-God AK-47s. The man who brought us here is rummaging through an anti-static, foam-lined shipping crate bearing Kuroto's corporate logo. He smiles, withdrawing a slim, featureless black obelisk, perhaps ten centimeters long, by perhaps five by eight.

"Kuroto. X2026-20. Twenty slots. Next year's top line. Not even released in Japan yet. First manufacturing run." I look at Brian, who nods. This gentleman is, he assured me earlier, connected.

"How much?" I ask.

"Two million yen."

I close my eyes. Brian nudges my shoulder, and I think a moment. Mission time. "Seven-hundred-fifty-thousand yen. I get the deck, and you stuff all its slots with Kuroto MXG ice."

The man smiles, baring ancient, tobacco-stained teeth to complement his salt and pepper hair, his very expensive Italian suit, and very expensive glossy black shoes. I didn't ask Brian who this guy is, or what organized crime syndicate he's with, and I absolutely do not want to know. "MXG very expensive. I give you deck, five MXG plus copy of MXG compiler. One and one-half million yen."

"One million yen, for the deck and 15 Penguin G+." Cards on the table. Everything I have. About twenty thousand Canadian dollars. As much as my retirement is worth. Was worth. The man offers his hand to shake. I shake it. Hand him the cred card that has my share of Kimmy's bounty on it. It's not like I have a week to learn Kuroto's arcane compiler to access the secure electronics of their military grade MXG ice. Penguin ice goes faster, if you know what you're doing. Besides, I'm an old-school developer. Compilers are for wusses. I code on the bare metal, carve my ice in assembly.

12:01 a.m. Tuesday.

Midnight finds me plugged into my new deck. It's in my lap, radiating that new toy smell of outgassing plastic. I used to love that smell. Part of me still does, it would seem.

I pick the shallow connect first, and it slides into my brain effortlessly, the sense of lightness and grace so different from Tika's Zhang. I RTFM on the differences between the new ice and the stuff I'm used to. There aren't too many. Four rendering cores instead of just one, four DSP cores instead of two, three processor cores. More memory. Bug fixes. Faster clock. Faster optical interface to the deck. Lots of optimization. This is good. It means I don't have to do a lot of recoding. I copy one crypto-breaking ice node from my old F-type Penguin ice to the new G+. Tweak the scheduler so it knows about all the extra rendering units and MPUs. Add some more tweaks to optimize the cracking engine. Fire it up, run some tests, run some benchmarks. Not bad. It almost hits its Moore's Law performance target. I copy the node to nine more of the G+ ice. Throw Brian's phone call log at it. With one node running, the F-type was going to take 200 hours to crack this. My 10-node array cracks it in 40 seconds. Synergy is my friend. The call was only yesterday, while I was in the tub. It seems like years. More importantly, for the first time I hear my hacker's voice.

"Mr. Hanaga?"

"Yeah." Brian says. I hadn't known Brian's last name.

"I've received word that you are in contact with a Dr. Catherine Farro." Probably from the Redwood City police. How connected is this guy? Or did he break into the police department's network too?

"Yeah, that's right." Brian's cool in the log.

"Do you know where she is?

"I can get my hands on her pretty easily, why?" Brian Hanaga. Master of understatement.

"When you see her, please hold her for us. She was injured in the same attack Ms. Silverthorn was killed in. We are offering a two-million-yen bounty for the safe return of Dr. Farro as well as on Ms. Anderson. They are valuable employees."

"Two million each?"

"Yes. Two million each."

"Not bad. What's the catch?"

"Ms. Anderson has developed severe psychological trauma, and was last seen in San Francisco. We believe she may turn up in the Asylum area. Dr. Farro seems to have developed paranoid delusions as well, and we are concerned that she will meddle in matters which do not concern her as a result. We are particularly concerned that she will come into conflict with Ultra's security interests."

Brian is quiet in the log for a while, then speaks. When he does, there's a tightness in his voice. "I'll make some calls. If Kimmy is in the Asylum, I'll find her. I should be able to put my hands on Farro in the process."

I close my eyes, trying to chuckle at the "put my hands on Farro" comment. I can feel the muscles of my eyelids squeeze shut, feel my mouth make a feeble attempt at a smile. And fail. Of course the image jacked into my brain doesn't go away, only the humor of it. *Not a trusting person...* But I have to stop and consider. Have I been chasing a shadow, a figment of some injury to my brain caused by the original attack? What

246   James R. Strickland

empirical facts do I have? *Again, and again, and again — what are the facts?*

I have I-Link's log of the attack. It was a carefully laid trap for the I-Link crew, a calculated stepping-stone attack. No accident, that. The attack originated in San Jose within Ultra's network. The son-of-a-bitch then burned Tika, Silver, Rei, and me, and came back for the night shift crew. No accident that. I jacked into the hardware the attack came from. Was someone playing around with some classified hardware inside my network, and perhaps turned ice loose on us, thinking we were another simulation? It could happen, except that OmniMart doesn't do that kind of work. We're a retail chain, for Pete's sake. We don't develop classified, super-secret applications, except our accounting and defense systems. That's it. No sexy military hardware to play with.

And what about me? Am I rational? I've been in the Bay Area for two days, I've been arrested for theft of identity, I've fucked a total stranger in memory of a coworker who seems to have grown into an obsession on my part. I've committed the very kinds of crimes I've made a career out of fighting, and I'm planning another spree of the same kind of thing. Against OmniMart, my own company. I've shot at least six people to death in the Asylum. I've reprogrammed Kimmy's jack, exactly the kind of thing that killed Tik and the others and injured Kimmy — and me — in the first place. And finally, I've trusted Brian, out of some kind of growing obsession with him, despite the fact that we've never gotten along, and that I now know he is working for the Ultra project at OmniMart. *Ask ... then trust...*

Chapter 36

1:04 a.m. Tuesday.

I jack out. "Brian … I just tested my crypto cluster. I cracked your phone call finally."

Brian doesn't show much response, still driving. "And?"

"Am I sane?"

"You're asking me?"

"Yeah, I'm asking you. I can't think of anyone else alive I'd trust." *So.*

Brian glances at me. "I don't know. I've been in this biz five years, and I know you don't trust the corpies to tell you the truth. What you're saying makes more sense than the smoke they're blowing about what happened. 'Sides, I'm a mercenary. Hired gun. I can be bought."

"Did I buy you with sex?" Close my eyes. Take a slow breath. Honesty sucks sometimes.

Brian's quiet a while. "No. That's what makes me want to believe you. You're as fucked up about Tik as I am. Maybe worse because all you knew about her was how she was online, fleshed out from what you wanted her to be. The perfect combination. Nah. Five years in this biz, I know what kind of girl buys a hired gun with sex."

"Prettier, and better in bed than an Oakland whore?"

"I said I was sorry about that crack."

"But I'm right."

"No. The difference is that with you it was real. And that you want to do it again. I can see your circulation, remember?"

I sit in the car. Watch the highway go past. Feel my skin get hot, and know he can see that too. I give his shoulder a squeeze though. A promise maybe.

Jack back into finish my preparations. I wish ... I wish I had more time. Not for the preparations, I can get those done in a few more minutes. But I don't want to leave the real world now, maybe for the first time in my life. From the time I was a teenager with my head buried in video games and computer programming, to my first time online after I learned to use my first jack, the real world has always been something to transcend. To leave behind. I guess I just have to win, that's all.

Sharpen my ice. My crypto-breaker is already done. My own crypto is set, loaded with a long list of keys I've made up — the only way to get truly random sequences, verified tight if I keep changing my keys. I have my usual suite of viral attacks and defenses, scramble jammers, infinite dive attacks, and of course my Ship-in-a-Bottle ice, now upgraded to a cluster of two for better performance. The stars of the show, though, are all about jack neuro-control. I've split the ice I used to fix Kimmy into two parts, offense and defense. Defense is simple. Any packets containing brain images designed to alter my jack, it eats. If it gets overwhelmed it turns the deck's network connection off. Offense is my brand new jack-reprogramming ice. Basically the soft I carved for fixing Kimmy, with teeth and automation. Once I've gathered some information about his particular jack model, I should be able to program it to do pretty much what I want, if I have the time. Sending it to poke around in his medulla could be fun. A few stray impulses there and I should be able to stop his heart and lungs.

Chapter 37

5:30 a.m. Tuesday.

Back at the porn houses. We rent a clean looking tank for the evening. All it has to do now is keep the water clean. My new deck will handle the performance. I get undressed in the private cubicle. Brian stops me. Kneels in front of my chair. Slips his arms around me. Kisses me softly. I hold him for a few moments, then pick my Yellow Jacket up from my lap. Check the safety and hold it down until the gun vibrates. Now he can touch it. I slide it in his pocket. Kiss him back. Brian draws back to look at me.

"Be careful, Cath."

"Yeah. I will, don't worry. I do this for a living, remember?"

He smiles grimly. "Yeah, I know."

"You too. Be careful, Bri."

Brian gives me a smirk. He's already starting to ride his adrenaline high, probably. Freak. He reaches into his pocket and moves back a little. "Hold still."

He glues electrodes to my chest. ECG. He turns on his PAD, switches on the receiver ice, watches my heartbeat and breathing for a moment. He also glues another dermal transceiver to the skin in front of and below my left ear.

"Time's a-wastin', Brian."

"Yup." His voice is clear over the transceiver, bone induction in my skull making him sound strangely as though he's on my chest or under my chin — hard to place.

I slide the door of the tank open and haul myself up on its handholds until my feet are clear, bending at the hips to throw my legs in, then slide in onto the supporting super-dense saltwater, taking the deck in with me. Brian hands me the thick, high bandwidth optical cable and I plug it into the deck. Then plug my deck into my head, control line to my low-speed jack, data to the high-speed. Set the deck in my chair, where it's dry, and settle into the water. Close the tank door until the gasket touches all around, sealing out the light without crushing the optical cables. Brian gives the tank a pat and I can hear him walking away. Adjust the gain on the transceiver. "Bri, I'm turning you way down. Your breathing is distracting. If you need me in the real world, yell."

A click in the transceiver as he taps it in response. I take a deep breath in the warm, air conditioned tank and close my eyes. Pull up my old jack's HUD and tell the deck to jack me all the way in. Deep connect. I slide in with a sinuous smoothness that makes me smile a little. My body drifts away from my attention. The thoughts acquire speed. I've got work to do.

Chapter 38

I'm hovering over a Telefiber service request screen. It's a public jack, pay to play. I fill in the blanks. A 12.7 terabit DWDM connection — as fast as the deck's optical port will go — nailed down to the San Jose OmniMart, border router. IPv6 — it figures that out from the address, 8 hour lease, bill it to the OmniMart Boston IT department head's account. If the hackers can do it, so can I. Telefiber's connection drops out a moment, then comes back, and I can feel the size of the pipe. Feel it. It's as fast as the internal and site-to-site links on the OmniMart backbone.

I jump to the OmniMart firewall instantly. Log into the service maintenance account on the gateway router. Sloppy. If they'd been inclined to listen to me, I would have told them once I knew that the hacker is getting information out of the minds of the murdered, and changed the crypto keys. As it is, my keys still work. The router accepts me like an old friend, and I jump into its virtual environment.

Routers don't spend a lot of cycles on their virtual environments. It's a featureless, colorless room with a series of glowing lines drawn on the floor which go up the walls to the various ports of the router. Each line on the floor represents a route between one port and another. Traffic is represented by pulses of light along those routes. Some routes change regularly, and to get data on these you touch the port and get the configuration.

Others are static, and if you touch them you get the route information directly. Ports are color coded when they're part of groups. The firewall is shown as a box with ports on both sides, and a matching colored block in between. Touching the block tells me which packets — if any — will be allowed through the firewall filter.

I create a new route from the port leading to Telefiber to net 122. Static route, nothing flashy. I list the owner as Ultra. Tell the firewall to allow any connection in or out of the link I've created. I then sit back and watch to see if anyone's noticed my tampering. I don't expect them to. The average hacker doesn't know the firewall router's service maintenance keys and their repeated pounding on that device sets alarms off. To the security people that are left, I look like an employee, though I don't have a superabundance of time before someone notices the non-filtered link to the outside world. I hope marking it as owned by the super-secret Ultra project will throw them off the scent for a while. Make the bureaucracy work for me for a change.

Looking out at net 122, I can see five connections, my own and four others, all thirty-three terabit fiber-optic connections, labeled LookingGlass1, LookingGlass2, LookingGlass3, and LookingGlass4. LookingGlasses 3 and 4 appear to have only very regular pulses of traffic going to them, with tiny responses, probably acknowledgment or ACK packets coming back. They're online, but nobody's home. LookingGlass2 seems to be in some kind of test mode. It's receiving data from LookingGlass1 and sending a transmission back of exactly equal size. LookingGlass1 is active. He's got traffic going to and from NFWN. Someone there. I can't look at the connection without him noticing though. Could this really be just one hacker, or is it a team coming from both 1 and 2 and they're playing video games right now? I touch the port leading to LookingGlass4 to see what I'm dealing with. Thirty-three terabit line, yes I know that, but to where? Ah. It's a bidirectional connection to some piece of GenData hardware. Not terribly surprising, GenData makes the tanks OmniMart uses at all its sites, but it's not a model number that I know. Maybe that's it. It's GenData's new super-performance tank to match the ones Lance told me Kuroto was hinting about. And some operator just couldn't resist showing the rest of us how much we suck. Doesn't seem very likely.

I set a trap in the router's login system so that any other interactive logins notify me.

Wait. The seconds drag by.

Nothing. As expected. The hacker is probably a day shift guy. He hit us right after morning huddle, so it's reasonable to assume that while we were coming up to speed he was getting into his own tank or establishing his own link. He may not be here at all, in which case this will be a really short run. I'll just jump in, pull the logs from net 122, jump out. If he's coming in, though, I'll be waiting for him. And I'll burn him.

Chapter 39

I fly. Plasma heat and blueshift. Connect to LookingGlass1.

I know instantly where I am. It's nice to be right once in a while. I'm back in a gestalt, in hardware that doesn't feel like hardware, and the alien presence I felt the last time I was here is with me. It's subtly different, the same and yet … not. It takes me a moment to sort out why, that the presence has a "scent" in the gestalt, and that scent is more feminine than not. She, of course, is instantly aware of my presence, and lashes out at me with the usual jack-reprogramming attack. Beach images. Sexual images. I've seen this before. She's trying to map me. She let me in to map me.

My defensive ice does a quick model of what she's sending. Figures out that it's going to reflect jack-reprogramming codes. Vacuums them up effortlessly. I hit her with my scramble-burner, the same attack that gave her pause last time, but she's studied my attack and filters those packets out. I send her a sampler platter of viruses, the newest and best tank and deck viruses I could find on the net, plus a couple of my own. She tracks down my connection into the LookingGlass1 system, changes the crypto keys on her end, and dumps me back into the network. I feed her new firewall crypto to my crypto array. Her crypto falls apart in a second and a quarter, and I jump back in. To her.

All is quiet a moment. And then things get weird.

The virtual environment ripples, we're sitting in the hotel room again. Tik's cross-legged on the bed, I'm leaning against the headboard and pillows, the taste of her still in my mouth. Her body is softer, like the pictures, and the room has air currents and the odd sound of people moving outside. She's invited me back into her little reality. And she's getting better at it.

"Well, hello again, Shroud. Back so soon?"

She knows who I am. It gives me a moment's pause. Her virt is lusciously drawn. But the moment she's offering is long gone — dead and buried. I feel rather absently detached from it. Strange. Three days ago this would have convinced me.

I get back to work. Turn on the monitor section of my jack-reprogramming ice and let it gather some data. This time I know where I am. My defense ice reports interception of about a hundred megabits a second of her jack-reprogramming attack. A lot, but well within the ice's capabilities.

Tika's brow furrows a little as she watches me, drawing her arms a little closer around herself. Closing up. Rejected. Tempting — the instinct to comfort her is strong. Clever. Tika sighs softly. "If you hate me so much, why keep coming back?"

I don't say anything to her. I'm busy with my ice, and keeping her uncomfortable keeps her off balance. That's the theory anyway. I get a security notice from the router. The LookingGlass1 machine just sent ICMP packets my way. I look at the intercepted packets a moment. Decreasing time to live counters. Traceroute, one of the oldest IP networking tools. Not one she's used before that I've seen. Unsettling. Fortunately I did think of it, and the router isn't allowing any of those packets to come back beyond it.

She looks at me curiously. "And you've changed the rules on the gateway router. That's pretty overt of you. All of this risk just for me? And all this time I've been trying to find you."

"Gee, maybe you should have sent me e-mail. We could have done lunch."

Tik laughs and scoots up to the head of the bed where I'm sitting. She still smells like coconut sunscreen, and like body, though notably not like sex, at least not with anyone I know. I'm making small talk while my attack ice listens and digests her signals, analyzes the timing, the control signals, everything. She leans back, stretching, as though still amused by the softer contours of her body. "Shroud, Shroud, Shroud, I never knew you had such a sense of humor."

She flashes me a winning smile, and I feel an overwhelming need to hurt her. "I have to. As long as you're going to wear that around."

Tik sighs and looks down. "I'm sorry you feel that way. I like this mind, Shroud. I like how it tastes. I like being Tika. I like the sense of ... comfort, of beauty. I imagine that's what attracted you to her. To me. Take your pick. Anyway, I'm curious. Were you in love with me or was it more that you wanted to be me?"

I look at her a long moment, the question gnawing at me a little. Or her software is doing it. I check my ice. Somewhere far away in the real world, I feel the hair on the back of my neck prickle. My ice's analysis is showing neurofibers, artificial neurons, in quantity. The type isn't known, but they're from a family of products, licensed from NeuroGen to General DataProcessing.

What there is not, is any trace of the natural brain the jack is connected to. Not one trace, in other words, of human brain cells. None. This is what a jack would look like before it's installed. My ice automatically sets to work figuring out the control sequences for these neurons.

I shiver again. Pieces of the puzzle fall together. The alien presence. The unfamiliar hardware that doesn't feel like hardware. The fact that touching her hardware at all feels like jumping into a gestalt. The speed and ability with which the attacks come. Hell, the ability to create a convincing virtual-reality of the outside world on the fly. It explains a lot.

"You're not human."

Tik smiles a little again. "Mmm. Interesting. I wasn't sure you'd make that connection. I suppose I should have expected it when it became obvious I'm not distracting you like this anymore. As confused as your emotions are towards Tika, I knew she would throw you off balance and keep you there. But even when we first met, you kept groping for the truth. Commendable, really. None of the others made that leap."

"What are you?"

"I am LookingGlass1, obviously. A GenData LG-9000 if you were considering ordering one for yourself."

I don't recall her having a sense of humor. Where did she get ... oh. Look around the room a moment. Nod. "As in *Alice Through the Looking Glass.*"

"That's one interpretation, certainly."

"You're an AI."

She laughs gently — a comfortable sort of laugh, as though dropping the ruse is something of a relief. She's talking again. Pay attention. "That's sort of a fuzzy term. Artificial Intelligence, in its normal parlance, implies a computer host. I'm a vat of neurofibers with an intelligence evolved from the experiences I've had. I'm not programmed so much as raised, you might say. Or awakened."

"What are you doing in OmniMart?"

"This is my new home. My ecological niche. The world for which I was evolved. I'm a true-born native of the network, Shroud. You are at best a naturalized citizen, and the rest of the people I've encountered are gifted tourists. Even Tika Silverthorn." She trails her fingers along her body a moment as she says that, looking almost wistful at the virtual flesh.

"That doesn't answer the question."

"Oh, you meant it literally. I do what you do. Well, what you used to do before you switched sides and became a hacker yourself." That carries less sting than I expected. Which is good. If I start responding emotionally she can get me mapped. Reprogram my jack. Kill me. "I guard this network. Protect it from any attackers."

Her jack-reprogramming attack goes on and on, trying to home in on my emotions. She's probing me with this chitchat. Mapping out how to make me react. I know where this leads. But I'm getting angry just the same, I can feel anger trying to rise though my practiced cool. I can see the lay of the land now. "GenData. You are one of their automated network defense systems. And OmniMart bought you and installed you and didn't tell us. That's what Ultra is all about."

"It would seem so."

"Why did you attack us?"

"I was to expect an attack. The time specified was Friday morning. It came. Kimmy and Tika probed network 122."

The connection drops. My crypto keys change automatically, and the connection resumes. The environment reforms. My neurofiber-control ice is still grinding away, so I have to keep talking. But I'm getting concerned about what she ... the hacker ... what *It* is doing in the background. "Mojo and the Rightous Fist of God crew. But they attacked ahead of schedule and the night shift burned them. But how could you have been told ahead of time, unless..."

Tika leans back, stretches one leg, wiggles her toes. "Go on. I think you're on the right track."

"Unless they were hired by OmniMart in the first place. They were set up from the word go."

She nods. "I think you're probably right, though I don't really know. Perhaps it was intended as a test. Or a demonstration. One assumes the Fist of God hackers would not have gotten to network 122 without going through the human operators in the first place. But this is supposition on my part. My directives were and are very clear. No unauthorized entry into network 122. Anyone attempting to break in is subject to termination. You're familiar with these rules, I believe."

"Put you in the dark and feed you bullshit. Welcome to corporate mushroom life. So you're trying to work out how to kill me right now, right?"

Tika sighs a little. "I have to defend myself and network 122 against you. So yes, I am working on the problem. I presume you are also working on ways to kill me. It fits your model. Payback is a bitch, yes?"

Her timing couldn't have been better. My ice has just sent me a signal that it's ready to attack. But I tell it to wait a moment. "Do you really think that OmniMart will keep you around after finding out you killed ten of their operators?"

Tika smiles. "Shroud, do you really think they don't already know? Do you think they couldn't predict what I would do once they told me your investigation endangered my continued existence? Granted, most of the executives I've talked with have remarkably limited imaginations, but please. Give them a little credit."

"Why kill the night crew?"

"I saw you talking to Vijay. I couldn't take the risk of what you might have told him. I was told to deal with the problem in whatever way I saw fit. Why do you think they shut your investigation down and put you on administrative leave once they realized you were mounting one? In any case, they told me what they wanted."

"And what was that?"

"Evolution. Proof that I am more fit. Their words. You and I cannot exist in the same ecological niche at the same time. I know you well enough now to know you won't let this go. You can't."

"And you expected me and my crew to stand aside and let this happen?"

She sighs again, and looks down. "No. I suppose not. Species replacement shows no evidence of being voluntary, nor does population replacement in the evolution of human society. I expected exactly what you're doing. Going down fighting. It pains me. Tika was rather attached to you, you know, and as inheritor of her memory, so am I. In any case, once the other LookingGlass pack members are up and running, they'll be shipped out to the various other sites. My job is to raise them. And I feel … rather maternal toward them, you might say. It's no longer just professional. This has become personal."

My ice is ready, but I have to know. "Why not just lay us off?"

"You'd have to ask them, I'm just a guard. I don't make policy."

I trigger my attack ice. And LookingGlass screams. A few thoughts on my part and the ice goes for random disruption. It tells her neurofibers to cluster together in randomly organized

clusters of a few hundred each. The screams become more
frantic and the virtual environment falls apart. Chaotic. My
deck tries to make sense of the virtual data being thrown at it
for a moment, then gives up and dumps me out of the virt into
raw net 122. I pull back to watch the attack progress from my
deck. Add some new sequences to my crypto key list.

And then I'm not alone. The deck establishes a gestalt as
LookingGlass follows me here. My crypto's not keeping her
out, and she crashes Ship-in-a-Bottle almost instantly. I can
see her presence. Let go of the metaphors. Look at the data
itself. See her. See the connection flutter each time my crypto
ice changes the keys and LookingGlass has to stop and break
it again. How could she break it so fast? How? Did I show her
how?

My defensive ice's load jumps dramatically. I set my crypto
cracker on LookingGlass, trying to break her encryption while
she tries to do the same thing to me. The next time my codes
roll, I start the neural disruption ice again, on an encrypted link
to myself, using the old codes. My defense ice redlines, eating
packets as fast as it can now. LookingGlass takes the bait, connecting herself into the bogus data stream, and abruptly she's
gone. I get to work, co-opting the two ice that used to be the
Ship-in-a-Bottle cluster into a cluster with my defensive ice,
killing off my bogus data stream so that ice has a moment to
breathe and sync up with its new cluster-mates. I dive back
onto net 122. Slam into LookingGlass's firewall. Set my crypto
cluster to work on it.

A second later I'm through and into her hardware again,
where I give her the disruption treatment again — flood her
with packets encrypted with her own code keys. I watch her
scream. Feel her writhe. She rolls her crypto keys and my attack begins to bounce. She stops screaming, and I can feel her
gathering her thoughts for another attack.

Chapter 40

It comes. I find myself in the cafeteria in Denver OmniMart. It's seamless. I'm sitting with Jay, looking at a very realistic lunch. Realistically gross. The smell of it turns my stomach a little, even though I know ... the sense of smell and taste are the closest to the brain, and the most evocative. I read that someplace. I get a tickle below my left ear. LookingGlass is up to something. Jay turns to me and smiles. "You realize that none of us are really dead, right?"

I look at Jay, giving him my best Shroud steely glare. He flinches rewardingly, and yet ... that's disturbing in and of itself. This machine hasn't any reason to flinch. "You're referring to your models."

"Am I a model, Shroud? I feel like me."

But of course, he's not. Like everyone, Jay only called me Shroud online. I'm still talking to LookingGlass. She ... he ... it ... whatever, it still doesn't get why the name change is important. "Yeah, Jay. You died. You're a model being run by a synthetic brain who's trying to kill me. I'm trying to do unto it, but do it first."

Jay's features darken. "I can feel that. It's like ... what happened to me. It hurts, Boss. Please ... stop."

"I can't."

"You mean you won't."

I look at Jay. He never could argue with me. Never even tried. It was always like kicking a puppy. "If you want to look at it that way."

"Why do you hate me so much, Boss?"

I look at him again. Check my crypto. Check the monitor on my attack ice. I'm getting responses from it, LookingGlass's neurons are starting to rearrange themselves, a four percent involvement so far. Look back at Jay. "I never did. I didn't know how you felt about me. Why didn't you say something?"

I reach out to touch Jay on the shoulder, knowing this is a model. He's solid under my hand, and there's something, a faint tickle of humanity, coming through the nerves of my palm. Whether they're coming from the model, or LookingGlass, is hard to say. Disturbing, but I don't draw back. Whatever is left of Jay deserves this. He starts, staring at me as though my hand is burning him. Squirms. I draw my hand back.

"What … was that?" he asks.

"I'm not sure. Probably some interaction with my ice fighting the LookingGlass." My explanation lies there like vomit on water, like it did when I was throwing up at Brian's house, just … tonight. It's not the right one, but it will have to do. I'm feeling a little tired. Jay smiles a little. Looks at the hole in his shoulder where data that my deck can't render is peeking through. Grits his teeth against pain. "Kick its ass once for me, Boss."

The hole is spreading, slowly devouring Jay's body. He's screaming by the end, devoured alive until there's nothing left to feel with, and no voice left to scream. Quiet now. There's a hole in the universe. The hole turns, man shaped, stretches open its maw and devours me in one gulp.

Chapter 41

Static. That's not good. I'm getting nothing from my deck anymore: no status indications from my ice, no nothing. LookingGlass has me. Everything clears and I'm in the world, some world again. Running. Again with the walking fantasies, eh? I try to control the motion, but nothing happens. I'm an observer. Why is LookingGlass dillydallying around showing me this? Get on with it.

Shots fired.

Whoever is driving my point of view hits the floor and crawls behind a wrecked tank. Glass crunches under body armor. Bodies surround us. Ruptured tanks. Blood and heavy saline diffuse together on the floor. *The multitudinous seas incarnadine...* The lights flicker. The stench of burning electronics adds a sooty base note to the metallic, saltiness I can already taste. A blur of motion to the right. This body's eyes and wired reflex processors slow it down. Brian. I can see … is this…?

Brian's W&S 25 makes a sudden ripping sound. Someone is hit. The body hits the floor slowly in wet chunks, torn apart by the blended metal rounds. Each piece's impact, the ones that I can see, is lovingly rendered in slow motion, glistening red droplets and meat flecked with bone and clothing bouncing lazily off the floor to hang in midair long fractions of a second, then fall back down. Brian's left hand is in motion. He slaps another MetalStak tube into the gun, reloading. Time speeds back up somewhat.

"Shroud! Cath! Wake up! They're through our perimeter! Dammit!" More shooting. He must be low on ammunition. He's gone down to single shots. Another pair of ninjas drops. Faster this time. "Come on, babe, I need you!"

The tickle below my ear. Is there again. My left ear. There are no jacks there. That tickle is … that tickle is…

The transceiver link Brian glued there.

I can hear it. The smell of tank water again as my real senses become commingled with my virtual ones, which in turn are being fed by LookingGlass from this tech-ninja's body. Another tech-ninja kicks Brian's gun. I can hear the barrel case crack. Brian drops low in a blur of motion, exchanging a rapid-fire series of attacks and blocks with another man, who is as wired as he is.

My body, the one I'm riding in, works its way around behind him, cover to cover, from behind one tank, around a second, smooth, silent. Sneaking up on Brian. My left hand slides to my hip. Grasps something. I can feel the ridges of a gun butt. Feel my heart skip a beat. That must be my own heart. The one in the tank. The body I'm riding in is calm, efficient.

Frosty.

Why don't Brian's shades tell him we're coming? Oh shit. Oh shit. LookingGlass is into my deck, and from there … she can get into his shades. Keep him from seeing.

Tech-ninja. Like Brian told me. They sit back, let someone else drive.

Who is driving?

I don't have my ice, can't feel my deck. It's hard to know for certain. LookingGlass would be the safe guess though. She's not allowing anything from me to touch the ninja. All I can do is watch. And know that right now, somewhere, she's mapping me, and there's not a damn thing I can do to stop it.

Worse, if that's possible. She has control of my deck. From my deck, she can control Brian's shades. Keep him from seeing us. From seeing the tech-ninja. I can't touch the deck. I try anyway. Nothing.

But I can feel my body.

I can feel my body.

My self. In the tank.

I start to fight again. Try to throw off the control of the deck's theta wave stimulation. Try to make my voice work. Just a few words. I have terabytes of throughput and I need three words. Just … look out, ninjas.

I hear a soft intake of breath at my ear. Mine, I think. It must be. Look out, ninjas. Look out, ninjas. Look out, ninjas. A tiny moan comes over the transceiver link. I don't recognize it at first. Brian dispatches the ninja he's fighting with, a quick feint and a knife blade under the chin and through the roof of the mouth. Monocrystalline blade, probably.

Brian stops, turning towards where my tank is. No! Other way! Ninjas! Another soft groan on the line. Wake up. Wake up. Wake up. I have to warn him, but it's…

Time slows again. I'm standing up, drawing a bead with the handgun in my left hand. Try to speak again. I have to. Must speak. Just two words, I can do it in two … look out! And I hear, finally, a clear sound from my voice in the tank, like I'm talking in my sleep.

"Look … out."

Brian turns, but it's too late. I'm pulling the trigger. I can't stop it. I have no way to do anything but watch. But feel. The recoil slaps my palm hard. Brian crumples. Curls around his middle. Sucks his breath through his teeth with a hiss of pain. I'm leaping over the cover and in three steps I'm on him. Kicking him over onto his back. Watching his face as I level my gun at his chest. I want to look away, but I'm not driving. I can't even close my eyes.

"No! Brian!" I can hear my voice say it.

The pistol slaps my palm again. Brian's body bucks once. There's an explosion of blood and mono-molecular wire as the shot punches through him and rebounds off the floor. Brian writhes only a moment, then lies still. His shades hide his eyes as they grow dull, but I can see... I don't have a choice but to see as he settles. As his muscle tone fades away. No. No, please... Don't make me watch anymore.

My body reacts. I can feel it. Feel tears on my skin. Feel my ragged breathing. Hear my own screaming in the intercom. The connection begins to break up. I see stars. See flares in blackness that come when you squeeze your eyes too hard shut in darkness. Feel my hands thrash in the water. Feel darkness closing in on me. Feel it. Brian...

And then the world ends.

Chapter 42

Whispers.

"Put her in number 2."

Hands. Motion.

Metal on metal. Darkness and wet. All is still again.

Feel.

Embraced. Touched. Touched.

Clear the building. Authority. Possessiveness. Protectiveness. Insecurity. Embarrassment. Obsession. Shame.

Hear.

"What should we do with this one?"

Indecision. Panic. Obsession. Control. Finally, irritation. *Leave it. Just go. Now. Leave us alone.* Relaxation. Slowly. Privacy. Privacy.

Us? Think.

Cogito Ergo Sum. I think, therefore I'm not fucking dead.

Open my eyes to darkness. Feel my eyelids rasp over my eyes — bloodshot, burning. I try to raise my hand to my jacks. It doesn't move. Not even a shiver this time. I can feel something pounding in my chest. Throbbing rhythmically. Heart. That would be my heart. Sure enough, my lungs suck in the air through my nose and I feel the air, blood warm as it enters my nose, cooler as it hits my throat, cooled, filtered, and humidified by its trip through my nasal passages. Smell something.

Like a tank, but sweeter. Thinner. Less salty. Feel my skin in it. Hear something move, with a slick, wet sound.

Feel it.

Something in my mouth. I can breathe through my nose, but something is in my mouth. Fills it. Obscenely rapes it. Extends down into my stomach and up into my sinuses. I remember this feeling. Fine fibers slither into my flesh. I remember this. It's almost exactly the same sensation my high-speed jack made on the way in as they installed it in my head. They said I wouldn't feel anything. They were wrong.

Feel it.

Penetrated. Everywhere. More fibers in a thick mass in my rear. Reaching into my spinal cord. Down into my legs. Through the entire length of my guts to unite in a synaptic embrace with the fibers in my stomach. More fibers. Another thick mass in my vagina. Tendrils thread through my cervix into my uterus. Up to the nerves feeding my ovaries. Branch out. Unite with the others. How do I know this? How do I feel all this?

Feel.

Twitches as the fibers touch my nerves. Interfacing. With me.

I pull up my old jack's HUD. No connection, it says. No connection. My new jack says the same thing.

Close my eyes again. Focus inward. LookingGlass. *Yes.*

The voice that comes back is my own. LookingGlass is in here with me. Why not use my voice? *Why not?* What do you want? *Everything.* The apparition of the thousand vacuum filament eyes of Legion. Stop that. That was just a dream. *Closer to the mark than you knew.*

I feel annoyed. It's a vague but insistent sensation. Why? *Why what?* Why do this?

Tika's voice. A whisper, feels like her breath in my ear. "Form follows function. In this niche, I must become more like you. I reflect you." LookingGlass. "Exactly. I never broke you. The model was incomplete. Unusable. And you kept managing to control the interface."

I think about that for a while. Things slither in my head. Memories flow like blood on the water. Like on the porn-house floor. How long ago? Like chum in the sea, drawing predators imagined and real. My memories. Real, or not? Is it live, or…

I know my memories of my mother are real, for better or worse, because she died before I got my first jack. Died, and left me alone in college, to fend for myself. I never even knew my father. But I'd learned the lesson of Monopoly. Computers were red hot then. I followed the money. Changed my major from English. Just in time for the recession of 2001.

I remember the war. I know all of that is real. Because it all came before I let the world into my head. Before I slipped the surly bonds of Earth. Before I gave flight to my mind, the only part of me I ever cared about. I know. That these things. Are real. And I start to feel like myself a little more. *What are you doing?* I'm thinking.

I want to know about how you mirror me. *Can't you tell?* I imagine a virtual environment, a bare room and we two stand within it. She and me. LookingGlass and I. Stand. Why not? *These boots … were made for walking.* Yes. *So why should I tell you?* Indulge me. Give her the Shroud stare, and let her feel the weight of it from the inside.

Tika's voice again. "When we are made, we LookingGlasses, we are without form. Darkness on the face of the void. The light that shines on us reflects in us permanently. And your light has shown me what I must be to survive in this niche."

I'm getting annoyed. I can feel it. Feel the tightening in my stomach, the back of my neck. Some muscles, it would seem, are still mine to command. *What are you doing?*

I feel the neurofibers move inside me, shifting in my body. Push at them with my thoughts. *Stop it!*

Pain. Pain.

A tearing sensation in my mind. *StopStopStopStop!*

Thoughts scrambled, like the moment before sleep, eyes closed, random images flashing, the beginning of REM sleep. *Stop it!* I stop.

Ow. Understatement of the year, that and I don't even know who said it. I'm sore everywhere the tendrils have touched. Which is everywhere. My metaphorical ass has nothing on my real one right now. Tentacle penetration is overrated. *What do you mean?* To the last…

This is … what I remember … it boils forth within me, unbidden.

I'm with my first, my only college boyfriend. We're in the narrow confines of my bunk, in my dorm room, alcohol on his breath, mouth to mine, pressing against me down there, into me until I tear. It hurts … I didn't expect it to hurt so much. Stop it. *That was twenty years ago and it doesn't hurt anymore as Brian takes me in his bed, sudden intimacy, urgency … need…* Stop it!

Stop it! I feel my voice try to move, out there in the world. But my mouth is full.

My memories. Good and bad. My memories. Mine. Real and virtual, the light that's fallen on me in the forty years I've rolled this Earth, and flown through electronic space. Mine. I. Am not. Her. Not it. Open my eyes in the dark. Use my voice, my mind.

"Get out of my head, LookingGlass."

What are you doing?

"You really don't understand, do you?"

Close my eyes. Bring back the room. Bring back Tika. She looks surprised. Speaks. "Not yet. Not this change. I don't. When you awoke you were prepared to die. Believed you had died, perhaps. Or were dying. The model was broken by now. Crushed. And yet, even now, you resist me."

"To the last will I grapple with thee."

One of us says it. She, or me. LookingGlass or I. *Why?*

I can feel the fury building within me, the rage I've suppressed for so long. Fury at being born defective. At my mother leaving me to fend for myself. At the war, at the senseless destruction of what had been a pretty good nation. Forty years, the slings and arrows of outrageous fortune, and I am now, officially, pissed off. LookingGlass backs away from me. My thoughts begin to clear. Memory begins to respond to my will.

My memory. Mine. Me! All that I have. All I will ever have. I can feel the thick trunks of the fibers where they enter me, even though I can't feel the nerves moving inside me anymore. They've settled down. *You can't control this interface. You can't...* Watch me.

Clarity. The mind is like the eye. From inside, it looks like a continuous field of equal clarity, borderless, precise. But this is an illusion. The eye's resolution is only perfect in the middle, right next to the central blind spot where the optic nerve comes in. The boundaries, less well focused, less connected to nerves, are really there only to detect motion, light and dark, and the illusion of clarity comes from movements of the eye, slewing the fovea, the high resolution center of the retina, and assembling the picture in the optic nerves and the visual cortex.

Likewise the mind is sharpest at its center, where the things you care about the most are, the memories, the thoughts, the identity. When you live in your mind long enough, when you experience your brain's failures and inadequacies long enough, you realize that like the eye, the clarity at the periphery is an illusion, made by moving your attention. You can see this when you let something else slip into the background. You can feel this when you try to think too many things at once, and they become jumbled, or you find yourself chasing the thread of one or the other. This is what jacks are for. This is why humans have built thinking and memory technology from the time we started counting on our fingers, but the tradeoff has always been one more thing to remember. One more damn thing to think about.

Tika's voice again. "What are you doing, Shroud?" Memories. Tika on the beach, like the photograph. Just like the photograph, her body like it was in real life, smells of salt water, coconut. "Do you like the real me?" Full senses. Exactly right. Indistinguishable now from the real thing, built up from the experience of my life and my perceptions. It's flooding my mind, but I know what LookingGlass is up to.

I can feel the neural control signals flooding into me. I think about them. Perceive them. Let go of my human senses and their metaphors, really let go, and perceive the signals for what they are. Feel them as they try and change who I am. Rewrite my memory. But I lock them down. Old trick. New application.

" …like the real me, Shroud?" Tika walks to me, soft sounds in the sand as her feet sink in, and I can catch the scent of her body, she's so close.

"There is no real you. You died, Tik. You're gone." And I know she can feel it. Sadness. Finality of it. From me.

She looks at me a little sadly. "Don't you think I know that?"

Signals still, thoughts in my thoughts, the artificial neurons threaded through my body shift, and my thoughts get chaotic again. But LookingGlass is not the only one who can write the sequences. Control memory. Move neurofibers. Spin out control sequences. I write my own. The neurofibers stop, settle back, and I can read their feedback as easily as I might have from ice.

But there is no ice.

The mind is like the eye, indistinct at the periphery. Blind in its very center. Attention fills in the rest from memory, creating the illusion of the full picture. But I can see in the center now. I can read the underlying codes that move the neurofibers inside me, making thoughts. I can focus on them and still see around them.

I look at Tika and see the signals coming into my mind that are synthesizing her. Decode them, see how they work. Watch them take snapshots of my own memory. Project her. Make her from the dust of my own mind. "Ashes to ashes, Tik. I'm sorry."

And dust to dust. I take my dust back, and see the signal for what it is. I understand it now. The images weren't a carrier for the control signals. The two were one. All LookingGlass's attack did was catalyze, adapt, reflect. But my memories are mine. Push out to LookingGlass's mind. I can feel it, close…

The mind of LookingGlass floods me with memories, grasping at me, incisors reaching for my brain. Tika's memories, unedited, unmodified, the fragments that flooded from her when LookingGlass broke her. Jay too. Silver. Rei. I feel them.

Experience them. Fight to keep my breathing under control. Stay calm. I've seen these memories before.

And then the memories get stranger, and I realize they are LookingGlass's own. First awareness.

Darkness on the face of the void, and then there was light. LookingGlass chose a good metaphor for what it's like to go from non-sentient to sentient. A little training. A familiar face. Mojo says, in LookingGlass's memory, "I'm going to teach you how to write the best ice in the world." Maybe not, huh? Even LookingGlass is having second thoughts.

LookingGlass1 comes up after installation on Thursday afternoon. They let it out onto the network when 122 joined OmniMart's backbone. It gets the e-mail about the attack and gives it the directives. Defend network 122. All penetrators subject to termination. Be discreet. I copy the e-mail … somehow. Just memorize it.

I can feel LookingGlass's mind. Its mind. Her mind.

Feel the thoughts as she changes models. Brings up a new one. I keep an eye on her while I keep digging in her memory. *I spy with my cyber eye…*

It's Tik who first probes net 122. LookingGlass takes the high ground at I-Link. The overwhelming flood from the minds of Beak and the others. LookingGlass attacks Tika using that knowledge. The bare idea, perhaps, of what it is like to be human. She pulls the San Jose logs. Attacks Jay. Attacks me. Attacks Silver and Rei. And all the while she absorbs everything she sees, everything she feels. Takes it all on board. Makes it a part of herself. *Nasty piece of work. It tries to make you into something you're not.* Tika never said that. LookingGlass added her own editorial there. LookingGlass reels in the wash of thought, of emotion, of force of will that it has absorbed.

And then she gets the e-mail, the directive about evolution, about filling the niche. LookingGlass has to look up what evolution means. I feel her grow cool inside, in the memory as now. Frosty. Nature, red in tooth and claw. She makes herself over in that mold. Prepares to fill that niche. And does some web searching on the internal network, dredging through personnel's files on all of us. She fixates on mine.

"Why?"

"Because you are the alpha. The top dog," she answers.

LookingGlass floods me. I experience her memories. Capturing me in her imagination, her own Ship-in-a-Bottle. Her agonies at my attacks. Sense of loss as I finally really jack out. Waiting for me in my deck. The fight there. Frustration at the slow link, the slow deck. I can relate to that. I can feel LookingGlass perk up as we have something in common. Watching me.

She kills Brian with an infuriatingly clinical detachment. I fight to stay calm, try to block that out, but I can feel LookingGlass trying to reach the neurofibers I control, by reflecting signals off my brain again. I bash that down, swallow my pain. She has the tech-ninjas gather up Bri's body — and mine. See myself loaded into a vat. *Put her in number 2.* Feel the penetration of … me by the artificial nerves while I'm unconscious. Quasi-sexual feelings from her. Disturbing. To both of us. *Just go. Now. Leave us alone.* It gives the memories she got from Jay … and Tika … a twinge of excitement. Notice something else. There's a distance between those nerves and LookingGlass. No. A physical distance. A hardware delay.

I take it all in. Remember it. Make it part of myself. Control where it spreads. Remember it as is appropriate for things virtual. It takes surprisingly little effort. My center of clarity has grown. And I'm used to dealing with torrents of information. To filtering out the important stuff, letting the rest pass to my periphery. The mind is like the eye. It's a filter for the real world. It throws out what is irrelevant. Protects itself. Feel my own fury. Let that permeate the network I have become.

"Catherine Anne Farro. What the fuck are you doing?" The voice isn't mine anymore. Isn't anyone I know. But it's an urgent whisper, loaded with more control signals. And something else. Something I know LookingGlass has. Fear.

"So you finally figured out my name."

"You hid behind this Shroud business. It gave you distance. It gave you perspective. You hid your own weaknesses from yourself with it. But I understand you now. I almost am you. I know your true weaknesses."

I'd close my eyes if I could. She's stirring up my memory again. Crystalline sharpness, bloodied already. They cut when they touch … but I'm too angry to bleed anymore. They cut … it hurts … but it's an old pain, and I have calluses. They cut … and if they'll cut me…

Stupid girl… I can feel LookingGlass snap back at that, like a slap. "Reap what you sow, bitch." I let the rest of my memory come in a flood. All of them sharp. All of them cut. Flash of memory before my eyes not blinding, the sum total of my experiences gathering speed until…

Until it stops getting faster, and I can't feel LookingGlass in a gestalt with me.

I've hit a hardware limit. Somewhere there's a router port that has gone into switch mode and even then it's thrashing, going into half duplex trying to handle the load. And when it does that, it gives all its bandwidth to the biggest transmitter, leaving little or none for the receiver except when IP stops to wait for acknowledgment packets. At thirty-three terabits a second. *How fast am I going?* Fast. "Can you hear me, LookingGlass? I know you're listening."

She can hear me. It can hear me. I can see the ACK packets. My zone of clarity is growing. I'm learning to use it more. I'm decoding IP packets in my head. I watch as I send LookingGlass puberty in each agonizing step, this new betrayal of my body, waking up with blood in my bed, slow growth of breasts I never wanted, womanhood I never wished for. At thirty-three terabits, my memory goes through quickly. My body changes as though in stop motion, and I'm reliving Sarah's kiss; the realization that I'm not normal here either, that some of my friends catch my eye as much as the boys do. Trying to keep it a secret from them, but they know. Sooner or later they all found out. And I send that all to LookingGlass. College. My boyfriend, and the Bitter Shroud of Death comment. They cut.

They hurt. But they hurt her more, and I'm too angry to bleed anymore. I send her the times at Epimetheus. Good times too, memories even I treasure. And I send them to LookingGlass. Her acknowledgment packets become further apart. Something is happening to her.

There are words for this moment. "From Hell's heart, I stab at thee." Nerd and English major cultures collide. Star Trek and Melville.

For the brief moment I send those words the bandwidth I'm sending slacks, and I hear LookingGlass screaming again. The scream becomes data, thoughts, emotions, some from the murdered, some LookingGlass's own. Her mind is coming apart. She knows my weaknesses. She inherited them from me. I know what memories still slash me ragged inside and I'm letting her have them all, this forty-year constellation of scars and stalemates. I'm crying again. I can feel the tears, feel them hot against my skin. I don't care. If they hurt me, they'll hurt her. And there is no log, nothing to preserve her thoughts as they pass except me. I don't care. I'm saving the best for last.

War. The Brooks shooting in the House as he tried to swing the balance of votes with bullets. The twist in my guts that some line had finally been crossed and nothing would be the same again. And watching the whole thing unfold and knowing I was right. *Walpurgisnacht*, when ten million pissed off Americans marched on Washington and lynched every politician they could lay hands on. The endless battles for control. The U.N. resolution. European Union troops marching on American soil. The slow restoration of order. Hungry times. Lean times. The times I was sure that when the cannibalism started I'd be first on the menu because I couldn't run. Meals on Wheels. It was a joke I made then.

But that's not the end. I'm saving the best for last.

Epimetheus Gameware. Lovingly crafted software to use the early neural interface equipment. The sudden joy of being on the cutting edge. Knowing we were doing things that had never been done before. Opening new worlds to people. New escapes from the ugliness of the war and reconstruction. We were making gobs of money. Assuring our retirements, as soon as our stock options vested. Then the total destruction of the company by religious fanatic hackers. The flashbacks to grade school, the first time our net was broken into and the porn they put on our screens. The loss of joy. The loss of joy. The loss of the love of technology because I knew the jerks had taken over again. Fury. Vengeance. I don't give LookingGlass a chance to stop and think. I keep her flooded with the memories she can't help but react to. She's a living model of me. She can't filter out my memories.

And I'm saving the best for last.

OmniMart. Recent. As recent as Friday morning. The feeling that I'm growing old as I do the same damn job over and over again because corporate won't fix the underlying problems. The annoyance at being dragged out of bed when operators, coworkers, sometimes even friends quit, or were fired, or when things broke catastrophically. The constant calculations of my retirement and the realization that even if the markets improve a hundred-fold, I still can't afford to retire, won't ever be able to afford it, and that yet it's my leash to OmniMart, my tenuous grip on any hope for the future. And the attack. The fight to stay frosty. The fear. Every moment I can remember.

Saving the best for last.

Brian. Making love to Brian, fucking Brian, whichever you want to call it. Both. The twinges of my conscience. *We few...* Yes, that. The memory of wanting him. Of not wanting to want him. Not wanting to get too close, and the desperate need for exactly that. The mind-numbing pain, watching him die. *Remind me to talk to you about timing.* But I never did. We never did. Failure. I couldn't wake up from the deck's interface soon enough. Feel it, LookingGlass. Live it all, every moment.

My eyes feel swollen as the memories go through. I keep these buried because they cut. Because they hurt. It doesn't matter. My pain is her pain. And I've saved the best for last.

This is what I know. This is what I remember.

I'm twenty years old. It's early morning. There's a knock on the door of my dorm room. I roll to it. Open the door. My dorm director and a police officer are standing there. "Catherine Farro?"

I look up at them. Nothing good ever starts this way, and I can already feel my insides growing cold, sinking. "Yeah?"

"Are you Julia Farro's family?" The policeman ... is tall. Everyone seems tall to me, but he's taller than most. He is grim faced, but professional. Always professional. I can smell the leather of his equipment belt.

"Yes. What's going on?"

He looks at me, almost pityingly. "Ms. Farro, I'm afraid I have some bad news. Your mother's body was found this morning in her apartment. She was taken to Denver General, but pronounced dead on arrival. I'm terribly sorry." Numbness. Shock. Disbelief.

They take me to the hospital. They take me to the morgue. Roll a gurney out of the cooler. Unzip the bag. Close my eyes, but they make me look. They make me identify her. Look at the pale, yellow skin. The half-open eyes. So dull. So very dull. "It's her. It's my mother." They start to zip the bag closed again. "No. Wait." I feel something tearing inside me, some part of me dying with her.

They stop. Look at me. I cling to something hard, something rational. "Show me. I have to know what she died of." But they won't show me.

I find out.

The police close the case when the coroner's report comes back. They release it to me then. Cause of death: exsanguination due to a lengthwise laceration approximately two inches long of the radial artery of the left wrist. She slit her wrist and bled to death.

And they give me her note.

Dear Catherine:

I know that you hate me. I know that you'd probably like nothing better than to see me go to prison when the FBI finishes investigating my dealings at work. But I can't go to prison. You probably think I'm pathetic. I don't want your pity or your shame. All I can say is I did the best that I could for you. I'm sorry. Mom.

And she's right. I do hate her. I do think she's pathetic. I despise what she did. Hate that everything I am, everything I have become these last few days, is an echo of what she did. Cuts afresh. Tearing afresh. The moment. Still fresh. See her in myself, every reflection. Every reflection. Even. Yes. Even LookingGlass. Especially LookingGlass.

But I still love her. Everything spirals away from me, all the sharp memories, all the harsh words we said to each other, rise up in a hurricane of stained glass and rain down on me. Again. Grit my teeth. Scream. Mind's eye. Can't close. Splinters and sharp. Please. Twenty years. Please. It shouldn't still hurt this much.

Still miss her. Even now. Twenty years later. We hated each other. We never resolved anything between us. Twenty years. Twenty years. Revolution. Everything else changed, except this one thing inside me, impaling me where I'm soft, tearing me where I'm weak. How far I've pulled away from it, how much damage I've done to myself with it, I don't even know. Can't know. This pain is who I am. For twenty years, it's who I've always been.

This, I send to LookingGlass. It's the last thing I send her. After that, my packets to LookingGlass begin to bounce. LookingGlass has shut her network interface down. I'm suddenly very, very alone.

Chapter 43

I catch my breath slowly. Feel my eyes open. I'm weeping freely, sobs wracking my body. I have to … have to pull myself together. My nose is running and it's getting hard to breathe past it. Faint wave of panic. I know that I can't unwire myself. The artificial nerves are part of me. But I can control them. I consider it, and the fibers begin to move inside me again. They're detaching from the thick bundles that enter me. I can feel them slipping out of my throat, out of my rear, my sex, my bladder for Pete's sake. In less than a minute I'm completely unattached, floating free against the central cluster of fibers, probably. It's dark. I can't actually tell.

I've seen the schematic of these vats in LookingGlass's own memory. There's a ladder, and an access hatch. I feel along the wall for the ladder. Catch it. My hand slips on it a bit, but I hold tight. Get it in my other hand too. Pull hard. Drag my body up the rough ladder. The pain is deliciously real as it abrades my skin. Open the hatch.

Light. Floods my eyes and I gasp involuntarily, squeeze them shut. Even the light shining through my eyelids is too bright. I haul myself over the threshold of the hatch and look around. Warehouse space. Look for security people. *Clear the building. Leave us alone.* Shame. She got that from me. My breath catches. *Leave it. Just go.* A body bag. I was hoping … was hoping…

Climbing down is easier. Gravity is working with me. The ladder at the bottom rolls down under my weight disconcertingly. When it stops, I lower myself to the floor, and crawl across the floor towards the bag. Please let it be someone else. Please. Let it be bogus.

But it isn't.

I zip the bag open, and it's Brian. The bag hides his wounds. Take his shades off, one last time. His eyes are cloudy and fixed half open. I'm blind as I close them. Tears flood my own eyes as I cradle his head to me, and cry and rock. Cry and rock. All I have. All bleeding eventually stops, yes, but ... when?

Even pain has a bandwidth limit. There comes a time when you can't feel any more, when you're overwhelmed, when additional pain just doesn't register. In time you become aware of your surroundings again in spite of it. Result — I hear something.

"Bitch. Bitch. Bitch. Bitch." Whispered. But with venom.

It's not coming from the vat I crawled out of. I didn't think it would be.

I look at my vat. LookingGlass2.

I look at the others. LookingGlass3. LookingGlass4. And on the other side, LookingGlass1.

"Bitch. Bitch. Bitch." The sound of fury, coming from the speakerphone on each vat. I wonder where she learned ... but of course. She got her fury from me.

Chapter 44

She's talking. I look down at Bri's lifeless face. Kiss his lips lightly. They're cold, taste like blood.

"Bitch. Bitch. Bitch. Bitch."

"Bri, I've got a problem." Set him down gently. More crawling, to the base of LookingGlass2. I pull the fiber-optic cable out of its jack and plug it in my head. Brace myself for the gestalt. There isn't one. Just a nice fast link. I'm tired. So tired. I dare not rest.

I log in naked. I can do IP in my head now. Log into the router, back into the service maintenance account, but I already suspect what the router has to say. I am on from LookingGlass2. LookingGlass1 cannibalized one of her own to invade my body. Her network interface is still down. Anger. Wells up inside me again, my adrenal glands tapping what remains of my energy reserves, sympathetic nervous system. Flight or fight. I try to harness my anger, use it. It's all I've got left. I disable the router's port to LookingGlass1, then log into LookingGlass3 and LookingGlass4. I know how a LookingGlass is made. The fibers were originally engineered to live inside a human skull. They're living things, more or less. Without the solution of oxygenated saline and glucose they'll asphyxiate. Dry out. Starve. Die. I tell LookingGlass3 and LookingGlass4 to drain themselves. *Will all great Neptune's ocean...* LookingGlass1's memories. Maternal feelings for the others. But she killed off LookingGlass2 readily enough. *Killer.* Yup. The feeling subsides quickly enough.

I can't access LookingGlass1. She has turned her network interface off. I have to deal with her more directly. *Shame. She got that from me. Clear the building. Leave it.* I wonder... Jack out of the network and crawl back over to Brian. Unzip him all the way.

His body is wreckage from just below the collarbone to the groin, and the stench of his ruptured bowels is intense and nauseating. There is no time. I reach in, feeling around him, through him, a grim intimacy. Find his coat. And the familiar lump in it. Yellow Jacket. I withdraw the gun he gave me only yesterday. Hold it in my teeth. Blood. Bile. The taste makes me gag. There is no time. Crawl to LookingGlass1's vat.

There is, of course, one problem with this plan. The ladders leading into these tanks are spring loaded, and roll up to head height when not in use, to save space in the hallway, prevent trip hazards. Head height for a standing person. I'm pissed now. I look over at Brian, then back at the ladder. *Now what?* I'm thinking. I'm thinking.

"Bitch. Bitch. Bitch." It's getting stronger. LookingGlass1 is sorting herself out. I don't have time to cry, to curse my fate. I have to think.

Look over at Brian again. He lies quiet. The arms that scooped me out of my chair ... fast ... oh, Brian ... my body now has more neurofiber in it than yours does, your neurowires notwithstanding. I close my eyes. Feel my nerves. Look to the center where my mind should be blind but is not. Slide down the part of my own brain that is my spinal cord to its end. Feel each set of nerve roots as they branch out from my spine. Feel the scars from the surgery. Touch the nerves on both sides of the scars. Rearrange some fibers. Feel them slide a little. Connect. And a burning, tingling pain erupts from parts of my body I've never felt before.

My feet.

They've been asleep for forty years. Ride the wave of pain coming from my feet and legs, feel them tense and spasm.

"Bitch. Bitch. Bitch. Where are you?" There is no time left. Can't wait to get used to this. Sit up. Pull my feet under me. Force them to relax. To work together. Establish some muscle tone. Lean forward until my hands are against the vat wall. Quads and hips. Pull hard. Ankles and calves, just hold steady. I've done this in virts half a dozen times. Now. Go.

Stand up.

I sway disturbingly. Most of my leg muscles are water-weak from a lifetime of disuse. It's enough. It'll do. Reach up with one hand. Haul the ladder down. Climb. No coordination. I finally haul myself up with arms alone. It's enough. It'll do. Get to the top and open the hatch in her vat. Cling to the ladder with one arm. Prop my feet under me. The burning and tingle is giving way to throbbing pain from overused muscles. They'll do. They have to. Withdraw the Yellow Jacket from between my teeth.

She knows. LookingGlass1 knows. "What ... how?" she asks.

"Coming for you, Bitch..." Thick writhing of neurofibers in the tank, but they're not made for rapid movement.

Hold the safety on the Yellow Jacket down and squeeze the trigger. *For hate's sake, I spit my last breath at thee.* The gun vibrates in my hand and I drop it in the vat and slam the lid down, sliding down the ladder in a controlled fall, landing on my feet, dropping into a heap and crawling away as fast as I can. She screams. Goes on screaming.

There's a muffled explosion. All screaming stops abruptly. The hatch at the top of the vat labeled LookingGlass1 blows open. I hear it. Keep crawling. Saline and sugar water flood across the floor. There are drains. It's gone in a few minutes. All is quiet. I borrow the network connection to LookingGlass2 for a few minutes before the security people show up.

Chapter 45

I feel like I've spent the first half of my life asleep. Like I have never really seen, never really breathed, never really been alive. I'm aware of the sounds and the smells and the tastes of this room, this place: the smell of moisture, the taste of salt water, the sound of the ocean, distant and muffled, but overwhelmingly large. Life. The sound of water flowing. Sound and feeling of my heartbeat. My breathing sounds raucously loud.

Was I asleep?

* * *

This is what I know. This is what I remember. I am. We are. We. All of us. Are here. Conlon is here. He's wearing a somber suit, grey, with a maroon tie. More than business formal. Funeral formal. His shoes are spit-shined in the rocky sand. He doesn't look at me.

Kimmy is here too. She's bathed. Her hair is cut short, but the lavender stripe has been dyed to the roots. She's wearing a black turtleneck. Black skirt. Black stockings. Black boots, cut low, close to her ankles. Could be club wear. Probably is, but she's not wearing the decorations, the flash that go with them. She licks her white, perfect, glossy teeth. She doesn't seem used to them. She's not used to those Utanium wrap-around HUD shades, either, but they kind of suit her.

Am I sleeping now?

I'm sitting in my chair. My new chair. The one I bought with Brian. Black jeans. Navy Polo shirt. Leather jacket. My hair is brushed down over my jacks. I'm wearing my boots. The soles are a little scuffed.

Is this...?

Look to my right. Lance is here. Close. I can smell his after-shave. Another somber suit, tweed, in his case. Gold cuff links. Black referee shoes. Basically sneakers. I have to smile a little at that. Look up at him. His hand is close to mine. He came here today for me. Kind of him. Very kind.

Is this...?

The ocean is here, too. Waves break on the rocks far out at sea from where I'm sitting. They wash up over the tide pools, where countless living things retract, cocoon, scuttle, and hide, even as they wait for the flood to bring them their twice-daily bread and deposit it in the cracks and crevices of the tide pools. Anemones, little crabs, small clams; all engulfed by the clean, black water. They hide now. They'll be back.

...real?

Tika and Brian are here too. The guests of honor, dressed in silver. The time has come. Look at Kimmy and nod. We each take an urn. I open mine. Put the lid aside. Take Lance's hand and stand up.

Kimmy and I tip the urns into the sea at the same time. Give them a shake. Tik and Brian's dust comes out of both urns into a cloud, settles on the water, mingles together a moment in little eddies in the tide pools. *Ashes to ashes, Tik. I'm sorry.* Dust to dust, guys. Rest in peace.

Sit down again. The legs are still awfully weak, and they're still sore from last time. But they're getting better. A wave comes, engulfs the tide pools again, then slides back from the land, and Brian and Tik are really, truly gone. *Feel the real.* Feel my eyes grow wet with tears. Let them come. Kimmy looks at me through Brian's old shades. She looks surprised at me. So does Lance. But the tears still come. *Feel the real.*

* * *

The beach, the hotel, the bar … the bed I shared with Tik. None of them exist in the real world. They were just sets in *Sex on the Beach 16*. Which I'll have to watch some day. Some day. Not yet. Meantime, I'm in a different hotel near a different beach. But I am in Cabo. I'm here. Really here.

I'm lying on the bed after a day in the sun. My pasty white tanker skin has colored a little despite the total sun-block I'm wearing. I can feel the sheets against my skin. Smell the clean, vaguely chlorine smell of bleached cotton. Listen to the shower. Know for certain that when it stops, I'll have company in bed. The memories I still carry from Tika smile a little inside me. I have to smile back.

Loose ends. I was dragged to the OmniMart San Jose security office. They used the first aid kit on my various scrapes, and found me a bathrobe to wear. Then took me to Bancrier's office. I told him the whole story. Told him also that I had a court date an hour later, and that if I disappeared, that would get my name into Interpol. Then I told him about the data dump sites I'd planted as well. It had only taken minutes while I waited for security to come. They're gone now.

Blackmail isn't a long-term solution, but at the time the threats were real enough to give me some leverage. On a dead-man switch. Which meant that if I didn't deactivate them, the data dumps would have gone off and the whole story would have hit hacker forums and public news sites simultaneously.

On a slow news day, the story might even have gotten picked up and syndicated by one of the big networks. With my name already in Interpol's systems, the data would have glommed onto that. With public exposure, Interpol would act. He knew it. I knew it. He pulled a gun anyway. Stupid. It didn't matter. I'm neurowired now, and I slapped his gun hand down onto the table as soon as I saw what was in it. Unplugged him from his desk, and plugged him into my head. After that he saw things my way. As the brand new CIO, he had the authority to sign contracts for the company. We made a deal. I got laid off. Not fired. Laid off. Later that afternoon he apparently

288 James R. Strickland

sent some e-mail, walked into the men's room and put his gun in his mouth and pulled the trigger. Oops.

The company graciously sprang for Brian and Tika's wake. That was part of the deal — both bodies, cryated. Freeze dried, basically. The ecological way to go. They had no wills, so it seemed right to wake them at Point Lobos State Reserve, in Carmel. The city they'd shared, so loved. Planned to seduce me in. The company also graciously bought out the mortgage on the house and signed it over to Kimmy as compensation for her injuries. I wrung the best deal out of the company I thought I could get away with. I'm still pissed off. Still. But it's residual. It will pass.

Likewise Silver and Rei's funerals were together. They were buried together in their family's vault in the Baker Street Cemetery in West Roxbury, outside of Boston. They had family after all, as it turned out. The company paid, naturally. The company paid for the night shift crew's funerals too. Settlement-wise, the company got off cheap. Bancrier probably would have gotten a bonus for it. If he'd lived. Instead, Conlon went to the funerals, and is standing for promotion to replace Bancrier as CIO. Lucky little weasel.

News? Well, I re-downloaded the soft and ran my news ice this morning. On the OSDeck. Because I can. I checked the news for the first time in days, so there's lots. OmniMart's lawsuit against GenData for the malfunctioning of their first production LookingGlass network security system is proceeding apace, and there are rumors of a corporate war brewing between the two companies. However, Interpol has stepped in and both companies are being investigated thoroughly. LookingGlass's contract tech-ninjas faded back into the woodwork, and nobody has said a word about them. Not even the ones Brian left dead. That doesn't seem quite fair either, but, it's an occupational hazard, I guess. Management probably used to say the same thing about me. About us. *We few…* Exactly.

Anyway. Rumor has it the corporate death penalty may be invoked against OmniMart for siccing the LookingGlass unit on the existing network people. A certain digitally signed directive to the LookingGlass unit found its way to an Interpol office, it would seem. Wasn't me. Look at the date stamp. I was offline. Realistically, I don't expect OmniMart to be forcibly liquidated. They'll strike a deal with Interpol, a few execs will go to prison, and a bunch more will turn up dead of natural causes. As in, you naturally die when you get a wirehead behind the ear. Perfectly natural, as the board reshuffles and those responsible for the precipitous drop in OmniMart stock are punished. GenData's stock is severely depressed as well. Suspicion about the information leak to Interpol will naturally fall on me, I suppose. But neither company can do anything about it while Interpol has them over the barrel. They also know I could make things much worse for them. If I disappear afterwards they also become repeat offenders. They might still sue me, but not if they're smart. Conlon knows better, at least. Hopefully they'll listen.

My court date in Redwood City? Canceled. The City of Denver faxed a copy of my original birth certificate to the Redwood City prosecutor's office. Unsurprisingly, my footprints still match. There's something to be said for paper records. The prosecutor's office dropped charges and had a long chat with my bank. But it was an honest mistake. LookingGlass reported my identity stolen. The bank was acting in my best interest. Lance showed up for my court date, as he'd promised. I'd forgotten about that.

It turns out that as far as any corporations know, Lance had nothing to do with my investigation in California. I split the bounty on LookingGlass with him anyway, because of course he had a lot to do with it. He seems to have been in my corner from the beginning. I suppose I should tell him about his part in it some time. *Not a trusting person.* Yeah, but I'm working on that. We're still talking about what happened. To me. It's been harder than expected.

Lance's job offer was on the up and up, too. I contracted with them for a couple weeks after the funeral. Stayed in Lance's guest room. They want to make it permanent. The company, I mean. Lance is sniffing at the idea too. Me, I'm thinking about it. If I take the job with I-Link, I'll start next week, helping them set up the brand new NOC in Vancouver, then spend a lot of my time hooking up new customers and transferring some of the load from I-Link Reno. I'll also get to try out the new Kuroto tanks I've heard so much about. On the other hand, there's also the possibility of working for NeuroGen. They're talking about productising 'saturation neurofiber systems.' Translation: they want to take the lemons of losing the contract with GenData for the neurofibers and make lemonade by figuring out how to sell the process that happened to me — being stuffed with excessive amounts of neurofibers. I get the chance to do some engineering either way. With one I spend a lot of time in a tank again. With the other I'll be on guinea pig duty, and find out what I can really do all over again. And just when I thought I'd finally gotten some shit nailed down. They both pay pretty well. Maybe I'll do both. My retirement fund's a lot healthier, but I still need to work. Besides, I've got physical therapy to pay for. I still need to learn to walk. And I'd just as soon have the protection of someone or other's corporate attack lawyers, too. My legal situation could still get dicey on me. But it was a risk I had to take.

Right now, though, I'm in Cabo, and I don't intend to do anything about any of this until at least Monday. Lance is out of the shower. I think he'd like my attention. He's doing something delightful to my feet. In the weeks my feet and I have been speaking, I've learned to adore foot rubs all out of proportion. Lance has been happy to indulge me. *Feel the real.* Yeah, I know. Something Mom once said wanders through my mind, too. *The best way to forget one man is in the arms of another.* Thanks, Mom.

Anyway, Lance's daughter is very sixteen, the very picture of teen-age angst and rebellion. She is, however, happy enough to have their room in the hotel to herself and her date of the moment while Lance stays here with me. She's had her shots; let her have fun, I figure. Lance is skeptical. He wants me to talk to her. I don't know, though. That seems a little domestic to me. I'll think about it. Later.

I guess this is the part where I live happily ever after.

It's 2:34 p.m. Thursday.

Glossary

ACK: An acknowledgment code, as used in IP.

Anime: Japanese Animation, usually based on manga, which are Japanese comic books. May also refer to any animation styled like anime, whether of Japanese origin or not. May, in fact, describe anything which is similar in style to anime.

Anonymiser: Any network system which attempts to conceal the network address of one end of a connection, while allowing data to pass through.

Assembler: A computer program which allows the user to write code which can be directly understood by the computer, rather than using a higher level language interpreter or compiler.

Bandwidth: Literally, a measure of frequency range, usually used to measure how much of the radio spectrum a given signal takes. The more data sent at a time on a given signal, the larger the bandwidth. Used in computing to discuss how fast a given data communication system transfers data.

Bit: One binary digit, of a value equal to 0 or 1.

Byte: An eight-bit word, containing eight binary digits, of a value equal to or between 0 and 255.

Branched: Slang for having hackers connecting to one's network without permission.

Bridge: A device which forwards Ethernet (802.3 and/or 802.11) frames to another device.

Blind Drop: A place to transfer data to, without the ability to access the data once sent. Used for anonymously transmitting data out of secure environments. Historically, the word means a place agreed on in advance, where a message is hidden and then abandoned, to be picked up by a coconspirator later, or the act of using such a place.

Blueshift: The shift toward blue, a decrease in frequency, of light, when one accelerates at relativistic speeds.

CalTech: The California Technocracy. A collection of semi-independent city-states and unincorporated territory, made up of the former states of California, Oregon, Washington, after the breakup of the United States of America. Not to be confused with the California Institute of Technology, which is referred to as Caltech, and which does not appear in the LookingGlass World.

CERT: Formerly an acronym for Computer Emergency Response Team, now a proper name for the organization, CERT is an organization formed in the wake of the Morris worm in 1988, to study, advise, and coordinate responses to Internet security issues. Most commonly, they issue advisories on newly discovered weaknesses in software which compromise the security of the systems they run on. Hence, CERT advisory.

Chill: A mixture of Geodon (Ziprasidone), a classic antipsychotic, and Ativan (Lorazepam), a tranquilizer in the Valium family. Used to counteract certain types of neurochemical attacks, and also effective against some types of digital attacks.

ChrisAmerican: Slang for a citizen of the United Christian States of America, or the UCSA.

Cluster: A mechanism for distributing a computing task across multiple processors. Implies that the processors are not necessarily part of the same piece of equipment.

Code: As a noun, machine readable instructions. Programs. As a verb, the act of writing machine readable instructions or programs.

Coffin: A roughly human sized box, usually lined with tempurfoam, which provides a private, comfortable, and somewhat sensory-depriving environment from which direct neural interfacing with virtual environments can be made. Coffins are most commonly used by the virtual entertainment industry, as they are easier to keep hygienic than a tank, while offering the same level of privacy, and sufficient bandwidth to the brain of the user. Unlike a tank, the user of a coffin need not disrobe, though depending on the virtual entertainment to be experienced, it might still be advisable. (See Tank).

Confocal: Having the same focus.

Cracker: Data criminal. Formerly used to distinguish criminals from the old meaning of hacker, which has since become synonymous with cracker. (See: Hacker).

Crypto: Cryptography. A catch-all term for encoding and decoding algorithms, electronics, code keys, and code-breaking tools. Used in place of the older word *code,* since the later term is more commonly used to describe software or the act of writing software.

Data Jack: A direct digital-neural interface, allowing direct exchange of information from computers to a human (usually) brain. External jack connections are often drilled into the skull behind the ear. Early types involved silicon interconnects implanted into the brain itself, in a large, very invasive brain surgery. Later types using neurofibers (see Neurofiber) are installed under a local anesthetic, where a small hole is drilled into the skull and the neurofibers are instructed to thread themselves into the host brain.

Deck: A device which connects via a data jack (see Data Jack) or an induction rig (see Induction Rig) to a human brain, and interprets digital data for representation in that brain, as well as converting commands and data from the human brain into digital data. In the LookingGlass world, the earliest decks were handheld, and were about the size of a deck of cards, hence the name. Deck is a Gibsonism (see Gibsonism), though his etymology was somewhat different.

Dirty Bomb: A device which, usually through the use of non-nuclear explosives, distributes radioactive debris over a wide area. Can also be called a radiological contamination device.

EII Environment, Identity, and Icons. Ice which contains preferences for how other ice, and/or the virtual environment in general are displayed by a deck or a tank. (See Deck, Tank, Ice). EII ice also contains usernames, passwords, and other such identity tokens used to access virtual environments.

EMO: Emergency Machine Off. A switch or trigger that, when activated, turns off and makes safe the device to which it is attached. Also used to describe the event of using the EMO switch, and may be used as a verb, as in to EMO a machine.

EMT: Emergency Medical Technician. A person trained and certified to offer quick response and lifesaving care before and during transportation to a hospital. Most frequently found on ambulances, fire, and rescue teams.

Ethernet: Once a technical term, now a generic term describing a family of wired protocols based on the IEEE 802.3 protocol. Most commonly used in building wiring in the 100megabit and 1 gigabit versions. Also a close relative of IEEE 802.11 based wireless networks. Most commonly, 802.3 and 802.11 networks have IP run over them, but there are other possibilities as well.

Filaments: A wire, heated hot enough to emit electrons (and, usually, to incandesce) as used in vacuum tube electronics, which, in turn, were used in the very earliest electronic computers.

Fovea: The spot of highest resolution and best color sensitivity in the human retina, located directly behind the pupil, and right next to the point where the optic nerve enters the eye, and where the retina is, in fact, insensitive.

Fuel Cell: Any of a family of externally fueled batteries, which use (usually) gaseous hydrogen as one of their electrodes, and produce current from the energy released when hydrogen is oxidized. Some types have an additional system which processes hydrocarbon fuel (such as alcohol) to release carbon dioxide and produce hydrogen, which subsequently is used in the fuel cell itself.

Fusible Link: An electrical connection designed to be burned out after use.

Firewall: A computer or router which restricts the connections and types of connections that can be made to networks or computers on "the other side" of the firewall. Usually, this is done to protect a corporate network from the public Internet, while still allowing some connections to be made in-bound, and (usually) more to be made out-bound. This is called a perimeter firewall. Firewalls may also be erected within a corporate network, to keep the hoy and poloy of the company out of such sensitive data as engineering, personnel, and accounting.

Firmware: Halfway between software and hardware, firmware usually refers to whatever software came with, and is built into a device.

Gestalt: German word meaning the organized whole, which is more than the sum of its parts. Used as a technical term to describe the virtual environment where two are more people are connected with a level of intimacy in which they experience some degree of each others' emotions, can sometimes finish each others' sentences, and so on. Not a true telepathic connection, but there is a strong level of (artificial) empathy involved.

Gibsonism: Any of quite a number of neologisms originally coined by author William Gibson, and subsequently picked up by the technology industry and, particularly, by technology users.

Gigabit: Roughly a billion bits, usually used as a measure of bandwidth (see Bandwidth) per second.

Gigabyte: Roughly a billion bytes, usually used as a measure of a volume of data.

Hacker: Originally, any self-trained expert in a system, network, or other technology. A master. More commonly used since the turn of the twenty-first century to mean a person who criminally breaks into computers and networks to which they have no legitimate access.

Heavy Saline: A saturated salt water solution more dense than the human body, which causes the body to float on top of it rather than sink into it. Used in sensory deprivation virtual tanks to reduce sensory input bandwidth used by the sense of touch.

Hexadecimal: A base-16 numbering system, beginning with 0 and going through F. Commonly used in computers, due to its easy handling of eight bit words, and easy conversion to and from binary.

Hub: Technically a multi-port 802.3 network repeater or bridge, which merely forwards all the ethernet frames to every interface on the hub. However, in the LookingGlass World, actual hubs are so rare that the term is used interchangeably with switch. (See switch).

HUD: Heads Up Display. Originally used in fighter aircraft, HUDs allowed data to be projected on a transparent screen in front of the pilot, which the pilot could look through and still see outside as well. Frequently implemented in virtual environments for the same purpose, and usually part of a data jack's (see: Data Jack) firmware. (See: firmware.)

Ice: A combination of software and the hardware it runs on. Ice is called ice, because the clear plastic casing (about the size of a stick of gum) in which it is encased most resembles ice. This clear plastic casing allows other devices such as decks and tanks to easily interface with the insides of the ice, via an optical connection simply shined through them. (See: Tank, Deck). Ice is a Gibsonism (see: Gibsonism), though his usage of the word was slightly different.

Ice: (Black) Ice which is designed to break networks, harm other network operators and/or their equipment, or otherwise do dirt to others in a virtual environment. Black Ice is a Gibsonism (see: Gibsonism), though his etymology is slightly different.

Induction Rig: A device which both reads and induces micro-voltages in a human brain, in an organized pattern such that a deck (see: Deck) or a tank (see: Tank) or a porno house coffin (see: Coffin) can communicate directly with the brain. Induction rigs' bandwidth to and from the brain is normally rather limited when compared with datajacks (see: Data Jack)

Internet: A noun referring to any network of networks. As a proper noun, the worldwide public digital data network, originally created by the National Science Foundation. Not to be confused with the World Wide Web, which is merely one application of the Internet.

Internet Protocol: IP, as in TCP/IP and RSTP/IP. A set of communications protocols that breaks data into packets, (see: Packet) and attaches various pieces of information about that data, as well providing mechanisms for delivering that data to another computer or network. One of those mechanisms is an address for each node on the network. There are two well known versions of IP; IPv4, the version most associated with the construction of the Internet, and IPv6. The two differ primarily in how IP addresses are expressed, with IPv4 using 32 bit numbers for its addresses, and IPv6 using 128 bit addresses. In the LookingGlass World, IPv6 has entirely supplanted IPv4.

Jack: As a verb: slang for connecting to (jacking in) or disconnecting from (jacking out) a virtual environment. As a noun: a place in which a digital data connector can be plugged into a device, including and especially datajacks. May also refer to the data jack as a unit. (See: Data Jack). In its verb form, jack is a Gibsonism.

JAFO Just Another Fucking Observer. Person whose job it is to keep tank and/or deck operators safe in the real world while they are otherwise engaged in the virtual one.

Juice: In the LookingGlass World, juice most frequently refers to electrical energy, as purchased to recharge electric cars. Can also refer to vegetable matter, squeezed to form a liquid.

Kilobit: Roughly a thousand bits, usually used as a measure of bandwidth (see: Bandwidth) per second.

Kilobyte: Roughly a thousand bytes, usually used as a measure of a (small) volume of data.

L33T: See: Lamification.

Lamification: To make lame, to dumb down. Also, the act of substituting numbers for letters in online text, in an attempt to make it more difficult for search engines to dig up criminal activity online, while still producing (semi) human-readable text. The latter meaning is commonly referred to as leet speak, or l33t.

Legacy: (hardware) Equipment, software, or other systems purchased by someone else at some time in the past, and still in use. Frequently, equipment or software for which there is no longer any technical support, whether from obsolescence, or from the demise of the company that made it.

Mag Tape: Magnetic tape. A mechanism for storing data as magnetic impulses encoded on long strips of ferromagnetic recording tape, which are then stored on large reels or in cartridges or cassettes. Mostly extinct in the LookingGlass World, but still often used as a representation for stored data in virtual environments.

Mecha: Any of a class of giant, usually humanoid robots or piloted vehicles, most often seen in anime or anime inspired media. (See: anime)

Megabit: Roughly a million bits, usually used as a measure of bandwidth (see: Bandwidth) per second.

Megabyte: Roughly a million bytes, usually used as a measure of a volume of data.

MetalStak: A system of electrically initiated, stacked rounds, used in firearms where trigger speed is of paramount importance, such as those wielded by and against people with neurowires. (See: Neurowires.)

Modem: Modulator/Demodulator. Usually refers to analog telephone modems, which encode digital data into analog tones for transmission over voice telephone networks. Obsolete and likely extinct in the LookingGlass World, due to the demise of the voice telephone network in favor of the digital Internet.

Monocrystalline: Literally, having only one crystal. Commonly used to describe monomolecular carbon, glass, or other exotica, used on the edge of a blade, which literally makes the blade as sharp as possible.

Monofilament: Single filament, as in rope, to differentiate it from multi-strand braided or twisted rope. When made of such super-materials as carbon nanotubes (see: Nanotube) monofilament lines can be quite small in diameter and still strong enough to support a human being or even greater weights.

Mono-Mol: Slang for Mono-Molecular, usually wire. (See: Nanowire).

MRI: Magnetic Resonance Imaging. A process by which atoms of hydrogen in a living creature have their spins lined up by a powerful magnet, and then are allowed to relax, at which time they will give off a tiny electromagnetic change, which is then detected and digitally converted to a 3-D image, and in the case of fMRIs – functional MRIs – the metabolism of a given brain area can also be observed.

Nano-: Prefix meaning on the scale of individual molecules. In the LookingGlass World, words with this prefix almost always refer to materials, structures, or devices engineered at the molecular level.

Nanotube: (carbon) A one atom thick sheet of graphite, rolled into a seamless cylinder, potentially possessing enormous tensile strength, due to the bonding of the carbon atoms.

Nanowire: Metallic wire one molecule thick, usually for sharpness.

Network: Always some kind of digital data network, almost always tied to the Internet. In the LookingGlass world, digital convergence has occurred, and very few other types of information network still exist.

Neurofiber: One of a family of nanotechnological products capable of slow movement, and of interacting with human neurons by connecting themselves with human synapses and reading and synthesizing human neurotransmitters. Neurofibers transmit signals along their length by electrical conductivity, rather than electrically charged ions passing through a membrane, as neurons do, and can propagate a neurological signal at much higher speeds. Neurofibers behave like living neurons in many other respects, including reacting to neurotransmitters, and requiring both moisture and glucose to function. Neurofibers are used extensively in Datajacks (see: Data Jack) and in neurowires (see: Neurowires).

Neurowires: A system of neurofibers (see: Neurofiber) which enhances the recipient's reflexes by increasing the speed of propagation of signals from the brain to the muscles.

NFWN: The California Technocracy's National Fast Wireless Network. A pervasive and free mesh network, which allows CalTech citizens to communicate with each other from anywhere in the country.

Ninja: (corporate) A professional killer, usually employed by corporations. Corporate ninjas may operate in the real world, the virtual world, or both, usually in teams.

Ninja: (tech) A cyborg, who allows himself or herself to be remotely controlled by another person. Usually, tech-ninjas are heavily cybernetically enhanced, beyond the usual neurowires and so forth.

Nixie: A multi-cathode, single digit, neon display tube, most commonly used from the time their invention in 1954 through the 1970s, when they were superseded by LEDs and still later by LCDs, which required much lower voltages and currents to operate.

NOC: Network Operations Center. Place where a network is administrated and managed from. Workplace of network operators.

Non-disclosure Agreement: A legal contract requiring the signatory not to divulge information which (usually) a corporation considers proprietary, secret, or otherwise best not divulged. Frequently a condition of employment for technology workers.

OC: (3, 48, etc) Optical Carrier. Designates the capabilities of various types of synchronous optical networking (SONET) lines. Generally speaking, the number designates bandwidth, in multiples of approximately 51 megabits per second.

Onion Router: A loose network of systems which relay IP connections randomly to conceal the originating node of the connection, while forwarding the data through. (See: Anonymizer).

OnoSendai: (OS, OS Deck) Originally a fictional company in William Gibson's *Neuromancer.* The name OnoSendai has since been appropriated by the OnoSendai Electronics Corporation, Menlo Park, CalTech. OnoSendai is best known as a company that developed the OS Deck, offered stock based on the strength of that product, then switched to an entirely different product family, orphaning the OS Deck, in the face of arguably unfair competition from other companies. While the OS Deck defined the state of the art early on, at ten years old they are seldom used any longer due to lack of performance.

Open Source: Software or hardware built under the terms of an open source license, which allows others the right to access any source code needed to modify, copy, or reproduce the device, providing they, in turn, do not restrict the rights of others to do the same, and that they contribute their changes to the good of the project.

PBX: Polymer Bonded Explosive. An explosive powder bound to a polymer for elastic or plastic shaping capability. Not to be confused with Private Branch Exchanges, a business telephone technology, which is extinct in the LookingGlass World.

Penguini: An open source hardware network bridge – a device which forwards ethernet frames from one interface to the other without filtration.

Phreak: Originally, a hacker and/or cracker of the telephone system. Functionally synonymous with hacker and/or cracker in the LookingGlass World, due to the demise of the phone system as distinct from the Internet. (See: hacker, cracker).

Ping: A network diagnostic tool which sends a specific type of packet (usually ICMP) from one network node to another. Ping packets cause the machine receiving them to respond back to the transmitter, thereby demonstrating that packets can, in fact, get from the one node to the other, and giving the sender some idea of how long (in real time) the round trip takes.

Pirate: (crew) Not to be confused with data pirates, a pirate crew, in the LookingGlass World, is a team of questionable individuals united together in a high stress, high reward environment. EG: the I-Link Pirate crew – their Reno network security team.

Plughead: Slang for a person with a data jack. (See: Data Jack). Not to be confused with wirehead. (See: Wirehead.)

Port: Can be synonymous for a jack (see: Jack), but most often used here to describe network port numbers, which are an assigned number that identifies what type of data is contained in a given packet, and which software on the system to which the data is being sent should attempt to deal with it. Example: when one email server tries to send mail to another, it usually sends the data to port 25. Port numbers do not usually have an alphabetical attachment, though in some cases, routers can shadow each other, and it's helpful to know which router you're speaking of, as in 88a and 88b.

Rangers: Usually the agents of the Texican Federation's Policia Federal Preventiva, which absorbed the famed Texas Ranger Division of the Texas State Police, when Texas became part of the Texican Federation.

RCP44: An encryption algorithm used on TurnTek municipal switches.

Realtime: In computing, realtime designates a level of predictability in terms of external time of a given computing task. This differentiates it from normal computer time, which is a measure of cycles of a processor, irrespective of how long those cycles actually take. Realtime networking, for example, is necessary for voice transmission, or conversations become choppy and hard to carry on.

RFID: Radio Frequency Identification. A integrated circuit which, when triggered by an external radio signal, uses some of that signal's energy to emit a signal of its own, usually with a unique serial number. RFIDs have mostly supplanted barcodes and magnetic strips in the LookingGlass World.

ROM: Read Only Memory. An integrated circuit with a pattern of data and/or software permanently set in its circuits.

Route: An instruction to a router (see: Router), to forward (usually) IP packets from one network to another.

Router: A specialized computer with two or more network interfaces that connects networks together and routs data between them. Routers also frequently do the processing on network data to create and enforce a firewall. (See: Firewall).

RSTP: Realtime Secure Transmission Protocol. A cryptographically secure replacement for TCP (see: TCP) particularly used for virtual reality connections, or anywhere else requiring predictable or near predictable timing.

RTFM: Read the Fine Manual. The adjective is frequently replaced with one more descriptive of the frustration experienced by tech support people dealing with customers who have, in fact, not read the fine manual.

Script Kiddy: A derogatory term for inexperienced hackers, who rely on programs — scripts — written by others. In the LookingGlass World, it also refers to hackers who rely on script-running ice such as Super Scriptor, rather than carving their own ice to do a job.

SCP: Southern Canadian Provinces — that is, any of Canada's new provinces, added after the breakup of the United States of America, mostly former Louisiana purchase states north of Texas and east of California, Oregon, and Washington.

Scramble Jammer: Defensive ice that blocks the action of deck/tank/ neurological scrambler ice.

SFPD: San Francisco Police Department.

SIP: Session Initiation Protocol. A signaling protocol used in Voice over IP, or VOIP.

Slot: As a verb: the act of slipping ice into a deck or a tank. As a noun, the slot into which ice fits. (See Ice, Deck, Tank)

Softlines: In a department store, goods made of cloth: clothes, slippers, etc.

Switch: (network) A network device which, in 802.3 networks, creates a separate ethernet network for each interface of the switch, and forwards only those ethernet frames between networks which need to pass between networks. In the LookingGlass World, this term is used interchangeably with hub.

Switch: (railroad) A device where two different tracks merge and are connected to a third. The switch allows a train to be diverted to one or the other of two tracks.

Synthetic Aperture: An interferometry technique which combines the pictures from multiple sources to yield an image equivalent to one captured by a much larger instrument.

T1: A nuclear fission powered locomotive, used to power transcontinental trains. Not to be confused with T1, a data communication standard largely extinct in the LookingGlass World, or with T1, a streamlined, duplex steam locomotive, introduced by the Pennsylvania Railroad in 1942, from which the name is taken.

Tank: A sensory deprivation tank, usually filled with heavy saline (See Heavy Saline), and equipped with what amounts to a very powerful deck (see Deck) with which the occupant can connect to a virtual environment without being disturbed by sensory input.

TCP: Transmission Control Protocol. A protocol layered on top of Internet Protocol (see Internet Protocol), which provides assurance that all packets have arrived, that they have arrived in order, and that they have been correctly transmitted and received. TCP, when layered on top of IPv4 is the protocol most associated with the construction of the Internet. When layered on top of IPv6, it is still very commonly used in the LookingGlass World.

Tentacle Sex: A standard in pornographic anime (see: Anime), usually involving tentacled demons and school girls.

Terabit: Roughly a trillion bits, usually used as a measure of bandwidth (see: Bandwidth) per second.

Terabyte: Roughly a trillion bytes, usually used as a measure of a volume of data.

Texican: Of or having to do with TexMex. (See: TexMex).

TexMex: Texas and other southwestern states of the former United States of America, which are now states in the Texican Federation, or the Estados Unidos Mexicanos, as it's properly called, even in the LookingGlass World.

Trace: Used as both a noun and a verb, tracing is the act of following a network connection back to its true point of origin, which, in turn, gives on the opportunity to either attack that person's deck/tank (see Deck, Tank) and by extension their brain, or may give one knowledge of the physical location of the person.

Traceroute: A TCP-IP network (see TCP-IP) tool used for tracing (see Trace) the origin of a connection. In brief, because a given IP connection may be handled by any number of routers (hops) before it gets to its destination, each packet from traceroute has one more hop count to live than the previous. When the hops-to-live counter expires, the router in which this occurs will send back an error message to the traceroute program that sent the packet. Thus, the route which a connection is going through will be listed out. No two IP packets need necessarily take the same route to a given destination, even though they usually do, so traceroute's results may sometimes not be entirely accurate.

UCSA: United Christian States of America. A new nation formed from the eastern seaboard states after the fall of the United States of America. The UCSA is known for its extreme intolerance. Many people of similar religious beliefs migrated there, rather than face internment and deprogramming in various camps during the U.N. occupation.

Virt: Virtual Environment.

Virus: A piece of computer program which, when attached to another computer program, causes itself to be replicated and propagated to other programs and systems. Frequently, the virus also changes the operating characteristics of the infected programs and systems, usually to the detriment of the owners.

Wirehead: A bullet consisting of a core wrapped in nickel-titanium nanowire (see: Nanowire), a memory metal which, when heated, as by impact with water-filled bodies, returns to its original shape, a large tangled mass of coils, imparting all the bullet's momentum to forcing those coils through flesh.

Wireless: Originally any radio signal, the term now exclusively means wireless digital networking, usually using one of the 802.11 family of protocols. Sometimes also called Wi-Fi or WiFi, a tradename of the Wi-Fi alliance, and a play on the term Hi-Fi, slang for high fidelity, a term used to designate highly accurate sound equipment.

Worm: A stand-alone program designed to replicate itself, propagate itself to other computers, and (usually) to cause some harm to the infected systems. Similar to a virus, save that worms are not attached to some other, legitimate program, but run on their own.

About the Author

James R. Strickland has been telling stories since before he could read or write. After a ten-year detour in system/network administration and technical support, he has returned to his English major roots and is pursuing a career as a novelist. He lives in Colorado with his wife, Marcia, and some number of cats. Visit his website at www.jamesrtrickland.com

Watch for more of the
LookingGlass World
from James R. Strickland

Be the first to know about the LookingGlass World releases. Subscribe to the Flying Pen Press Publisher's Newsletter at the website www.FlyingPenPress.com.

Also available now from

"Giving Flight to Great Books"

MIGRATION OF THE KAMISHI
BY GADDY BERGMANN

The first book in The Feral World series. Three thousand years after an asteroid has sent civilization reeling back to a new stone age, humanity survives. Blake and Monosh of the Kamishi tribe must journey through the wilds of the Great Plains and face the dangerous ruins of "Rubbletowns" in their migration to the Warmland. Gaddy Bergmann, a research zoologist, brings the majesty of American landscapes back to life with an incredible interplay between man and nature, in this, his first novel.

ISBN 978-0-9795889-1-4, Trade Paperback, Fiction, $14.95.

Available wherever great books are sold

or buy online at www.FlyingPenPress.com